BRINGER OF
STORMS

THE BINDING OF THE BLADE

BY L. B. GRAHAM

Beyond the Summerland
Bringer of Storms

Book 2
THE
Binding
of the
Blade

Bringer of
STORMS

L. B. Graham

P&R
PUBLISHING
P.O. BOX 817 • PHILLIPSBURG • NEW JERSEY 08865-0817

Page design by Tobias Design
Typesetting by Michelle Feaster

Printed in the United States of America

Library of Congress Cataloging-in-Publication Data

Graham, L. B. (Lowell B.), 1971–
  Bringer of Storms / L.B. Graham.
    p. cm. — (The binding of the blade ; bk. 2)
  Sequel to: Beyond the Summerland.
  Summary: As Aljeron plans the final battle between Shalin Bel and Fel Edorath, Rulalin must make a horrible choice, while Queen Wylla is forced to accept that it is Allfather's will for her son Benjiah to face the ancient enemy of Kithanin, Malek.
    ISBN 0-87552-721-3 (pbk.)
    [1. Fantasy.] I. Title.

 PZ7.G75267Br 2005
 [Fic]—dc22

                                                          2005042983

For Anna, my mother,
who read to me.

CONTENTS

Prologue: What Was and What Will Be   9

GATHERING

  1. The Streets of Shalin Bel   29
  2. A Time for Peace   50
  3. Choices   75
  4. All That Remains   97
  5. His Father's Son   116
  6. First Steps   138
  7. Midautumn   161
  8. Into the Mountain   182
  9. Looking Back   204
10. Farimaal   220
11. The Calm Before   242

BREAKING

  1. Gyrin   273
  2. Blood on the Mountain   289
  3. Inside the Walls   313
  4. Cheimontyr Comes   336
  5. The Storm Breaks   355
  6. Allegiance   375
  7. Convergence   393
  8. Face to Face   413
  9. Zul Arnoth   433
10. Home   452
11. Into the Sea   474

    Epilogue   495
    Glossary   499

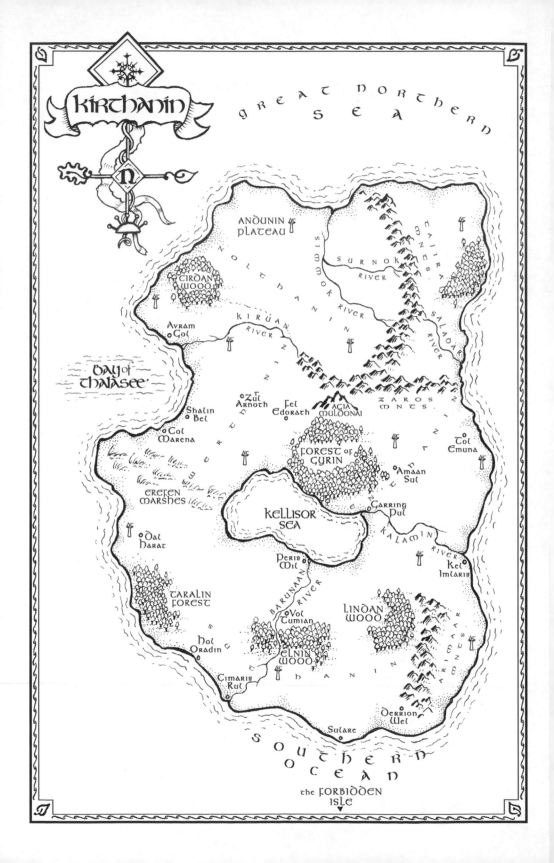

PROLOGUE:
WHAT WAS AND WHAT
WILL BE

ALAZARE SAT ON THE rocky precipice, his feet dangling from the ledge. His eyes were squeezed shut because the constant spinning of the world around him had begun to make him feel sick. He had tried to get a good look over the side of the Mountain, to see where Malek had fallen, but looking down had been a bad idea.

He opened his eyes. The spinning wasn't nearly as bad now. He blinked a few times and found he was even able to focus, but his relief was tempered by the return of the ringing in his ears. The ringing had accompanied him as he had chased Malek through the streets of Avalione and up the long stair that ascended the northern slope behind the city. When he had thrown Malek from the Mountain, the ringing had stopped, only to be replaced by the spinning.

Gingerly, Alazare reached up and touched the side of his head above his right ear, where Malek had struck him with the hammer. When he thought of the fury of that blow, Alazare knew he was fortunate to be alive. Ringing ears and blurry eyes were the least he should have expected. In the end, he knew that he was alive only because Allfather had seen fit to spare him. What else could account for his survival? Alazare had watched Malek slay Volrain with that same hammer just moments before it had shattered when used against him. It wasn't the solidity of the blow that had destroyed it, for he had dodged it just enough that it struck him and glanced off his head, and he was spared the full force of the impact. For a moment, they had both been immobilized by that curious turn of events. Alazare had seen shock, anger, and even fear as Malek looked at the broken pieces of the hammer. Alazare knew then, as Allfather's spirit filled him, that Malek had been delivered into his hand.

Alazare looked up. The sky above the Mountain was a glorious blue. The brightness hurt his eyes, even though they were focusing better than they had been. He shifted his position on the rock and gazed out over the rough landscape of Nolthanin, out beyond Agia Muldonai. With a sigh, he managed to muster the will to try looking down once more.

This time, the spinning did not return, and he did not get dizzy as he gazed down the side of the Mountain. The precipitous drop fell for hundreds of spans. The rocks on the side of the Mountain were jagged and rough. It was an impassable surface, much like the upper reaches of the eastern and western sides. The bottom of the Mountain was difficult to see, but even without complete clarity, it was obvious to Alazare that the impact of Malek's fall had changed the terrain. The rough and uneven ground that sloped slightly downward from the foot of the Mountain had been broken open. Now, a large crater interrupted the consistency of the landscape. Alazare could not see the bottom of that crater, which frustrated him, but he couldn't imagine how Malek could have survived that fall. For all his might, surely even Malek must have been broken by that impact.

Alazare started to rise but quickly thought better of it. The ringing in his ears became a deafening buzz, and the spinning returned to his eyes. He sat back down with a thump and cradled his own head in his hands. The wound above his ear pounded with pain, and he thought his head might explode. With his legs still dangling over the edge of the rocky ledge, Alazare gingerly lay back on the ground. Maybe it was premature to think he was going to survive the hammer blow after all.

When next he sat up and opened his eyes, the sun had dropped below the western peak of the Mountain. The light it cast was a bright red, and while it couldn't really be said to be the color of blood, that was what it brought to Alazare's mind. Blood. The Holy Mountain was stained with blood. Malek had destroyed the peace that had reigned in this place for a thousand years. Malek had lifted his hands in violence against his own brothers, and he had incited others to do the same. Alazare touched the dried blood that clung to his matted hair. Somewhere, behind and below him in Avalione, the blood of his brothers was drying where it had seeped out of their lifeless bodies.

As he sat, thinking of what had become of Avalione and the Twelve, he noticed a windhover alight nearby. The bird hopped across the warm rock to the place where he was sitting, cocking its head sideways as it peered at him.

"So you've come to keep me company, little fellow," he said. "I'm sorry, but I think I will prove to be a poor companion. I have nothing to say, and it is probably better that way. Darkness is coming, and it may never pass."

The bird hopped nearer. It stopped just shy of his enormous legs, which still dangled over the edge. For several minutes, the windhover perched there quietly, looking out over the wide land still visible for leagues in the light of the setting sun. It turned its head to look at Alazare. Then, suddenly, the bird leapt into the air, wheeled around, and flew south over the city behind them. Alazare turned to look over his shoulder, but the bird quickly dropped out of view.

Immediately, Alazare wished he hadn't turned around. Just the sight of the tops of the city buildings, Allfather's Temple, the Council Hall, and the rest made him sick to his stomach. For the first time, as the sun set over the Blessed City, it set upon a graveyard, not a living place. Only he remained, and likely not for long.

He turned and gazed back out over Nolthanin. He could not yet face what lay behind. He could not yet descend the long, winding stair back into Avalione. Thinking of what was there, he started to wish that he had not survived at all. If it had been necessary for Allfather to grant survival to one of them, even if only for a while, why him? Why had he been left alone to face what could not be faced? Surely nothing could be worse than this.

Behind him rose a sound—the flutter of many wings and the cry of many birds, and when he turned, half a dozen windhovers came into view. Each King Falcon carried something in its talons and brought it to Alazare. The first four carried pieces of fruit from the vineyard and groves that grew on the eastern slope of the Mountain beyond the edge of the city. The last two carried strips of cloth that had been dipped in water. As Alazare placed the pieces of fruit on the ground beside him and took the two wet cloths, he realized they had been soaked in the water of the Crystal Fountain. They were cool and refreshing, and with one he wiped the grime and sweat and blood from his face. He held the cloth to his skin and pressed the moist surface against his sore eyelids. The other he held against the side of his aching head. It was immensely soothing and provided a welcome measure of relief.

The birds stood by silently, almost still, as though waiting his command so that they could provide for his need. He took up the fruit they had brought and ate. It tasted sweet and good, and he repented of his haste in despairing of this life. "I am rebuked by your goodness," he said to the windhovers. "There is still joy in the sweetness of a grape and the coolness of water. May I have some more?"

Instantly the King Falcons rose, wings flapping, and sped back down into the city. They returned momentarily, each bearing the same gifts they had brought before. This time, Alazare took the two cloths and squeezed the water into his mouth, then sucked what remained from each. Though both contained little more than a mouthful, that mouthful was exactly what his parched throat needed. He swished the cool water around in his mouth and closed his eyes as the liquid slid down the back of his throat.

When he had finished the second round of fruit, he turned to the gathered windhovers and said, "Blessed are you, little ones, for you have ministered to me when I thought myself forsaken by all living things. Whatever is to come, and wherever Kirthanin is to go from here, you will be blessed as long as this world shall last."

As he spoke, each of the birds settled down upon the rock. There they stayed, and whenever Alazare turned to look at them, he found them waiting, watching. As the last rays of daylight faded and darkness fell even upon the northern face of Agia Muldonai, the odd group remained: Alazare, his eyes more closed than open, immobile on the edge of the cliff facing north; and the windhovers, their piercing dark eyes steady on the great Titan, keeping his lonely vigil.

In the grey morning light just before dawn, a great golden form came gliding over Avalione. Sulmandir swept up and over the top of the precipice on which Alazare still sat, looking with wonder at the curious scene, for the Titan was almost statue-like in his lack of motion, and a cluster of six wind-hovers sat almost as still just a short distance away. Sulmandir circled overhead for a few minutes, but even when he passed almost directly in front of Alazare, he could detect no sign of life in the Titan. He had seen the bodies of the others, and now he feared that he was looking down upon the final victim of Malek's crazed mutiny.

Sulmandir landed on the rocky ledge not far behind Alazare, and the heads of the King Falcons turned almost in unison. They, at least, were still living. Alazare in Titan form was a good seven spans tall, so that even when Sulmandir raised himself to his full height, he was shorter than his friend. Now, because Alazare was seated, Sulmandir stood a bit higher than he, and as he approached him from behind, he lowered his mouth to whisper in his ear.

"Alazare, if your heart beats still, come back from wherever you have gone. I have need of you. Kirthanin has need of you."

Alazare did not reply, and Sulmandir straightened as he considered what to do next. He was reticent to touch Alazare, perched as he was in a precarious position. He had finally decided simply to repeat himself when Alazare suddenly moved. It wasn't a dramatic movement, just a barely perceptible sinking of his head. Sulmandir paused, wondering what it meant. For all he knew, Alazare's dead body was just slipping forward. Perhaps he would eventually tumble off the heights into the depths below. It was a grim thought, for Sulmandir knew that if Alazare was in fact dead, then both he and Kirthanin would have to face its doubtful future alone, for the first time without the guidance of even one of the Titans.

But then Alazare spoke, just as softly as he had been addressed. "What Kirthanin needs, Sulmandir, I cannot give. It is beyond me. What was broken and destroyed here is impossible for anyone but Allfather to put back together."

"That may be true, but I do not speak of fixing or finding. I speak of fighting and defending."

At these words, Alazare turned, though from the grimace of pain that crossed his face and the way he lifted his hand to hold his head, Sulmandir could tell that the sudden movement had cost him. "What do you mean? Malek and his followers are dead. Anakor, Charnosh, and Daegon lay fallen where they were slain, and I threw Malek from the Mountain myself."

"I know. I have viewed the crater at the foot of the Mountain, but I am not sure that Malek died in the fall. The crater is empty."

"What?"

"There is no body in the hole. I made a preliminary sweep of the area to see if I could find him, but I could not. I fear he has shifted into human form and hidden in one of the many caves or crags below."

Alazare stared at Sulmandir, his heart sinking. If Sulmandir spoke the truth, the battle was indeed far from over.

"Alazare, some among the humans are preparing for war. I flew north, into Nolthanin, and I saw that Andunin has given his people weapons with blades of metal, carefully crafted and well-made. Even from the height at which I flew I could detect Malek's handiwork. His rebellion appears to run deeper than it first appeared, for the farther I flew, the clearer it became that almost all of Nolthanin has made ready for war."

"Andunin," Alazare whispered. "What did Malek promise him, I wonder? Long life? Power? Or perhaps he did not make a promise, but a threat. Perhaps it was not what Malek could give so much as what he could take."

"Perhaps both," Sulmandir added. "Fear of Malek and a promise of glory would be hard for a man like Andunin to resist. He loves his family and his people, and fear for their lives might have caused him to succumb, especially if the possibility of greatness was rolled into the offer."

"If Malek is dead, then we could stop whatever is happening below before it even starts. But, if Malek is still alive, then we may well be looking out over a world about to go to war. But surely Malek, even if he survived, surely he is broken in some way? We must find out, Sulmandir, for if he has been injured, even in some small measure, then we may yet stop the war. If Andunin sees that Malek cannot secure victory, then maybe he will put down his weapons before more ruin falls upon Kirthanin. Perhaps the world below can avoid the complete destruction that has befallen Avalione."

"You may be right, Alazare. I will summon some of my children to help me look for news of Malek and to watch the developments in Nolthanin. I will return by nightfall with word of what we find."

Sulmandir paused, looking at Alazare, whose gaze had strayed from the dragon to the city. Reading the sadness in his eyes, Sulmandir looked away. "Before I go, Alazare, is there anything I can do here, to help you?"

Alazare shook his head gently. "No, great Father of the Dragons. What I need to do, I need to do alone. Go, find as many of your sons as you can, and do all that you have proposed. I must rise at last and go back into the city. I must attend to the fallen faithful, and dispose of those who betrayed our house."

Sulmandir nodded as Alazare swung his body around, away from the rock ledge, and slowly stood to his full height. Though Alazare was clearly in great pain, the power and magnificence of his Titan form was still evident. "You were victorious here, Alazare. Though all may feel like ruin and despair, you triumphed. Though all may feel like death and destruction, you live today because Allfather has chosen you to live."

Alazare held his head. "For now, Sulmandir. I live for now, but my ears ring so that I can hardly hear, and my eyes blur so that I can hardly see, and my head aches and throbs constantly. I fear I will never be well. Even so, I thank you, for you speak the truth, and I have only Allfather to thank."

"You would tell me that continued service is the only thanks he requires."

"You're right, but what that service will be, that is a mystery."

"Yes. Who can know what lies ahead?"

"Allfather alone."

"Indeed," Sulmandir nodded and, after leaping from the rock, circled above Alazare once before flying north.

For a moment, Alazare watched the Golden Dragon, both beautiful and powerful in flight. It was comforting to think that Sulmandir had not been claimed by Malek's rebellion, at least not yet. As Sulmandir disappeared from view, Alazare shook his head slightly in disbelief. He stole another quick glance down the side of the Mountain at the crater created by Malek's fall. How could he have walked away? He didn't know, and at the moment, Alazare guessed it didn't really matter. The only important fact was that Malek, it seemed, was somehow still alive.

Alazare turned from the edge, and the windhovers leapt into the air and circled overhead. With a glance from them to the city below, he began to make his way down the long winding stair. It was time to bury his brothers.

The stairs descended for more than a hundred spans back and forth from the northern ridge of Agia Muldonai. Even when Alazare reached the bottom of the stairs, he was still about seventy-five spans above Avalione. Gently sloping terrain led the rest of the way down, so that stairs were unnecessary. Moving as carefully and slowly as he could, Alazare made his way to the bottom. At last he was on ground that was more or less level, and he walked across the intervening space into Avalione, which he entered from the back. Most of the buildings faced south, and he wound through them until he reached the rear of Allfather's Temple, just before the court-yard of the Crystal Fountain.

He stopped and rested his head against the smooth, solid stone of the Temple walls. On the other side of the Temple, in the courtyard, he would find some of the slain. He knew already what he would do with the bodies of the three traitors; he would drag them one by one through the city and out the southern gate, where he would leave them exposed on the ground beyond the city walls. He would leave them for the birds to pick their flesh and gnaw their bones. They deserved no burial and would have none.

Rejuvenated by anger, Alazare moved forward again. He would feel better when these three were no longer in the city, defiling it.

As Alazare entered the courtyard, he saw the scene was just as he had left it. The water of the fountain sprayed high into the air, just as it had done for a thousand years, but floating in the pool at its base was Daegon, who had fallen into the water when Alazare struck him down. Sitting slumped with his back against the fountain was Volrain, the last of the faithful Titans to fall. He had fallen by Malek's own hand, struck and killed by the same hammer that had shattered moments later against Alazare's temple.

He walked to the fountain and stepped up into the pool. He waded through the cold clear water, but despite his thirst, he refused to drink. Vowing even as he crossed the pool that he would not drink until the three were expelled from the city, he plunged on until he reached Daegon.

Daegon was facedown, and Alazare left him that way. He had no wish to see this Titan's face again. Taking hold of the body under both armpits, he pulled it across the pool to the southern side. With a great heave, he lifted the torso onto the side of the fountain pool, and giving the feet a great push, he managed to shove the whole body out. It fell with a wet thud on the paved courtyard, and Alazare climbed out onto the stone. Once out, he renewed his hold on the body and started down the central street that led through Avalione to the gate.

It was a difficult job. The body was stiff and heavy with water, and Alazare's eyes were acting up again. He had to stop frequently, release his grip with one hand and feel around in front of his face to make sure he was still on course. Eventually, though, he reached the gate, which was still partially open from when he and the others had entered silently the previous morning. Shoving that side of the gate with his shoulder, it swung open, and he hauled Daegon's body out of the city. He didn't stop in the wide, lovely meadow of soft green grass that surrounded the city walls. Instead, he kept on dragging Daegon until the grass gave way to a sloping surface of large rocks and loose gravel. Then, with a great heave, Alazare sent Daegon's body sliding down the side of the Mountain. It slid, still prone, and head downward, for about fifteen spans before coming to rest against a large boulder. Alazare tried to focus so he could see the place where Daegon was lodged, but he couldn't get a clear look. After a moment, he headed back to the city.

Just inside the gate, to the western side, were three more bodies. Here lay both Stratarus and Haalsun, not far from one another, with Stratarus's killer, Anakor, lying almost on top of them. Alazare grabbed Anakor by the leg and began to pull him out the gate. He was greatly relieved that he didn't have to take Anakor as far as Daegon, and that he was not soaked with water. He brought him to the same place where he had thrown down Daegon, and he gave Anakor a similar solid shove over the side. Anakor slid across the loose stones but missed the boulder and slid a good bit farther down. Eventually, he too came to rest.

Alazare found the last of Malek's allies, Charnosh, in one

of the groves east of Avalione, lying in the cool, soft grass. He had been struck down by Rolandes, who had avenged Haalsun's murder by the gate, but Rolandes had been unable to escape Daegon, who had come on him from behind just after the faithful Titan had killed Charnosh. Stooping over, Alazare gently rolled Rolandes off Charnosh, again doing his best not to look at the traitor. Securing Charnosh by the feet, he began to drag him back through the city toward the gate, finding grim satisfaction in the rough treatment Charnosh's body received along the way.

As he passed through the gate a third time, his muscles aching, his body sweating, and his eyes and ears malfunctioning, he closed his eyes and pictured the cold, clean water of the Crystal Fountain shooting high above the pool. By now, the blood from Daegon's body might have even been washed away, out of the pool itself, but even if it wasn't, Alazare knew he could stand in the pool and drink right from the source, right from the Fountain without fear of any contamination. How he looked forward to that drink.

Stumbling, he opened his eyes again and continued to pull Charnosh through the field. He had drifted off course but soon righted himself and headed for the place where he had deposited Daegon and Anakor. He brought Charnosh to the slope and without hesitating for a moment hurled the body down it. This time, the body followed Daegon's path precisely and soon lay nestled against his treacherous brother. Alazare paused long enough to pray that the birds come quickly or the bodies rot completely, that even this barren place on the Holy Mountain would not be long defiled by these wretches.

As he passed through the gate yet again, he paused again over the bodies of Stratarus and Haalsun. He could put off no longer what to do with them. They needed to be buried, but where? He looked out through the gate at the beautiful green meadow. It was big and broad and in some ways would have been perfect for a final resting place. But Alazare wanted to lay his brothers down within the blessed city itself. He needed to find a place in Avalione for them all.

He started back up the center road, toward the Crystal Fountain, for he was eager for that too long delayed drink. As he walked, he realized that the grove on the eastern edge of Avalione was the only place large enough and peaceful enough to hold them all. Rolandes lay there already, and neither the two at the gate nor Volrain by the fountain would be hard to move there. The three in the Great Hall, though, would have to be carried all the way across the city, for Alazare would not drag the bodies of the faithful.

He reentered the courtyard and then the pool of the fountain. He waded through it until he stood under the spray. As it fell over him, he leaned his head back, feeling the wonderful refreshment of the water that ran down his face and arms and body. With his eyes closed, he opened his mouth and drank. Each time his mouth was full, he would take long, delicious gulps. He didn't want to open his eyes or move from that spot, for he knew the hardest part of his task was still ahead.

But when he had finally satiated his thirst, he left the fountain and climbed out of the pool. Stooping by the fallen body of Volrain, he gently cupped his brother's chin in his great hand. Dried blood covered the paving stones, the side of the fountain pool, and Volrain's face, clothes, and hair. Placing his shoulder against Volrain's chest, Alazare lifted him until he was resting more or less upon the side of the pool. Carefully, with his arm beneath his brother's shoulders, he leaned Volrain back into the water. With his free hand, Alazare began to wash the blood off of Volrain's face. When it was clean, he moved to Volrain's hair, which was floating in the water, and started to untangle it, pulling out the dried clumps of blood with his wet fingers. It was unpleasant work, and he knew he couldn't get Volrain completely clean. Still, he would do whatever he could to prepare him for burial.

Eventually, he hoisted Volrain up over his shoulder to carry him out to the grove. He walked slowly through the city, grateful that his eyes had stopped bothering him for the moment. The buzzing in his ears was low and steady, and he realized that the sound of his own feet on the pavement sounded faint and far away. Alazare sighed. If he lost both his sight and his hearing, he wouldn't be much use against Malek. He could only hope that Malek had fared worse than he.

In the groves, Alazare laid Volrain with care beneath one of the trees. He then retrieved Rolandes and lay him beneath a neighboring tree north of Volrain. For several moments, Alazare gazed at them, but he pulled himself away and headed down to the gate.

There he took Stratarus first upon his shoulders, and he carried him back to the grove. He put him down beside Rolandes, under the next tree over, and then did the same for Haalsun. He massaged his sore arms and shoulders. The sun stood almost directly overhead. It would soon be midday, and he still needed to dig the graves and retrieve Balimere, Therin, and Eralon from the Council Hall. He would need to move quickly now.

He decided to dig the graves next. The three in the Hall were out of the sun, and he didn't want to disturb them until the heat of the day had passed. Besides, he hadn't been into the Hall since his return to the city, and he wasn't sure how he would handle the scene when he went.

Seven graves he dug, as the sun rose higher, passed midday, and began to descend again. He laid out the graves under seven trees, parallel to one another but a little staggered, for the tree line was not completely straight. He would have liked to make the graves deeper, but time was against him. When all seven were complete, he headed back into the city, pausing only for another drink from the Fountain before making his way to the Council Hall.

He found the doors wide open. Entering, he scanned the Hall apprehensively. The great square council table was where it had been, chairs pushed in, three to a side. Had Alazare not known what to look for and where, he wouldn't have noticed anything amiss, but on the far side of the Hall, beyond the table and below the great western window, a pair of feet rested on the stone floor. The attached legs were not in view, blocked by the table.

As he walked slowly across the large room, the rest of the carnage gradually came into view, and for a moment he had to stop and lean upon the corner of the table to steady himself. The sunlight flooding in through the western window highlighted the dark stains on the light grey stones, and the cold, mangled bodies of his brothers. As he approached them, he looked down on Therin and Eralon, who had tried to resist after Malek struck down Balimere, but against the four traitors, they had stood no chance. Moving past them to the body under the window, Alazare knelt down beside Balimere and rolled him over.

In death as in life, Balimere was beautiful. Of all the Twelve, he was the most beloved, both among the other Titans and among the people of Kirthanin. Perhaps that was why Malek had killed him first. Alazare sat down and cradled Balimere's lifeless head in his lap. Despair and grief welled up in him, and he began to weep. He wept for Balimere, wept for the others, wept for all of Kirthanin. All was misery and ruin. Rage welled up in him too, and he felt bitterly angry that Malek had not been killed when he threw him from the Mountain.

Alazare lay Balimere back down and stood. He would take him out last. Lifting Therin in his arms, he carried him out of the Hall, through the city, and to the grove. After returning for both Eralon and Balimere, he stood once more in the grove, now with all seven of his Titan brothers lying still in the grass. He walked their length, taking one last look at each of them, from Volrain on the southern end to Balimere on the northern. Then, retrieving the shovel once more, he returned to Volrain's body.

Laying him gently in the grave, he paused before shoveling the dirt back in. He felt the spirit of Allfather come upon him. "Farewell, Volrain. Faithful and true you lived, and faithful and true you died. Rest well until the end of time. Rest well until the Holy Mountain is cleansed. Rest well until all things are made new, and the way is prepared for your return. Go to Allfather's side and rest!"

Alazare covered Volrain and moved to Rolandes. Again the words came, and again he wept as he spoke them. And so he spoke and wept over Stratarus, Haalsun, Therin, Eralon, and finally Balimere. But before he covered Balimere's body, he dropped to his knees beside the grave and reached down into it to touch Balimere one more time. He was struck by the peace on Balimere's face. It contrasted dramatically with the turmoil in his own heart. Had Balimere died in peace? Had he stood, looking Malek in the face, at peace? Had rejecting Malek's mutiny stood before him so clearly as the right thing to do that there had been absolutely no concern over what would happen if he refused?

"Allfather," Alazare whispered, "I don't know why you have spared me, or for what purpose I still live, but I pray that you would grant me just a small portion of the peace you have granted Balimere. Can I not have some of this rest you promise now, if not for my body, for my soul?"

His answer came immediately. Alazare's sobbing stopped, and the trembling in his fingers and hands disappeared. Calmly, slowly, he laid Balimere in the earth. Gently, he kissed his forehead and then whispered in his ear, a single word. He spoke so quietly that no living soul, however nearby, could have heard it. Even so, it resonated in Alazare's mind, and as he stood to cover Balimere, it was all he could think of. Louder and louder it echoed within until the ringing of his ears was drowned out completely and his blurred vision was pushed from all conscious thought. And when at last he had smoothed out the ground that covered Balimere, and he had turned from the seven fresh graves to return to the city, he whispered it one more time as he gazed upon the devastation brought to the beauty that was Avalione.

"Resurrection."

GATHERING

THE STREETS OF
SHALIN BEL

THE BEAUTY OF SHALIN BEL was evident even in the
autumn twilight. Though a sprawling city, with many buildings
of carved stone rising along seemingly endless streets in every
direction, it was also a vibrant and living city, with trees lining
the streets as far as the eye could see. Autumn was an especially beautiful time in Shalin Bel, and anyone who visited in
that season treasured the colorful memories they took with
them when they left.

Oblivious to the beauty around him, a solitary man hurried along one of the smaller side streets. The sun was well below the western horizon, and if the man had been able to see
past the buildings and beyond the edge of town and into the
many leagues of farmland, villages, and farmhouses, he would
have been able to see the sunset reflected on the peaceful Bay
of Thalasee. But the man did not even take in the resplendent

beauty around him. The trees, tall and stately, with leaves turned brilliant hues of orange, red, and yellow, and illuminated by the last light of the day, went unnoticed. He was late, and he did not like to be late. It wasn't so much that the friend he was meeting would be annoyed, though he might be. No, it was more his own conscientious nature that drove him onward. He didn't like to keep anyone waiting, especially when the news was good.

Turning the corner, he almost ran into the lamplighter, who was coming the other direction and had already lit the many lampposts along the street, though it wasn't even yet the beginning of First Watch. The days were growing ever shorter. As the man apologized and moved on, he was reminded of how much remained to be done before winter. It was hard not to be excited about the prospect that soon, the war could be over. Victory was within their grasp, and barring some unforeseen catastrophe, all that remained for them was to reach out and seize it.

A strong, cold wind whisked down the next street, and the man pulled his heavy cloak even tighter around his body. He was not a native of Werthanin, but he had been here the better part of seven years now, long enough to know that this was unseasonable cold. If this was Full Autumn, he shuddered to think how cold Full Winter would be. With any luck, though, everything would be over by then and he could be on his way back to Suthanin with his family.

He tried to envision a warm summer day at home, but it didn't do him much good. His wife seemed able to visualize home easily and be comforted, but he lacked some crucial ability that made this possible, for he was rarely able to conjure up anything more than weariness and homesickness. Almost as quickly as the thought of home had come, he was busy pushing it away again. It was a distraction he didn't need right now. The less he thought about going home, the more he could focus on doing his job, and the better he did his job, the sooner he could think about going home.

Turning onto one last street, he finally reached his destination. Two young men had just emerged from a large wooden door to a popular inn, The Flute and Fiddle, and when they had passed him with a nod, he entered.

The accumulated warmth of several large fires and many bodies hit him, and he gladly removed his heavy cloak and draped it over his arm. The sword dangling at his side made him feel self-conscious. Even in days like these, he felt awkward bearing arms in a friendly inn, but as he had often reminded his friend, they couldn't afford to be unprepared or caught off guard, not when they were so close.

He stood in a narrow hall, which had three large common rooms branching off it. On a busy night like tonight, he had no idea where his friend would be. He poked his head into the largest common room, the one immediately on the right. True to its name, The Flute and Fiddle was providing music. A trio of young women were playing, rather beautifully, a sad, old song that he felt sure he had once known, even though its name eluded him now. One of the women played a flute, another a fiddle, and the third sang with her eyes closed and hands clasped. Though most of the men and women in the room were busy conversing with one another, they showed their obvious approval for the song and for the musicians when they finished. Then, after a brief pause, the trio began again, playing a much livelier song to which the singer also danced.

Scanning the room quickly, the man saw that his friend was not there, which was a pity, for he would have enjoyed the music. He continued down the hall, the music and song drifting along behind him. The second room was about half the size of the first, though equally packed and dense with smoke. Though he saw a few familiar faces, including a few officers who had been injured earlier in the war, he didn't see the man he was looking for, so he stepped across the hall to the common room on the left.

The last of the common rooms was almost as big as the first, and two large fireplaces lit and heated it. His friend sat near the fireplace farthest from the door. He was always easy to spot, not only because of the large scars that ran down the right side of his face, but because Aljeron was the only man around who always had a tiger with him, even when he was taking a late supper in a public inn where tigers were generally discouraged.

"Sorry I'm late," Evrim said as he approached Aljeron at the table.

"Never mind that now," Aljeron said, looking up with an expressionless face. "Did the messenger come?"

"He did."

"And?"

"Gilion says that things are right on schedule. Brenim is back and they'll be ready as soon as we can get there."

"Good." Aljeron leaned back in his chair. He sipped from a large mug and looked thoughtfully into the fire. Reaching down with his free hand, he stroked Koshti's head. The tiger closed his eyes and signaled his approval with a contented growl that Evrim had come to recognize as the tiger's version of a purr. While Aljeron was lost in his thoughts, Evrim caught the attention of one of the stewards and ordered a cider.

He had received and finished half of it before Aljeron's attention returned to the table. "Sorry, but I've already ordered. Are you eating?"

"No, I grabbed a bite while I was waiting."

Aljeron nodded. "You dispatched my message to Gilion in return?"

"Yes."

"Good." He reached over and patted Evrim on the shoulder. "I can't tell you how much I appreciate having you with me. It makes all the difference in the world to have competent people around. I don't even know why I bothered asking. You've never failed to do what you've been asked."

"Not if I could help it."

Aljeron sighed. "As glad as I'll be to see this finished, I'll be sorry to see you go home. I've gotten used to having you around. You're not just a good officer; you're a good friend. Any chance you'd consider staying in Shalin Bel?"

Evrim took a drink. "I don't think so. Kyril wants to go home and so do the girls, though they've adapted to life here pretty well. I want to go too. Shalin Bel is truly amazing, but we'd like to finish raising the girls in Dal Harat. It's home, after all, even if it is just a little place."

Aljeron nodded. "I understand. Though I'll likely never marry now, if I were to, it would be hard for me to settle down somewhere else when I could be here. It isn't so easy to leave home in the end, is it?"

"No, it isn't."

"That was the only thing about marrying Wylla that was bittersweet for Joraiem, you know, having to leave Dal Harat. He knew he'd be happy in Amaan Sul with her, but leaving the family, leaving you, well, it pained him. "

"I know," Evrim answered, finishing his cider and signaling to the steward for another. "And it wouldn't have been easy to see him go. It wasn't the same when he left for Sulare, and it hasn't ever been the same since. But things are what they are, right?"

"Right."

Evrim looked at Aljeron as he stared across the room at nothing in particular. For a moment, Aljeron's face had softened, and he had seen a glimpse of what others called "the old Aljeron." But the cold, hard look had returned upon mention of Joraiem's name, and Evrim had a pretty good idea what he was thinking about.

"Fel Edorath is going to fall, Aljeron, and we'll get him. He won't escape justice this time."

"I hope so, but he isn't mine yet."

The steward reappeared with Evrim's second cider and Aljeron's meal, a large bowl of steaming hot stew with half a loaf of bread and cheese. Aljeron thanked him and ordered another cider. When the man had gone, Aljeron leaned over the meal and looked intently at Evrim. "I've waited seventeen years for this, Evrim. Seventeen years. It infuriates me to think he has been alive and well all this time. He'd better hope that he dies defending his city, because if I take him alive, he will be sorry that I did."

Evrim leaned over the table too. "I've waited just as long, and I despise him just as much. I know how much you want to be the one to kill him, but I'm not making any promises that you'll have that chance if I get my hands on him first. He was my best friend and my wife's brother."

Aljeron stared at Evrim, and Evrim knew his own eyes mirrored the intensity in Aljeron's. Evrim rarely betrayed his feelings, but on a few rare occasions, he had shown Aljeron a glimpse of the fire that burned within. Evrim knew this shared passion was why Aljeron trusted him absolutely, even though they had barely known each other when Aljeron had first made Evrim an officer in his army. Both men had loved Joraiem Andira as though he had been their brother, and they both smoldered with the desire to make Rulalin Tarasir pay for taking his life.

Aljeron smiled, and the fierce fire in Evrim's heart dissipated. He leaned back in his chair. "Don't worry, Evrim. I wouldn't begrudge you the right to do what you had to do. If there is any hand in Kirthanin other than my own that I could accept his end from, it would be yours, and maybe Brenim's. Of course, that would go for Monias too, but his support for what we are trying to do here has always been reluctant."

"He wants to see justice done, Aljeron, believe me. But even before Joraiem died, he was never very keen on the use of weapons. He accepted their necessity with Malek and Malek's creatures living right in the middle of Kirthanin, but I'm not surprised that he finds it difficult to support a war like this between men."

"I know." Aljeron swallowed some of his stew. "It would just be easier to make our case to the Assembly with his full support. For that matter, it would be easier to make our case to the Assembly with Wylla's full support. Their voices clearly and unashamedly supporting us would go a long way."

"We have Wylla's support, Aljeron, but you know why she isn't going to go before the Assembly and give a fiery speech about the necessity of this war. She was Joraiem's wife, but she is also the Queen of Enthanin. The war will end, and we will need to knit Kirthanin back together. It is going to be hard enough to reunite Werthanin and restore peace between Shalin Bel and Fel Edorath without bringing Enthanin into it all. Besides, she's trying to raise Benjiah without bitterness. She doesn't want him to be consumed by the hate that burns in you and me, and I don't blame her."

Aljeron sighed. "No, I don't blame her either." He paused from his supper and reached down to stroke Koshti some more. "Do you think we will be free of it when this is done and he is dead?"

Evrim shrugged his shoulders. "I don't know, but I hope so."

Aljeron continued eating, but Evrim remained silent, gazing into the fireplace. The room wasn't quite as full now, as several of those who had been eating when Evrim had come in had finished and gone. Five men still wearing their heavy outer cloaks entered and took a table across the room. Evrim glanced up, but he didn't recognize their faces.

"Have you heard from Kyril and the girls recently?" Aljeron asked.

"Not since their arrival in Amaan Sul in the spring. I'm sure they are enjoying themselves, though. They always do. Kyril and Wylla get along well. From the moment they met, even with circumstances being what they were, they were close. Kyril looks to Wylla as an older sister for guidance and for help, and from what I can tell, Wylla loves to have Kyril around. Maybe she's the little sister Wylla never had. Goodness knows Pedraal and Pedraan wouldn't have given her many opportunities to fulfill her natural big sisterly inclinations."

"No, I imagine not."

"And the girls, well, they adore Benjiah. He can do no wrong in their eyes. Halina and Roslin could barely wait to go and see him again."

"What is he like, Benjiah?" Aljeron asked, looking up from his supper thoughtfully.

"He's a handsome boy. His hair is blond like his father's was, but it is hard to tell who he resembles most in the end. He has his father's eyes, but I think his face resembles most clearly Wylla. The last I saw him, three years ago, he was only thirteen, but I could tell already he was going to be a tall, strong boy. I am sure that he has changed a lot since then."

"What's he like as a person?"

"Strong, quiet . . . angry."

"I can imagine."

"You know," Evrim said, setting his cider down and leaning in over the table toward Aljeron, "you really should go and see them when this is done. I know it would be hard, but I think it would be comforting too, and I don't just mean for them. Wylla would love to have you visit, and meeting Benjiah might help you to be more at peace with Joraiem's death."

Aljeron seemed to consider this. "Perhaps you're right. Maybe after Rulalin is dead, maybe then I can go and see him. I have often felt like I have failed the boy by not avenging his father sooner. Maybe afterward I'll be able to look him in the eye and know that I have done what justice required."

"You haven't failed him, and no one sees it that way but you. If you don't visit, you will do both Benjiah and Joraiem a disservice. You were his father's friend, and he should sit beside the fire with you and hear your stories of his father. I have told him mine, and of course Wylla has told him hers, but I'm sure that he would love to hear of his father in the Summerland and Nal Gildoroth and the rest from you. I know that he admires you."

"Benjiah admires me?"

"He does."

"How do you know?"

"The last time we were together, Benjiah was playing a game with Halina and Roslin, where he was running around with a stick, slaying imaginary enemies while they were sitting together under a bush. They were supposed to be prisoners in a cave or something. I asked him what he was doing, and he said that he was killing the Malekim so that he could set the girls free. He was re-enacting your pursuit of the women after they were abducted on the Forbidden Isle. I told him that his father had used Suruna, not a sword. Do you know what he said to me? He said, 'I know, but today I'm pretending to be Aljeron.'"

Aljeron finished eating quietly and looked up at his friend. "Thanks. I hadn't considered what it might mean to him to meet me. I will go when this is through, Evrim, and I will tell him how much I loved his father."

They sat in silence, the warmth of the fire heating their faces as they gazed into it. Koshti's eyes were closed, and from his even, rhythmic breathing, it appeared that he was asleep. The room was now almost completely empty, and the music, which had been steadily drifting down the hallway the entire evening, had stopped now. The crackling and popping of the warm fire filled the silent void in the room, and though it wasn't especially late, Evrim and Aljeron knew that most of Shalin Bel would have already retired for the night. The shops were closed, and while most of the inns would be open for several more hours, even they would have few people eating and drinking within. It was cold outside and most people in the city would be home by their own bright fires and in their own warm beds.

"Well," Aljeron began at last. "We should probably get back. Tomorrow I have to convince the council that seeing this through to the end is the only reasonable path before us, and after that we still have many things to do before we head back to Fel Edorath. Let's get some rest."

"Sounds good," Evrim said, standing and stretching. "Whenever I know the time is approaching to return to the front, I always savor those last few nights in a real bed. You know what I mean?"

"I know exactly what you mean."

"When do you think we will be ready to go?"

"If we are ready to go by Midautumn, my thought would be that we could celebrate the rites here, then head out the following morning. That should give Gilion and Brenim plenty of time, and as soon as we get there, we will bring Fel Edorath to its knees and end this war."

After listening to the innkeeper remind him how much he had loved Aljeron's parents, Aljeron stepped outside, followed closely by Koshti and Evrim. Aljeron was certainly glad he had wrapped his cloak tightly before going out. The wind was blowing twice as hard as he remembered, and the evening air was twice as cold. It was very dark now, though the moon was almost three-quarters full and shone brightly over the city. The lamps along both sides of the street gave off a soft glow that illuminated most of the roadway, though patchy spots here and there remained in darkness.

Aljeron tried to say something over his shoulder to Evrim, but the whistling wind obscured his words so much that he doubted Evrim understood. Even Koshti looked up intently at Aljeron as though to say he had heard his voice but didn't know if the words had been meant for him. Evrim shook his head and shrugged his shoulders. Aljeron tried again, a little louder, but Evrim still didn't hear. This time, Aljeron waved it off as unimportant with a look of frustration and kept walking.

They made their way down several streets. They passed the occasional pedestrian, invariably walking quickly and clinging tightly to a cloak. The usual social niceties were replaced by simple nods as everyone seemed anxious to get where they were going. In addition to the cold, small droplets of rain were beginning to fall. Aljeron felt the first drop hit his hand. Looking up, he took the next one in his eye. He rubbed it to get the water out. The drops started to fall faster, and Aljeron stepped up his pace as he glanced over his shoulder with a look at Evrim that he intended as, "It figures."

They weren't far now from the Council Hall of Shalin Bel. The Council Hall was an enormous stone building that was really more of a complex than a single structure. At the center was the Hall proper, where the Novaana who lived in and around Shalin Bel met with the prominent merchants and city elders to discuss the city's affairs. Since many of these people owned extensive lands outside the city itself and traveled into town for meetings of the city council, one large building off of the Council Hall was dedicated to two large kitchens and five separate dining areas, and two more large buildings were full of chambers in which visitors stayed when they came into town for the council. Most of those chambers were allocated more or less permanently to their users. Evrim and his family were a case in point, and Aljeron had seen to it that they received some of the best quarters to be found. So a spacious four-chamber suite had been dedicated to them ever since.

Aljeron's use of the facility was more typical. The Balinor estate lay an hour's ride beyond the western gate, just south of the road to Col Marena, so his parents had kept a suite of chambers at the Council Hall when staying in the city. In fact, their quarters were undoubtedly the best, for the Balinors were generally acknowledged to be the most prominent of all the Shalin Bel families, though they had never asserted any such position and happily functioned as one family among many in the city council and in the Werthanin delegation to the Assembly.

That was exactly how Aljeron's father had seen it and how Aljeron had been raised to see it, but at times like this, it was a decided inconvenience. Reining in the Shalin Bel council and getting it to support the war had never really been easy, even in the early days, but especially as the conflict had dragged out longer than anyone had expected, the number of dissidents had steadily grown. Aljeron might not have minded so much if the objections had been principled, as Monias's were, but he was sick and tired of economics and pragmatics dominating the debate when justice was the more important consideration. He cared of course about the well-being of those merchants and farmers who depended on commerce and trade between Shalin Bel and Fel Edorath, and he found no joy in their sustained hardship, but he couldn't just abandon justice so that business would pick up again. Many men had sacrificed more than profits or fortunes in the last seven years on the plains between Werthanin's two great cities. He wasn't about to let their efforts die in vain when the end was within sight.

The Council Hall was still some distance away, and the rain became heavier. Aljeron's soaked hair lay in clumps on his shoulders, and his hands were trembling with the cold. He rubbed them again on his wet clothes to try to dry and warm them, even if just a little bit. He looked over his shoulder at

Evrim and noticed that he was having much the same problem. He was holding his hands up to his mouth, blowing on
them fiercely. Aljeron tried it too, but it didn't really help and
the bottom of his cloak kept blowing open.

At the next corner, he crossed the street, and a faint
sparkle of light caught his eye. He turned his head in time to
see a flash of steel pass less than a hand in front of his face and
hit the side of the building beyond him. The resulting ring
was just barely audible above the wind. Ducking quickly
around the corner and drawing his sword, Daaltaran, at the
same time, he turned to see Evrim and Koshti close behind,
though he could tell Koshti was likely to go dashing back out
into the street if he heard any sign of further danger.

"What was that?" Evrim shouted as he leaned over Aljeron's shoulder.

"A knife meant for my head, I imagine." Aljeron pointed
out through the rain at a cloaked figure darting from a dark
doorway across the street. "Come on," Aljeron added.

He ran out into the rain with Koshti at his side and Evrim
just behind, and he focused as well as he could on the elusive
figure that ran ahead of him. For a moment he thought he
had lost sight of him altogether, but suddenly he saw the man
turn into a dark, narrow alley. The alley ran a long way between two rows of buildings and emptied out onto a lit street.
Aljeron paused just long enough to pick up the silhouette before plunging into the alley after him.

"I'm not sure this is a good idea," Evrim shouted as black-
ness swallowed them. "He may not be alone."

Aljeron didn't reply but kept on running through the alley,
which was so narrow that they were forced to proceed single-
file. Koshti had taken the lead. One second Aljeron could see
nothing before him, and the next Koshti had broken back out
into the light and so had he. They paused again, but this time
Aljeron could see no hint of his attacker. Koshti, though, took

off to the left up the street. The men followed, trusting that Koshti's senses were doing what theirs could not.

Not far ahead Koshti led them into another alleyway. This one was dark like the first, but seemed to have no outlet and threatened to dead-end in darkness. There was no way without light of some kind to know just how far back the alley went. Immediately they halted, sensing that unless the man had made a mistake, they could be in a very precarious place.

A knife whistled through the darkness, slicing through Aljeron's sleeve and making a clean if passing cut in his arm. Immediately they backed out of the alley and around the corner into the lighted street. As they did, several men in dark cloaks with swords drawn pursued them, and soon they found themselves trying to gain firm holds on their swords' slippery hilts.

As Aljeron gradually processed what was happening, he realized that about half a dozen men were pressing them back, each wielding their swords as if they knew what they were doing. Clearly these men had seen combat, probably recently and against his own army. He gripped Daaltaran tightly and soon had shifted from defensive strokes to offensive attacks against two of the assailants.

One of them slipped on the wet paving stone and Aljeron found the opening he needed. With a quick, furious attack at the other man, Aljeron forced him back half a span. Wheeling rapidly toward the man who had slipped, he caught him still off guard and drove Daaltaran completely through him. As quickly as he had buried Daaltaran, he withdrew it, now dripping with blood and shimmering red in the rain, and turned to meet the counterattack of the other man. The attack was quick but predictable, and Aljeron had soon driven him back to the corner of the street and alley, where he made quick work of him.

Turning, he saw a third man dead at Evrim's feet, and a fourth lay before Koshti with one of the tiger's massive claws resting on his chest. Koshti's teeth were bared and bloody, and

Aljeron recognized in his eyes the glint of battle fury that came over him in the middle of combat.

Running to Evrim, he called, "Where are the others?"

Evrim still held his sword warily before him. "I saw only five, and the other one ran back into the alley when he saw Koshti tear his friend open like a feather pillow."

The sound of something metallic falling on stone rang out from the alleyway, and before Evrim could even think of protesting, Aljeron was running back into it. As it turned out, the alley didn't go very far back, and it took only a moment to realize that the man wasn't there. Something loose under his foot told Aljeron that he was standing on the cause of the metallic ring. He bent over and picked up a sword. Groping in the dark, he found a tall, slender ladder tied up against the side of one of the buildings that faced the large street. It was common in the city for homeowners and even some of the shop owners to use their rooftops, which were generally flat, for a number of different purposes. Holding up the sword before Evrim's face, which he could now make out in the alley's darkness, he said, "I bet he didn't want to drop this. Let's go up and get him."

Koshti remained in the alley, pacing at the foot of the ladder, as Aljeron and Evrim went up. Soon both stood on the roof, swords ready. The building was attached to a line of shops, and Aljeron and Evrim began to make their way carefully from rooftop to rooftop.

The lights from the street illuminated at least a portion of their passage. Still, it was fairly dark and puddles of water met their feet at every step. After they had crossed perhaps a dozen buildings, Aljeron grabbed Evrim's arm. With Daaltaran he pointed to a dark figure, perhaps three buildings ahead, paused at what must have been another street, for lamplight framed his dark form nicely. Quickly and quietly they turned slightly and took a more direct path toward him.

They were about to step onto the roof where the man was standing, peering over the edge of the building, when he turned and looked at them. They both froze instinctively, and the man took a step that put him right at the edge of the roof.

"If you surrender we will take you as a prisoner of war," Evrim shouted through the storm, though Aljeron wondered if the man could hear.

The man made no reply but began move slowly along the edge of the roof toward the corner, where the light wasn't so bright. Evrim called out again, "Stop moving and kneel! We will take you prisoner and spare your life."

The man stopped, but didn't kneel as they came closer. He turned and looked quickly over the edge again, then looked back at them. They had crossed half of the roof and in a few moments would be in a position to take him prisoner. The man seemed at that moment to realize this fact as well, for he suddenly leapt out over the street and disappeared.

As both Aljeron and Evrim raced to the edge, they heard the crack of his body hitting the street. The man lay almost directly under the light of a street lamp and did not move. Aljeron looked up from the street after several moments. "Fool," he said to Evrim as he turned away from the edge. "Come, let's see if the bodies tell us anything about these men."

Koshti was waiting impatiently at the bottom of the ladder, and he seemed to discern almost immediately from Aljeron that the fighting was over. His body relaxed and he fell in behind them as they went to examine the dead men.

The bodies didn't tell them a thing. All five were dressed in nondescript clothes and cloaks, and none of them carried anything except for a sword and a small pouch of silver and gold coins. Two carried knives. When it was clear they weren't going to learn anything from the attackers' possessions, Aljeron and Evrim headed off to inform the city guard so that the bodies could be removed before morning. There was enough tension in the city and concern over the war without people thinking that they were no longer safe in their own houses and in their own shops. Something like this the night before he met with the council could be quite a nuisance.

When everything had been taken care off, they arrived at last at the Council Hall. And after doing their best to converse nonchalantly with the guard at the gate, they passed through.

Evrim followed Aljeron through the long maze of hallways to his chambers, and they stepped inside with Koshti. Aljeron quickly kindled a fire, and the two men gladly removed their soggy cloaks and huddled by the fireplace. After the fire was burning strong, they sat back in two wooden chairs beside it and warmed their hands until they were positively glowing with the heat.

During all of this neither of them spoke; in fact, they barely looked at one another. But when they were just about completely dry, Evrim broke the silence. "They were the men from The Flute and the Fiddle."

"I know."

Evrim shook his head. "Can you believe the temerity? To think that they showed themselves to us, sitting right across the room for the better part of an hour. They might as well have waved and said hello."

"They were having a drink before going to work."

"Well, at least it was their last."

"I should have known they were trouble."

"How?"

"They never took their cloaks off. It was warm in there, and they sat cloaked the whole time to conceal their weapons. I saw it, but it didn't register."

"That's twice now," he said turning to Aljeron again. "I don't think you should go out alone or at night again until after we return from the Fel Edorath victorious. Even then you might want to think twice about it."

"I'm not going to live like a prisoner in my own city," Aljeron growled. "Besides, the last attempt was over a year ago, and that was just one man. He could have been anybody with a grudge or grievance."

"But he wasn't. You know that."

"Even so, Fel Edorath barely has enough men left to slow down my entrance into the city. They won't waste any more men on what even Rulalin must realize is a suicide mission."

Aljeron reached down to stroke Koshti's head, which was still drying. The tiger, for all his heavy fur, seemed to tolerate the heat more than Aljeron could. In fact, neither heat nor cold seemed to wear on Koshti, as long as he was dry. He didn't enjoy being wet in either.

"I think you underestimate Rulalin's desperation and determination," Evrim continued, undeterred. "We can't be the only ones who see his end is near. Do you really think he's just going to accept defeat and bow out gracefully? Let you walk into his city and take him captive? He means to get you if he can."

"I don't doubt either his desperation or his determination. I'm just not going to allow him to take anything from me, my freedom or my life."

"Aljeron, why—"

"Look," Aljeron said, turning toward his friend and speaking firmly. "I understand what you're saying, but I'm not going to cower in my room. Besides, we've only got a few days left here before we head back to Fel Edorath, and unless he sent more than the five we encountered tonight, there is no way anyone else is going to arrive in time to find us, much less attack us. Don't worry about it."

Evrim apparently recognized the finality in Aljeron's voice. "All right, but at least let me stay here tonight and take me with you wherever you go the next few days. I can sleep here in the parlor."

"Don't be silly. Who was talking tonight about savoring his last few opportunities to sleep in a real bed before going back to the front? You're going to trade that in for the floor of my parlor? And for what? You think a band of assassins is going to try to overpower the guard and make their way into the Council Hall?"

"Why risk it?"

"Look," Aljeron said, sitting back in his chair and gazing into the fire. "I appreciate your concern, even if you are obsessive, but I don't want you sleeping on my floor. Koshti will already be sleeping there, and he's as intimidating and effective a bodyguard as I could ask for. I want you to go back to your own chamber and get a good night's rest, not only tonight but every night you get the chance."

Evrim gazed at Koshti and sighed. "All right, Aljeron. I give up. You're going to do whatever you want to, but at least think about taking me with you outside the Council Hall, especially if you are going out at night."

"I promise to think about it."

"That's a start. Think of it as being kind to a lonely man. With Kyril and the girls in Amaan Sul, my chambers feel big and empty. An invitation out and about could be your gift to me, your mercy offered to a friend."

Aljeron laughed. "You don't give up. Poor Evrim, all alone, eh?" He stopped laughing and turned back to the fire. "Sure, I'll try to include you whenever I can, that way you can make sure I'm not killed by assassins, and I can make sure you aren't wasting away from loneliness."

"Deal," Evrim said quickly.

"Well, now that that's settled, would you like a drink?"

"No thanks," Evrim replied, standing. "It's late."

"Do you want me to come with you? You know, I could check under the rugs and tables and even in your bed for possible threats."

"Funny. Do you want me to meet you here tomorrow, or in the Hall?"

"Here is fine. Meet me at the beginning of Second Hour, then we'll have some time to review things before the Council begins."

"All right," Evrim replied as he walked over to the door to the hall. "I will be here at Second Hour."

"See you then."

Evrim slipped out into the hall and down the corridor. Aljeron closed the door behind him and then returned to the fire. He sat beside Koshti and stroked the fur along his back, which was not only dry now but warm and bristly. "You were great tonight, old friend," he whispered softly as he rubbed him gently. "You are always there when I need you. So many years now, and you never fail me."

Koshti rolled on his side so Aljeron could stroke his stomach and looked up at Aljeron. Not for the first time, Aljeron wondered what the tiger was thinking. Despite their close bond, the intuitive communication they shared, and their many years together, he didn't know. It was a question that not even Valzaan had been able to answer.

Valzaan. The name brought back so many memories. Aljeron slipped out of the chair and lay next to Koshti. It had been many years since he had last seen the prophet, and many more since they had first met in that great field of grain near the dragon tower on the road to Sulare. How much those days came to him now like a wondrous, golden era of youth. He saw it now as one of the best years of his life. The friends he had made there, especially Joraiem, had filled the one void he hadn't even realized he had, close companionship outside his family with a real person. That was what he had found with Joraiem. Though it had been difficult and even terrifying at certain points, he looked back at their adventures together as one of the highlights of his existence.

But then Rulalin had murdered Joraiem and robbed Aljeron of that friendship. How clearly that morning remained in Aljeron's memory. Wylla had come into the Great Hall for breakfast without Joraiem, and Aljeron had asked her where he was. Her answer had made Aljeron shudder. He had sensed something was wrong, but there had been no opportunity to do anything about it. Word had come immediately after that Joraiem was hurt down on the beach, and they had all raced to him. He had often wondered if Joraiem was alive when he'd asked Wylla where he was, or if the cold shiver that rippled through him had been some kind of supernatural awareness that his friend was dead.

That moment had changed everything. Life ever since had been misery and toil. He had taken Joraiem's body back to Dal Harat and grieved his loss anew as Joraiem's family grieved it for the first time. He had returned to Shalin Bel and grown ever more frustrated by the inability of the Assembly to bring Rulalin to justice. And as his anger and bitterness had grown, he had been forced to deal with the loss of his mother, and then several years after, the loss of his father. He had buried them both, and now he was more alone than ever.

He rose and walked into his bedroom. It was dark, and he was glad. He opened the window. The rain was still falling steadily, and the cold air that rushed in made him shiver. He inhaled deeply, shut the window, and got into bed.

Loneliness. Evrim had spoken of it, and Aljeron didn't doubt Evrim was lonely. He was afflicted with the loneliness of a man used to being surrounded by family. He had a loving wife and beautiful children.

Aljeron's loneliness, though, was of another sort. It was bone-deep. The emptiness threatened at times to consume him. His parents. His best friend. All he had ever had. All lost. He had nothing now, except this war, and the council would decide tomorrow if he still had even that.

2

A TIME FOR PEACE

ALJERON WAS DRESSED AND WAITING when Evrim returned to his chambers in the morning. It had been a restless night, and despite his weariness and desire for rest, sleep had come neither easily nor deeply. He awoke several times and even passed a small portion of the night in a chair before the fading embers of his fire while Koshti slept on the rug. He had tried leaving his window open for fresh air, and then closing it for warmth. Neither helped him much, and in the end he tossed and turned and stared at the rafters of the ceiling most of the time. The more he reminded himself how important the council in the morning was, the worse it became, and even though he knew it wasn't helping, he couldn't help but keep up the periodic reminding. So the night passed slowly, almost tortuously, and he was glad in the end when the morning light illuminated his room.

"How'd you sleep?" Evrim asked as he entered the room.

"Fine," Aljeron answered, ashamed of the lie but more

ashamed of the truth. He couldn't tell Evrim that he had gone to bed feeling desperately lonely, and that this melancholy state on top of the importance of the day's convocation had kept him awake. That was not the kind of thing to tell a subordinate. Evrim might confide his burdens to Aljeron, but Aljeron could not hand his down to Evrim. Of course his men knew that he was human and had his share of worries and concerns, but he couldn't afford to give those worries and concerns shape and form. As long as they were a mere abstraction they were barely taken into consideration, but if they became concrete and therefore real, they could threaten his ability to lead.

He shut the door behind Evrim and walked to the round table by the larger parlor window. The slight breeze blowing in this morning didn't have anywhere near as sharp an edge as the cold wind of the night before, but it was nonetheless cool, so Aljeron poured himself some of the hot mint tea that one of the stewards had left by his door earlier in the morning. "Would you like some?" he asked Evrim.

"Yes, please."

Aljeron poured the hot tea then took a seat opposite Evrim. "What do we know?"

"We know what the Merchants' Guild is going to say, because they've been saying the same thing for seven years. We also know that the other Novaana have been supportive of the war on the main and will likely continue to be."

"Agreed, but I don't feel like I have a good handle on where the city elders are in all this, despite their past support, and I don't like walking in there this morning without it. It seems too much like fighting a battle without knowing the ground, and we both know what a disaster that can be."

"We do," Evrim answered with a nod. "But what can we do about it?"

"Nothing." Aljeron shrugged. "Today is the day, and we need to go in and do what we have done from the beginning.

Not one thing about why we started this has changed, so if it was right and just seven years ago it is right and just now. We simply have to keep that before ourselves and before them."

"I suppose it's too much to hope that Dorant won't be here."

Aljeron scoffed. "Dorant wouldn't miss this if his own children were home in their deathbeds. There's a lot of money on the line, after all. He'll be here."

"I wonder what it's like to have a world so simple," Evrim mused. "Everything reducible to entries in your ledger of accounts."

"I don't know," Aljeron answered, "but I don't know that the problem with his view of the world is its simplicity. Maybe the world is supposed to be simple. Take this meeting and this war. We believe they are the right thing to do. We believe justice requires it, so we do it. That's simple, isn't it?"

"Sure, but knowing what is just and what justice requires isn't always that simple, is it?"

"No, it isn't," Aljeron agreed. "I didn't mean that everything in life was simple, but maybe the bigger things, you know, the guiding principles, maybe they aren't as complicated as the details. Maybe doing what is good and just and right as an idea is really very simple, even if the details can be tricky."

"Perhaps, but I still think a world that values money alone would be a lot less complicated than a world where money is but one of many values. We have to deal with the same questions of money, how to make it and how best to spend it, but that is only one small part of how we view the world. When he's dealt with those questions, he's finished."

"True, but don't envy him. I suspect that he isn't nearly as happy with his simple world as he appears."

"I don't envy him, believe me. I don't even really understand him."

They sat a little while longer, discussing which questions should be addressed candidly and in detail if asked, and which should be tactfully avoided. They had been over all of it before, but they both went through the motions of the conversation, knowing that they would benefit from having warmed up, as it were, before the council actually began. When they had run through the essentials, they slipped out of the room with Koshti and headed down to the Council Hall.

Aljeron and Evrim were standing in the antechamber to the Council Hall, exchanging polite pleasantries with a few city elders, when two stewards entered from the outer courtyard, followed by three massive forms. Conversation all over the room came to an immediate halt as everyone turned in unison to see the unusual visitors. Aljeron smiled and excused himself as he crossed the room to greet the visitors.

"Sarneth," he said, a smile breaking out on his face. "What a pleasure and a surprise. How long has it been since you were last here?"

"Too long," Sarneth replied, his voice deep and strong but gentle. "It was a year or two before the war began, I think."

"Well, it is good to have you here now. And what timing? The city council is about to meet today to discuss the state of the war, and it would be a pleasure to introduce you. We haven't had the pleasure of visiting Great Bear since you were with us last."

"We would be honored to be introduced before the council, though you should know that the position of the draal's elders hasn't changed. We will not take part in a war among men, Aljeron. And to be prudent, I think that I should also stay out of a council that meets to discuss that war."

Aljeron shrugged. "I understand. Of course, you know my feelings about the matter, but I respect the decision of the draal. The clan must do what it believes to be best. Anyway,

I've been rude. Here I am rushing to business, and I haven't even greeted your companions."

"Yes, let me introduce you." Sarneth motioned to one of the Great Bear beside him. Aljeron looked at him carefully for the first time, and as far as he could tell, this Great Bear appeared to be about the same age as Sarneth, his face and body marked by grey hair scattered among the darker brown, and his eyes deep wells of wisdom and understanding. "You may not remember Arintol, but you have met before. He journeyed through Lindan with us and fought the Malekim alongside you."

"Yes," Aljeron said, nodding his head, recognition dawning at last. "Of course I remember. My friends and I owe much to you, Arintol, even our lives. I am happy that you have come to my city so that I can repay some of the debt we owe."

"You are kind, but you owe me nothing. We, like you, simply did what needed to be done."

Sarneth motioned to the third Great Bear, who had no grey hair and deferred to his elders both in attitude and posture. "This is Erigan, my son."

Aljeron stepped over before Erigan, looking thoughtfully at him. "It is truly an honor to have you with us, Erigan. I'm sure your father has told you about our adventures, but knowing him, he hasn't told you nearly enough about his own part in bringing us safely through. We will have to rectify that while you are here."

"You are as welcoming as my father said you would be," Erigan said. "It is an honor to meet you."

"The honor is mine." Aljeron turned back to Sarneth. "I want you to consider yourselves my personal guests. I will leave instructions with a steward that you are to have all you need."

"I'm sure everything will be well," Sarneth answered.

"We are just about to begin the council, so I will make some arrangements now. Please wait here until we start. I'll introduce you first, then after the council has had an opportunity to welcome you as you deserve, you can go to your rooms. I will check in on you later today, all right?"

"That would be fine. We are here to see you, Aljeron, but we don't need to talk today. It sounds as though you already have much on your mind."

Aljeron looked carefully at Sarneth. If the clan elders had not changed their position on the war, he wondered what mission or message had brought Sarneth to Shalin Bel. It was a question that was going to have to wait, though, for the Council Hall's doors had opened.

The Council Hall was dominated by the large triangular table in the middle of the almost-square room. Rooms and hallways extended from every side, and numerous windows set high in the walls provided ample light. Only on the cloudiest of days were candles or torches required.

The council table was full, more so than Aljeron had seen it in a long time. There were always some empty places, for rarely could all the Novaana, merchants, and elders be present at the same time. Today, though, there were precious few open chairs. In fact, with Evrim seated near the center of the side dedicated to the Novaana, holding a seat for him, he could see that there would be no spare seats on their side of the table. Aljeron sensed that despite his attempt to be ready for any argument against him, today's meeting might hold some surprises.

He sat down, knowing that the eyes of many around the table were focused on him. The war had come to be known among some who opposed it as "Aljeron's war," as though it was being fought for his own personal pleasure. He also knew that while it couldn't be fought with only his support, it would end tomorrow if he withdrew his support. He always reminded himself of this fact when he took his seat at this table. He was essential, but not sufficient.

The council always began with a prayer to Allfather, of-fered by the chief elder of the city. The elders comprised twenty Shalin Bel citizens, chosen from among those at least sixty years old. Once elected, elders served on the council un-til the time of their death, and the chief elder was always the oldest of them all. Though in some ways the real power of the council lay in the hands of the Novaana and the Merchants' Guild, the council had only succeeded in functioning well and peacefully because of the wise and able presence of the elders, who often arbitrated disputes between the other two groups. Aljeron had witnessed this himself as the consistent objections of the Merchants' Guild to the war had been overruled by the support of the city elders for the just causes of the war. They, as much as his fellow Novaana, had spoken eloquently from the beginning about Allfather's love of justice and the need to do right regardless of how difficult it might be.

The chief elder invoked Allfather's presence and called on Him for wisdom and guidance, then prepared to call the meeting to order. Aljeron rose to his feet. "Elder Curran, I'm sorry to interrupt, but a matter has come up that should be at-tended to before turning to the business at hand."

Elder Curran looked up, surprised, but most around the table had seen Aljeron conversing with the Great Bear before the meeting, and regardless of their position on the war, all knew that a visiting delegation of Great Bear should be ac-corded the utmost respect.

"Yes," Elder Curran said, "go on Master Balinor."

Aljeron signaled to a steward who was standing by the en-trance. He pulled the door open. The three Great Bear ap-peared, and Aljeron waved to them to come in as he spoke. "Ladies and gentlemen of the council, as you no doubt saw in the foyer this morning, we have the unusual pleasure of wel-coming three Great Bear to Shalin Bel. Most of you will re-member Sarneth, who visited with another elder of the

Lindandraal many years ago. He sojourned with the Kirthanim Novaana in Sulare when I was there and was a great help in rescuing the women with us when they were taken captive on the Forbidden Isle."

Sarneth bowed low as the members of the council clapped and nodded in return. Then a man with a full head of grey hair and a neatly trimmed grey beard on Aljeron's own side of the table stood and began to speak. Aljeron was startled to realize that the man standing was Garek Elathien, Mindarin's father. Now in his mid-sixties, Garek was notoriously unwilling to travel the few hours that lay between his home and Shalin Bel to attend the council. Though hospitable to visitors and friendly enough when present, he was something of a recluse and an independent spirit, and Aljeron wondered what his presence this morning could mean.

"Elder Sarneth," Garek said. "I was not in the city when you last visited Shalin Bel, and I have long hoped that you would return one day when I was here. My daughter, Mindarin, was one of those taken by the son of Vulsutyr and the Malekim, and I wanted to thank you personally, as a father, and indeed to thank all the Great Bear in the Lindandraal, for helping to get her back. I am very grateful, and I cannot fully express it."

Sarneth bowed low again. "Also as a father, I appreciate your heartfelt thanks. We were glad to help."

There was a momentary silence as Master Elathien took his seat. Aljeron hesitated, still recovering from the surprise. But aware that he was as yet not finished with the task at hand, he returned his attention to the Great Bear.

"Joining Sarneth is his son, Erigan, and his friend Arintol, who also fought the Malekim on the border of Lindan Wood."

There were more murmurs and nodding and more applause as the council rose to its feet to welcome the Great Bear. When the murmurs had died down, Elder Curran addressed the visitors. "You are most welcome here, friends. All that we can offer you is at your disposal. We even invite you to stay and partake of our council. Heavy matters lie before us and the wisdom of the Great Bear would be timely indeed."

"You flatter us with your courtesy, but with your permission, we will withdraw. From what I have seen, you have no need of my advice to govern Shalin Bel wisely. Even so, we will pray for Allfather's wisdom and blessing as you consider your affairs. We know that weighty matters lie before you. Thank you all for your gracious welcome."

The chief elder bowed slightly to Sarneth. "As you wish. We trust that you will find rest from your journey, and that we will have opportunity at some future point to talk further with you."

Each of the Great Bear bowed once more, and turning, walked back through the open door. When they had left the room and the door had been shut behind them, the members of the council took their seats again, with much whispering and murmuring. Elder Curran waited for a few moments, then turned once more to begin the council proper.

"Friends, we are gathered this day to discuss the matter of this war, which has lasted now for seven years. It has not been our habit in years past to open the matter for complete reevaluation, but it seems to me, and also to some of you, I know, that perhaps it is time to look carefully again at whether or not the course we have set is the best for Shalin Bel, for Werthanin, and indeed for all Kirthanin."

Tension rose in Aljeron as the chief elder spoke, and though he longed to stand and object, to insist that nothing had changed at all since the day the war had begun, he held himself back. He gripped the sides of his chair firmly and scowled as Elder Curran sat and Tergan Dorant stood on the side of the table occupied by the Merchants' Guild.

"Elder Curran, as usual, has spoken with much wisdom. I think we would do well to heed his advice and consider carefully, all of us, what would be the best course of action for the city from this day forward. I know that much of our discussion of this matter in the past has been marked by division and dissension, but I for one hope that today we will be able to talk reasonably, without malice or acrimony, as fellow citizens of a great city, who stand at a very important crossroads. And, what's more, I extend to those with whom I have disagreed most severely in the past, an offer of peace. I hope that today at last, we will see eye to eye and find the path of wisdom together."

There were some murmurs of approval, though many waited to hear what he really wanted to say before reacting with enthusiasm. Aljeron, for his part, struggled not to betray his irritation at Dorant's ingratiating manner and mock humility. His transparent appeal to "peace" among the council members was no doubt his prelude to a larger appeal for peace in all Werthanin. Though Dorant hadn't named Aljeron directly, everyone knew exactly who Dorant had meant with his appeal to "those with whom I have disagreed." It was Dorant's habit to speak first, calmly and with many references to words like peace, so that when he indirectly attacked Aljeron, the war, and everything he stood for, he could feign shock and disappointment if Aljeron retaliated with anger. Aljeron had taken the bait before, and he had come today determined to speak plainly and firmly but without anger.

"Though there was some disagreement about the wisdom of undertaking this war," Dorant continued, "the council decided that it was the right thing to do, and so we began to raise and train an army for a military campaign against Fel Edorath that was supposed to last six months. We were assured when the preparations began that winter and spring, that Rulalin Tarasir, the accused, would be captured and turned over to the Assembly by the following winter.

"That was seven years ago, and still Rulalin Tarasir hides

safely within Fel Edorath's walls. Meanwhile, we are embroiled in an extended conflict that none of us wanted. Some might even say it was unwarranted. It does not seem overly hasty to suggest that our original course of action has proven ultimately to be a failure. Countless young men from both cities have died as we have fought numerous battles across the plains of Werthanin with nothing to show for the effort. Of course, had Master Tarasir been taken and justice served, we could have consoled ourselves that the war had accomplished its goal, even if at a high price. Sadly, we cannot say that as we sit here this morning.

"So, my question today, the logical question I believe, is how long? How long are we to cast all other cares and concerns aside in the pursuit of this war? How long will Werthanin be divided, and how long will we be estranged from our brothers and sisters in Fel Edorath? Already I fear that the division will be difficult to heal. However noble the quest for justice, is it not time to consider compassion for the poor people of both our city and theirs? I say we should sue for peace immediately. By all means, let us continue to insist on the necessity of turning Rulalin over to the Assembly for trial, but let us also open the door for the free exchange of ideas, of discourse, of trade and commerce between us. Let us foreswear the foolish pride that pushes us to continue in this failed venture, and let us, let all of us, humble ourselves in a newfound commitment to peace. After all, have we forgotten that we are fighting over a crime that took place seventeen years ago? Is righting one distant wrong worth all this? So again I say to us all, how long? Is it not time for peace?"

When no one spoke immediately, Aljeron could not resist the fiery urge to object any longer, to denounce Dorant's despicable attempt to dress his self-interest in the garb of love for mankind and desire for peace universal. He stood, drawing all eyes to himself, and paused to check his anger. He would not lose this battle to emotion. "Master Dorant speaks of seeking peace, of pursuing what is best for Werthanin, and I agree with him. I agree that we should eagerly seek peace. But what peace should we seek? The peace he offers is the peace of inactivity. The peace he proclaims is a peace that turns a blind eye to murder so that the peace will not be disturbed. Is this the peace we want? Is this the peace you want your children and grandchildren to inherit?

"That is not the peace I want. I want the kind of peace that only comes from doing what is right. I want the kind of peace that flows from obedience to the just laws of Allfather. I want the kind of peace that comes when I stand in a mirror and see that I did not shrink back from doing what needed to be done, no matter how difficult. Though costly, is that not better than the peace Master Dorant offers?

"What difference does it make that the murder of Joraiem Andira took place seventeen years ago? Are we to reward Rulalin Tarasir because he has eluded justice successfully this far, or should we all the more ardently pursue him that justice might finally be done? And what message do we send to others who might follow in his footsteps if we turn away from justice simply because so many years have passed?

"Have we forgotten why it is justice has eluded us so long? Allow me to remind you that Peredin Tarasir hid his son for ten years. Ten years! He lied to everyone, including the Assembly, that whole time, swearing that he didn't know where Rulalin was. And, all the while, he was quietly and persistently campaigning among the Novaana and the first families of Fel Edorath that this whole thing wasn't really about justice after all, but was an issue of politics and ill-will, jealousy and envy between Shalin Bel and Fel Edorath. He convinced most of the Novaana of Fel Edorath that Rulalin had been unfairly and falsely accused, that the Assembly would never give him a fair hearing. So, in spite of the uniform testimony of all those who had been in Sulare with Rulalin, including Allfather's prophet, Valzaan himself, Peredin and his followers turned their backs to the will of the Assembly.

"Have we forgotten that we still might not know of Rulalin's whereabouts if not for a fortuitous tryst between a boastful servant girl from the Tarasir household and the boy of a Shalin Bel merchant? But Allfather brought this information to light so that Rulalin could be held accountable for his crime.

"And in case you have forgotten, let me remind you, that we did not choose war, they did. Ambassadors from the Assembly rode to Fel Edorath to present both the charges and the evidence in the case so that Rulalin could be turned over, not to us, but to the Assembly. Fel Edorath refused, knowing full well that the price of refusal might well be war. They were willing to risk their sons and husbands to defy justice; should we be less willing to risk our sons and husbands to defend justice? Or are we less committed to what we know to be right than they are to what they must know to be wrong?"

Aljeron paused and the room remained silent. He could feel his hands trembling. He was always nervous when he had to speak about this matter. It was so clear to him, but he worried that he couldn't say it as well as he would like. He worried that he might lose the war because of a stumbling or stammering tongue, not a failure in the field, though he knew there had been plenty of those along the way.

"Now, listen to me," he started again, his tone softer, more gentle. "I know that there have been mistakes." He paused and rephrased his point. "What I mean to say is, I know that I have made mistakes. You entrusted the army to me, and I made a rash promise. I assured you that when we marched out to war in the spring, we would return victorious by the start of winter, and that was a promise I didn't keep. Had I been wiser in the ways of war, we might well have returned victorious as promised, but I wasn't. I have learned though, by success and failure, how to conduct a war. What I say to you now, I do not say lightly. I have seven years of painful experience to draw upon. Members of the council, we stand on the brink of victory. Even as we gather together here, my army, our army, surrounds Fel Edorath almost completely, save only for the easternmost portions that face Agia Muldonai. For the last two years, we have slowly and methodically established a stranglehold on the city, as I promised to do when last we met to discuss the war two years ago. All spring and summer we have feasted on Fel Edorath's crops, and we have slowed the flow of food into the city to a trickle. When I return to the front in a few days, we will march into Fel Edorath and end this war once and for all. We cannot turn back now. The promise I made to you seven years ago was naïve, but the promise that I make today is a promise born of sweat and blood. We will take Fel Edorath before winter this year, and we will come home victorious."

Aljeron sat and surveyed the council. He had labored over just how to make his plea, and now that it had been made, he searched anxiously for some sign of its reception. Gradually small discussions broke out around the room. However, before the deliberations could go very far, Tergan Dorant interjected, "With all due respect to Master Balinor, we have heard such promises before. Why should we believe them now? I say again—"

"You have said enough, Tergan," Aljeron said coldly, cutting him off as he stood again. "You have no right to question me or doubt my word when I talk of military matters."

"Why? Have you not made such promises before?"

"What do you know of war, you are—"

"Enough! Both of you, enough." Aljeron leaned forward and looked down the row to see who had interrupted. *Garek.*

With his hands outstretched as though to calm and quiet

everyone, Master Elathien had stood, addressing both directly. "Your views on this matter were clearly and persuasively presented, Master Dorant. I think we understand your point, and I ask that you indulge me a chance to speak before you reiterate it. If you are dissatisfied when I am finished, by all means add whatever you like. Master Balinor, I say the same to you."

Looking a bit ruffled but trying to accept the gentle rebuff gracefully, Dorant sat down. Aljeron sat also. "The matter before us is not an easy one, and while the deep division between the two sides we have just heard from is well known, I suggest that a compromise is not as impossible as we think. Master Dorant has asked us to consider how long. It is a good question. When is enough, enough? When do we lay aside a pursuit, even a just pursuit, when it proves vain and futile and costly? Can the cost of what we believe to be just ever be so high that we must leave justice in Allfather's hands because it is out of our own? All good questions.

"At the same time, Master Balinor urges us not to reward wickedness and deceit with weakness and lack of resolve. Master Balinor reminds us that Allfather calls us to follow Him, even if success does not come easily and the road is difficult. What's more, we are all but guaranteed that victory lies right around the corner. Would it not be foolish to fight a war for seven years only to turn aside just as we stand ready to claim victory? No doubt it would be, which brings us to the compromise I would like to propose. It was in my mind to speak to this effect when I came, and all that has been said has confirmed my thoughts on the matter.

"I recommend that the council empower Aljeron to return to the front with our complete support to end this war by taking Fel Edorath. However, I also recommend that we further specify that if he cannot take Fel Edorath by Midwinter as promised, or, if Rulalin Tarasir evades capture when Fel Edorath is taken, that he nevertheless return home immediately.

To both Tergan and Aljeron I say, we have heard you. The answer to your question of how long, Tergan, is until Midwinter, just one season more. The answer to your question, Aljeron, of whether we should finish what we have begun, I say yes. Go and finish. You say Fel Edorath is ready to fall, go and take it. If Allfather blesses you, then both of you shall have what you desire by the first day of the New Year. This is my recommendation, and I submit it to the council for approval."

Excited chatter broke out around the table. Aljeron leaned over to Evrim. "I have considered so far only that we might win or lose here, but I'm not sure I know which this is. Do you?"

Evrim shrugged. "If we take the city as we expect, it's winning I guess."

"And if we don't, or if Rulalin slips away?"

"I guess we can't let either of those things happen."

Aljeron grunted his agreement and scanned the room again. Dorant was huddled with the other members of the Merchants' Guild, talking with emphatic gestures. They seemed to be disagreeing over whatever it was, but Aljeron couldn't really tell. They had to be happy with the proposal. If it was accepted by the council, then they were guaranteed an end to the war by the start of the New Year. It would probably take them the three months in between just to be ready for it. What's more, if Aljeron and the army could manage to conquer the city in the intervening months, then Tergan and the other merchants would not only benefit from the newly made peace but also from the position of strength Shalin Bel would enjoy for at least a time.

Aljeron was not held in suspense for long. Elder Curran rose and tried to quiet the room. The task was considerably more difficult than it had been at the start of the meeting, but he managed at last to restore order. "Members of the council, we have three alternatives before us. We could take the road suggested by Master Dorant and call for an immediate end to the war. We could take the slightly modified suggestion of Master Elathien and grant the army one more season to take Fel Edorath and end the war. Or, we could leave things for now as they have been, entrusting the war effort to Master Balinor as we set a date for our next meeting, when we will again consider our options. As I see it, those are the three choices before us, and the decision we make now could have far-reaching implications. So, it is my suggestion that we adjourn for now, take some time to think, and come back together this afternoon."

"With your permission," Master Dorant began as he rose and faced the chief elder, "I would like to say something."

"You may," Elder Curran said, looking as if he was bracing for what might come next.

"For our part, the Merchants' Guild is willing to concede that at least the first of those options need not be considered. We believe that Master Elathien has spoken wisely, and if it pleases the rest of the council, we will happily agree to his compromise without adjournment if enough of the council is in agreement. So, I submit to the council that the Merchants' Guild unanimously supports the decision to grant the army its wish to proceed with its current plan, so long as it is understood that whatever might happen, the war ends by Midwinter."

Murmurs rippled along the Novaana's side of the table and along the side with the city elders, and as Aljeron watched the reactions around the room, he realized that the matter was already decided. A member of the Novaana had suggested a compromise that had been accepted completely by the Merchants' Guild, and it seemed to offer everyone the best of both worlds. Even though he did not now doubt what he had believed wholeheartedly just a moment ago, that Fel Edorath would fall when he pressed the attack, he didn't like having his hands tied. He worried at times that securing Rulalin would be more difficult than taking the city, and now it looked like a deadline had been set for that part of his mission as well.

Elder Curran raised his arm to silence the room. "It would appear that the Merchants' Guild and the city elders are in agreement. We also unanimously support the suggestion of Master Elathien. And, since Master Elathien is one of the Novaana, it would appear that we have at least some support among them as well." He gazed up and down the row of Novaana. "Are there others among the Novaana who would assent to this suggestion?"

Several heads nodded both to the right and left of Aljeron, and a few of them gave their verbal agreement as well. Aljeron did not nod in agreement with them, but he did not protest either. He knew enough of battle to know finality when he saw it. "Well," Elder Curran continued, "it seems to me that we have come as close to unanimity on this matter as we have ever been. We are agreed."

Neither Aljeron nor Evrim spoke much during lunch. There wasn't a lot to say. "I should have seen this coming," Aljeron sighed.

"We both should have."

When they finished, they sat silently at the table in Aljeron's parlor while Koshti slept on the floor, his tail twitching every so often. Evrim was about to leave when Aljeron suggested they go find the Great Bear.

"I've never really been around one," Evrim said, and with that they were on their way.

They wound their way through the corridors until they reached a pair of rooms set apart from the others. "Well, I don't know which of them is where," Aljeron said, "so I guess it doesn't matter which door I knock on."

He knocked on one of them, and the other door opened. At the door was Sarneth, and even down on all fours, he stood just about as tall as the doorframe and as wide. Aljeron and Evrim passed inside, where they found the other two Great Bear resting on the floor of the large parlor. Most of the furniture had been stacked neatly against the far wall. A single chair remained in the middle of the room, and it was occupied by an older man with long, grey, braided hair. He rose and said, "My, my, Aljeron Balinor. After all these years."

"Caan?" Aljeron said with a mixture of surprise and excitement. "What in the world are you doing here? How . . . how did this happen?"

"I traveled here with Sarneth from Lindan Wood."

Aljeron turned to Sarneth. "You didn't say anything about Caan being here."

"Sorry about that, Aljeron," Caan answered for Sarneth. "That was my doing. I had so looked forward to the look of surprise on your face when you saw me—and, by the way, you didn't disappoint—that I told Sarneth not to say anything if he saw you first. My horse lost a shoe as we approached the city, and I was making arrangements for him at the gate while the stewards showed the others in."

"Well," Aljeron started, then he stopped and stepped across the room, wrapping his arms around his old friend. "It doesn't matter now. It's just great to have you here. I can't believe my fortune."

"Yes," Caan answered, sitting down again and motioning to Aljeron and Evrim to bring over two chairs, "it is good to see you too. Of course, I am sorry that it is under these circumstances. I know you bear the weight of many things. Why don't you introduce me to your friend."

"Yes, I'm sorry," Aljeron turned to Evrim as he handed him a chair so he could sit down. "This is Evrim Minluan. He married Joraiem Andira's sister, Kyril, the spring after our time in Sulare. He was Joraiem's closest friend in Dal Harat, and he came to Shalin Bel when the war started to offer his services.

He's become a good friend. You would like him Caan, he is a great tracker."

"Glad to hear it," Caan said, extending his hand to Evrim. "Though long belated, please accept my condolences on Joraiem's death. He was a wonderful man, and his death was a terrible thing."

"Thank you," Evrim said as he took his own seat. "It's a pleasure to meet the man behind the legend. Aljeron is always talking about things he learned from you in Sulare."

"Well, he was a good pupil, at least for me. I think my classes on fighting and battle strategy had a special interest for him. I don't think he paid nearly as much attention to Ulmindos or Berin. Even as a lad, Aljeron seemed to have only swordplay and warfare on the brain. Not much has changed, eh?"

Aljeron took Caan's remark as an opportunity to vent some of his frustrations about the morning's meeting. "Well, it looks as though my days as a soldier will be coming to an end pretty quickly."

Sarneth and the other Great Bear glanced at one another as Sarneth asked, "What do you mean? Is the war over?"

"No, not yet. But I've been given a deadline of Midwinter to finish it."

"Can you?" Caan asked.

"I think so. I know I can take the city, but taking Rulalin could prove a bit more complicated."

"So," Sarneth continued, "you have been directed to finish the war by Midwinter, whether or not you succeed in your goal?"

"Yes. I am told that I have the support of the city only for one season longer. So either we get him now, or I guess we never do."

A few moments of quiet hung in the room. "Well," Caan finally said, "though it sounds like this wasn't exactly what you wanted to hear from the council, Aljeron, I can tell you that it is a big relief to us."

"Why?" Aljeron asked.

Caan looked intently at Aljeron, "Because it is time, Aljeron. I was sent by Master Berin to come with Sarneth so that we might make essentially the same request."

"You came all the way from Sulare to ask me to end the war?"

"More or less, though I think you will see it is a little bit more complicated than that."

"But why? You were there. You know what Rulalin did. How could you come asking me to end it when we haven't accomplished what we set out to do?"

"Because there is a growing fear that there is a lot more at stake in all of this than simply the punishment of one man, Aljeron. You know why old men all across Kirthanin trembled at the thought of an army from Shalin Bel marching on Fel Edorath, no matter how deeply they believed it to be right. They trembled because the War of Division was a civil war that engulfed all of Kirthanin and gave Malek the opportunity to invade from the Forbidden Isle. The longer this war stretches on, the more people fear it might become something that Malek could use for his third attempt."

"This kind of thinking is not new to me, Caan. I have heard it a thousand times before, and I certainly didn't need you to come all the way from Sulare to tell me this. You know something else."

"I do. As you know, in the aftermath of our return from the Forbidden Isle, several things changed in Sulare. The visits every seven years of the young Novaana were suspended indefinitely, and the Assembly approved a decision to patrol the Southern Ocean more carefully, especially along the coast below Sulare, to guard against Malek's use of the island. Ulmindos recruited several captains and their ships, and Sulare was once again manned at least a little bit like it once was of old. You would not have recognized it, Aljeron. Many of the houses in the city were filled with the families of the sailors and captains, and the tables in the Great Hall were full most nights. Farmers from nearby towns and villages came to work the long fallow fields and vineyards, and almost overnight Sulare became a city again. Some twenty or more ships could be found at dock on any given evening, and easily that many again would be out at sea at the same time, patrolling the coast and watching the long-forgotten waters.

"Throughout the years this vigil has been maintained. Many of the sailors who work the ships now are children of those who first came, men who have come to see Sulare as their home. They sail with their fathers and brothers and uncles and understand that in some larger sense they are serving all Kirthanim with their labor.

"All seemed to go well and without incident until the springtime, a year and a half ago. It was early in Spring Rise, when one of the ships out on a routine patrol for three weeks never came back. Other ships went out looking for it, but it was never found. Neither Cimaris Rul nor any of the other coastal towns had word of her. It was concluded that she had been lost at sea. We held a memorial service for those who had been lost, and we continued with the patrols.

"Thing returned to normal until this past winter. In two separate incidents, ships out on patrol did not return and could not be found. Rumors and worries began to ripple through the community. Three ships lost at sea with not even a hint of storm or bad weather at the time they were out was alarming. These were all good ships with good captains and good crews. The growing suspicion was that somehow Malek had destroyed them.

"The patrols were increased, and no ship sailed any section of the Southern Ocean alone. All ships went in pairs, and everyone was on edge. Then, this past spring, two more disappeared. Panic spread through Sulare like wildfire. It intensified when two sailors from one of the ships returned to Sulare, bruised and battered and with a remarkable story to tell. At first we believed them to be delirious, because they spoke only of terror in the deep, of a massive and terrifying shadow that lived on the ocean floor and that had come up out of the sea to destroy the ships. Their descriptions were vague and changed over time, but they agreed on the essential facts that whatever had attacked their ships had done so with amazing strength and speed, and had been wholly unlike anything they had ever seen or even imagined.

"Their stories were believed by many but not all, for no other testimony could confirm or deny their stories, and none of the five lost ships were ever found. Even so, it did not take long for most of the families to leave Sulare. They had come to guard against ships sailing to and fro between the Forbidden Isle and the mainland, not to risk their lives with some mysterious ocean creature. Even those who argued adamantly that such a creature did not exist were shaken by the loss of five ships. In the end, Master Berin urged Ulmindos to suspend the patrols until we could receive guidance from the Assembly. An embassy was sent just after Midsummer, and I was given the task to come and see you. Sarneth, who had been visiting at the time of the most recent disappearance, volunteered to come with me. And so we have come by way of Lindan Wood, so Sarneth could speak with the other elders of his clan."

"A strange and fascinating tale, to be sure," Aljeron said, "but I don't see the connection with me or this war."

"Do you not?" Caan replied. "Look, I have no idea what happened to those ships. The creature those sailors described sounds like a legend to me, the kind told to frighten children. What I do know is that in the space of a single year, we lost five ships after losing none in the fifteen years before. That doesn't sound like a coincidence to me. Malek is involved somehow, and if Malek is up to something, then this is a really bad time to be fighting a war among ourselves, no matter how just the cause. Do you see now?"

Aljeron sat quietly, then turned to the Great Bear. "And this is why you have come too, Sarneth? You wish to ask me on behalf of the Lindandraal to end the war?"

"Actually, I am here on behalf of all the draals. We do not wish to interfere in your business, but we would like you to consider at least suspending the war for a while."

Aljeron rose and walked to the parlor window. He gazed out at nothing in particular. "So, if I tell you that the war will be over by Midwinter, will that answer be satisfactory?"

"It is as speedy an end as we could have hoped for," Caan answered.

"Well, if things go well enough, it may not even be that long," Aljeron answered without turning round. The sun outside was very bright for such a crisp, autumn day.

"Aljeron." Caan stood and walked over toward the window. "There is another reason why it is time."

"What's that?" Aljeron said blankly.

"It is time for you to move on to something else. I think your council has recognized that too. You've done all that a friend could reasonably have been expected to do. I doubt that many people could have done all that you have done. Rulalin deserves to be tried and punished, I know that as well as you, but even if he is, Aljeron, even if you succeed, I do not think that you will find that justice gives you all you seek."

Aljeron remained at the window, his body motionless as stone. "I know you, Aljeron, and I have followed your life with interest since you left Sulare. You are a good leader, and you could use that gift for more than warfare. You have to let this go."

After several moments, Aljeron turned away from the window and walked across the room to Evrim's chair, motioning for him to stand. "Sarneth, Arintol, Erigan, we are delighted to have you here, and I look forward to discussion of happier things in the few days before I must return to the front. Caan, it has been too long. I would love to discuss our situation at Fel Edorath and our plans for concluding the war swiftly, if you would have the time before I leave."

"I would be happy to be of service, though I doubt I have much left to teach you."

"A fresh perspective is all I ask." Aljeron walked to the door, followed closely by Evrim. "We will check in to see how you are faring later."

They slipped into the hallway, and Evrim followed as Aljeron walked silently away.

3

CHOICES

THE DOORS TO THE GREAT HALL were open and the light from the windows high above the chamber floor fell in bright squares on the council table. Some rooms were conceived and constructed and then put to quite ordinary uses: a parlor or bedroom or kitchen or merchant's shop. Then, of course, there were other rooms. They were conceived and constructed and then dedicated to extraordinary things. They became reservoirs of power or the scenes of momentous decisions.

People aren't so different, Aljeron thought as he moved on past the Hall. Some were born to quite ordinary lives, farming or trading or crafting. They grew up, learned a skill, and then put it to use until they died. Others, well, their lives seemed set apart for greater things. At times, he had felt like one of the latter men, but more frequently now he wondered if he really was. Perhaps Caan had been right. He had always been interested in the details of warfare. Maybe that was just his trade, like Dorant was a merchant. Maybe people who seemed set apart for greater things were just ordinary people who plied their trade or used their one skill or gift at a particularly important time. In the end, he didn't suppose it mattered all that much, save that in less than a season's time he would have little use for his particular skill. With the matter of Rulalin no longer before him, he would have to figure out what to do with the rest of his life.

Aljeron walked down the hallway that led to the front of the building and stepped through it into the sunshine. It was indeed very bright and very crisp. He pulled his cloak around his shoulders and shielded his eyes as he looked at the front gate of the compound across the courtyard. He had told Evrim he wouldn't go out into the city, but he hadn't said that he wouldn't go outside. He turned and walked along the front of the building, eventually going around the far side. About midway along the wall was a set of stairs that led up to a large rooftop garden above the main dining room. Though Aljeron didn't typically frequent rooftop gardens, he paused at the foot of the stairs. It occurred to him that walking alone on the roof and looking out over the city might be the very thing he wanted to do.

Upon reaching the garden Aljeron stepped off the stairs and kept straight ahead along the rail at the side of the building toward what would have been the back of the dining room. At the back corner of the garden he faced the city as it stretched out south and west of the Great Hall. He could not see into many of the streets beyond the walls of the Great Hall's courtyards, but he could hear the people and animals. The city's sounds and smells were alive, and he wondered what the streets of Fel Edorath sounded like and looked like right about now. He wondered if the people there went about their business in an attempt to sustain some semblance of normal life, or if the expectation of imminent ruin hung over them, seeping into the most mundane details of the day.

He started along the back end of the garden, where the rail separated it from a slight drop to the neighboring building. As he moved along the roof, he turned his attention to the side of the garden opposite the stairs, and for the first time realized that he was not alone. A slender woman with long, dark brown hair looked over the rail with her back to him. She wore a light red dress with a matching red coat, both embroidered with intricate black stitching. The vista before her extended past the towering walls and roof of the Great Hall, a building much taller than the others in the compound, out over the center of the city, which sprawled north and east for as far as Aljeron could see. She appeared oblivious to his presence.

"Hello?" Aljeron called as he walked around what appeared to be a rose bush, though without blossoms Aljeron didn't really know.

"Hello, Aljeron," the woman said without turning. "I heard you on the stair and saw you come up, but you seemed so preoccupied that I didn't want to disturb you. Please don't think me rude."

She turned her head and looked over her shoulder, her eyes bright with warmth and welcome. Aljeron was surprised but managed a reasonable greeting, "Aelwyn, welcome. I didn't know you were in the city."

"You remembered my name," the woman said, laughing.

"Of course."

"I didn't really doubt you would," Aelwyn said, reassuringly. "I just spent so many years being known to you as Mindarin's little sister."

Aljeron reached the place along the rail where Aelwyn stood. He stepped up, avoiding a prickly bush, like holly, to stand about a span away from her. She watched him, still smiling. She had not changed much in the few years since he had seen her last. She was tall for a woman, probably half a hand taller than Mindarin. Her skin was olive and her eyes bright green. She was slender and graceful, every bit as pretty as Mindarin, though lacking the same fiery tongue.

"I assume you came in with your father."

"Yes, when he announced he was coming in, I seized the opportunity to visit a few of my friends in town."

She looked over at Aljeron with a penetrating gaze. Aljeron shifted nervously. He had never thought of himself as either adept or awkward around women, but he had found Aelwyn a little unnerving since she came of age. In truth, he had always thought of her as Mindarin's little sister, but she had grown well past that. "It's nice to see you again. It's been a few years."

"Yes it has," she said gently, stepping a little closer to him. "Three in fact. I haven't seen you since we came into Shalin Bel for your father's funeral. We've been here since, of course, but you were always at the front."

"Yes," Aljeron answered, "I've been away more and more as this has gone on."

She put her hand on his arm. "You know, Aljeron, I really liked your mom and dad. Your mother especially. She was always very nice to me. I can remember being left behind as the 'baby' when the older Novaana would play together during council meetings and seasonal festivals, and she would always take pity and spend time with me. She was wonderful."

"She was."

The silence following made Aljeron uneasy. He straightened his cloak unnecessarily before moving to just about the only topic he knew to bring up with Aelwyn. "How is Mindarin?"

"All right, I think. I haven't seen her for a few weeks."

"I never really had a chance to extend my condolences to her."

"Ralon's death was sudden, but I'd say that Mindarin is doing pretty well. He's been gone a couple years now. It was hardest on the children, who still miss him of course. I'm sure I'm not telling you anything. You knew Mindarin never really loved him. Then again, he never really loved her either. He married Mindarin for the status he could gain from marrying one of the Novaana, and she, well, who knows why she married him. In the end, though, I think they did about as well together as they were going to. They learned to respect one another, even care for one another to a certain degree."

Aljeron listened as he gazed out over the city, a cool wind brushing against his face. "When the war is over, I will make it a point to catch up with her. I've neglected a lot of things and a lot of friends these last seven years."

"I think your friends will understand, don't you?"

He looked back at her. "Why didn't she come into town with you?" he asked.

Aelwyn's smile faded and she looked away. "She has been away the last few weeks. She didn't know that we were coming."

Aljeron watched her, looking out over the rail. She stole a quick glance at him. "Ah," Aljeron said softly. "Away. Now I understand." He shook his head and clenched the rail tightly. "So she's back at that, is she? She just won't lay it down."

"Aljeron, she means no harm," Aelwyn said, stepping closer and taking hold of his arm. "Don't hold it against her."

"She could get herself killed."

"I know. I warned her. Dad warned her, but she is convinced that if she maintains a friendship with Rulalin, she might be able to talk some sense into him and end this war."

"This war will end when I lead him away in chains, or when we find Rulalin's dead body on the battlefield."

"Maybe, though that isn't the only way it could end. In fact, wouldn't it be great if he left Fel Edorath voluntarily? Wouldn't it be great if you could bring all of your men home now? Why does this bother you so much? The important thing is that the war ends, isn't it?"

"Of course, Aelwyn. I just don't think Rulalin deserves her kindness and devotion."

"She's always loved him," Aelwyn said, sadness in her eyes. "I love her dearly, but I can't explain it."

"Love is a strange and unpredictable thing."

"It is indeed," she answered, her laughter returning. "Well said."

Aljeron didn't know what else to say, the subject of Mindarin being exhausted. After a moment, Aelwyn continued. "I promised my father I'd meet him to go out shopping in the city this afternoon."

"I hope you enjoy your time here," Aljeron said as she started across the roof.

"I already am." She smiled as she waved and then walked briskly across the garden to the stairs on the far side. In a moment, she had disappeared below the roofline. Without really knowing why, he started across the roof after her, but when he reached the top of the stairs and could see her in neither direction below, he did not descend. Instead, he leaned against the rail and looked down into the narrow courtyard on this side of the Great Hall complex.

So different from Mindarin. Were I young and handsome, I'd love to linger here with her on a summer's day. He stroked his scarred face, and after a few moments returned to his chambers.

The sitting room just outside the bedroom was really quite nice, though Mindarin had often complained of it in the past. The first time she had come to Fel Edorath after the beginning of the war, Rulalin had given her this room to stay in, and he had put her here every visit since. It had grown on her over those years, to the point now where she was actually a little bit fond of it, even the wretched statuette under the window of a boy with a contorted face riding the back of a large dog. Rulalin seemed offended when she had first mocked it. Evidently it had been given to him when he was himself a boy, and for some mystifying reason it still held a special place in his heart.

The rest of the room was not quite as hideous, being decorated with the skins of animals Rulalin had hunted, most of them in the years before Sulare. The large bearskin on the floor beside the table still disturbed her, as it had from the beginning. Having met some of the Great Bear and in fact owing her life to them, she found herself ill at ease around this trophy, even though she knew it had been taken from quite an ordinary bear.

She stood and walked to the large window that looked out over the city, and the sorrow that had welled up inside her when she arrived the previous evening returned. There was a semblance of ordinary life out in the streets of Fel Edorath, but it was a mockery of the city's pre-war state. Shops and merchants had almost nothing to sell. Inns and taverns were closed, for there was little drink and less food, and no one could afford to buy it anyway. A general air of resignation and defeat surrounded everything and everyone Mindarin had seen since her arrival. It was madness for Rulalin to even consider taking the field against Aljeron again, but she had no doubt that this was precisely what he intended. She sighed and moved back to the table as she fidgeted with her smooth black dress. This was her last chance.

She drummed her fingers on the table impatiently. It was Fifth Hour at least, and she had been guaranteed an audience with Rulalin before lunch. She scowled at the thought that he might be putting this off. It was true that she didn't have much new to say, but surely even Rulalin could see with all that had transpired since last she came that if she had been right then, she was certainly right now. There was but one choice left for anyone who possessed even a modicum of common sense. He had to surrender now and throw himself on the mercy of the Assembly.

There was a knock on the door. "Come in," she called.

One of the stewards opened the door just enough to pop his head through, and before he could open his mouth to speak, Mindarin unleashed her frustration. "Look, this is getting ridiculous. I've come a long way and don't appreciate being made to wait in this tiny room all morning. Don't even give me one of his stupid excuses, just turn around and toddle off to wherever he's hiding and drag him here by his ears if you have to, or so help me, I'll come and do it myself.

"And don't think I won't," she added before the steward could reply.

"Actually, he's right behind me, Mistress Elathien. I was just going to announce him."

"Oh, very well then. Send him in."

The steward was pulled from the opening by an unseen hand and the door opened wide enough for Rulalin to stride in, a frown plastered on his face.

"What is this 'Mistress Elathien' business?" he asked.

"I never did like Ralon's name. Orlene. What kind of name is that?" Rulalin kept frowning at her. "Don't look at me like that. I'm not going to make the children go by Elathien. I'm not trying to blot his name out or anything, I've just decided I like 'Mindarin Elathien' better, that's all. What's wrong with that?"

Rulalin walked to the table and poured himself a cup of water from the pitcher there. He drank thirstily and filled the cup again. "I wasn't hiding, Mindarin. I have a siege to worry about and a war to manage, or have you forgotten?"

"Don't get snippy with me. I'm the one who's been waiting all morning. I know there is a war on, but it isn't like there's anything terribly pressing at the moment, is there?"

"There are always matters that need addressing."

"Well, I'm sorry to interrupt you, but if you didn't completely lack common sense, I wouldn't have to."

"Mindarin," Rulalin said, stepping right in front of her as she stood by the table. He put his hands on her shoulders and gripped her tightly. "You have to stop coming here. It isn't safe. You come riding in here through both battle lines as though nothing is going on. One of these days, Aljeron's army is going to suspect you of something less noble than trying to talk me into surrender, and my own will greet you none to gently, no matter how much I protest that you are not a spy."

"I'm not a spy for anybody." Mindarin wrenched free of Rulalin's grip.

"I know, but a lot of people think it."

"Well I don't care what people think."

"Oh no? Then I don't suppose you'll care that those who don't believe you are a spy have their own story about why you keep coming to see me, and the purpose they have attributed to you is even less noble."

Mindarin grew red from embarrassment and anger, but she did not speak. "I don't like your character being attacked, either way," he added gently, taking a seat on the opposite side of the table.

Mindarin sat too and refilled her own cup with water. "I appreciate your concern for my good name, but that is a trivial discussion now. If you continue on the course you're on, most of your people aren't going to have opportunity to do much of anything, let alone gossip among themselves about you and me."

"Mindarin," Rulalin began.

"Why don't you listen?" Mindarin cut him off. "Everyone in Fel Edorath but you knows this war is over. Everyone in the world knows it, but you're too proud or too stubborn or too . . . *something* to give it up. It's over. Your soldiers and your people are starving. There is no fight left in them. I saw them as I came in, with listless eyes and frail bodies. They will be unable to stand up to Aljeron's men when they come, and they will come. You know that. You must surrender. The only chance you have is to appeal for clemency and pray that Allfather spares your life."

"Clemency? Aljeron knows nothing of clemency. He wants me dead, so I might as well fight to the death."

"The Assembly does know clemency. Send me to Aljeron. I will tell him that you'll surrender, but only to the Assembly. A delegation from the Assembly can take you into custody. But you must surrender. It's the only way."

"Mindarin, even if Aljeron lets them take me, the Assembly will sentence me to death."

"You are wrong, Rulalin. Your fate has not been decided yet. You might yet avoid death. Not everyone in Kirthanin is as firmly set on seeing you dead as Aljeron is. Both my father and I are prepared to speak against a death sentence if you surrender, confess to what you have done, acknowledge your sorrow, and appeal for mercy. If you will do this, we will argue in favor of permanent imprisonment or house arrest, and I think many will agree with us. They believe far too many lives have been lost already, and their hearts will be soft if you will give them reason to believe you are worthy of their mercy."

Rulalin rose and walked to the window, his arms crossed. He stared at the city, and Mindarin hoped that perhaps he was considering her proposal. Without turning from the window, he said, "Maybe I'm not worthy of their mercy, Mindarin. Did you ever consider that maybe, just maybe, death is what I actually deserve?"

Mindarin rose and walked to the place where Rulalin stood. She reached up to put her arm on his but thought better of it, clasping her hands before her instead. "I have considered it, Rulalin. What you did, all those years ago, was a terrible thing. I don't like to think about it even now. But that was seventeen years ago. You aren't the same person you were then. I don't believe you even knew what you were doing. You had just recovered from a terrible injury. You had been on the brink of death. And"—Mindarin hesitated—"you came back from death only to find Wylla lost to you."

"I did know," Rulalin turned to Mindarin, a fiery glint in his eyes. "I knew exactly what I was doing. I went over that meeting with Joraiem a thousand times before it happened. I laid awake at night and played the conversation through in my head over and over and over."

"See, you weren't in your right mind."

"You aren't listening to me. I hadn't lost my mind, and I wasn't governed by rage. I don't know what I was, though perhaps despair is closest. I simply knew that everything I had dreamed of since I first met her was over."

Mindarin turned away and went back to the table. She had never spoken of what Rulalin had done, though she had often wanted to ask. Now that he was speaking of it, she wished he wouldn't.

He turned from the window too, facing her but gazing at the door. "I went to meet him, Mindarin, perfectly willing to die. I lacked the strength to take my own life, but I was willing to let Joraiem take it from me. I was willing to lay myself down so that he and Wylla could be happy, but I knew before he ever came that morning that he wouldn't. I knew Joraiem wouldn't kill me. So I had no other choice; if he wouldn't kill me, then I had to kill him.

"So you see," he continued as he came and sat down at the table beside her. "I knew exactly what I was doing."

Rulalin sat back in the chair, sighing. "My problem is that I have always been afraid of dying. If I'd only died when the Malekim wounded me, I would have died a hero. If I'd only had the strength to take my own life in Sulare, at least I would have died before my name became synonymous with villainy and treachery. Even now, I fear death every bit as much as I long for it."

"If you fear it," Mindarin said with renewed vigor, "surrender. Put your life in the hands of the Assembly."

"Surrender? I may fear death, but I've no wish to live locked up like a bird in a cage."

"You do already."

Rulalin didn't reply. He gazed down at the table. "I can't do it, Mindarin," he said eventually. "I'm guilty of all I'm accused of and more. That, I must live with."

"Rulalin," Mindarin began.

"No, Mindarin," he interrupted her firmly. "Enough. I have decided. It has been good to see you, but you must leave the city by nightfall. That was the agreement I made with my officers when we admitted you this time. And you must not come back. You will not be given entrance to Fel Edorath again while we are still in control of it. It is for your own good."

Mindarin wanted to protest, but she knew it would be pointless. She rose, went around the table to Rulalin, and crouched beside him. She took his hand in her own. "There are so many regrets in life, Rulalin. I know you feel terrible for what you did, but many of us have done awful things. You aren't the only one. I just want you to know, if I don't see you again, that I am sorry for the various ways I have wronged you, and I forgive you for the times when you wronged me."

As she stood, she leaned in and kissed his cheek gently. "I can sympathize with the loss of love, you know, and with making poor choices because of it."

She stepped into her bedroom to retrieve her riding bag, then spoke to Rulalin for what she thought might be the last time. "Please thank the stewards for my breakfast this morning and for the offer of food last night. It was very kind considering how hard food is to come by in Fel Edorath these days."

"I will."

"Goodbye, Rulalin," Mindarin said as she paused at the door.

"Goodbye, Mindarin."

Before pulling the door to behind her, she said, "Rulalin, throwing your life away needlessly won't atone for what you did, but acknowledging it and humbling yourself before the Assembly might be a start."

Rulalin made his way through the narrow halls of the enormous house that had been in the Tarasir family since the Second Age, or so he had always been told. Of course, the original building had been expanded over the years so that now it reached up and out in many directions, a sprawling labyrinth of rooms. It had been a magical place to grow up, with endless hours spent by Rulalin and his friends running down dim passageways and slinking up and down narrow stairs, both straight and spiral, as they played. Since the beginning of the war, though, little mirth could be found within these walls, as it had become the military headquarters and residence for many of Rulalin's chief officers.

Rulalin made his way down to the kitchen from the second floor where Mindarin had lodged. The kitchen was Mistress Brahan's domain, and it was no surprise to Rulalin that he found her presiding over the house stewards, talking to them as they sat around the large open fire. It had been her habit for many years to give the stewards daily instruction, generally in matters of food preparation, which she always maintained was the first responsibility of a good steward. "Feed your employer well," she often told the stewards under her, "and they will overlook almost any other fault."

As Rulalin entered the kitchen, though, the lesson for the day was put on hold, and Mistress Brahan crossed the room to meet him. She was by no means jovial, but she had always been, as far as Rulalin could remember, a pleasant person. Even when presented with legitimate opportunity to rebuke those under her authority, her reprimands were nevertheless quiet, measured, even humble. For all this, her stewards never showed any proclivity to take advantage of her kindness, but rather worked as hard as they could to serve her and the house well. Rulalin had tried to model his own treatment of his officers after Mistress Brahan's manner, though these attempts had not always been successful.

"Could I borrow you for a moment, Mistress Brahan?" Rulalin asked softly as she drew near.

"Of course. What can I do for you?"

"I just wanted to finish the conversation we were having last night about our dwindling food supply. I'm sorry we were interrupted."

"That's quite all right," Mistress Brahan answered gently, putting her wrinkled hand on Rulalin's arm. "I know that you have much more to attend to than my concerns over our larder."

"Your concerns over our larder are as important as any of the matters before me. Our options for the future are directly related to our food supply."

Mistress Brahan nodded. "Well, I'm sorry to say that the situation is worse than I'd first guessed. I thought we might have a solid season of stores left, but I'm afraid I've had to cut that estimate in half. We can last at our current rate of consumption to about the beginning of Winter Rise, but no more."

"Only until Winter Rise?" Rulalin repeated, shocked. "Why has the situation changed so dramatically? Only a few weeks ago you thought we would survive until Midwinter."

"I've had opportunity to inspect our stores more closely. Rats have devoured no fewer than three barrels of grain, and another barrel of salted pork that was improperly sealed has rotted. And, to make matters worse, the last shipment of dried fruit that we were expecting was intercepted as it was being smuggled in, and I'm afraid it has been eaten by the soldiers from Shalin Bel, who sit watching our gates like hawks watching mice in the grass."

Rulalin nodded. Mistress Brahan was clasping her hands and looking nervously at the long table beside them. "It is unfortunate that once again we have furnished a meal for our enemy, but it isn't your fault," he said. "We knew there were risks to smuggling the food in that way. At least we were successful a few times."

"Yes, that's true."

"At any rate, I suspect that you also have a suggestion for me?"

"I do. I propose that we continue to prepare a full breakfast, followed in the early afternoon with a half portion lunch, and that we get rid of the evening meal altogether. I will try to make a light broth with our breakfast and lunch remains to stave off the hunger pangs at dinner, but I can't promise much."

"Do you think we could make it until the New Year if we make the change?"

Mistress Brahan grimaced. "I can't promise, but we will get a whole lot closer if we do."

"All right. Make the change immediately. Have the stewards inform everyone that I have ordered the change. If they don't like it, tell them to talk to me about it."

"I will, Master Rulalin," said Mistress Brahan. "And thank you for understanding."

"You're welcome," Rulalin answered kindly. "There are many things I don't know, but I am certain that it is never a good idea to ignore the advice of Mistress Brahan when it comes to matters of the household."

Mistress Brahan smiled as she turned and made her way back to the stewards. She clapped her hands together twice, quickly, and they rose to their feet and gathered around her. Soon, several of the stewards were moving briskly around the kitchen carrying out her orders. "If only my men obeyed me like that," Rulalin whispered to himself.

As Rulalin approached his own quarters, two large rooms set apart in one of the more recent additions, he heard his name called from behind. He turned to find Soran Nuvaar walking quickly toward him, the sword that Rulalin had given him and that he wore everywhere as though it were a priceless treasure hanging at his side.

Soran's father was well known in Fel Edorath as one of the most unsuccessful merchants ever to dwell within the city. He had undertaken half a dozen commercial enterprises in his lifetime and failed more miserably in each of them than almost anyone had ever failed at even one such venture. He seemed to have a gift for making spectacularly poor judgments about his investments and had eventually been forced to work as a servant in three different households to pay off debts that would never fully be recouped. For all that, he had been well liked and had many friends, though all of them knew better than to even consider loaning him as much as the price of a cup of cold cider.

Soran, for his part, had worked alongside his father for years, trying to help him repay those debts, until his father died about the time the war began. While the war was to many a grievous misfortune, it was to Soran a glorious opportunity. Here at last was a chance to succeed at something and make a name for himself that would put distance between himself and his father's reputation. To Soran's credit, he had done exactly that. He had distinguished himself enough to be made an officer in the first year of the conflict. Almost anything entrusted to his command succeeded, even the almost impossible assignments sent his way by envious superiors. At last Rulalin himself had taken note of him and brought him out of the regular chain of command to serve as his own assistant and main advisor, which he had been the last three years. Though ten years Rulalin's junior and only thirty-one years old, few doubted that Soran had one of the sharpest military minds in

Fel Edorath. It was widely believed that if he could not help Rulalin find a way to victory, it would never be found.

"Soran?" Rulalin inquired.

"Do you have a few minutes?"

"Yes," Rulalin answered, turning back to his door. He slipped a small black key out of his pocket and unlocked his door with a single, deft motion. He didn't remember when he had first taken to locking his personal rooms, though it had been several years ago.

"The last of the streams on the eastern side of the city has been dammed. There is no fresh water coming into the city."

"We knew this would happen eventually."

"I know. They should have done it a long time ago. I would have."

"My guess is that some of them didn't have the stomach to face what cutting off our water would do to our people."

"Then why do it now?"

"Because they think this will be over before the full effects of the water shortage will be felt."

"I think you're right, Rulalin. When I heard about the water, all I could think was that the end was here at last."

Rulalin turned and motioned Soran to follow him. He walked across the large outer room of his chambers, which also served as a meeting room, and entered the inner quarters. It too was large, and along the far wall a simple wooden bed with a small nightstand marked the only part of his room dedicated to personal space. Along the near wall was a table piled high with a wide variety of maps and letters and papers. He poured himself a cool cider from the pitcher on the table and then handed the pitcher to Soran. He pushed the door between the rooms mostly to and sat down at the table.

"If we are to speak of the end of things, we should probably do so here. I wouldn't want anyone who was still clinging to hope to hear that we haven't any."

"It's hard to believe that anyone in this city might still be clinging to hope. Surely no one believes we will last much longer. The food supply will be exhausted in the next few weeks, and we are already too weak to put up much of a fight if Aljeron comes in the fullness of his strength. We will fall before Winter Rise."

"So that takes us back to where we were yesterday, before we were interrupted."

"Speaking of," Soran interjected, "is everything all right there? I saw her riding away, crying."

"She thinks I'm going to die soon."

Soran nodded. "We may both die soon."

"Unless I do what we've discussed. I could get my horse and ride out there right now. I could sue for peace and ask for favorable terms for the rest of you."

"No, Rulalin." Soran shook his head. "I'm not laying down my sword for anybody. Call it foolishness, call it pride, call it whatever you like. But I'd rather die tomorrow with my sword in my hand than go crawling out to them, even if it bought me fifty more years."

"I know," Rulalin said, leaning back in his chair with a sigh. He wasn't the only one unable to countenance surrender.

"There is another option," Soran said, leaning in close to the table. "You could sneak out of the city on the eastern side. The patrols between Fel Edorath and the Mountain are still light compared to elsewhere. You could slip through if you aimed for the foot of the Mountain. From there, you'd have to go north, since they have the south blocked, but if you could cross the Kiruan into Nolthanin, you could probably get away. It would almost take away the sting of defeat if I could see the fury in Aljeron's eyes when he found you gone."

"I'm not going into hiding again," Rulalin answered firmly. "I spent ten years hiding, and while those ten years kept me alive, it wasn't much of a life. I won't do it again." He hesitated. "Unless you promise me that you will surrender as soon as I am safely away, you and all the officers. If I leave, you must promise me this war ends now."

Soran glared across the table at Rulalin before looking away. He rose suddenly and strode across the room. "I can't do that, Rulalin. You know I can't."

"Then I will stay. I will not go if you are going to fight and die needlessly even if I'm gone. I will only leave if you promise to lay down your sword."

Soran turned and came back to the table. The glare in his eye had taken on a new dimension. "There is still one hope for victory," he whispered.

Rulalin stood. "No."

"It's the only way."

"No."

"Why not?"

"Because I won't, that's why."

"But what is there to lose?"

"Everything."

"Rulalin, if you fight, you will die. If you surrender, you will probably die anyway. So it can't be your life you're worried about. If it's your reputation, well, that's pretty much ruined too, isn't it? So why not?"

"Because even if my reputation is ruined, my name is not mentioned along with Andunin and Corindel as traitors to all mankind. If I accept the offer, then I'll be seen as the very worst of them all."

"Only if he fails," Soran added.

"He won't fail, I assure you," a third voice said from the doorway. Rulalin stepped away from the table as Soran drew his sword and whirled. The man was of medium height and build with short light-brown hair. He was well dressed in dark grey riding clothes with a black outer coat that swept the floor. He was fair-skinned, and his face might have been considered handsome if not for his permanent insolent smirk.

Soran's drawn sword flashed up to the intruder's exposed throat, the point less than a hand away. Rulalin stepped up beside Soran quickly. "What do you want here, Tashmiren? And how do you come to be inside my inner chamber without invitation?"

"It is most impolite even for a sour fellow such as yourself, Rulalin, to welcome an important guest with sword and rude questioning."

"Answer the rude question before I cut off your head," Soran said.

"That would be unwise," Tashmiren said, not taking his eyes off of Rulalin. "If you think Aljeron Balinor poses a threat to your city, just kill me and see what Malek will unleash against you."

"Even Malek can't kill me twice," Soran answered. "I could kill you now and ride out to my death against Aljeron's army this afternoon. Then, whatever Malek sent would come too late, wouldn't it?"

A flash of anger glinted in Tashmiren's dark green eyes as he looked at Soran for the first time. "Simpleton! If you so much as cut me with that sword, you had better pray for a swift end, for if it doesn't come, you would know why all living things tremble at the name of Malek's dread captain, Farimaal."

At this Soran's sword did quiver, and a shiver ran through Rulalin. He pushed Soran's sword toward the ground. "Put it away, Soran."

Soran reluctantly sheathed the sword, and Tashmiren walked around them to the table, where he helped himself to a drink and sat down.

"Now answer my question," Rulalin continued. "Why are you here, and how did you get in?"

"You know why I'm here, and getting in was easy. The patrols of your enemy are not vigilant in watching the eastern side of the city. How ironic that your only hope and their imminent downfall lies in that direction."

"Imminent?" Rulalin repeated.

"Imminent." Tashmiren took a drink from the cup before him. "Twice you have rejected Malek's offer. This is your last chance. I will slip from the city in the dark before morning and go back to my master. You must choose by then whether you are coming. You can accept his terms and live, or you can refuse them and die. No one will stand before the enemy about to emerge from the Mountain."

Soran glanced sideways at Rulalin as Tashmiren poured himself another drink. Rulalin's fingers were trembling, but his words did not betray his nerves. "The terms are the same?"

Tashmiren nodded. "They are."

"I have until morning to consider the offer?"

"I will leave before dawn."

"And you are sure that despite two failures already, Malek will win this time?"

"Of course. Sulmandir is dead and his children scattered. The Great Bear hide in their draals and turn their eyes from the affairs of men. The war between Shalin Bel and Fel Edorath has drained Werthanin of both men and vigor. What's more, all that is to say nothing of what Malek is prepared to unleash. The Bringer of Storms will end this world as all of us have known it. Malek's rule, which has until now merely been postponed, will come."

Tashmiren rose, stepped around them again, and walked to the doorway. "I will show myself to the guest room where I have stayed before. I am both hungry and thirsty from my journey, so a large lunch as soon as possible would be just the thing."

He slipped from the room, and a moment later they heard

the outer door click quietly shut. Soran turned to Rulalin, who raised his hand before he could say anything. "I need to think, Soran. I'll send for you later."

Soran nodded reluctantly and left the room. The door clicked shut again, and Rulalin was alone.

Mindarin had talked about choices, but she could not have imagined just what his choices really were. It was an abhorrent road, but Malek's offer tempted. Not with the promise of life or escape, but of her. After all these years, she was the only thing he still desired, but at what cost?

4

ALL THAT REMAINS

THE SPIRES OF AMAAN SUL gleamed in the afternoon
sun, which hung a rich gold in the autumn sky. Tall white towers within the thick high walls loomed above the ordinary
buildings of the city and presented a vivid picture to approaching travelers even many leagues distant. Amid the towers and spires were tall trees with dense multi-colored foliage,
fluttering ceaselessly in the stiff breeze that blew out of the
north with a distinct wintry chill.

Wylla wrapped her shawl more tightly around her shoulders as she stood on the northern wall of the palace. She
hated that first clear glimpse of winter, when the wind told her
that the scales had tipped and the autumn season was leaning
closer to winter than to summer. Today held such a chill, even
though there were still four days till Midautumn.

Her face tingled with the cold, and she turned away from
the beautiful land to the north and looked back over her own
palace to the picturesque lane that lead from the front gates

to the central courtyard. The palace and palace grounds were situated just inside the northern wall of the city, about equidistant between the eastern and western gates. A large east-west road ran through the city, intersecting an equally prominent north-south road. The city, lying in four roughly equal quadrants, was well serviced by many interlocking smaller avenues and alleys.

Though not as populous as Shalin Bel, Amaan Sul was far and away the largest city in Kirthanin in terms of land. A visitor from any of the other great cities of Kirthanin instantly felt the difference within Amaan Sul's walls. Such spaciousness was not present in any other comparable city. The houses and shops were often separated by gardens full of flowers, tall hedges creatively trimmed, and even fully grown trees that provided an unusual amount of shade for a city. While walking down some of the smaller side streets, it was possible to feel as if strolling along some country lane under a canopy of boughs thick with leaves.

The royal palace also added to Amaan Sul's distinctiveness. Not only was it the only royal dwelling in Kirthanin, the palace was also an architectural wonder built late in the First Age. A wall some four spans high and about two-thirds of a span wide ran around the entire palace and grounds. Where the palace wall paralleled the city's northern wall, also about the same dimensions, the two were so joined as to create a wide walking path on top, and was lined with several stone benches and bowers. Since childhood, this had always been one of Wylla's favorite places, for she could walk high above the earth and in the same spot view both the beautiful land outside the city and the lovely courtyard inside, as well as the fountain and gardens. Though these were perhaps not as spectacular as the fountain and gardens of Sulare, they were nevertheless quite lovely. The spot had become even more precious to her over the years, as her son, Benjiah, had more frequently ventured out of the palace and city through the wide northern gate.

Though he was sixteen now, and both capable and strong, she was frustrated by the distance that had grown between them and found herself drawn up to the wall on days like today when he was out hunting with his uncles.

It hadn't always been like this. Benjiah had always been tender as a boy, especially toward her. As he'd grown, though, he'd pushed her away. This she had expected as he reached out for the independence she'd always intended him to have. What had surprised her were the flashes of anger and the long stretches of coldness.

On top of this frustration was another change, this one in her. Her anxiety had grown each time he left the city. She had taken to pacing this high wall at such times, her heart ill at ease. She could not escape the growing fear that Benjiah would be taken away from her in the midst of their happiness, even as Joraiem had been. She had survived the loss of Joraiem, largely because of Benjiah's arrival, which brought joy despite her pain and light despite her darkness. Even now, with this tension between them, she feared his loss most of all. He was all she had left, all that remained.

Thinking of Benjiah drove her to turn back into the cold wind. The broad green plain that stretched out beyond the northern walls toward the scattered trees in the distance was still empty, as she had known it would be. Pedraal and Pedraan had said they would try to be back before sunset, though they had looked mildly annoyed when she pressed the point, but that was still many hours away. Benjiah had left without saying goodbye, and that always left her out of sorts until he'd return and something peaceable would pass between them.

She glimpsed movement along the wall and turned to see Kyril, Joraiem's sister, walking toward her. She wore a long woolen cloak of dark green, and it was tied snugly around her to protect her from the cold. Her long blond hair was braided in two places, and the twin braids hung down the length of her back. She smiled sweetly as she approached Wylla, and her greeting brought warmth to Wylla's heart.

"Do you feel better after your nap?" she asked as her sister-in-law drew closer.

"I do, though it's a bit embarrassing, isn't it?"

"Why?"

"Because I haven't slept in the afternoon in ages. I feel so lazy."

"Nonsense," Wylla replied, taking Kyril by the arm and leading her over to one of the stone benches nearby. "There is no reason to feel lazy. You came here to have a break from all the tensions of war, after all."

They sat down and Kyril's eyes glistened as she leaned closer to Wylla, all but whispering, "I have to say that it did feel wonderful."

"Good, I'm glad." Wylla leaned back in the bench, turning her eyes from Kyril to the land beyond the city. She had wondered whether to talk to Kyril about Benjiah. She trusted Kyril and would have liked to talk about him to another woman, another mother, but her sister-in-law seemed to get along so well with her girls, she just didn't know if she'd understand.

"What is it, Wylla? I've interrupted some soul-searching here or deep contemplation, so you'd might as well let me in on it."

"I don't know, Kyril," Wylla answered.

"Don't know what?"

Wylla hesitated, looking closely at Kyril. "What to do about Benjiah."

"Ah," Kyril replied, nodding.

"What?"

"Oh, nothing." Kyril blushed. "I just wondered when this would come up."

"You did?"

"Sure, he has changed dramatically since we were here three years ago. He is harder, angrier too. Even the girls see it."

"Has he mistreated them?" Wylla asked, turning sharply to Kyril.

"No."

"Tell me the truth, Kyril."

"He hasn't, Wylla. Nor me either. I meant with you. We've all noticed the change. Has something happened?"

"Yes, but I don't know what it is. It hurts to have him close, and it hurts to have him out of my sight. Sometimes I fear I'll lose him like I lost Joraiem."

Kyril put her arm around Wylla and pulled her in close. Wylla rested her head on Kyril's shoulder, the warm woolen cloak a comfort against her cold cheek. "This time of year must be especially hard for you."

"It is," Wylla replied, "but it's bittersweet and not bitter only. Autumn is the season in which I lost him, but it is also the season in which we had our brief life together. My happiest memories are of autumn days in Sulare, where we would walk among the groves of fruit trees in the early morning, not long after the sun had risen, and we would speak together of the future."

"Sounds beautiful."

"It was, and the turning leaves and changing season always take me back to the time before my great sorrow."

"Do you think, now that he's older, he is showing more anger over what happened to his father?"

"Perhaps, but why is he so angry at me? He doesn't rail against Rulalin like my brothers do . . ."

"Or like Evrim," Kyril added.

"Or even like you and I used to," Wylla finished.

Wylla nodded. "Perhaps you feel the echo of the war in the west," Kyril said. "Though I have left Werthanin far behind, I still feel the discord in my bones, sometimes even when I close my eyes as I lay down to sleep. Maybe he feels it too."

"That may be part of it," Wylla answered, "but I think not all of it. He has been asking since he was thirteen to join Aljeron in the war. Though I refused to let him go, it was Pedraal and Pedraan who insisted most vehemently that he wasn't ready."

"Maybe he dreams of avenging his father. That desire might well disturb a boy more visibly than it would a man."

"He does, and I find it hard to fault him for that. There was a time when I would have gladly avenged Joraiem's death with my own hand." Wylla's voice grew quieter.

"You wish it no longer?" Kyril asked softly.

"I do not," Wylla shook her head firmly. "I'm not saying that he shouldn't be brought to justice. His offense should be lawfully punished by death. I'm only saying that I no longer have any desire to be the agent of that punishment. I'm happy to leave that to someone else."

Kyril was quiet, and both women drew their cloaks tighter against the wind. Wylla added, "There is something else. It is more than Rulalin and missing his father. There is something between Benjiah and me, and I don't know what it is."

"Have you asked him?"

"Not recently. I can't even get close. The coldness, the hardness, the anger, the distance—he just shuts me down."

"What do you do?"

"At first, I came out fighting. I tell you, I let him have it a few times. We really got into it on a couple of occasions. But, the last time, he didn't fight back at all. He just got quiet, really quiet. I mean, he didn't talk to me for weeks. It was scary. I've dropped that approach. I do want him to give me some answers, but I don't want to lose him over this."

"So now?"

"Now I keep trying, softly, gently, persistently. I want him to know I'm not going anywhere, and I'll be ready to talk as soon as he's ready to tell me what's going on."

"Sounds wise," Kyril said. "I hope that'll be soon."

"So do I," Wylla echoed. "He's driving me crazy."

Kyril laughed, and soon Wylla was laughing too. When they were finished, Wylla rested her head on Kyril's shoulder. "I wanted to talk to you about this sooner, Kyril, but I was afraid you wouldn't understand. I'm sorry."

"Don't be. I don't understand, not really, but I don't need to understand to listen."

Wylla smiled and sat back up. "I'm getting cold. Do you want to go down?"

"Sure."

They stood and walked the length of the wall to the corner stair that led down to the courtyard. Looking northward out over the open ground one last time, Wylla sighed as they descended.

In Wylla's personal parlor, a sizeable but cozy room with an enormous fireplace outside Wylla's private chambers, she and Kyril stripped off their outer cloaks and warmed their hands by the brightly burning fire. As she stood soaking in the heat of the fire, Wylla found her thoughts straying toward Benjiah with the more common maternal concern that he might not be prepared for this degree of cold so early in the autumn season. Pedraal and Pedraan would have been no help, for they wore it as a badge of honor that weather had absolutely no effect on them. Wylla didn't think this was actually true, but it was certainly the case that they had regularly defied the elements when considering their attire.

A persistent rap at the door interrupted Wylla's thoughts, and turning from the fire she called, "Come in."

One of the palace stewards, a young woman of perhaps twenty, pushed the door open but did not enter. "Your Majesty wanted to know when Madame Karalin and the young ladies returned."

"I did. They're back?"

"Yes, they've just arrived."

"Good, bring them in."

"Yes, Your Majesty," the steward answered as she pushed the door closed.

Soon thereafter, the sound of footsteps and voices came echoing down the hallway, and the door swung open once more.

Wylla watched as Halina and Roslin came bursting into the room, their faces sparkling with excitement. Both girls had shoulder-length, straight brown hair that was fine and silky like their father's. Halina was fourteen years old, pretty and warm, but almost always unable to get a word in edgewise around her younger sister, Roslin, of whom the term "vivacious" was dramatic understatement. Not surprisingly, though both girls entered with mouths ready to proclaim their story, Roslin's determination and skill at dominating a room managed to secure for herself the floor.

"Mom, Aunt Wylla, you wouldn't believe what happened to us today! We were walking in the city past that little trinket shop that I so love but we can't go to anymore without Aunt Wylla because I knocked over the shelf with the glass horses, when a group of jugglers in brightly colored cloaks came strolling down the street with balls and blocks and even knives and torches flying way up in the sky even while they walked. They were really great and a whole bunch of people were following them since there wasn't much else going on in the city just right then, and Karalin let us join in the crowd and follow them down the street. Well, they kept right on going and juggling all the way, never even stopping to take a break, not for ages and ages, when all of a sudden a bird came swooping in from one of the trees and snatched one of the balls, a bright yellow one, right out of the air. I've never seen anything like it and apparently neither had the jugglers because they were so distracted that everything started to fall down around them with a crash and they were ducking and dodging and blocks and balls and big knives and hot torches were falling all over.

At the same time the juggler whose ball had been taken started running through the city after the bird with the bright yellow ball, and he was shaking his fist at the bird and shouting words that I can't even repeat and lots of people went running after to see what happened. I went tearing after them too because I just had to find out if he got his ball back, didn't I? And I never even heard Aunt Karalin yelling after me not to go or of course I wouldn't have, but I didn't hear it and I did go, as fast as I could. And pretty soon we were winding back through lots of little streets and alleys in a part of the city that I don't even know very well but I didn't care because even though I was falling back behind the others I saw something they didn't. I saw the bird turn back low over the houses and fly back the way he had come from and I turned around too and kept right on after him even though the others had lost sight of him and were going the wrong way now. Anyway I managed to keep right after him and all of a sudden I saw him set down on a branch not all that far up above the road. I called up to him, 'Hey, drop that ball,' and you know what?"

Wylla, who had been looking intently into Roslin's eager face the whole time, understood that she had been graciously granted a chance for a monosyllabic reply while Roslin gathered herself to continue her breathless tale. "What?"

"He dropped the ball right there over my head and even though I've never been any good at catching anything all my life I caught it. I don't know if the bird meant to drop it, in fact I think that he just couldn't carry it around anymore since it had been rather big for his beak from the beginning, in fact it had been pretty silly for him to fly off with it in the first place, hadn't it? I mean what good would a bright yellow juggler's ball do a bird anyway? Nothing, right? There isn't anything he could do with it, so I just think he had realized that all the fuss he'd created wasn't really worth the ball and he just happened to drop it when I called up after him and it just looked like he was obeying me when probably he wasn't. And just as soon as he dropped the ball the bird took off through the sky again in another direction all together and before I knew it he was gone way away and there I was holding the juggler's ball. I still didn't really know where I was and it took me a while but eventually I heard the sound of the crowd of people who had been following the jugglers in the first place but hadn't gone running after the bird like me and the others, and all of them were walking around calling my name. Aunt Karalin had gotten the whole group of them out looking for me because she was worried I would get lost which I kind of did but not really. So I found one of them and they took me back to the place where the jugglers had gathered their things and were waiting for their friend and I gave them the yellow ball that the bird had taken. They were really happy to get it back and one of them, a really nice grey-haired man with a big bushy beard, asked me if I wanted him to teach me how to juggle and I said I did and he said he'd be happy to teach me. So I asked him if he'd teach Halina too and he said he would so I asked him when and he said he'd come any evening I wanted if I'd just tell him where I lived. I told him I lived a long way away from here but that I was here visiting my Aunt and he asked me who my Aunt was and I said 'Queen Wylla' and he almost fell over he looked so surprised. I don't think he knew what to say when I told him you were my Aunt and I was worried he wouldn't teach me how to juggle now so I asked him if he would still come and teach us and he stumbled around but finally said that he would if it was all right with you and Mom. So I was wondering if you would mind because he was really nice and I'd love to learn how to juggle and wouldn't it be great if we went back home and could juggle for Dad? He wouldn't believe that Halina and I could do it and he'd be so surprised and I think he would really love it. So what do you think? Because we should send him a message right away and tell him it's all right before he forgets."

The silence that followed this rush of words felt so strange to Wylla that for a moment she didn't realize that she had actually been asked a question. Suddenly, like shaking off a daze, she turned to Kyril and asked, "Well, sister, I think this is a question for you."

Kyril, in turn, looked from Halina and Roslin to Karalin, who stood behind them with a slender hand on one shoulder of each. "What do you think, Karalin?"

The girls looked up eagerly, and Karalin smiled. "As far as I could tell, he certainly seemed like a very nice, respectable man."

Reading the excitement in the girls' faces, Kyril nodded. "I can't see where the harm should be."

"Then we shall invite him right away," Wylla said, stepping up to Roslin and stroking her hair. Roslin seemed so excited that she couldn't speak, and all she could do was jump up and down, spin around, and throw her arms around her sister.

"Thanks, Mom, Aunt Wylla," Halina said happily while Roslin kept squeezing her around the waist.

"With that settled," Kyril said as she turned her daughters toward the door, "let's go and get changed for dinner."

"Bye girls," Karalin called.

"Aren't you staying for dinner, Aunt Karalin?" Halina called back over her shoulder as they stepped into the hall.

Karalin looked at Wylla, who nodded with a smile. "Yes, I'll see you then," Karalin called back.

As the sound of the girls talking excitedly with their mother faded away, Wylla motioned for Karalin to have a seat by the fire. Wylla knew that Karalin's bad foot would be aching, and even more than dinner, she would be wanting a rest. "They really love you, those girls," Wylla said.

Karalin, happily settling into the cozy chair, turned her

pleasant smile on Wylla. "Yes, they do, and I thank you for that, for sharing your nieces with me. I think they really do see me like an aunt."

"Of course they do. So does Benjiah. You're one of the family, Karalin."

"Thank you," Karalin answered softly. "It means a lot to me."

For several moments they sat quietly, but Wylla's thoughts did not linger over Roslin's story of the juggler for long. A nagging feeling in the back of her mind suggested her attention should really be elsewhere. Wylla's gaze was drawn to the crackling fire that leapt and danced in the great stone fireplace. It was warm and comfortable in the parlor, and as Karalin slid her heavy outer cloak off and adjusted her seat, Wylla found her thoughts slipping away from the palace. Somewhere out there in the cold, in the fading daylight, was her son. She knew he would soon return, but even then, he would still be far away.

Benjiah remained hunched in the dense thicket where he had hidden himself. The cold wind made him shiver, and he rubbed his hands together. Suruna lay across his knees, nestled firmly between his legs and his elbows. To anyone else, it would have appeared an awkward position to keep the bow, but he was already very skilled in its use, and he knew that when he had his chance he would be ready to take his shot.

Suruna was Benjiah's most beloved possession. His grandfather had given it to his father the year he died, and his father had used the bow against Malekim, Black Wolves, and even two Vulsutyrim. His uncles all told him that his father had worked wonders with it, and when Benjiah had not shown much aptitude or interest in training with other weaponry under his uncles' tutelage, his mother had encouraged them to teach him the bow. They agreed, and he took to it immediately, training year-round. Day after day and arrow after arrow, he became increasingly adept at use of the weapon, so much so that all of them had tried to urge him to turn his attention toward something else, lest he become obsessed. Benjiah knew, however, his devotion to Suruna was not about his love for archery, but something deeper. By everyone's account his father had been a master of the bow, and when at last Benjiah also mastered it, he felt for the first time in his life a connection with the father he had never known. The bow was more than a bow; it was a bridge into the unknown past and an unbreakable bond joining father and son.

As he crouched, he traced the long sweeping curve of the bow with the chilly fingers of his left hand. The wood was a mixture of light brown and an almost tan color, which swirled from end to end in curling, interlaced patterns. How often in the dark of his room, when he was supposed to be asleep, had he sat by the window and traced those patterns in the moonlight. He knew every last mark and was comforted to feel the cold, smooth wood beneath his fingertips.

A slight movement beneath the tall trees and the snap of a small twig arrested Benjiah's attention. He peered through the thicket branches, scanning the forest floor in the fading twilight. His deep grey eyes zeroed in on a young stag, its horns just beginning to mature even as his powerful frame showed the promise of the fullness of his years. The stag moved gracefully, unaware, and Benjiah slowly raised Suruna. He slipped the long arrow with its dark brown fletching onto the taut bowstring, and adjusting his body precisely, took careful aim.

He gazed along the shaft of the arrow out at the stag, now bending down to nuzzle something on the ground at his feet. It was a beautiful animal, and for a brief moment, Benjiah hesitated to take the shot. The moment passed though, and he fired. In a single heartbeat, as the arrow flew, he raised his head and saw the arrow take the stag down. Benjiah broke out of the thorns and ran across the forest floor to the place where the majestic creature had fallen.

Kneeling beside the dazed animal, he pulled a long, heavy knife with a finely sharpened blade from out of the sheath that hung at his side. The stag, still stunned by the arrow that had almost pierced him all the way through his side, looked at Benjiah from the corner of his eye with a wild look of terror. "Shh," Benjiah whispered, as he placed his hand lightly against the side of the stag. "Soon it will hurt no more."

Taking the knife, he slit the stag's throat open with a quick, deft slice. The creature shuddered for a moment, but soon lay still, as its warm blood poured steaming out onto the dark, cold ground. Benjiah remained by its side, running his hand back and forth along the animal's thick hide until he at last lay still.

Benjiah carefully extracted his arrow and then placed both hands on the animal's side. He closed his eyes and felt its fading warmth pass into his fingers. "Your death is not in vain. I promise you that. I have not poured out your life's blood for my pleasure, but from your flesh I will find sustenance, as from your body I now draw warmth. You are a creature of Allfather, beautiful and noble, and I take your life as a gift from his hand. Know this as your spirit departs, that you serve your Maker's purpose, even in the manner and hour of your death." For a long moment, Benjiah crouched silently beside the stag, his hands resting quietly upon it, before finishing, "As Allfather wills."

Benjiah opened his eyes. The stag lay still, its big dark eyes gazing emptily straight ahead. The blood continued to drain out of its neck, creating an ever increasing dark patch on the already dark forest floor. Benjiah stuck another arrow with a bright orange fletching in the ground beside the stag, then rose, still gazing down, turned, and ran back through the woods.

It took him perhaps half an hour to collect his horse, return to the stag, and tie the animal on his horse's back. When he had secured the stag, he started back through the woods, pushing the horse at a steady trot, looking for Pedraal and Pedraan.

He had been hunting with his twin uncles many times, and he knew enough to have no idea what to expect. Though they meant well, they were terrible hunters, and rarely did they have the patience to actually be successful. Unlike Benjiah, who like his father was slender, tall, and deft in his movements, both Pedraal and Pedraan were large, muscular men. They were larger than anyone Benjiah had ever seen, and though they were powerful men and fearful warriors, they were not especially adept at stalking or lying in wait for their prey. To be sure, they could be stealthy when required, but they were more interested in sneaking up on one another or on Benjiah in order to work some piece of mischief than to employ what talents they had in the hunt.

Benjiah found his way to the edge of the road they had taken into the wood, and looking up at the evening sky, saw for the first time how close to dark it really was. Even if he found Pedraal and Pedraan immediately, they would be hard pressed to reach Amaan Sul by nightfall. This meant both he and his uncles were going to be in trouble when they got there, for his mother had been in one of her moods when they left, and they all had been made to swear that they would be back by dark.

His mother. She acted as if there was something wrong with him, when really there was something going on with her. She was keeping something from him. He didn't know what it was, but he thought it was connected to the dreams and the strange certainty in his heart that something was coming. She had avoided his early questions about these things, and he had seen in her that she was hiding something. He would find out what it was, though, somehow he would.

He started back along the road toward the edge of the forest, but he saw no sign of his uncles. As he drew near the open plains, though, he heard the sound of metal on metal. He rode quickly to the open land beyond the forest's edge, and sure enough, there were Pedraal and Pedraan, weapons drawn, circling each other with sweat pouring down their brows.

Had Benjiah not seen similar scenes before, he might have been worried, for the concentration on their faces belied the fact that this was a mock fight, staged for their mutual enjoyment. Pedraal held his battle-axe, swinging it in a smooth, arcing pattern, eyes on the war hammer in his brother's hand. Benjiah sat on his horse as they circled, observing the spectacle with curiosity. He found the scene fascinating, though he had seen them spar many times. Suddenly, Pedraan stepped toward Pedraal, his war hammer flashing through the fading light, only to be met by Pedraal's counterstroke. The two great weapons clashed and rang out as the two stood locked in a ferocious struggle of will and raw power, but then Pedraan's war hammer slid along the shaft of Pedraal's battle-axe. With as much force as he could muster, Pedraan wrenched the axe from his brother's hand. It fell into the soft grass, and Pedraal looked in frustration at the place where it lay.

He raised his arms above his head and slapped them together in frustration. "You win again," he said with disgust as he bent over and picked up his battle-axe.

"It was luck. It could easily have gone the other way. I didn't have much strength left in me."

"Well, you may not have had much strength left, but it was enough. I felt it coming but couldn't stop it."

They were standing side by side, now, their backs to the road and Benjiah, and as Pedraal slapped his brother on the back, Benjiah called from his horse, "If the two of you have quite finished playing around, we'd better be getting back. We're going to be late as it is, and you know what that means."

Pedraal and Pedraan swung around to face him, the smiles on their faces dimming for a moment. "Yeah, your mother is going to let us have it." They faced each other and grimaced.

Pedraal and Pedraan walked toward Benjiah. Pedraan, looking suddenly serious, looked up at him. "Responsibility is a very serious thing, young man. As your uncle, I think it is very important that you learn to be responsible, just like the two of us."

They looked at each other again and laughed. Pedraan turned back to Benjiah. "Sorry about that. I tried, but it doesn't really sound like me, does it?"

Benjiah shook his head. "No, it really doesn't. After all, we were supposed to be hunting, and while I'm away in there, doing the hard work, here the two of you are playing at fighting."

"Well, it looks like the right man did the job," Pedraal said, walking around to look at the stag. "You got a nice one. I bet he'll taste grand."

"I think he will, but I'm not sure you'll ever know. I'm hungry enough that I might just eat him myself. Where are your horses?"

The twins looked around absentmindedly, scratching their heads. After a few moments, they spotted their horses quite a long way away along the edge of the wood. They ran along beside Benjiah as he rode to them. After reining them under control, the brothers mounted and prepared to ride back to the city, one on either side of Benjiah.

Just as they regained the road that headed south to Amaan Sul, a particularly icy wind blew out of the west and made them all shiver. It was a freezing wind that felt far more like winter than autumn. All three men turned and gazed west across the wide, open land. For a long moment, no one spoke.

"It's strange," Pedraal eventually said, "but that wind felt as though it came from the Mountain itself."

"I know," Pedraan answered without looking at his brother. "It has the feel of more than cold, doesn't it?"

"Yeah, its unnatural."

Benjiah shuddered. He had grown up in closer proximity to the Mountain than most, but it was still an overwhelming thing at times. Sometimes, the adults around him would stop in the middle of what they were doing, like Pedraal and Pedraan had just done, and simply stare in the direction of Agia Muldonai. Then, just as suddenly, they would resume their business.

Even more than the general awkwardness of trying to live a normal life within sight of Agia Muldonai, there were the dreams, strange visions of isolated images he did not understand: bright light, dark skies, rain and water, a wooden crate or cage, and the most recurrent image of all, a great white courtyard. With each dream, his certainty that change was coming grew. He felt it inside, the same way he could feel the coming of a storm. He was being drawn, pulled even, into something, but he didn't know what it was.

"It seems darker over there, doesn't it?" Benjiah asked, noticing the grey and overcast sky was especially grim in that direction.

"It does," Pedraal said, and Pedraan nodded.

Wanting to change the subject, Benjiah added, "I wonder how things are going in the west? I wonder if Aljeron and Evrim will be able to take Fel Edorath soon and get Rulalin."

Pedraal looked intently at Benjiah. "Aljeron will take Fel Edorath, don't worry about that. He'll bring Rulalin to justice. He'll avenge your father."

Benjiah looked at his uncle and saw the same fire there that he always found when the war or Rulalin was brought up. He understood, now that he was older, that one of the reasons he had grown up so despising Rulalin, was that the name alone had always evoked just this kind of concentrated hate. If

Aljeron was half the warrior that Pedraal and Pedraan said he was, and if he hated Rulalin as much as they did—then Rulalin had better hope that death found him before Aljeron did.

Benjiah turned his face west again. Just mentioning Rulalin's name stirred in him a deep and powerful rage, and he knew that this was not just because others had put it there. Coming to understand how he had lost his father by Rulalin's hand had been sufficient to plant the seed of hatred, a seed that had been watered and fertilized by the hatred of others.

And yet Rulalin's name stirred up more in Benjiah than simple animosity. Increasingly, discussion of the war, of Aljeron's burning passion to get Rulalin, of anything related to Rulalin at all, penetrated deep within him and tapped a deeper well of sorrow and grief. Oh, he hated Rulalin all right, but along with his hunger to see Rulalin pay for his deed, another hunger grew, a hunger to understand why. Why had this man killed in cold blood someone who had called him friend? What had his father done to deserve such a death, and who was this Rulalin that he would dare to take the life of one of Allfather's most precious creatures?

This growing desire for answers alarmed Benjiah. If Rulalin was brought to justice, then Benjiah would never be able to look the man in the eye and ask these questions. He felt, almost with each passing day, that something in him would never be at peace if he did not have this chance, but he didn't know what to call the desire or how to understand the need.

"Benjiah," Pedraan said, "we should head back."

"You're right," Benjiah said, turning away from the west and spurring his horse forward. They rode quickly, and Benjiah pulled his cloak even tighter, mumbling under his breath that the icy wind was as unnatural as the darkness, and that if they were the harbingers of this coming change, this storm, he didn't want to be caught out in it.

5

HIS FATHER'S SON

THE SUN WAS FULLY DOWN when Benjiah and the twins reached the northern wall of Amaan Sul and the royal palace. The thick, iron-lined gates had already been shut, so Pedraal had to call for the gatekeeper to come wind the great wheel that opened the outer gate like a yawning mouth. They passed below the outer wall and waited as the inner gate, which swung inward on creaking hinges, was likewise opened to receive them.

As they passed through the broad, well-lit courtyard, they felt immediately the difference of temperature within the enclosure. No longer exposed to the full force of the wind, their skin warmed instantly. Benjiah slipped from his horse, and rubbing her damp side gently with his hands, whispered his gratitude for her faithful service that day. Pedraal and Pedraan likewise dismounted, and together the three of them began to lead their horses to the stable on the eastern side of the courtyard. Benjiah looked up at the sky, dark with clouds as well as night, and knew that wind or no wind, it still smelled like a storm.

Before they had reached the stable door, a figure appeared in the torch-lit entrance to the palace on the southern side of the courtyard. Before her face could even be properly illuminated by the flickering lights, Benjiah recognized his mother's manner. She stepped just far enough out into the courtyard to be seen, then stopped.

Wylla stood there, motionless, gazing at them across the courtyard with an eerily vacant expression. After a few moments of total silence, she slowly turned away from them and disappeared back into the hall.

"Why don't you leave me alone?" Benjiah muttered as his mother walked away.

"What did you say?" Pedraal asked.

"None of your business," Benjiah shot back, walking away from his uncles into the stable.

"Benjiah!" Pedraal called after him. "Hey, who do you think you're talking to?"

Benjiah ignored his uncle and kept walking. The twins thought they had a right to insert themselves into his life when it suited them, especially if they thought they were protecting their sister. Benjiah knew that when push came to shove, they were on her side. For all he knew, they might be well aware of what his mother was hiding from him.

"Hey, I was talking to you," Pedraal said when he entered the stable.

"Leave me alone," Benjiah answered, motioning for the steward to go away. He would tend to his own horse tonight.

"I'm not your enemy," Pedraal said after a moment. "I don't know what's going on in you these days, but you don't have to treat everyone so badly."

Pedraal and Pedraan turned their horses over to stewards and walked out of the stable. Benjiah watched them go. He ran his hand through his hair as he turned back to his horse. He felt kind of bad about snapping at Pedraal. His uncles were generally pretty good to him. They weren't really the issue, and he knew that he needed to learn to control his anger and frustration better.

Benjiah finished grooming his horse, saw the stag safely into the hands of the steward who supervised the palace kitchen, and hurried to his room to change for dinner. His mother would wait for all three of them before starting, and though grooming his own horse would make him last and irritate his mother, he didn't want to push it too far.

Changing quickly out of his hunting clothes, he stowed his gear and laid Suruna gently against the wall in the corner of his room. He always felt he was leaving part of himself behind when he set the bow down after keeping it at hand all day, but he did not linger over it. He left the room and headed down to his mother's private dining hall.

He was surprised to see that he was not the last one to arrive. Not only were Pedraal and Pedraan not there yet, but his mother wasn't in the room either. Perhaps they'd sought her out to discuss his behavior. Or she might have sought them out to find out why they were all so late.

He didn't have long to consider the matter, for hardly had he arrived when his cousins came rushing over from where they had been seated with his Aunt Kyril and his Aunt Karalin. As Halina and Roslin grew nearer, he could see in the excitement in Roslin's eyes that a tale was coming, and sure enough, before she had even stopped walking she was well into a story of jugglers and a thieving bird. He only heard about half the story before the door opened again and his mother walked in, followed by his uncles, both looking serious and neither looking at him.

"Oh, Benjiah, Pedraal and Pedraan are here and they need to hear too," and before he knew what was happening, Roslin had grabbed his arm and begun dragging him toward the twins. With a new audience she shifted seamlessly out of the story as she had left it and took off again from square one with remarkable enthusiasm.

When all had finally been told and when Roslin's good work in following the bird had been duly acknowledged, she proceeded to invite all three men to the juggling lessons. "You really must come, Benjiah, as it isn't every day one gets to learn to juggle from someone who is really good at juggling. And you will both have to come as well," she continued, nodding at Pedraal and Pedraan, "as it's never to late to learn you know. I mean I've never seen either of you juggle so maybe you can and I just don't know you can but if you can't this is a great opportunity to learn and I would imagine that juggling skills might come in handy in all kinds of ways. If we all got really good we wouldn't even have to go looking for jugglers to entertain us we could just pick up the dinner plates or whatever was at hand and—"

"Roslin." Her mother's voice was firm.

"Yes?" Roslin looked only slightly taken aback at being interrupted.

"There will be no juggling of dinner plates, or any other breakable household item. There will be no juggling of knives or other sharp or dangerous implements either. If I let you have this man here to teach you, you must promise me that you will only practice your juggling with what I tell you that you can use. Understood?"

"Of course, Mother," Roslin answered, "we won't be ready for knives or even the dinner plates for a while, but—"

"No 'but,' Roslin. Only what I approve. Do you understand?"

"Yes," Roslin said, sighing as her eyes dropped to the floor.

Benjiah, knowing his cousin's vivid imagination, knew she had foreseen herself flinging various dangerous or exotic items high into the air in the castle courtyard, and now those visions would slowly slip away from her.

He stepped up beside her and put his hand on her head and stroked her hair. "I'd love to learn how to juggle, Roslin. When is he coming?"

She looked up, the excitement back in her face. "We don't know yet but hopefully soon because we sent him a messenger earlier this evening and maybe we'll find out before too long if he doesn't take too long to answer the message which I don't think he will because people don't usually keep a queen waiting when she sends a message to them do they? So I think we'll hear tonight, maybe even before we finish with dinner and then we'll know for sure."

"Speaking of dinner," Wylla said from across the room, taking advantage of a pause in Roslin's pulsating rhythm, "perhaps we had best eat, now that we are all here."

There was no hint of accusation or annoyance in her tone, but Benjiah bristled as they all stepped over to the table, which was set and waiting. Benjiah was careful to avoid looking at any of the others and took a seat between his cousins on the near side of the long table. His mother sat on one end and his Aunt Kyril sat at the other. Pedraal and Pedraan took their seats along with Aunt Karalin on the other side.

The food, which Benjiah knew had probably been ready for a while and waiting in the kitchen, came out warm and delicious. Benjiah, who always fasted on days that he hunted until the hunt was over, was famished, and he devoured everything set before him with eagerness, enjoying the satisfaction that only comes from having waited for something much desired. For a while it appeared as though he might even out-eat his uncles, who were semi-legendary for their appetites, but as though stirred by a challenge, they rallied as he grew full and by the end of the meal their pile of rib bones was far greater than his own.

Conversation at the table remained pleasant, though the initial silence from Wylla, Benjiah, and the twins proved too tempting to Roslin, who saw a rare chance to dominate the dinner table, a place where her tongue was generally restricted. However, her attempt to wax eloquently once more about the many apparent virtues and practical uses of juggling was effectively cut off by her Aunt Wylla, who seemed roused as from a daydream by the return to the subject.

"Roslin, dear, I am so happy you are excited about the juggler, but if you are going to make a good student for him, you will need to listen well. Why don't you practice listening now? I'm sure you can do a good job of it if you try."

"Oh I listen great, especially when it's about something really important. Once back in Shalin Bel when Mom wanted me to be quiet when an important guest was coming she told me that—"

"Roslin," Kyril reached out and put her hand on her wrist gently, "listening means not talking."

So Roslin had done an admirable job of keeping quiet, though she squirmed in her seat a lot more than usual as she struggled with silence. Meanwhile, into the conversational gap had charged Pedraan, despite his sober countenance and remarkable appetite.

"That's a lovely dress you're wearing, Karalin," he said, a little hastily as he wiped his mouth with the cloth napkin that lay in his lap. "That light blue suits you."

Karalin's face colored slightly as she looked up at Pedraan, sitting between her and Pedraal. She took a small drink and swallowed the bread she'd been chewing. "Why thank you, Pedraan." She smiled. Her voice had always seemed to Benjiah like the sound of gentle music. "It's kind of you to say so."

Benjiah watched Karalin's lingering smile and Pedraan's silly grin curiously in the silence that followed. Pedraal gave his brother's leg a jab with his finger that he probably thought was under the table and out of sight. When Pedraal saw that his poke had gone unheeded and that his brother continued to stare at Karalin, he tried to rescue the situation by inquiring after Karalin's day in the city. After some time, he managed to guide the conversation into a discussion of the relative skill of the city's more prominent dressmakers, which allowed Pedraan to recover his faculties and return to the business of eating. His work done, Pedraal also returned to the food and ate while the dress discussion carried on quite ably without him.

When they had finished their meal, they retired to the parlor chairs around the warm fire, which several of the stewards had stoked beautifully as they were finishing at the table. They settled in comfortably, each in their favorite chair, with Halina and Roslin sharing a lovely couch and with Benjiah stretched out on the thick rug, lying on his stomach and gazing at the dancing flames. As he had stooped in the dense thickets and pulled his cloak tight, bracing against the freezing wind, it had been just this moment he had kept before him. He closed his eyes and felt not only the warmth of the fire against his face, but the delight of a full stomach. Even if his mother would want a word before bed, it had been a pretty good day.

"I think we need a song," Kyril said as she sat with her feet drawn up beneath her in a great big armchair. "Any volunteers?"

"Yes indeed, an excellent idea," Wylla said. Benjiah opened his eyes and glanced across the room at his mother. "Though she keeps it carefully hidden in her modesty, Karalin has a wonderful voice. This is the perfect moment to share it with us all."

"Secret talents? You are full of surprises," Pedraan said, looking curiously across the room at Karalin.

"Yes," Wylla continued. "I didn't know about it until only a few months ago. She not only sings beautifully, she even loves to write her own songs."

"A songwriter too?" This time it was Pedraal, sitting up and paying more attention.

"Yes."

"Well," Karalin interjected, her face even redder than it had been at the table. "I like writing poems, and some of them I've put to music."

"She's a wonderful poet," Wylla continued. "She remembers everything Master Berin and Valzaan taught us about the history of Kirthanin, and she has put a lot of it into verse. I think she should pick one of her originals and sing it for us. Would you, Karalin?"

There were numerous encouraging murmurs, and they watched Karalin for her response. She was still blushing, but she nodded and everyone clapped for her as she stood.

"Well, there is a new one that I'm working on, about what life must have been like in the First Age before Malek's Rebellion, but I didn't know I'd be giving a command performance, so the words and the melody are still a little rough."

"I've no doubt it will be beautiful," Wylla said, smiling from her chair at Karalin as she moved to a comfortable spot beside the fire. She looked at the floor as though deep in thought, and then, raising her head, she began.

> *When rose the morning free of care*
> *And rode the midday unaware,*
> *And evening fell across the land*
> *Like soft raindrops upon the sand,*
> *Then was a time beyond compare.*
>
> *And without fear all creatures grazed*
> *While golden light around them blazed,*
> *Or even when the moon did rise*
> *To join the stars and light the skies,*
> *While all the world its Maker praised.*

For man Allfather's will embraced
And knew His good was interlaced
With fish and fowl and plant and tree
Each one alike, alive and free
And all with purpose planned and placed.

And though the Twelve were given reign
Over every dale and plain,
They shared with man the sober charge
The good of all things to enlarge
That peace enduring might remain.

But Malek longed the world to rule
And craved the Mountain as a stool
By which to reach Allfather's throne
To seize it for himself alone
And make the sun into his jewel.

And to his cause Andunin swayed
Who promised power all things betrayed,
And lost to all both then and now
Was life arrayed around a plow,
Replaced by life under a blade.

And what it was to know not strife
To live by neither sword nor knife,
To know a world without the hate
That rests upon us like a weight,
No one can say. These things are life.

But how I wish that world to see
And know a life of these things free,
And how I hope the promise true
That one day all will be made new
And what was once again shall be.

Karalin finished and for a moment the rest sat hushed and still. The tune's melancholy longing lingered, and Benjiah tried to hold onto that longing as the final notes slipped away. As the spell of the music began to wear off, they began to applaud her beautiful singing, and at that moment a tremendous thunderclap shattered the sober stillness. All turned their heads upward as though to penetrate the ceiling of stone and see into the distant heavens.

"That's strange," Wylla said. "I don't often hear thunderstorms in here."

"I've never heard one in here," Pedraal said, looking from his sister to his brother.

"We're safe, aren't we?" Roslin asked timidly, huddling in close to her sister.

"Of course you are, darling," Kyril answered, gliding over to the couch and squeezing in between her daughters. "It's just a loud noise, that's all."

Suddenly, the large double doors from the main hallway burst open, and a striking figure strode in, followed by some startled palace stewards. The man appeared to be at the same time ancient and ageless, his wiry white hair protruding from his grizzled head at all angles, despite the fact that it was soaked and streams of water were running off his brow and chin. His long green robe was soaking wet as well and hung heavy upon him, drooping in sagging bulges around his body and limbs. He carried in his hand a long wooden staff, topped with a magnificent carving of a King Falcon, or windhover, its wings tucked in and its head held proudly erect. Perhaps most striking of all were the man's eyes, which were completely white, revealing their loss of function.

"Valzaan!" Wylla exclaimed, rising to her feet. The others quickly followed suit and rose to meet the guest bearing this legendary name. "What . . . what a surprise to have you here in Amaan Sul . . . what a pleasure."

"To hear your voice again after all these years is indeed a pleasure, Your Majesty," Valzaan replied, his voice seeming to Benjiah to be every bit as melodious as Karalin's, though stronger and deeper, like the sound of a mighty river as opposed to a stream. "However, I come on business as urgent as any I've had since Allfather called me to be His prophet. I apologize, but I need an audience with you immediately."

"Of course," Wylla replied, laying aside her relaxed demeanor. In an instant, she stood transformed, Wylla the queen. "Do you need to speak with me alone?"

"There are children in the room, are there not?"

"Yes, my son, Benjiah, and my nieces, Halina and Roslin."

"It would be wise if they left for now, though we may all need to speak together before long. Otherwise, there are only your brothers here and a few others?"

"Yes, Valzaan," Pedraal answered. "We are here, as is Karalin and Joraiem's sister, Kyril."

"I am sorry that we must meet in this way, Kyril," Valzaan answered, giving a slight bow. "And Karalin, it is good to find you well."

"Benjiah," his mother said, "take your cousins to your room, and we will send for you if necessary."

"I'm not a child," Benjiah started, anger and disappointment in his voice.

Valzaan moved in the direction of Benjiah's voice, then reached out and placed his hand upon the boy's shoulder. "The time will come when you and I will speak together, of things past, of things present, and of things to come. For now, though, do as your mother says."

A chill rippled through Benjiah's body as Valzaan spoke, and his deep certainty that something was happening, both inside and all around him, sent shudders from head to toe. Benjiah replied softly, "Will you speak to me of my father?"

"Yes, Benjiah, for that time has come."

"And will you tell me what's happening to me?"

"I will."

"Benjiah," Wylla interjected, walking quickly to her son's side and guiding him away from Valzaan, toward Kyril and the girls, "do as you are told, and I will send for you when I'm ready."

Benjiah jerked away from her and took Roslin's hand, putting his other arm around Halina's shoulders, and he led them out of the room.

The palace stewards closed the doors on Wylla's signal, and Wylla guided Valzaan to a seat before the fire.

"May I get you a towel, or food or drink, anything?"

"A drink, yes, but the rest must wait. I've ridden three days and nights to reach Amaan Sul, and I haven't come a moment too soon. The raging storm is but a foreshadowing of our doom, for Malek's hour is at hand."

Wylla felt the blood drain from her face. "You mean the time is here at last?"

"Yes."

"His third attempt," Pedraal said.

"Yes," Valzaan repeated, his voice firm and clear. "And now Allfather calls me and all who serve Him to stand together, though Malek's strength may appear indomitable."

"Is there any chance, any at all, that maybe . . ." Wylla looked at Valzaan's ancient face.

"That maybe I am wrong? Listen, and I will reveal to you what Allfather has revealed to me, and how.

"Four days ago I was many leagues north and east of here, not far from Nolthanin. I was sitting by my fire in a small glade in woods far from any human habitation or road. The air was alive with birds singing in the twilight and taking shelter in the boughs of the trees. The Full Autumn air was not then so brisk, and I reclined comfortably beside the fire as the stars came out above me one by one.

"What happened next I knew later to be a vision, but at the time, it felt real enough. Dark storm clouds appeared overhead, obscuring the glittering canopy, and a howling wind began to rip through the woods surrounding the glade, bending the mighty oaks as I could bend blades of grass were I to fall to my hands and knees and blow across the ground. The birds fluttered through the air, trying unsuccessfully to remain aloft. My fire dwindled until at last it went out completely and the embers were scattered by the wind. I rose, though I felt that at any minute the howling wind would carry me away with the birds. But it did not.

"Soon, I heard a great cracking, as though a mighty ship were being rent in two, and right in front of me a great oak was ripped out of the ground and flung up into the air and carried off into the distance. It was the first stone in a great avalanche of sound, as the rending came again and again and tree after tree was ripped from the earth and thrown into the sky. Before long, my ears ached with the sound of splitting wood and sundering roots, and the air above me was like a log-jam in a great river.

"I held my ears, but I could not drown out the noise. Finally, it began to fade, and I let my hands fall to my side. The woods had been completely uprooted and blown away. Nothing remained, save great holes in the ground where whole trees had been torn up, and scattered stumps where others had been broken off. The ground also had been swept clean, and there was no sign of the usual debris left by a great storm, let alone any indication that a wide wood had once stood there.

"The wind slowed and disappeared. The storm clouds slipped away, and once more the stars twinkled in the sky. But the birds were gone, save a single windhover, which fluttered down, bedraggled, to rest its weary wings. It perched on top of my staff. The singing of the birds had given way to the howling of the wind, and the howling had created the ear-piercing shattering of the wood. Ultimately, both the howling and the rending had stopped, and an eerie silence had settled upon the land. Nothing moved, crawled, flew, or creaked.

"Then, a quiet voice whispered to me. It did not come from above me or below me, nor from before me or behind me. It was both inside me and beyond me, and it spoke as clearly as I speak to you now. The voice said, 'Valzaan, do you see?'

"I replied, 'Allfather, you know that I see only what you show me.'

" 'And what have I shown you?'

" 'A great wind, destroying a beautiful wood and driving away the birds of the air.'

" 'Is that all?'

" 'You have shown me storm clouds above and chaos below, my fire being extinguished, and everything carried off but me.'

" 'Look and listen again.'

"I turned around in the remains of the glade, hearing nothing and seeing in my mind's eye only scattered images of the destroyed glade, for though my physical eyes no longer see, Allfather still grants me vision sometimes, even in the waking world. After turning three times, I was about to answer that I could see nothing else when I saw what I had missed.

"A single tree, much younger and smaller than the mighty ancient trees that had surrounded me, remained standing in the distance. The branches still bore leaves, and it stood unbroken.

"I said, 'I see a single young tree, unbroken by the great wind, still standing amid the ruin of this place.'

"The voice beckoned me to approach the tree, and I did. As I grew near, the voice continued. 'Remember the words I have already spoken concerning what is now coming to pass.

For though your enemy rises again, to try once more to rend from me what is mine, and though he brings with him darkness and great destruction, all hope is not lost. For from of old I have known him, from of old I have seen this, and from of old I have spoken:

> 'With a strength that stoops to conquer
> And a hope that dies to live,
> With a light that fades to be kindled
> And a love that yields to give,
>
> 'Comes a child who was born to lead,
> A prophet who was born to see,
> A warrior who was born to surrender,
> And through his sacrifice set us free.'

"When I heard the words of the ancient prophecy, I trembled. I knew they referred to the days of darkness before the restoration of all things, and I knew then that Malek was coming, so I asked, 'How long, Allfather?'

" 'Soon. Before the birth of a New Year, he will have swept aside the first line of our defense. He will strike where we should be strongest but are not, and he will send forth from the Mountain a terror until now unknown to the world that will cause hearts to melt with fear, but be strong! For though he may triumph for a day, he does not know that all tomorrows are mine.'

"And before I could say anything else, the voice was gone, along with the vision. I found myself some distance away from the glade, standing before a young tree just like the one in my vision but surrounded by the towering oaks of the wood and hearing the songs of birds in my ears. I returned to the glade and found my fire still burning brightly. I slept because I knew that there would be little sleep ahead, and I set out for Amaan

Sul with the dawn. I have been traveling ever since, until I arrived at your gates not even an hour ago."

Questions filled Wylla's mind, and fear, but she composed herself as her office required. "And why have you come first to Amaan Sul? Is it here that you think he will strike?"

"He will come here, but I don't think he will come here first."

"Then why?"

"You already know why, don't you?" Valzaan, his face finally dry, faced Wylla.

She stood, keeping her eyes on Valzaan. "Would the two of you make sure all of Valzaan's belongings have been stored safely in one of the guest rooms? Kyril, could you check on the children? And, Karalin, please go to the kitchen and see to it that a proper dinner is prepared for Valzaan."

Kyril and Karalin rose to go, as did Pedraan, who looked reluctantly at his sister. "Wylla," Pedraal said, still seated.

"Brother, I speak now as your queen, not your sister," Wylla said firmly, still looking at the prophet.

"Yes, Your Majesty." He followed the others out of the room and closed the doors behind him.

Valzaan's face now turned toward the warm fire. Wylla walked over to the fire herself, where she stopped and looked down into the flame. The light flickered and danced and the warmth made her bare skin uncomfortably hot, but she stayed rooted to the spot. How many times, late at night after Benjiah had gone to bed, had she sat or stood before this very fireplace, staring into the flame, wondering if this day would come? No, not if, but when. She had always known it would come. Especially since Benjiah had first spoken of the images in his dreams and the feeling in his heart.

She had always felt it an honor that Allfather had put His hand on her husband in a special way, but she had spent a lot of time hoping He had not likewise gifted Benjiah. She didn't blame Allfather for Joraiem's death—that had been Rulalin's work—but at times she'd found herself angry that Allfather had done nothing to protect him. If Joraiem had been called to be a prophet, why had he been allowed to die when his prophetic gifts were just coming into use? Why had neither Joraiem nor Valzaan foreseen the danger Rulalin posed?

And, more to the point, what price would Benjiah have to pay if she was right about why Valzaan was here? What would be expected of him? To what dangerous or sacrificial job would he be summoned?

"Wylla," Valzaan said gently. "There is no need to keep your burdens from me. I know what troubles you, even as you know why I'm here."

"I am silent because I don't know what to say." Wylla turned from the fire to face Valzaan. "I am a queen, but I am not a prophet."

"Then I will speak, and you will no longer need to wonder." Valzaan took his staff and laid it across his lap. He folded his hands and rested them upon it. "I have come about Benjiah, for it is time he knew who he was."

"You mean what he is?"

"No, I mean who he is."

"He knows who he is," Wylla said firmly, striding over to the seat beside Valzaan and sitting down. "I have raised him to know who he is. I have spoken to him in detail of his father. He knows our story and the story of our families. He knows that he is the heir to the throne of Enthanin. All this he knows."

Valzaan didn't answer. He continued looking straight ahead toward the fire, as though Wylla had neither spoken nor moved. She grew uncomfortable and turned away.

"It's true," she continued, this time with not quite as much vehemence, "that he doesn't know the whole story of Joraiem's calling and gifts, but I had thought that this was something best left until he came of age. I thought he needed to grieve his father as a man before he tried to digest the news that he was also a prophet. It is hard enough to bear the weight of being heir to a royal title and royal responsibility without also wondering if he was the heir to his father's legacy. It has been a heavy enough burden for me; I could not ask him to bear it too."

"I understand, which is why I have stayed away until now." Valzaan turned to face Wylla. "But there is no time to withhold the truth any longer. He must know now, and he must know everything."

"What do you mean by 'everything'? You've never even met Benjiah before tonight. Maybe he isn't what or who you think he is."

"Wylla, I have long known who Benjiah is, for on the day you left Sulare, Allfather gave me a vision as clear as the noonday sun. You remember that day. The Autumn Wane air was still warm, as it often is that far south at that time of year. You and the others were preparing to leave, to head to Dal Harat with Joraiem's body. I watched with heavy heart alongside Master Berin as you and the others passed north over the causeway and out of the Summerland. As I sat there, I saw clearly a vision of you in Amaan Sul, holding a golden-haired boy in your arms. He was beautiful. I saw that joy would break into your darkness, and even as you faded from view, I was heartened to know that Allfather had given you a son.

"As I prepared to turn away, I was drawn instead to the causeway, and I rode midway out over the swiftly flowing channel. There, Allfather spoke to me. He said, 'The boy is the one you have sought. The time is coming.'

"I knew then that this day would come, when I would have to tell you to give your son up, at least for a time. And I knew that this would place a heavy burden on you. I have long dreaded this day, and I do not ride to your door lightly. I do not know all things, and I cannot see what lies in store for me, much less for Benjiah. I can only tell you that I will watch over him as best as I am able, and I will do my best to teach him all I know of his gifts and calling."

The fire continued to dance in the hearth, but it seemed far away now. "I didn't even know that I was pregnant when I left Sulare," she mumbled.

"Allfather knows all things, and He revealed it to me."

Wylla turned to Valzaan. "When you say Allfather told you Benjiah was the one you had been seeking, what did He mean?"

"Let me tell you of the day I first saw Joraiem."

"Joraiem told me about seeing you in his dreams and of how he saw you in real life, coming as from the dragon tower—"

"No, Wylla, that's not what I mean. I do not want to tell you of the day Joraiem first saw me, but of the day I first saw him."

Wylla looked mystified. "But I thought—"

"I know what you thought. I had not yet told Joraiem all before he died, as you will see in a moment. Like you, I thought we had plenty of time. But though I never had the chance to tell him, I will tell you."

"All right."

"Several years before I met Joraiem on the road to Sulare, Allfather summoned me from the eastern coast of Suthanin, to travel all the way to the northwestern coast, not far from Dal Harat. It was a long and wearying journey, but I reached the coast just west of Dal Harat not long after Midspring. Allfather led me to a place where large sand dunes stood on a small peninsula. He led me to a place among them where he bid me sit, and as I did, he granted me a vision of a family, which I realized was not far from where I was sitting on the beach. In fact, as I watched them in my mind's eye, I could hear their voices echoing in the distance as they played in the sand and waves. There was a father and mother, and three small children. I know them now to have been the Andiras, but I did not know their names then. Joraiem was perhaps fourteen, a few years younger than Benjiah is now. I could see without needing to be told that Allfather had set Joraiem apart.

"From that moment on, I paid special attention to Joraiem's childhood. He was the first prophet to be set apart in over a hundred years. More than that, he was the first in the Third Age that I had ever met as a boy. I began to wonder if he was the answer to the prophecy that I have mentioned here tonight.

"For reasons of His own, Allfather did not see fit to answer that question, and I was left to wonder. Even after traveling with Joraiem, I still didn't know. Even up to the moment of his death, I wondered. Part of me had become convinced that Joraiem *must* be the one, that until the vision on the causeway, I wondered if somehow the prophecy had failed. It was only as I heard Allfather's voice that I knew Joraiem's son, not Joraiem, was the child of prophecy."

Wylla had too many questions to keep them all straight. "Wait," she said when Valzaan paused, "you are saying that you thought Joraiem was the 'boy born to lead' that the prophecy speaks of? Even if you thought that when you first saw him, he was twenty-two when he went to Sulare. He was no longer a boy. If you were wrong about Joraiem, maybe you are wrong about Benjiah."

"My certainty about Benjiah comes not from myself, but from Allfather. As for Joraiem, I was aware of his age. I had expected a younger child, but everything else seemed to fit. Besides, though he was of age, the Novaana do not usually take their seat in the Assembly until after their time in Sulare. So, even though he was no longer technically a boy, it could also be said that to a certain extent, he was not yet fully a man. I have learned it is important when looking for the fulfillment of any prophecy not to be to confident about the means Allfather will use to fulfill it. Besides, my suspicions were confirmed by the fact that Malek also seemed to believe what I believed."

"What do you mean?"

"Didn't Joraiem tell you about the day before he left for Sulare? He killed a Malekim not far from Dal Harat. The Malekim's discovery was no doubt an accident, but I'm sure his presence that close to Dal Harat wasn't. Even Joraiem had begun to wonder if he was drawing trouble to us all when the black wolves attacked Sulare. A black wolf had been killed near Dal Harat some time before his leaving, and another near Peris Mil not long before his arrival. What's more, we were attacked on the road south as well as while we were there. I know now that Malek had sensed Joraiem's presence, and knowing the prophecy, he desired to eliminate any danger Joraiem posed."

"Then surely Malek must know about Benjiah too! Why have you not warned me? His life may be even now in danger!"

"I don't think so," Valzaan answered, raising his hands to calm Wylla. "Trust me. I have not been idle. I have many eyes and ears in this world, and I have been keeping a closer watch on Amaan Sul than you know. Besides, for all his power, Malek is no more omniscient than I am. For several years after the day Joraiem was revealed to me, Malek had no apparent interest in Dal Harat, not until Joraiem was already of age. Benjiah is younger still, and with Joraiem dead, Malek may not be looking for another. Besides, his present attention is bent most particularly toward the West. So while the war may be a weakness of ours, it may also have been a diversion that has kept him from seeing who was growing up right here under the shadow of his hiding place. At any rate, it is too late now to be worried solely about Benjiah's safety. All our lives are in danger. Even if Benjiah were to stay here with you, you could not keep him safe."

Wylla sat with her hands clasped tightly in her lap. "So you believe Benjiah isn't just a prophet, he is this particular prophet."

"I know he is."

"And you want to tell him this now, tonight."

"Yes."

"And then what? You will leave?"

"Yes, at first light, if not before."

"Where will you go?"

"We will ride west by the fastest road possible. I don't think we can save Fel Edorath, but we may be able to help save Shalin Bel."

Wylla peered at Valzaan. "You want to take my son straight into the heart of this war, right to the place where you expect Malek will go, even though you know that when Malek discovers who he is, he will want to kill my son, perhaps more than anyone else in this world?"

"Whatever role Benjiah has to play, Malek cannot be defeated without him."

"Yet you can't say for sure that Malek will be defeated now, even with him, or that Benjiah will survive."

"No, I cannot. There is no guarantee that his service won't cost him his life, even as there is no guarantee that my service will not cost me mine. I am sorry for what I must do, but this is what must be."

Wylla shut her eyes tight for what seemed like hours. "All right, I will send for him."

6

FIRST STEPS

BENJIAH PAUSED OUTSIDE the large double doors. His mother's message had said he should come right away, but in spite of his earlier unwillingness to leave, now he felt reluctant to return. He was being summoned to a private meeting with a walking, breathing Kirthanin legend, for stories of Valzaan could be traced back to the beginning of the Third Age. And, as if this were not enough, Valzaan was also one of the few people who had shared the last several months of his father's life and could speak to Benjiah knowledgeably of those days. Though his mother and uncles had told him tales, it seemed to him that it all might be more real if he could learn the story of his father's last days from a prophet, from an official spokesman for Allfather.

Now he had his chance. Just beyond these doors the legend sat, no doubt enjoying a sumptuous supper beside the warm fireplace. Benjiah raised his hand to the handle, but his fingers trembled and again he did not open the door. As awe-inspiring as Valzaan's legend was, and as impressive as his appearance, even wet and bedraggled, there had been something else at work in him when the prophet had first entered the room. Valzaan's coming was tied to what was happening to him, he knew it. Even before Valzaan had spoken in that voice that carried an echo of divine authority, and even before his mother had dismissed him in the voice she always used when she thought she was being reassuring, Benjiah had sensed the change coming. Valzaan had seemed to understand without needing explanation the request that Benjiah had made of him. The answers just might lie beyond the door, but now did he really want them?

He forced his hand to close around the handle, and by an unprecedented act of will, he turned the handle and went in. He had been right about Valzaan, who sat in one of the plush high-back chairs with an empty plate beside him and a cup of hot tea in his hand. The steam of the tea rose steadily out of the cup, except when an occasional sip interrupted its smooth ascent.

His mother, who sat on Valzaan's left, turned to look at him momentarily before returning her attention to Valzaan, who had not moved since he stepped into the room. Something in his mother's hasty glance caught him unaware. She had seemed nervous, even anxious when he'd left, and his first thought was that she must be nervous still. But as he walked toward them across the large room, he realized that he had not seen anxiety in her eyes, but something akin to sorrow, or perhaps "resignation" would be a better word. His apprehension grew as he stood in the space between their two chairs, waiting for guidance.

Wylla stood and moved to the seat immediately on her left, motioning to Benjiah to take the seat she had just vacated.

Benjiah sat, not wanting to look at his mother and not sure if he wanted to look at Valzaan, who had turned in his direction at last and seemed to be staring at him with those eerie, empty eyes. Rather than look at either, Benjiah gazed straight ahead at the fire, which had gone down a bit.

"Benjiah," Wylla began, "there are things that need to be spoken." She broke off there, her mouth slightly open as though she was going to continue, but she said nothing more. She closed her mouth and, reaching her hand out across the intervening distance between their two chairs, took his hand. He pulled away, and to Benjiah's surprise, she started to cry. She did not sob, but the tears rolled noiselessly down her cheek.

"Benjiah," Valzaan began from his other side. Benjiah, disconcerted by the rare appearance of tears in his mother and wishing he hadn't pulled away, twisted in his seat to see the prophet. "I am come on a long journey to Amaan Sul for many reasons, but most of all, I have come to see you."

"Me?" Benjiah whispered. That strange certainty was there again, swirling inside his head and heart like a windstorm, blowing confusion around his normally calm mind. He knew there must be sense and reason behind what Valzaan was saying, but he couldn't see it.

"Yes, I have come many leagues over several days to reach you. Things are moving in the world beyond Amaan Sul's walls that will forever change Kirthanin. More to the point, though it may seem farfetched to you, Allfather has called you to play a crucial role in these events."

"Me?" Benjiah said again. He knew he should be surprised, shocked even, but he wasn't. It was the beginning of an answer.

"You are not surprised?"

"Something has been happening inside me. I've felt it and known it."

"Allfather has been preparing you for his calling. You are his prophet."

Now Benjiah was shocked. He had heard what Valzaan said, but it was impossible. He turned to gauge his mother's reaction to Valzaan's words, but he couldn't read her. The tears stopped, and she returned his gaze as blankly as if Valzaan had just said that Benjiah was a nice boy or a fine bowman or some other innocuous pleasantry. He looked at her, and his anger toward her flared. He turned back to Valzaan. "Prophet? I don't understand."

"You are a prophet because Allfather set you apart for his service and consecrated you with prophetic gifts," Valzaan said calmly. "You are a prophet in exactly the same way your father was a prophet."

"Dad?" Benjiah said, looking back at his mother.

"Benjiah," Wylla said, her voice revealing that her emotions were still raw. She leaned forward in her chair. "You must listen to what Valzaan is saying. He is speaking the truth."

"He is? You knew this? You knew my father was a prophet and you've kept it from me all my life? You've hidden him from me and you've hidden me from myself?"

"Benjiah—"

"No, your chance to speak is over." He turned his back on her.

"Benjiah," Valzaan said firmly, "it is not fitting for any of Allfather's servants to disrespect their lawful authorities. You may be a prophet, but she is still your mother."

"She lied to me."

"She did not, and even if she had lied to you, you still wouldn't have the right."

"She did lie to me."

"She did? She told you that your father was not a prophet?"

"No, she never said he wasn't, but she never told me he was. She hid the truth from me."

"She did? You asked if he was a prophet and she wouldn't answer?"

"No, I never asked. How was I supposed to know? That's the point. She knew and could have told me, but she didn't."

"Ah, that is very different. You are not mad because you've been lied to. You are mad because you dislike your mother's decision to withhold this information from you until she thought you were ready to receive it. And yet, this was her right as your mother."

"Didn't I have a right to know about my own father?"

"Yes, eventually. Your mother never intended to keep this news from you always. When your mother told you as a little boy that Malek was in the Mountain, she did not tell, I'm sure, all she knew from firsthand experience of the terror his creatures can inspire. You were not ready for that information. It wasn't necessary to detail the true size and power of a Malekim or a Black Wolf for a child to understand the danger. Now you are older. Now you know and can understand. If she thought you should be of age before you knew the whole story of your dad, that was her choice and her right.

"Benjiah, it is not a simple thing to know how and when such things should be spoken, and I myself, who have long known both your father's story and much about your own, have chosen also to keep this knowledge from you until today. In fact, I have only confirmed your own calling to your mother this very evening. Before tonight she had no knowledge of it. What's more, until a few days ago, not even I knew that you would be needed now, so not even I, let alone your mother, could have foreseen that this hour would come so soon."

Benjiah shifted uncomfortably. He didn't want to discuss his mother with Valzaan anymore. "I still don't understand how I could be a prophet. Things like that don't just get passed along in the family, do they?"

"I know of no situation like it," Valzaan answered. "Be that as it may, you are what you are, even as he was what he was."

"You know this for sure?"

"I do. As I have already told your mother, I thought your father was a particular prophet, a specific fulfillment of a prophecy from long ago, but he wasn't. However, even before you were born, I knew that you would be."

"So I'm not only a prophet and the son of a prophet, but the answer to some ancient prophecy too?" Benjiah answered. A swirling sensation filled Benjiah's head, and he started to rise.

"Benjiah, you must—" Wylla began to reach out to him and started to speak. He didn't hear the rest of her sentence, for as he began to stand, Valzaan's hand shot across the space between them with remarkable speed and strength and grabbed Benjiah's wrist firmly. As he did, the dizziness in Benjiah's head intensified. The whole room began to swim as Benjiah's eyes momentarily blurred.

The room stopped spinning. Valzaan stood before him, still holding his wrist. "Are you all right?"

"Yes, I think so," Benjiah said as Valzaan released him. Benjiah lifted his hand to wipe sweat off his forehead. He didn't remember being so hot before standing, but his hand was soaked after wiping his brow.

"I think I'm getting sick," Benjiah said, and he turned to his mother. His mother's hand was still, hovering in the air between her chair and Benjiah's. For that matter, her whole body wasn't moving at all. Her head was leaning down and her eyes, wide and unblinking, were staring at the place where he had been sitting. Benjiah stepped closer. Even her hair, which should have been slipping off her shoulders as she leaned forward, seemed completely still.

Benjiah pulled his eyes away long enough to look back at Valzaan, who was stroking his wizened chin. He looked back quickly, but his mother had not moved. "What's happening here?" he asked without taking his eyes off of her. "Is she all right?"

"She's fine. Nothing has happened to her. It is you and I that are different."

"What do you mean? We're fine. She's, well, she's frozen or stuck or something."

"Like I said, she's fine. You and I have changed. Look around you."

Benjiah gazed around the room, but he could not see what he was looking for. The chairs were the same, and the long table where they had eaten was still clear and empty. The double doors were firmly shut where he had closed them after coming in. The rug before the fire was just as it had been, and the fire . . . the fire. He stepped closer to it. The flames weren't moving either. They neither danced nor flickered, and a thick billow of smoke that had just begun its journey up the wide stone chimney hung where it was, suspended in the air right above the fire and right below the flue.

He looked back over his shoulder at Valzaan, who had taken his seat again in the high-backed chair, his elbows resting on the arms of the chair and his hands clasped before his face. He looked deep in thought, and his face wasn't turned in Benjiah's direction. Benjiah rose, still looking at the surreal image of a burning fire that neither moved nor smoked.

"All right," Benjiah said. "What have you done to me?"

Valzaan continued to sit with his hands clasped. Benjiah, impatient with the silence, wondered what he should do now. Before he could do anything, Valzaan snapped out of his reverie and dropped his hands into his lap. "I haven't done anything to you."

"Then what is going on?"

"You've entered *torrim redara,* or slow time. We are no longer in time as we normally are, though shortly we will return and time will appear to resume, though properly understood, it is not resuming so much as we are entering into it again in the precise place where we left it."

Benjiah stared at Valzaan as he was speaking. "What you are saying cannot be."

"It can be because it is," Valzaan answered. "How it is, well that is another question altogether. Perhaps it would help to think of it this way: Time is like a river, flowing throughout history as a seemingly endless succession of moments, one after another. Well, to me, and to you, as to other prophets in the past, Allfather has granted the ability to climb up onto time's shore on occasion, even if only for a few moments. It is at times a very useful ability, because there are things that can be seen from the shore that are hard to see in the river. Do you understand?"

"No." Benjiah shook his head. "I think I understand what you are trying to tell me, but it makes no sense. A river is limited to the space it occupies, so climbing out is understandable. But time, time is everywhere. How can one "climb out" as you put it?"

"I'm not sure, Benjiah." Valzaan shrugged his shoulders. "And even if I did know, I'm not sure I could explain it. But I suspect time may be more limited than you imagine it to be. At any rate, before long you will be pulled back into time and find yourself beside your mother at exactly the same moment you left when you entered *torrim redara*."

"How did I get here?"

"You are a prophet and have many prophetic abilities, though as yet you don't recognize them and don't know how to use them. The dizziness you felt was your body being drawn into slow time, even though you didn't know it. I reached out to touch you to help you in the transition, to guide you more smoothly into it. It can be a difficult experience the first time."

"I did this?"

"You did."

Benjiah ran his hand through his hair again, then peered at Valzaan suspiciously. "But how do I know I did. I mean, how can I really know. I'm here, true, but I came here after you touched me. Maybe you did bring me here. How would I really know?"

"You know already, don't you?"

Benjiah did know. He'd felt that sensation before, when Valzaan hadn't been around. "Valzaan, could my father enter this slow time?"

"Actually, when he first met me on the road to Sulare, your father slipped into *torrim redara* too. I seem to have that effect on young prophets who have the gifts but not the control over them, though admittedly Allfather's gifts to his prophets are never wholly under their control."

"This is what happened when you met my father?" Benjiah answered quietly.

"Yes."

"What happened?"

"I followed him into slow time, as I did with you, and we talked as you and I are now. It was while we were in *torrim redara* that he learned about who he was. He was a little older than you are, but it was still quite a shock."

Benjiah looked down at the floor. "I wish I knew what my father had looked like, then I could imagine what you are telling me."

"He looked a lot like you, actually."

"I know that I'm supposed to look like him, but that doesn't help me. I can't see my father when others talk about him. I can't picture his face."

Valzaan stood and walked over to where Benjiah was standing. "Our time here is short, but stand still. Perhaps you will be given what you seek."

Valzaan stepped to Benjiah's side and raised his hand to cover his eyes. With his other hand, he clasped the back of his head. Between them, he got a pretty strong grip on Benjiah's head. "What are you doing?" Benjiah asked.

"Shh," Valzaan replied, maintaining his grip. "Don't speak and close your eyes. Now wait."

As Benjiah stood there, he suddenly could see a wide open plain in the dark of night. There were no stars out that Benjiah could see, and yet it was light enough that he could make out the knee-high grass all around him.

"What do you see?"

"I see a broad, empty plain. It is grassy and empty. The sky is dark, but there are no stars and there is no moon."

Suddenly, the sun began to rise. It did not creep up over the horizon but shot straight up into the sky, perhaps a little more than halfway to its full noonday height. Then, just as soon as his eyes had adjusted to the sudden and complete transition to the brightness, the shape of three riders riding hard across the plain appeared in the distance. They rode at a furious pace, kicking up grass and dust as they came. Benjiah strained to see them as they approached, and gasped as they drew closer. The one in the middle did look like him, though older. He was fair-skinned with golden hair hanging down over his ears and down the back of his neck. His hair was matted with sweat from the warm sun and hard ride. He was bent intently over his horse.

Though his eyes lingered on the blond rider, who he imagined must be his father, or at least the image of his father, curiosity turned his eyes to the others. One at a time, he gazed carefully at them as the riders approached and then suddenly passed him. Then the sun slipped beneath the horizon, and before he knew it, Benjiah was back in darkness on the plain.

"The image is gone."

Valzaan released his head, and Benjiah opened his eyes and let them adjust once more to the light of the room. "What did you see?"

"I saw the sun rise above the plain, and then I saw three men come thundering by on horseback. The one in the middle, he had hair like mine, and a face like mine. I think he was my father."

"And the others?"

"Well, the one on the near side was Aljeron I think. He was big and strong, with long dark hair hanging down past his shoulders, and scars marked one whole side of his face. He had a fierce look, and he rode as though his life depended on it."

Valzaan was nodding. "I think you are right. The third?"

"I don't know," Benjiah said, concentrating on remembering the face of the third rider.

"But you have a guess."

"I do," Benjiah said, a little reluctantly. "I think it was Rulalin. He was not as big as Aljeron, nor even as big as my father. His hair was also dark, and his face brooding. He seemed deep in thought and wore a scowl. Do you think it could have been him, Valzaan?"

"I believe it was."

Benjiah looked more carefully at Valzaan. "How did I just see what I saw? Did you show me one of your memories or something?"

"No, I had no control over what you saw, though I had some idea what you were seeing as you saw it."

"Then how did I see three men I know of but have never seen?"

"You are a prophet of Allfather, Benjiah. As hard as that may be to accept, it is true. This doesn't mean you can see whatever you want, but it does mean that sometimes you will see things no ordinary man or woman can see. I am blind, and there are many things I cannot see that you or any ordinary sighted person might see every day. At the same time, I am Allfather's prophet, and I see more, much more than most people could even imagine. At the heart of being Allfather's prophet is the calling to see what He wants you to see, and to speak the words He wants you to speak."

"So, you're saying that Allfather showed me my father?"

"Though He will not always show you what you want to see, today He granted your wish to see your father."

"And Aljeron and Rulalin?"

"Did you not also wish to see them?"

Blood rushed to Benjiah's cheeks. "Yes, I suppose I did."

"There is no reason to be ashamed. And what do you think, now that you have seen them all?"

"I've seen my father's face. I've always wanted that." Benjiah was quiet for a moment, then continued. "As for Aljeron, he is everything that I had always imagined him to be."

"And Rulalin?"

"Well, I'm not sure. I had no idea what to expect. I've always thought of him as evil, but he didn't look evil. I guess I'm not sure what evil looks like. Maybe he looks normal because he isn't really evil through and through. Or, maybe the real insidiousness of evil is that it looks normal. Either way, I hope to meet him one day and ask him why he did what he did."

"Perhaps one day you will have that chance."

"Not likely," Benjiah said, shaking his head. "If what I hear of the war is correct, Aljeron will soon have Fel Edorath. When Fel Edorath falls, I think Rulalin won't live long."

"Maybe, though what is coming to pass will surprise a lot of people. A lot of plans are going to come crashing down, perhaps even mine."

Benjiah grew faint and dropped to the floor. Valzaan reached down and took hold of his shoulder. "What is it?"

"I'm in a great dark place. I think I'm inside, because I can't see the moon or stars or anything. A searing bright light has flashed before my eyes, and now the light and heat are overwhelming. It is hot beyond reckoning, but I'm not burned."

"And now?"

"It's gone."

"Can you see anything else?"

"Yes, it's raining, and I see thick wooden slats or bars, like a cage. I can feel the wood with my fingers. It's rough and the sides are splintered. Now the cage is gone too. I'm in a broad, open white square in a city. A great open space, larger than any city square I've ever seen. I've seen this place in my dreams many times. I've seen the light and wooden bars too." The images faded away. Benjiah opened his eyes and looked up at Valzaan. "What's happening to me?"

Valzaan stooped down. "Stand up, I'll help you."

They stood, and Benjiah held onto Valzaan's arm. "Dark things are coming."

"They are."

"I will have to stand alone, won't I?"

Valzaan's face looked suddenly very sad, and his grip on Benjiah's shoulder tightened. "Yes, you will."

A sudden flash of wooziness swept over Benjiah, and his knees buckled. Valzaan held onto his arm and led him back to his seat. "You are slipping back into normal time. Don't fear. It's uncomfortable at first, but you'll be fine. Time always pulls us back to the exact space where we were when we left it, so it's always good to be as close as possible to the place where you entered slow time, for your own good."

Benjiah's head was swimming as he stopped before the chair where he had been sitting. All of a sudden he felt a force pulling him down into the chair. Then, just as he reached a certain point right above the chair's cushion, he felt himself begin to rise back up out of the chair, but this time as though under his own power. He also realized as he stood that he could hear his mother's voice.

". . . lay aside your grievance with me and listen to Valzaan. He is telling you the truth."

Benjiah looked at his mother, who was no longer frozen. She leaned to the side, looking up at him, with her hand on the arm of his chair. Her face pleaded with him to believe her.

"I know."

A puzzled look crossed her face. "You do?"

"I do, and I'm sorry." Benjiah turned to Valzaan, standing beside him. He felt weak and weary. "What now, Valzaan? What do we do?"

Valzaan reached out his hand again, but this time, instead of taking Benjiah's wrist, he laid his hand gently on Benjiah's shoulder. "It means that you must come with me, right away."

"Tonight?"

"We will wait until first light, but we dare not wait any longer."

"Where will we go?"

"You will understand the answer to that question when you understand more about why I have come to you. Sit, please, and I will tell you what I have told your mother. It is time that you knew all."

At Valzaan's request, the adults reassembled. Quiet whispers were exchanged around the fire as they waited for some indication of what must be discussed. After several moments, even the whispers died away. Valzaan lifted his staff from across his knees and set the base firmly on the floor. "At first light, I am riding to Werthanin with Benjiah. As I said earlier, Malek is preparing to move, to come forth from the Mountain at last. I must go to help, and Benjiah must go with me."

"Benjiah?" Pedraal asked, looking from Valzaan to his sister, who sat looking at the floor. "Why do you have to take Benjiah? He is only a boy."

Benjiah looked at his uncle, who was now staring at him, puzzled.

"Valzaan and I have spoken of this already, Pedraal," Wylla said. "I must ask you to trust us. I am satisfied that this is necessary. I would not send Benjiah west unless there were no other choice. For tonight, that will have to be enough. There will be time later for more information, but for now, we must turn to other matters."

Pedraal and Pedraan exchanged a quick glance. "If Benjiah is going west with Valzaan, then we will go too," Pedraal said. "We will watch over him and lend our aid to the Werthanim when Malek comes forth."

"And what of Amaan Sul's defenses?" Wylla asked, having regained most of her regal composure. "Will my brothers and captains leave their city undefended?"

"Of course not, Wylla," Pedraal said, looking imploringly at her. "You know we will make the necessary arrangements as soon as we leave this room. You will lack for nothing because we are gone, but we must go. We belong in Werthanin now. Besides, Benjiah is as precious to you as this city, is he not?"

"If Wylla will allow it," Valzaan said, "I would be glad of your company on the road. We must be swift, but two companions will not be a burden."

"Surely there will be room enough for three more as well," Kyril jumped in. "I need to take the girls to Evrim. If Malek is about to go west, then Evrim will be at the first line of defense. We must go to him."

Wylla put her hand on Kyril's arm. "Kyril, don't you see? It's a blessing that you are here. Were you there now, in Shalin Bel, I would warn you to evacuate, to flee. I would offer my home to you as a refuge. But I don't have to, because Allfather has brought you here already. There's nothing you can do for Evrim by heading needlessly into danger. Stay here, and pray with me that Allfather will deliver all our loved ones."

"But my place is with him, and—"

"Kyril," Valzaan interrupted. "Wylla is right. I will not lie to you. Your husband is in great danger, but we are all in great danger. Even Amaan Sul will not be safe if Werthanin falls, for Malek desires all of Kirthanin. You must trust your husband to Allfather now, and take care of your daughters. Besides, we must travel with great speed. Even if I wished to take you with us, I could not. Your daughters are too young for the journey."

Kyril sat with lips pursed. Benjiah could see that she did not want to accept this answer, but there was nothing to say if Valzaan was against the idea.

"It will take several weeks," Pedraan added, as if to support Valzaan's point about the difficulty of the trip. "Most likely a month. It is a week to ten days to Garring Pul, and there we will need to find a ship to take us across the Kellisor Sea. From there to Fel Edorath will be tricky, even if Malek hasn't arrived. The lands south of Fel Edorath are unsettled and in no small amount of turmoil already."

"It will be a hard trip indeed," Valzaan said. "But for reasons other than those you have outlined. We will not be headed to Garring Pul, nor will we be crossing the Kellisor Sea."

"But I thought we were headed to Fel Edorath," Pedraal said, again exchanging a puzzled glance with his brother.

"We are."

"Then the quickest way is to Garring Pul and across the Kellisor Sea."

"No, the quickest way is to take the Old Mountain Road, which once connected Fel Edorath and Amaan Sul."

"What?" several said, and shocked disbelief rippled through the room.

"The Old Mountain Road runs straight through the Forest of Gyrin, and it has been abandoned by all but Malek's servants since the betrayal of Corindel at the beginning of the Third Age," Wylla said. "Surely you don't mean to suggest you will take the road into Gyrin?"

"I do indeed."

"This is madness!" Pedraal muttered. "What is the use of rushing out of here if we rush but to our grave?"

"I am no fool that I would choose a road of certain death," Valzaan said sharply. "I have much hope that we will not only pass through the Forest of Gyrin, but that we will pass through quickly and safely. For many centuries the Old Mountain Road has lain virtually abandoned, though occasionally Malek has used it. We will find it overgrown and forgotten. Further, the road runs south of the Mountain itself, and if I am correct, Malek will be amassing his forces in the west. And we may be able to reach Fel Edorath in fifteen days, cutting the time of the next fastest route in half."

Benjiah did not know a great deal about the Forest of Gyrin, but he knew enough to know that speaking of entering Gyrin was almost like planning to climb the Holy Mountain itself. It simply wasn't done.

Valzaan continued. "I am going on the Old Mountain Road, and Benjiah is coming with me. Pedraal and Pedraan, this is the road I have chosen, and if you come with us, it is the road you must take."

Pedraal shook his head but said, "We will come. We may never see the other side of the Forest, but we will go with you."

"Good, then let us be about our business."

Almost an hour later, Benjiah strapped shut his pack, full of clothes for both autumn and winter weather. He had no idea how long he'd be gone, but the chill wind today suggested that winter was already well on its way.

Carrying the pack from his bed to the wall beside his door, he set it on the floor beside Suruna. On the other side of the bow was a full quiver of arrows, most of them marked red to indicate that they had been tipped in cyranic poison. His uncles had talked as though they expected trouble on the Old Mountain Road, and even if trouble didn't find them there, he would likely find himself shooting at Malekim, or worse, soon enough.

He stood looking down at the quiver, the bow, and the pack. It seemed very little, but it was all he knew to take. He wished for some keepsake, some symbol of home he could slip into his pocket for days when he ached for his home. But though his room was full of trinkets, none seemed worth toting everywhere he went.

He extinguished the lamp beside his bed, but he did not get in. Instead, he walked to the window on the far side of his room and settled into the large comfortable chair drawn up beside it. Reaching over, he unlatched the window and pulled it open. The air was almost frigid, and a strong gust of wind blew splashes of raindrops into his room. His skin broke out in goose bumps, but he did not shut the window.

The sound of steady rain against the wall and roof was pleasant, even soothing. He had always loved to listen to the rain, and not even the occasional roar of ominous thunder or the constant flashing of dramatic lightning strikes could negate the positive effect of the sound. The lightning, as it streaked to the earth or filled the clouds, was as impressive and beautiful as it was frightening. Even the thunder, which from time to time would raise the hair on the back of Benjiah's neck, was something that was here and then gone again, while the music of the rain played on. He closed his eyes and leaned back in the chair. Let the lightning fall and the thunder roll. He was safe here.

He was not going to be here for very long. He opened his eyes and gazed blankly out the window. He had always wanted to travel, and to a certain extent, the prospect of seeing the larger world of Kirthanin under the direct supervision of Valzaan was exciting. Surely there was no one in all the land who could serve as a better guide to the geography, history, and story of the world than he.

And yet, this would not be a tourist's excursion. He was going into turmoil and chaos, facing difficulty and possibly death. How could he just mount his horse and ride away from Amaan Sul in the morning, not knowing if he would ever see it again? How could he say farewell to his mother, not knowing if he would ever feel her arms around him again or hear her voice calling his name?

Running through all these thoughts were the mystifying words of the prophecy. He could see how he would be considered a child, and it appeared that he was indeed a prophet. But in what sense could he be considered a warrior? And what did it mean that he was born to surrender? More than that, what sacrifice was he going to be called on to make?

Valzaan had not explained the prophecy. Instead, he had encouraged Benjiah simply to know it. Prophecy, he had said, was often a complicated business to understand. The mystery of the future was something Allfather rarely revealed with total clarity. While He might give direction, He usually left the details in the dark. It was, Valzaan insisted, necessary at times to point the way into the future, while at the same time placing our trust in Allfather alone for guidance and direction.

It was all a mystery, and there was too much of it for Benjiah to grasp. He pushed the words from his mind. Maybe in the light of day he would wrestle with them anew. But, for now, it was enough simply to know he had to go.

Maybe, he thought as he let his eyes close again, maybe he would have a chance to meet Aljeron at last. If they were successful in reaching Werthanin before the coming of Malek, perhaps he would finally be able to see for himself the man who had so zealously campaigned for justice. He wondered what Aljeron would think of him. Benjiah wanted to impress him. He didn't like the thought that Aljeron might be disappointed in what he had grown to be.

He thought of his father, Aljeron, and Rulalin riding across the plain. As far as he knew, Rulalin was still alive, and it was possible Benjiah might meet him after all. If they could arrive before the fall of Fel Edorath, then he could ask Aljeron for a chance to face his father's murderer. His request might carry some weight. Aljeron might stay his hand for Benjiah, even if not for anyone else.

But how likely was it that he would actually come through the Forest of Gyrin alive? All these hopes were based on a safe passage there. He knew no stories of men venturing into the forest since the time of Corindel, let alone stories of men going in one side and emerging safe on the other. How could anyone pass so close to Agia Muldonai undetected?

Benjiah rose, shutting the window. He was tired. The fatigue was deep and pervasive. Body, mind, and heart, all were weary beyond comprehension. He moved toward his bed in the dark, when a light rap came on his door. The flicker of lamplight slipped under his door from the hallway. "Yes?"

"It's me," his mother's voice answered.

"Come in." At least if they did this now, he wouldn't have to wait for it in the morning.

Wylla opened the door and stepped in. The lamp in her hand illuminated her and the part of the room closest to the door. She appeared calm and controlled, but he could see she had been crying.

"I just wanted to make sure you had everything you needed," she said as she glanced at his pack by the door.

"I'll be fine."

Wylla nodded. "I'm sorry if I got you out of bed. You'll need your sleep."

"I haven't been to bed yet. You didn't wake me."

"Good."

He looked at his mother. He didn't want to part badly, but he had to ask. "Why didn't you tell me about my father?"

"I wanted to protect you." Wylla answered quickly, and Benjiah realized she'd been expecting the question.

"Protect me from what?"

"From the questions and fear I've been living with since your birth. Knowing who your father was has always raised certain troubling questions, and I wanted you to have a chance to know him and grieve his loss as a father, without all the rest."

"Why would I need protection from the truth? How could I truly grieve him if I'd never been truly informed about him?"

Wylla opened her mouth to speak, and the hand that held the lamp faltered and the flame danced as the lamp jiggled. "I . . . I'm sorry, Benjiah. It's a lie that I was protecting you. I was protecting myself. When you were born, I could sense there was something special about you. I knew it. I tried to tell myself I was just being maternal, seeing a unique wonder in my child, but I knew there was more going on than I could see, and I was afraid. I kept the truth from you because I didn't want to open a door I couldn't close. I didn't want you to start asking questions of yourself that you weren't ready for. I'm sorry."

"And when I asked you about my dreams?"

"I know. I pushed them away. I didn't want to face them."

Benjiah stood, not looking at his mother. "I had a right to answers."

She stepped closer to him, setting the lamp down on a small table beside the bed. "Again, I'm sorry. I shouldn't have left you alone to wonder about the meaning of what was going on inside you."

"It was hard, and lonely."

"Benjiah . . ."

"I forgive you," he said, after a moment.

She hugged him tightly. When she let go, he said, "I'm sorry for the way I've been."

"I forgive you too," she said, wiping tears from her eyes. "We should have had several days or weeks to work through these things. I'm sorry we won't be able to. Valzaan will help. There are things he'll be able to explain that I couldn't."

"When I get back," Benjiah answered. "My duty lies now with Valzaan. Your duty lies here."

Wylla reached out to him and hugged him again. "Thank you," she said softly.

"For what?"

"For making this easier. When your father was taken from me, Allfather granted me a precious gift in you. I will pray for you every day, as I always have."

Benjiah stepped back. "Thanks."

Wylla put her hands on Benjiah's shoulders, and stood before him for a moment, looking at him intently, as though drinking in the moment. "Benjiah," she began, "there's something I'd like to send with you, if you would have it."

"What?"

Wylla extracted from her sleeve a long, slender golden cord. It was finely woven and knotted at both ends, where it had begun to fray. "This is the union cord that Valzaan tied around your father's arm when we married in Sulare. I want you to take it."

Benjiah looked down at the cord in his mother's outstretched hand. "But, Mom, this is yours. I don't want to take this."

"I want you to have it."

"But—"

"No, listen to me. This is a symbol of the union between your father and me, but you're a symbol too. In fact, you're a truer picture of the love and time I had with your father. I want to send this cord with you so you'll understand how much I love you, and how much your father would have loved you if he'd been given the chance. Though your journey may carry you far from here, this will ever remind you that there is also a bond between you and me."

Benjiah looked from the cord to his mother and finally nodded. Wylla tied it around his neck.

"I'm glad you'll be wearing it," Wylla said. "Now I should go, so you can sleep. I'll see you in the morning."

"All right, good night, Mother."

"Good night."

"And thanks."

"You're welcome." Wylla slipped out of the door, and as the door swung shut, Benjiah was left in darkness. He climbed into his bed, and it felt good to his weary body. He didn't go to sleep for a while, though, but lay there feeling the slender cord around his neck.

7

MIDAUTUMN

PEDRAAN STOOD OUTSIDE Karalin's room. A faint light beneath the door suggested she was not yet asleep, but still he hesitated to knock. He clasped his hands tightly, taking a deep breath. There were few things in the world he feared, and while fear might not have been exactly the word for what he was feeling at that moment, it was something very like it.

"All right, Pedraan," he mumbled, "you're going to miss your chance if you don't knock now."

He lifted his big hand and rapped lightly on the door. Karalin's voice, like music, called out, "Who is it?"

"It's me, Pedraan," he said nervously.

"Oh," came her simple reply, and then he heard the sound of a chair squeaking on the floor, and a moment later, the door opened.

Karalin wore a long, simple robe of light green wrapped around her nightclothes. In her hand she held a small candle, though behind her a lamp on her bedside table glowed brightly. She didn't look irritated, which greatly relieved him. Even so, she looked expectantly at him, and he realized that she was waiting for him to say something.

"Yes, well, I'm sorry to come by so late, Karalin."

"It's all right. I wasn't in bed yet. Is everything all right? You don't look well."

Pedraan wiped sweat off his brow. "I'm fine."

She looked at him closely. "Maybe we should go somewhere where you could sit down."

"That may be a good idea," Pedraan replied. "Let's go to the upstairs parlor. I don't think anyone will be there."

Karalin followed him through the corridors to the small parlor, which was both dark and cold. There had been no fire in its hearth this night, so there wasn't even a residual heat from dying embers. Still, both of them were warmly dressed, and the candle Karalin carried would serve sufficiently for light. Pedraan waited for Karalin to take a seat in one of the big chairs by the fireplace, and he pulled another one over close to where she was.

"So," Karalin said as he sat down. "You have me a bit worried, Pedraan. I don't like to think of you setting out tomorrow sick."

"Really, I don't think I'm sick, just a bit anxious is all."

Karalin nodded, "Anxious is understandable. It's no small task before you, and added to all the rest, you undoubtedly feel responsible for Benjiah."

"No," Pedraan scratched the back of his neck, shaking his head. "It isn't the trip or Benjiah or any of that. It's you."

"Me?" Karalin said, sitting back and placing her hands gently in her lap. "Why would I make you anxious?"

"Because there are things I need to say to you, but I've never been good at such things, and I don't know how to say them."

"Oh," Karalin said, visibly relaxing. She leaned forward again and looked at Pedraan in the candlelight, smiling. She placed her hand lightly on his and added, "Then don't worry about how you say it or how it sounds. Just say what you have to say."

Encouraged, Pedraan cleared his throat, coughed, and then began. "I think the first thing I should say, Karalin, is that I'm sorry I haven't spoken sooner. I've failed you in that, and I'm sorry. You know I've cared for you for years, and I shouldn't have waited until now to say so. I need to ask you to forgive me before I go."

"Of course I forgive you," she whispered, "you know how I feel."

"I know," he said, "and I'm grateful." He reached over and brushed a tear from her cheek. "I also wanted to explain, though I don't intend my explanation to be taken as an excuse."

"You don't have to explain anything to me."

"I want to. You deserve to know. I don't think I really understood how I felt for you, Karalin, until I rode away with Pedraal to join Aljeron in his first campaign against Rulalin almost seven years ago. Being away from you made me realize how much I had come to care for you. Not seeing you or hearing your voice convinced me I loved you. I couldn't wait to do what had to be done in Werthanin, come home, and then ask you to marry me.

"But when the campaign against Fel Edorath failed and we returned to Amaan Sul, I was torn. I wanted to speak to you then, but I felt that I needed to be available to Aljeron. I felt a burden of responsibility to help avenge Joraiem, who had been my brother, even if only for a short time. I didn't think it right of me to speak to you when I might have to leave at any time. And though I didn't go back right away, I did return a second time, as you know. But all the time I was out there, I dreamed of being here with you. So, while I was there, I wasn't really there, if you're following me. When we came back the second time, the war still wasn't over, and now so much time had gone by, I felt . . . well, I felt like I was bound to silence until all this was over, like I had made my choice and had to live with it.

"It must sound silly, I know, but as much as I ached to be with you, I just couldn't get rid of the guilt I felt for not having been of more use to Aljeron. At the same time I felt guilty for not coming to you first and giving you a say in my decision. I began to feel as though I didn't deserve you."

"Oh, Pedraan," Karalin said, lifting her hand from his and brushing his cheek. "How could you not deserve me? I don't know that I deserve you."

"Karalin, how can you say that? We've lost at least five years of a life together because I didn't go straight to you as soon as I came home. I've squandered so much of our precious time. Now here we are, Rulalin still at large, Malek on the move, and me on my way out with no real idea if I will ever make it back to Amaan Sul alive. I've failed you in every possible way."

"You did what you believed was right," she answered. "That is one of the things I love about you, Pedraan. You are very loyal to what you believe. What is past is past."

"Then you really do forgive me?" Pedraan asked, looking at Karalin as though she were out of her mind.

"Of course I do, what did you think I would do? I love you."

"I . . . I didn't know what you would do. You really love me?"

"Yes, I really do. You know that."

"I hoped. I didn't know."

Karalin leaned in and whispered, "This is where you say you love me too."

"Of course I love you too," Pedraan said, embarrassed by his oversight. "I love you more than anything in the whole world. I can't bear the thought of leaving you behind, but, you know I have to go, don't you?"

"I do."

"I can't send Benjiah out there alone. Pedraal and I, well, we feel like we need to be fatherly to Benjiah."

"I know."

"All that being said," Pedraan went on with a new tone in his voice, a layer of excitement. "If you really do love me, and if you really do forgive me, then there is one other thing I need to ask."

"Yes?"

"Karalin, I know I don't deserve you. You are the best woman I've ever met. You are beautiful. You have a voice like a songbird. You are the kindest and the gentlest person in the whole world. You are everything I could ever want in a wife, and if you will consent, I would like to make you my wife if ever it is my good fortune to come home again. If Allfather brings us safely home, will you marry me?"

"Yes, I most certainly will," she replied, coming forward out of the chair and throwing her arms around him. He clung to her, and wrapping his great big arms around her, squeezed her tight. Then, lifting her up onto his lap, pulled her in close to him and kissed her.

"I can't tell you how long I've wanted to do that," he said.

"Not as long as I've wanted you to do it," she answered.

She leaned her head down upon his shoulder, and her long hair hung around his face. He slipped his rough fingers through it and felt the soft strands fall through his fingertips. "I don't want to go," he whispered.

"I don't want you to go."

"I can't stay, though."

"I know."

"I'll do everything I can to come back for you."

"I know."

"If I don't make it back, I want you to know that this has been the happiest moment of my life."

"Mine too."

She sat up and looked down into his eyes, tears freely rolling down her cheeks. She lifted her slender fingers and brushed them through his short hair. "I'll be waiting."

He pulled her close again, and for a long time, they sat there in the flickering candlelight together. The candle burned low, and eventually went out.

Benjiah leaned forward in his saddle, hunched over the horse as the four riders pressed through the cold, grey morning. The sky hadn't cleared, but the rain had stopped. There was a crisp coolness to the morning that brought to Benjiah's mind the image of brown crumpled leaves on frozen earth.

The parting that morning had been a quiet affair. A small group of stewards and family members gathered to see them off beside the stables. Kyril had handed Benjiah a letter just after he mounted his horse. "For Evrim," was all she said as he tucked it carefully into his pack.

Before they left, Valzaan had raised his staff above his head and spoken a blessing upon Amaan Sul and those they were leaving behind. "May Allfather's eyes be ever upon you, His hands ever beneath you, His arms ever around you, and His power ever within you." Wylla thanked him for the blessing, and Valzaan replied simply, "We must look to Allfather alone for hope, for the gathering storm is bigger than us all."

And with that they had passed out of the northern gate and turned northwest immediately, leaving behind all sight of the city within an hour of hard riding. Not long after, they met the first of what would no doubt be several patrols. Though Enthanin did not keep a large standing army in the field, patrols between Amaan Sul and the Mountain were always active.

This patrol had hailed them while still at a distance, and Pedraal and Pedraan had led the way to them. The exchange was brief, with the soldiers spending as much time staring at Valzaan as they did listening to Pedraal's instructions. In the end, Pedraal had to satisfy himself that they were at least clear on the chain of command and the need for heightened alertness. Pedraal had agreed with Valzaan that the men did not need a lot of detail, but he had insisted that each patrol be directed to increase its vigilance.

And so they had ridden on the rest of that morning, before stopping for a quick lunch and a brief respite. Benjiah had not spent so much time in a saddle in months, and he knew that by day's end he would be sore. "How long, do you think?" Benjiah asked Valzaan.

"Until Gyrin?"

"Yes."

"Today is the thirteenth of Full Autumn. We should enter Gyrin by the twenty-second or twenty-third."

Benjiah nodded. His uncles, standing a few spans away, began to whisper together.

"And you, Benjiah, how did you sleep?"

Benjiah looked at his uncles, seemingly oblivious to the prophet's question. "All right, I guess," Benjiah said warily.

"Any dreams?"

"None."

"None while you slept, anyway," Valzaan added, smiling.

"No," Benjiah answered.

Valzaan leaned in close and whispered, "I'm not your mother, and I'm not your uncle. I am the only person who can help you understand who and what you are. Remember that."

Aljeron knelt in the grass beside Evrim. They were surrounded by a throng of people, gathered there in Shalin Bel's city square to celebrate the rites of Midautumn. The rites had already begun with the dawn, and Elder Curran was kneeling atop the city mound, praying. How long they would be kneeling was anyone's guess, but usually they passed several hours this way as the chief elder prayed for his own sins and the sins of the people, and as the men and women prayed for the return of peace and the restoration of all things.

Aljeron, though, found his thoughts bending toward war, not peace. In the morning, he would leave with Evrim and the others for Fel Edorath, hopefully this time to end the war begun so many years ago. How could he think of peace? Now was the time to steel himself for battle. There would be time later to think of peace, if indeed peace would ever return. Werthanin's wounds would be long in healing, and he could not guarantee that peace would inevitably follow the end of the conflict.

He squeezed his eyes shut, trying to push thoughts of war from him. He tried to focus on Elder Curran's earlier words. But again, his attempt was frustrated. Into his mind came Rulalin's face, impassive and hard and filled with bitterness. Though he hadn't seen Rulalin for seventeen years, not since the evening before the murder, his face was always before Aljeron. Sometimes he envisioned Rulalin laughing, laughing at Aljeron's failed attempts to bring him to justice, but there was no laughter now, just a cold, hard stare. Surely Rulalin knew his hour of reckoning was fast approaching. He'd been given an ultimatum, and Aljeron was going to throw everything he had at Fel Edorath with unrelenting fury until he crushed the city's defenses and brought Rulalin's army to its knees.

He wondered whether Rulalin's army was on its knees now. A sudden and striking image appeared before him. Could it be that they were beseeching Allfather for mercy, for strength, and for victory, even as he was? Would they dare to go before Him with their plight, even though they were fighting in defiance of justice? Aljeron was taken aback. He had never considered this possibility. No doubt many of the soldiers in Rulalin's army were faithful servants of Allfather. What of their prayers? Did Allfather hear them?

Aljeron opened his eyes and looked at the mound and

bowed assembly surrounding it. He believed, adamantly, that he was right to be doing what he was doing, that it was faithfulness to Allfather and Allfather's love of justice that drove him. At the same time, he wondered if his just cause applied to all those gathered here. Did his faithfulness place them on the side of good and all those gathered in Fel Edorath on the side of evil, or at least rebellion?

He wasn't sure, and the question was discomforting. He didn't like the idea that faithful servants of Allfather were gathered in Fel Edorath asking for mercy and victory. It was easier to think of Allfather marching with him and against Fel Edorath.

Allfather. I may not have all your faithful servants on my side, but I believe that my side is right and in accordance with Your will. Forgive us—forgive me—if the pursuit of justice in this war leads us, leads me, to slay any of Your faithful servants. Hold us not guilty of their blood, I pray, and give their spirits rest until You restore peace and make all things new. Help us, Allfather, to end this war quickly. Help us to bring peace to Werthanin again. Help me to bring justice to Rulalin. Let him escape it no more.

Aljeron knelt for a long time in silence, these same words and thoughts running over and over through his mind. Some time later, Elder Curran's voice rang out, and Aljeron opened his eyes.

"The promises of Allfather are sure. What He has spoken, He will do. This is so, always has been so, and always will be. Allfather has spoken of the future of Werthanin and all Kirthanin. His words are truth and His promises certain. Is this not so?"

"It is so," all the people answered as one, their many voices like one mighty voice speaking from out of the earth itself.

"Evil shall be destroyed. So be it?"

"So may it be."

"Malek shall be cast down and punished, once and for all. So be it?"

"So may it be."

"Peace and life shall be restored. So be it?"

"So may it be."

"Allfather shall make all things new. So be it?"

"So may it be."

"Allfather shall cleanse the blessed Fountain. So be it?"

"So may it be."

Elder Curran took up the great, shining golden bowl of water that had been sitting next to him in the grass and tipped a steady stream upon the top of the mound. Though Aljeron couldn't see it, he envisioned the water beginning to slip down the sides of the mound atop the cold-hardened soil.

"Allfather shall cleanse Avalione. So be it?"

"So may it be."

Again Elder Curran poured a steady stream from the bowl, this time tipping out a little more.

"Allfather shall cleanse Agia Muldonai. It shall be cleansed forevermore, as indeed all Kirthanin shall be cleansed. Never again will sword and spear be raised in battle or war, for even they will be made new. Every implement of war ever forged shall be unmade and recast. They shall become implements of peace to till the earth and work it. No one will harm or destroy on all His Holy Mountain. So be it?"

"So may it be."

Elder Curran tipped out the rest of the water into the grass. Aljeron remained kneeling beside Evrim as the chief elder encouraged the whole city to break their fasts and enjoy the feast of Allfather. People rose to their feet and began to talk among themselves. The sound grew to a din as the gathered city dispersed to homes and inns for feasting and celebration. Aljeron stood at last, as did Evrim. Placing his hand on Evrim's shoulder, he turned from the mound and started off into the city.

As they passed through the outer courtyard of the Council Hall, Aljeron peered into the sky, soaking in the first rays of sunlight in almost a week. Though the sun didn't bring much warmth, he was tempted to take the breakthrough of sunshine as a good omen.

He and Evrim passed inside, and sounds of feasting and celebration emanated from the main dining hall. Many of the Novaana who lived in outlying areas came to the city on feast days, and after attending the rites, they would often return to the Council Hall to celebrate the remainder of the day with one another. Aljeron didn't especially want to join their celebration, so he motioned to Evrim to follow him through a side door that led in a roundabout way to their rooms.

Back in Aljeron's quarters, both men slipped off their warm outer coats and warmed themselves by the fire that the stewards had prepared for their return. They had barely had time to pour themselves a drink and settle in when a knock came.

"Who is it?" Aljeron called.

"Caan," came the reply, "and I have Sarneth with me."

Aljeron rose and strolled across the room, unlocking the door and opening it. Caan nodded to Aljeron as he entered. Sarneth bent over and squeezed through the doorframe, which was just big enough to accommodate his massive form.

Caan took a seat and Sarneth sat beside him on the floor, and once his guests were settled, Aljeron returned to his chair. "Did you go to the rites this morning?"

"Yes," Caan replied, "though we stood at a distance so as not to distract anyone."

"Hopefully the people have been welcoming," Aljeron said.

"Yes, they have been. We cause a bit of a stir wherever we go, but people are usually quite polite after they've recovered from their shock."

"Good," Aljeron answered, leaning back. "I would hate to hear you'd not been welcomed properly."

They sat for a few moments, each of them gazing at the flames, an awkward silence settling over them. Caan scratched his head and then said abruptly, "Look, Aljeron, I'm not going to beat around the bush. I wanted to make sure you understood that I sympathize with what you're after. I think Rulalin deserves to be brought to justice, and I for one hope that this war not only ends quickly but satisfactorily in that regard. The fact that we believe the war poses a particular danger for Kirthanin doesn't mean we don't believe in justice. Speaking as one soldier to another, I believe that under different circumstances, pressing this war to its natural conclusion would be exactly the right thing to do."

"I understand, Caan," Aljeron replied, "though I was upset at first. I guess I expected that you of all people would understand what I was after, and I know you do. As for me, I'm sorry I haven't had more time to spend with you."

"No apology needed. I understand how important it is to be immersed in the details of battle. Never take anything for granted. That was one of the lessons I tried to teach you, wasn't it?"

"It was."

"Besides, there should be plenty of time on the way to Fel Edorath for you to explain in some detail what the plan of battle will be."

"What? You want to come with us?"

"Well," Caan said with a twinkle appearing in his eye, "all four of us would like to come, but that's really up to you, now isn't it?"

Aljeron looked from Caan to Sarneth, then back to Caan again. "But what happened to the idea that you needed to remain neutral?"

Caan shrugged. "Well you know, neutrality is a tricky thing.

In fact, one could say that having come to Shalin Bel, a truly neutral ambassador from Sulare would also visit Fel Edorath. And, if one was to travel in the company of an old friend along the way, who could find fault with that? And, if one was endangered during some part of this trip and so had to defend himself against bodily harm, who could find fault with that either?"

Aljeron sat shaking his head. "Even from here, you can smell the scent of war, can't you?"

"I can indeed."

"And you can't resist."

"I could," he said, "I just don't want to. I'd rather go along and see for myself what you've learned."

"And you're willing to come along too?" Aljeron said, turning to Sarneth.

"Yes, though not for the same reasons. I would like to be on hand when the war is concluded so I can bring a full report back to the draals. And, as that means going to Fel Edorath, I'd be delighted to travel once more with you, if you will have us."

"If I will? You will lighten my heart and bring fear to our enemies, even if they only see you from the city walls. Of course I will have you."

"Good," Caan said, rising to help himself from the pitcher on the table behind them. "Then it is settled. We will come with you to Fel Edorath and stay with you until the war is finished. And, if in the course of things, we can be of service to you, we will help as we can."

The gathering in the main dining hall had grown, and singing could be heard above the din. Aljeron and Evrim slipped past the open doors, and soon they had made their way to the main kitchen of the Council Hall. Aljeron took aside the senior steward and, having explained his wishes, led Evrim to the smaller dining hall, where they sat to wait for their dinner. They didn't have to wait long, for shortly after they had settled into one of the round tables beside the fire, five stewards bustled into the room bearing a broad selection of meats, breads, cheeses, steaming soups, and pitchers of cider both hot and cold. Aljeron motioned for them to leave it all, and they set down their trays and disappeared from the room as quickly as they had appeared.

They talked little as they wolfed down their dinner, and occasionally the roar of some outburst down the hallway would reverberate through their room as well. Even so, they kept their attention on their plates and ate their fill and more, until at last they had pushed themselves back from the table, unable to eat another bite.

"Feast days are one of the few things that remind me of life in Dal Harat," Evrim said as he leaned back in his chair.

"Big feasters, were you?"

"Not especially, but it brings home vividly to mind all the same. Even now, I don't have to close my eyes, and I can see it. Our village square is green and lush and the mound rises out of it in much the same way the mound does here. I can see the whole village gathered around in the early evening, eating and singing and dancing, their hearts filled to bursting with the joy of the day. Rivalries and disputes, feuds and arguments are put aside. Those who live hours from the village and those who live in town, those who have lived there for a single season and those whose families have lived in the village for as many years as anyone can recall, they are all neighbors. Everyone's good fortune is shared, and no one carries his burdens alone. I want that, Aljeron, as much as I want anything. I want to finish this war, ride home with Kyril and the girls, and become part of that world again."

Aljeron sipped his cider. "It sounds idyllic. I should like to come and visit you over one of the feasts."

Evrim looked at him. "You would be welcome whenever you like, for as long as you like. I think it would do you good. You could find rest there."

Aljeron took another drink. "Rest," he said softly. "That sounds good."

Evrim poured himself another drink. The images of home had been joined now by the picture of Kyril, her long hair flowing as she danced in the moonlight of a Midsummer feast night many years past. Her eyes glistened and her feet glided across the thick grass like the wind rippling across the water. She was graceful like no one he had ever seen, and she danced for him to see and enjoy. He could have watched her all night.

With an effort he pulled himself out of the dream, returning to the small dining room, beside the table bearing empty trays of food, across from his silent friend and the small fire. Aljeron had spoken freely with Caan of happy times in the Summerland just an hour ago, but now the melancholy that always overtook him when he was preparing to return to the front was settling upon him. "Surely there will be some rest for you when this is through."

"I suppose that depends on how it ends. I don't know what rest I will have if Rulalin escapes."

"He won't," Evrim replied. "If he was going to abandon Fel Edorath, he would have left before now. Anyway, let's not worry about that tonight. For the sake of argument, let's assume that we take the city as we should, and that at long last Rulalin is brought to justice. You will have earned your rest then, won't you?"

Aljeron shrugged. "I guess. Sure, I'll rest then. I certainly won't know what else to do. What else is there?"

"What else?" Evrim said, leaning in over the table to look at Aljeron. "Living, that's what else. When you've rested, you will have a whole new chance at life. Surely you remember what you once dreamed life would be, don't you? When you rode off to Sulare, you must have had dreams of what you would do when you returned. When this is over, you'll finally be able to turn your attention to those dreams, or to new ones if they will no longer do."

"That was long ago, Evrim. You speak of memories from another man's life. I can hardly remember the things of which you speak. Everything I've done or desired since Joraiem died has been tied to bringing Rulalin to justice. I can't really picture what I'll do after that goal is realized. It seems too fantastic to be real."

"But isn't that the hope that keeps us going? That this would end and we would be free of it?"

"Yes, and no. The hope that I might be able to dream of Joraiem at night and not wake up guilty because Rulalin remains free keeps me going. The hope that I will no longer have to send my soldiers into battle against other Werthanim keeps me going. And yes, the hope that one day my life would consist of more than this war keeps me going, but to tell you the truth, I don't really know what that means. This is my life, my identity."

"No, it is what you've had to do. It isn't who you are."

"How can you be so sure? Maybe what we do defines who we are. Maybe I'm already like Caan, an old warrior at heart, excited by the chance of getting another crack at the field of battle."

"Do you think Caan could be defined that simply? I know you can't be. There's more to both of you than that."

"Maybe you're right," Aljeron said, resting his head back on the top of his chair and staring at the ceiling. "I certainly hope you are."

"I think Caan was right. It's time we ended this, not just for Kirthanin, but for you. It's time you were reminded that there is more to you than this, more to you than that sword that always dangles from your side."

Aljeron looked down at Daaltaran, which even then hung

at his side. There had been a day when he would have taken the sword off to eat, but now he took it off only to sleep. He ran his fingers along the sword's scabbard and across the fine hilt. The weapon was his most prized possession. Though he might not object to leaving the war behind, putting his sword down might prove harder.

A light knock on the door interrupted their discussion, and Aljeron called out, "Come in."

They were both surprised when a tall, beautiful woman in an elegant blue dress stepped into the room. Her dark hair was pinned up in a complex knot at the back of her head, accentuating her slender neck and lovely face.

"Aelwyn," Aljeron said as both he and Evrim rose.

"Don't get up for me," Aelwyn said as she walked to the table. They remained standing. "I'm sorry to interrupt you, but I had hoped to have a word with you before you left in the morning. Would there be time later perhaps?"

Before Aljeron could respond, Evrim interjected, "Actually, I was just about to excuse myself. Feel free to have my seat."

Evrim stepped around and behind his chair, and Aelwyn, accepting the invitation, sat down as Evrim pushed it in for her. Aljeron continued to stand, looking as if he was having trouble keeping up with developments.

Evrim excused himself to Aelwyn, saying to Aljeron as he left, "I'll be in my room later if there's anything you need me for."

When Evrim was gone, Aljeron took his own seat again. "I'm sorry, Aljeron," Aelwyn began softly, "I really didn't want to interrupt."

"No, its all right," Aljeron answered. "I'm glad you've come. How's your visit in the city been?"

"Good, really good," Aelwyn answered, reaching across the table for one of the pitchers. "May I?"

"Of course," Aljeron said, "I should have offered."

"Don't worry about it. You learn to fend for yourself, being the youngest, unless you want to be left out of everything."

She poured a drink, then continued. "I do enjoy the city every time I come. It's a wonderful place; I'm just not sure I would like it all the time. I think if I were here always, I would miss the open spaces of home. There is something refreshing about waking up in the morning and looking out over the wide land and seeing little more than sun and sky, trees and grass."

Aljeron nodded. "I agree. I am almost never home anymore. When the war doesn't take me east, I'm usually here. I love Shalin Bel, and there are certainly worse places I could be, but it would be nice to be able to pack up and go home for a while."

"Maybe you'll be able to soon."

"We'll see."

Aelwyn, who had been sitting at the edge of her chair, put her cup down at the edge of the table and made herself more comfortable. "Speaking of home, do you remember that old gnarled tree at our house? The big one out front that was such a great climbing tree?"

"Sure. Why?"

"I was just thinking the other day of the time when you and the other Novaana met at our house on your way to Sulare. You remember? All of you, you came to the house to meet so you could travel together?"

"Yes, I remember," Aljeron said quietly.

"And do you remember that you rescued me out of the tree while you were there?"

Aljeron smiled. "Yes, I remember that too. I seem to recall you were way up there, and you didn't know how to get down. I went up and carried you back down."

"You did."

"You were only little."

"I was eight. And the fact that I was little was the whole reason I climbed the tree. I wanted to impress you."

"Impress me?"

"Yes. I was tired of being seen as Mindarin's youngest sister, the baby of the house. I wanted everyone, especially the great Aljeron, to sit up and take notice of me. I had this silly idea that if I could go all the way up the tree, and then call down from the uppermost boughs, then everyone would look up at me standing there and marvel.

"It was a cool day, as I recall, but bright and clear and sunny. I scrambled up and up and up, going farther than I had ever been. I just kept the vision of triumph in my mind, and before I knew it, I was almost at the very top. The problem was that I sat down on a branch to look back down, and I was paralyzed with fear.

"I was really stuck. I didn't want to call for help, because needing rescue was only going to make matters worse. I'd really be the baby then. So I sat for a couple hours. A few times, people passed by beneath the tree, but I didn't say anything. I just sat.

"Then you came out of the house, and when I saw you I began to cry. You looked all around, until you realized the crying was coming from up in the tree. When you saw me, you didn't even hesitate. You called up to me to sit tight, and then you climbed up to get me."

Aljeron was nodding at the recollection. "Yes, I remember that, but as I remember it, you were mad at me. You didn't speak to me and you hardly even looked at me the rest of the time we were there."

"No." Aelwyn laughed, shaking her head. "I wasn't mad. I was mortified. I was so embarrassed at having to be rescued that I just couldn't face you. Of course, after you left for Sulare, I realized that I hadn't minded being rescued by you all that much. In fact, I consoled myself that at least you had noticed me. From that grew the crazy thought that you had risked your life to save mine, which had to mean you liked me. I lived with that delusion for quite a few years."

Aljeron looked at Aelwyn's smiling face, full of life and warmth. "I know how that is. I certainly had my share of childhood illusions. Fortunately, they usually pass of their own and are replaced by new ones, unlike the illusions of adulthood, which simply pass."

Aelwyn's smile faltered and Aljeron felt awful. He hadn't meant to squelch her evident enjoyment of the evening. "Look, Aljeron," she said, moving back to the edge of her seat, "I didn't really come here just to waste your time with my childhood memories."

"You didn't waste my time. It's a good memory. I haven't thought of that day in ages."

"I'm glad, but I really did come with a different purpose."

"All right," Aljeron said.

"I wanted to tell you that whatever Mindarin thinks or believes or wants, I, for one, hope you not only end the war soon but succeed in bringing Rulalin to justice. He deserves whatever he has coming, and I didn't want you to go to battle thinking my family isn't on your side. My dad knows Rulalin deserves to be punished; he's just worried about what could happen if the war isn't resolved."

"I know," Aljeron said. "I respect your dad, and I understand why he said what he did. I'm not upset."

"Good, I wanted you to know that you have my support."

"Thank you."

"And more than that, I wanted you to know that now that I'm too old to climb trees to impress you, I'm glad to be your friend. You're important to me, Aljeron. I want you to know that."

"I'm glad to have you as a friend."

Aelwyn pushed back her chair and rose from the table. Aljeron stood as she rose. "Well," she said gently, "I won't take up any more of your time. I'm sure you have much to do."

"Thanks for seeking me out, Aelwyn."

Aelwyn smiled. She started to turn away, but stopped, and instead stepped toward Aljeron. Then, reaching up with her hand, she turned his face a little to the side so that the scarred side was facing her. Stretching up on her toes, she kissed it lightly and turned away, walking out of the room.

For several moments after she'd gone, Aljeron stood stunned, his fingers pressed to the rough ridges of his cheek.

8

INTO THE MOUNTAIN

RULALIN PULLED HIS CLOAK tighter and scooted closer to the fire, careful not to tip over the stone on which his dinner lay. Soran was already about as close as he could get without actually being set on fire, and he also had his hands extended toward the flame, which was just about touching his fingertips. It had been cold in the woods they'd passed through, but now they had left what cover those woods afforded and ascended a small fraction of the way up Agia Muldonai, where the wind seemed to have intensified dramatically. The chill penetrated their clothes and pierced their skin and bones, leaving them aching.

Rulalin pulled another strip of warm rabbit's flesh from the cooling carcass on the stone between his legs and slipped it into his mouth. The meat was a little tough from spending too much time in the fire, but his half-frozen fingers had been inept at handling the roasting stick. As they slowly warmed, he had fumbled his charge a few times and nearly let the rabbit fall into the fire. His attempts to compensate for the miscues had led him to move his dinner in and out of the ideal cooking range, producing a less than satisfactory result. Even so, he ate gratefully, because it had been two days since they had tasted fresh meat. He hadn't had the heart to plunder the meager food reserves of his own home before fleeing Fel Edorath. He was deserting his men in time of need; he would not take their rations to fuel his flight. He figured that the three of them could find their own food on the way to Agia Muldonai or go hungry looking. The absence of wildlife most of the way had meant they had mostly gone hungry. Still, he didn't regret his choice. Soon they would be in the Mountain, and Tashmiren had promised that plenty of food would be waiting.

"Can you believe we are sitting on the Mountain?" Soran whispered as he swallowed some of his own dinner and placed his hands back over the fire.

Rulalin looked over the fire at the rising mass beyond. "It is like being in a dream."

"It is," Soran agreed.

"Or a nightmare."

Soran peered at Rulalin, who had returned his gaze to the ground and his attention to picking over his charred rabbit. "It's not a nightmare. We're here. We're alive. If Tashmiren was going to betray us, well, do you think he would have brought us this close to everything? Wouldn't he have taken care of that before now?"

"Why would he have? Once he gets us inside, he can do anything he wants to us. What could we do, the two of us against Malek and all his hosts?"

"All right, so we could still be in trouble if he's planning something nasty for us, but we are on the Mountain, aren't we? I mean, I thought Allfather was supposed to have cursed the Mountain after the First Age. If he did, if going onto Agia

Muldonai was supposed to be forbidden and cursed and all, why hasn't anything happened to us? Why are we sitting here, eating fresh rabbit and enjoying the warmth of this cozy little fire? If He cared that we had come to make a deal with Malek, wouldn't He have tried to stop us? I think Tashmiren is right. Malek knows that Allfather doesn't really care what happens here. Alazare is gone. Sulmandir and the dragons are gone. There's nobody minding the store. Malek is going to walk out of this place and wipe his enemies off the face of the earth, and we're going to go with him. When he comes back to Agia Muldonai, in charge of everything, we're going to get our reward."

Rulalin watched Soran, noticing the excitement in his visage and voice. He was no longer really surprised, because it had been growing steadily over the last week as they journeyed from Fel Edorath to the Mountain. Still, it amazed him how quickly Soran had gotten used to the idea of joining Malek, but then again, Soran had not walked the Forbidden Isle or stood under the statue of Vulsutyr in the heart of Nal Gildoroth. He had not drawn his sword against Black Wolves and Malekim or been wounded in battle against them. He had not burned with a hatred that drove him across many leagues in pursuit of Malek's creatures to rescue the one woman his heart treasured in all the world, only to lose her anyway. Soran did not consider himself partially responsible for a victory over some of the forces of Kirthanin's ancient enemy, the seducer and destroyer, the betrayer of peace and hope. Rulalin did.

And now, with every step that took them away from Fel Edorath, Rulalin crawled closer to allegiance with that ancient enemy. Soran would not have understood why Rulalin thought of it as a crawl, but that didn't matter. Rulalin knew he was crawling. His knees were unmarked, but to him they felt chafed and bloody. His face was uncut, but to him it felt as though the brambles of the woods and untamed land around the foot of the Mountain had lashed and ripped his skin. He was covered in blood and dirt and filth, and with every span it became increasingly clear he would never be clean again.

But he crawled on. Soran still believed he was going to Malek because he had no other choice. Soran still thought this was all about saving his own neck and seizing an opportunity for power. He didn't understand what Rulalin saw clearly: Ransoming his body by selling his soul was a fool's exchange, and if that were all there was to it, Rulalin wouldn't have left Fel Edorath for all the power in the world. It was not really despair that drove him, though that was a factor. Despair alone would not have been enough. Rulalin knew that buried deep below his despair was a hope that had never been fully extinguished. He crawled on, hand after hand and span after span, because the road that led to the Mountain was the only road that might one day lead him again to her.

The sound of footsteps on loose rocks announced Tashmiren's approaching form. Rulalin bent toward Soran and whispered, "We will soon be inside the Mountain itself, and then we shall see what we shall see. Until then, I wouldn't think too far ahead."

Rulalin sat back up as Tashmiren appeared within the circle of the fire's light. Malek's warrior sat on the other side of the fire with his back to the Mountain, something Rulalin still found disconcerting. No one raised in Fel Edorath ever sat or stood or camped with his back to the Mountain. No one. Superstition and wisdom rendered such behavior inadvisable, and yet Tashmiren seemed to flaunt his lack of concern.

"Well," Tashmiren said, his voice dripping with its typical insolence. He looked through the flames at each of them. "Tomorrow we will enter the Mountain."

Rulalin turned his stone-faced stare to Tashmiren. Rulalin hated showing emotion in front of him, so despite Tashmiren's obvious desire for a response, he remained silent.

"Tomorrow you will see the place that has been Malek's home these last thousand years, the very focal point of power in Kirthanin. You will feel it oozing out of the stone, taste it in the water, and hear it in the mysterious winds that flow ceaselessly out of the deepest chambers. But you feel the power already, don't you?"

From the corner of his eye, Rulalin saw Soran nod in silent agreement. Rulalin pulled his hand back from the fire and placed it on one of the warm stones before him. Though a hunger for power had not brought him to this place, he could not deny that a current ran through the stones on which he sat. Despite what Soran had said, and despite the many arrogant comments of Tashmiren with regard to Malek, Rulalin wasn't so sure that what he felt coursing through the stones of the Mountain could be entirely explained by Malek. There was something older, something deeper at work. Perhaps the vibration was little more than a memento of Agia Muldonai's first inhabitants. Whatever it was, he had left his men and his home to come, and tomorrow he was going in.

The morning sun rose above the Mountain, but its rise was shrouded in a thin grey mist. Thin strips of fog rippled along the ground at Rulalin's feet, then graduated into wisps of low-lying cloud farther up the Mountain. Rulalin stood in the fog and smiled to himself as he looked down, unable to see anything below his own knees. It was a curious sensation, and creepy too. He felt a chill as he remembered the story of Corindel and the fog that had descended upon the Mountain. He shuddered and thought about the eerie emptiness of the land. Though Tashmiren had found rabbits the previous evening, he had not seen with his own eyes any living animal since they began their ascent.

Behind him, a little farther down, Tashmiren and Soran were both mounting their horses. Rulalin started toward their camp, picking his way over the loose stones, where he could see them. He mounted as well, glad to know that his horse would be selecting his path through the partially obscured landscape.

As they zigzagged back and forth but ever upward, the sun, pale behind the thick cloud cover, continued to climb as well. As the hours passed, much of the fog and mist was burned away, and though the land around them remained dusky from the clouds, it became largely clear and navigable. They were soon able to move faster, and their horses toiled further on, avoiding the dense bramble bushes and other wild growths that dotted this lower region of Agia Muldonai.

Sixth Hour came and went, but Tashmiren did not stop for lunch. Rulalin was not surprised. He had wholly ignored lunch a few times already on this journey, usually when he wanted to reach a specific destination. Rulalin took this as a sign that it would not be long.

He was right. Between Eighth and Ninth Hour, they started moving not upward, but sideways along a reasonably wide path that wound eastward around the face of the Mountain. They now looked at the Mountain in a profile view, the ground rising steeply to the left and falling away more gradually on the right. Not long past Ninth Hour, they came into view of a large, open cave. The road seemed to duck a little left into the Mountain, disappearing inside a wide, tall opening, right into the cave.

Rulalin hadn't known what exactly to expect, but he hadn't expected anything like this. He had imagined the entrance might be cloaked by a secret hole or tunnel, virtually impossible to find without privileged information or maybe even supernatural power granted by Malek. On the other hand, if the entrance to the Mountain had not been obscured and protected by secrecy, he had thought there might be massive and majestic gates, broad and wide and impenetrable, guarded by giants and Malekim and Black Wolves. Somewhere there must be such a place to allow the movement of armies and creatures as big as Vulsutyrim into and out of the Mountain. He had never imagined that he might come across an enormous entrance that was, as far as he could see, unguarded and vulnerable, both easy to find and easy to access.

Tashmiren came to a stop at the opening, which was sufficiently dark that Rulalin could barely see a dozen spans past the cave's mouth. Tashmiren dug around inside his pack and produced torches for each of them. As he did, Rulalin felt a gentle breath of wind upon his cheeks, blowing as Tashmiren had said it did, not into the cave from the outside, but from the inside of the cave out.

"Do you feel it?" Soran said, touching his own face with his fingertips.

"Yes," Rulalin said quietly.

"It blows here always," Tashmiren said as he lit the first of the torches.

"Where does it come from?" Soran asked.

"I don't know," Tashmiren answered as he handed Soran a torch and moved to light another. "It comes from the caverns and chambers in the heart of the Mountain, but I have no idea how or why."

He handed the next torch to Rulalin, who took it gladly. It would be good to have his own light ahead, so he would not be dependent on Tashmiren's lead. He had little hope that he would be able get back out of these caves alive if this was indeed a trap, but at least if he had to try, he would not flee in darkness.

Having lit his torch, Tashmiren turned to them. "Well, are you ready to see what is hidden from almost all human eyes but your own?"

"Then this is the gate," Soran said, looking up and around him one more time at the large opening.

"Of course it is," Tashmiren said. "What did you think it was?"

"I don't know," Soran said, turning red. "I just didn't expect this."

"Why? Did you think it would be hidden, a secret entrance? Why would we need that? Who comes looking unbidden for Malek's halls? Who would we need to hide our gates and doors from? Did you think it would be stronger, like the gates of a fortress or a strong tower? Why would we need that? Are not the Malekim, the Voiceless, here in greater numbers than you can imagine? Are not the children of Rucaran, the Black Wolves, waiting in the dark beyond? Are not the Vulsutyrim gathered within? Is not Farimaal here? Who would be foolish enough to bring war to Malek and Malek's hosts?" Tashmiren's face seemed to glow with pride and contempt, and his voice fairly hissed when he spoke of those who waited inside the gate.

"There are many doors and gates into Malek's caverns and chambers, and none of them are guarded. They never have been nor have they need to be. No one seeks entrance here. Rather, all Kirthanim pray Malek will never again come out. Every night they pray for it, but he is coming out, and soon."

Rulalin and Soran followed Tashmiren into the cave and down a gently sloping but smooth and wide passageway. Rulalin kept his mouth shut while Tashmiren boasted, but it had been an effort. He doubted that Tashmiren's arrogant demeanor was rooted in personal strength and battle prowess; rather, he had the pompous attitude of a bratty child who knows his father is nearby and able to protect him from other children. Rulalin gazed at Tashmiren's back, wondering why Malek had such a man running his errands for him. He wondered if accepting Malek's offer of allegiance included putting up with Tashmiren's unbridled arrogance indefinitely. He hoped not, or he might find his patience exhausted at last and end Tash-miren's miserable life, even if it cost him his own. He smiled. Such a death might almost be worth it if he could silence this braying donkey's big mouth.

The tunnel dimmed as they left the entrance behind. Rulalin was surprised to find a source of light aside from their torches. There were small, glowing stones near the base of the tunnel walls, every twenty-five or thirty spans. They gave off a faint bluish light that illuminated a couple spans around the stones themselves.

Rulalin had seen fireflies on a summer's evening, some-times in virtual swarms, their glowing lights blinking in and out of the darkness. As a boy he had chased them in the dark, try-ing to catch and hold them in his hand. In Sulare, Ulmindos had told them that far out at sea, there were whole schools of luminescent creatures, small and essentially formless, that wig-gled and squirmed deep below the surface of the water. At night, he said, they formed a spectacular panoply of purple, blue, pink, green, orange, and red. Sometimes, when the wind was down and the ship becalmed, they would rise and float near the surface as far as the eye could see. Rulalin had never heard, though, of any inanimate object giving off light like this.

When they passed the next one, he looked back over his shoulder at Soran, who was also studying them closely. Soran looked up and shrugged his shoulders. Rulalin nodded in re-ply and turned back around. He knew he could ask Tash-miren, but ignorance seemed preferable to another condescending explanation.

Suddenly, the tunnel passed into a large, expansive cavern. Many of the blue stones that had lit the passageway were scat-tered around the walls and embedded in the floor of the chamber. The light was by no means overwhelming, but it was sufficient to illuminate the whole cavern, and what it showed Rulalin made the hair on his neck stand on end.

Not far from them, several Black Wolves lay on the cavern floor in a large cluster. Their ears perked up as the three men entered, and Rulalin could see the faint glimmer of numberless eyes upon them. The far side of the chamber was filled with a host of Malekim, most of them sitting around half a dozen small fires, their bulky frames casting flickering shadows across the floor.

Soran, who had pulled his mount alongside Rulalin, nudged his arm. He pointed toward the far corner, along the same wall they had entered through. Rulalin turned and looked. Four Vulsutyrim sat around an enormous square stone table, their huge seated forms even taller than the standing Malekim. A small lantern in the middle of the table cast light on the grim face of one of the giants. Even from this distance, Rulalin could see the formidable gleam in the creature's eyes and hear their deep voices echoing across the quiet chamber.

Tashmiren, who had moved on a few paces, turned around and rode back toward them. "This is of course, the merest fragment of Malek's hosts," he sneered. "The labyrinth of chambers here is more extensive than you can imagine, so I warn you not to go exploring without me. The Wolves and Malekim know me and the other Nolthanim, but you they will not recognize. Until they do, walking unaccompanied through these halls could prove perilous."

"We'll keep that in mind," Rulalin said. At the sound of his voice, the conversation at the giants' table paused, and Rulalin could see four fearsome faces peering at him through the darkness. If he had felt uncomfortable before, the sight of four giants taking note of him made him even more so. They must not have been particularly concerned with what they saw, however, for they resumed their conversation soon enough.

Tashmiren moved quietly to the other side of the large room, where they entered another tunnel. For another half hour they traveled in this way, the ground beneath them sometimes heading up and sometimes down, going through several more cavernous rooms. Though they passed many Voiceless and Black Wolves, they did not see any more Vulsutyrim on their way in.

The farther they progressed, the more traffic they encountered. At first they met only wolves and Malekim, but eventually they began to pass men too. The first group of half a dozen or so surprised Rulalin. He had known there would be a certain number of men here, but he was still shocked to see them, walking in clusters and talking to one another. They stopped and nodded to Tashmiren as he passed, and then they stood and stared at Rulalin and Soran. It was hard to describe their expressions, which were neither welcoming nor unfriendly.

Rulalin wondered how long it had been since the men here had seen the full light of day. They were not made to live like moles. He shook his head at the thought that these men might have been born and raised inside this Mountain, perhaps unaware of the outer world. Or perhaps they went out from time to time, but that would hardly be sufficient. He had seen the ocean only on a few brief occasions, save for his trip to Sulare, but he was not a fish and the water was not essential for him to survive. He could not imagine seeing the sun so rarely. It would be like being teased with the beauty of sight but then being made to live the life of the blind.

Eventually, Tashmiren led them to a place where they dismounted. Their horses were entrusted to two young men who moved noiselessly in the permanent twilight of the cave, and Rulalin and Soran followed their guide into a much narrower passageway. This journey did not last long, and after winding down several small corridors, they found themselves at a small door. Tashmiren pushed it open and walked in.

A small lantern sat on the table of the simple room. Along with the table were two crude chairs. Beside them was a small bed with a straw mattress and a single blanket. "This is your room," Tashmiren said, pointing to Soran. "The temperature in the cave remains constant, day and night, all year round. If you are cold when you sleep, put your coat on."

He turned to Rulalin. "You are next door. Come with me." Rulalin followed him down the hall to another room. It was almost identical to the one Soran was in, save for a third chair around his small table. "Make yourself at home," Tashmiren said.

"Are we allowed to leave our rooms?"

"I wouldn't advise it."

"Then we are prisoners?"

"Not as such. You have come to Malek as friends, so we have no intention of treating you as a prisoner unless you show yourself to be untrue. However, as I said, this is not the kind of place where wise people go wandering."

"So I can go next door, and Soran can come here, but no more than that?"

"For now," Tashmiren said, moving to the door. "Be patient. You won't be confined long."

With that, he slipped out, leaving Rulalin to put his pack down and sit on the edge of the bed. He might be in a virtual prison cell in the depths of Agia Muldonai, but a bed still felt like a bed. He lay back, happily, closing his eyes.

Rulalin woke sometime later with a start. He sat up in the bed, surprised by the figure of a man sitting at his table. He rubbed his eyes and focused in the gloom. It was Soran.

"What are you doing?" Rulalin asked.

"Eating," Soran said, turning toward him with a mouthful of food. Rulalin looked at the table more closely and noticed for the first time the platter in the middle and the pitcher on the far side. Soran lifted a simple wooden cup and took a long drink, clearing his throat.

"It isn't great, but it'll do."

"What is it?" Rulalin asked, stretching as he stood up.

"I don't know. It's like venison, salty, but that might just mean it isn't fresh."

Rulalin stepped over to the table and reached down, picking up a hunk of meat. It was warm, at least a little bit. He bit off a corner and chewed it. It was salty, and he moved around the table and poured himself a drink of water, which was cool despite being a little stale. He had been on less than full rations for many months, and he was not going to be especially picky about what he was offered. Food was food.

He sat down beside Soran, rubbing the sleep from his eyes. "Did you sleep well?"

"Yes," Rulalin said, chewing, then added, "Mostly."

"Mostly?"

Rulalin nodded. "It was strange. I don't think I've dreamed much since we left Fel Edorath, but I dreamed just now. The dream, it was odd. At first, I was home in Fel Edorath, walking through the city on a warm sunny day. Everywhere I looked there were hungry children, searching through waste and trash for something to eat. Their faces were dirty and their bodies emaciated. At one corner, three women were arguing in shrill voices. What they were arguing over, I couldn't see, and I walked passed them into another street. Many if not most of the buildings had closed doors and closed windows, in some cases they were even boarded shut. It was hard to walk down street after street and see little more than misery and suffering. I started to cry." Rulalin paused, realizing. "I haven't cried in years.

"After walking a long way, I found myself in a part of the city I didn't recognize, and when I turned around to go back the way I'd come, I couldn't find anyone. Everywhere I went, everyone was gone. The buildings were still there, but there were no people. I called out, but there was no reply.

"I came to the city gate. I stopped—and this will sound crazy—because there was someone standing there that I both did and didn't recognize. He looked like Joraiem Andira." Rulalin looked at Soran, who didn't say a word. They had never spoken explicitly of Joraiem's death. Rulalin's father had claimed for years that Rulalin was innocent. Most in the city had eventually come to believe, or at least say they believed, in Rulalin's innocence. Rulalin doubted that Soran believed.

Rulalin continued, "He looked like Joraiem, but it wasn't him. He was younger. I must have been imagining his son, or what his son might look like. Anyway, this boy, whoever he was, was waiting at the gate. He watched me as I came up close to the gate and stopped. I could see now that the land outside the city was beautiful, lush and green, like it once was before armies trampled it under foot, spring after spring. I longed to go out into the open grassland, but I didn't want to get any closer to the boy.

"'Will you not come out?' he said after some time had passed.

"'Who are you?' I asked.

"He only smiled and said, 'Can you not see that it is better out here than in the city?'

"I looked past him again, admiring once more the beauty of Fel Edorath that I had thought lost. 'How can this be?'"

"He said, 'Many things now spoiled will be renewed and remade. Come out.'"

"Still I hesitated, caught between my desire to go into the beautiful fields and my reluctance to go near him. After a few moments, he turned away. I watched him, but I didn't follow. Before I knew what was happening, the sun had set and darkness surrounded me. When I turned back to the city, Fel Edorath was gone.

"That startled me, and I awoke to find myself in this room. When I saw you sitting at the table, for a moment I thought you were the young man from the dream. It was odd, very odd."

"Sounds like it. What do you think it means?"

Rulalin shrugged as he started eating again. "Dreams don't mean anything."

Soran didn't say anything for a while, then, "I still can't believe we are really here."

Rulalin scanned the dark room. "It's like prison, what's so hard to believe?"

"I know the room isn't great," Soran said, shaking his head. "That's not what I mean. We're inside the Mountain. This is Agia Muldonai. Kirthanin's history begins here. This has always been the center of everything."

Soran shifted his chair so that he was facing Rulalin. He leaned in as Rulalin continued eating, watching him out of the corner of his eye. "Rulalin, Malek is here, somewhere in this Mountain. Malek. He could be only a hundred spans away as we sit here, maybe even less. Doesn't the thought of it amaze you? The last of the Titans, the most powerful being in Kirthanin—he's right here. A week ago, we were cornered, on the brink of defeat. Now, just like that, we've escaped that dark corner and traveled into the forbidden places, into the light. We're out. We're free. When Malek marches out to war, we're going with him. When he brings Aljeron to his knees, we'll be right there. Who's going to stop him?"

Rulalin watched the gleam in Soran's eye intensify as he spoke. It was like seeing an ember being blown upon, increasing in heat and light and intensity "We're in the heart of power. I can feel it. Can't you?"

Rulalin continued eating, letting Soran sit in anticipation. He could see the young man's impatience mounting, but he held his tongue. He wanted to choose his words carefully. When he finished, he reclined in his seat with a drink. "You're right, Soran. We are in the presence of power. I can feel it.

You're also right, that when Malek marches from this place, he will crush those who stand in his way. What strength there was in Werthanin has been spent these past seven years. Our army and Aljeron's army, both are but shadows of what they were seven springs ago. We may well be at hand when Aljeron falls. I can't say I'll weep for him, but we will also be at hand when Malek and his creatures swarm over Fel Edorath. Have you thought of that? Have you imagined the Silent Ones running over the city? Black Wolves running through the streets and drinking from our streams? And what of the rest of Kirthanin? Who will make up for the strength that Werthanin has lost? Who will stand where we fall? Will Cimaris Rul? Will Amaan Sul? I don't think so. Malek will conquer everything, and we will go with him. He may indeed share both power now and rule later, but over what will we rule exactly? If you and I are to rule under Malek or for Malek or with Malek, what will we rule? Oh yes, I can feel the power here, but it is a fearful power. I long to rule and to win as you do, but I have no desire to rule over a barren wasteland. I have no desire to rule a land no longer worth ruling."

Soran stood, his frustration evident. "Then why did you accept Malek's offer? Why did you come? You were adamantly opposed to it before, and you've been clearly unhappy since we left. What's going on? I followed you here, remember? Don't do this to me. Don't tell me now that we're here that you wish we hadn't come."

Rulalin also stood and looked Soran in the eye. "I don't want to be here, and don't you ever forget it. I hate being here. I hate myself for coming here. I hate Tashmiren for bringing me. I'm here because I was going to die if I stayed. I'm here because coming was the only hope I had to see the only person I've ever loved, one last time. I'm here because Malek is that only hope, and for that, I hate Malek most of all."

Soran didn't back down from Rulalin's gaze. "Fine, I won't

forget that you really don't want to be here, as long as you don't forget that you came here of your own accord. This was your choice, your decision. I would have stayed with you in Fel Edorath had you chosen that."

The fire in Rulalin dissipated, and he sat back down to continue eating. Soran sat back down too. "Look, Rulalin, all I'm asking is that you don't leave me out on a limb here. We are in the Mountain. It's too late to be having second thoughts. Way too late. We made the best decision we could have made, and now we've got to see this thing through to the end. If we don't march out of here at Malek's side, we aren't going to leave here at all."

Rulalin finished eating what remained of his dinner. He gazed at the table, feeling Soran's eyes upon him. At last he nodded slowly, "I am trying to get used to this. I know you've come because I've come, and I'm sorry your service has led you here. At the same time, I want to give you some advice: No one, and I mean no one, ends up in life exactly where they thought they were going to end up. Sometimes we make messes of our lives, and sometimes life messes with us. Either way, things generally don't turn out the way we've planned. When you lie awake tonight in your bed, dreaming of a grand future in Malek's service, remember that, too."

Soran looked at Rulalin and shook his head. He rose and walked to the door. "No offense, but I hope you're in a better mood tomorrow."

Rulalin shrugged. "Better mood or not, I'm not going to think differently. This is just the way things are."

Soran closed the door behind him, and Rulalin sat at the table in the dim lamplight. He thought of Fel Edorath and wondered what was going on there. He wondered how long he and Soran would be left in these rooms, and whether they were going to meet Malek soon, if at all. He even allowed himself to wonder about Wylla, something he'd tried not to do too often, since the pleasure it brought was generally fleeting and followed by only more darkness. Even so, it was the only pleasant picture he could bring to mind, and he did not resist it.

Some time later, as Rulalin was preparing to put out the lamp and get into bed, someone knocked on his door. "Come in," he called, turning to see if it was Soran or Tashmiren. It was neither.

A lean man about Rulalin's height stepped into the room. He moved with an obvious limp, and his right foot was brutally deformed and discolored. It was a wonder that the man could use it at all. The man's face, hidden in shadow in the doorway, was illuminated as he stepped into the radiance of Rulalin's lamp. Rulalin's eyes glanced over him in surprise, taking in his deformity, his hair of mixed grey and black, his deep, brooding eyes, and his haggard and worn face.

"Synoki?"

"Your memory is excellent, Rulalin," the man said with the hint of a smile appearing at the corner of his mouth. "It has been many years."

"This is a strange meeting," Rulalin said, his mind reeling. Almost as though by habit, he motioned with his arm to the crude table and offered Synoki a seat. "Please, rest yourself here."

"Thank you," Synoki said, drawing out a chair and sitting down.

For a moment Rulalin sat there looking at his visitor, trying to grasp the incongruity. A thousand different questions ran through his mind. Before he could ask any of them, Synoki spoke. "Though I have not seen you for many years, I am not ignorant of your plight, Rulalin. I have heard of Aljeron's unjust crusade against you, and I am glad to see you well despite all you've been through."

Rulalin looked closely at Synoki, his mind churning. "Did you go back to Col Marena? It's strange that you see the war as Aljeron's unjust crusade if you've been living in the shadow of Shalin Bel these many years."

"Where I have been since last we met has little to do with my sympathy to you and your sufferings. I know Aljeron's cause to be unjust, because I know the injustice you received from his hands back then, even if it was not as great as the injustice done to you by Joraiem. As you know, I have always sympathized with your sufferings."

Synoki's eyes were bright and clear, but there was also an impenetrable air of mystery about him. This was undoubtedly the mariner they had rescued from the Forbidden Isle seventeen years ago, but Rulalin felt as though he was really seeing the little man for the first time. Suddenly, the whirl of questions in his mind disappeared. One single, disturbing thought pushed all others from him. "Synoki, where have you been and what have you been doing since you left us?"

"I've been about my master's business," came the simple, calm reply.

"Your master?"

"My master."

"You weren't really stranded on the Forbidden Isle, were you?"

"No."

Rulalin had known what Synoki's answer would be before he had asked, but still he stared with disbelief. Suddenly, this simple revelation loosed a whole chain of memories. The whirling began again as he struggled to reorder all that he thought he had known about those events so many years ago. Synoki sat, his blank expression still fixed, his body still unmoving.

"I don't understand. You fought against the Malekim and

the Black Wolves. I saw you crush the head of that wolf that grabbed Caan's leg."

"You did."

"And you rode with us to save the women, up the length of the Arimaar Mountains, didn't you?"

"I did."

"And did you not save my life from one of the Voiceless the night we rescued the women?"

"I did."

"And all that time you were a servant of Malek."

"I was and am."

"But why? You did no harm to me or any of the others, even though you had the chance. You helped us thwart the Vulsutyrim and rescue the women."

"I had little real effect on the outcome of that situation. I doubt my being there would have prevented you from leaving the island or rescuing the women. Don't you agree?"

Rulalin shrugged. "Sure, you didn't turn the tide of battle or anything, but you helped. Why?"

"It helped you to believe my story, didn't it? When I killed the Black Wolf, many of the questions that would inevitably accompany a man found alone on the Forbidden Isle went away."

"That's true, but why come with us at all? What did it accomplish?"

"Perhaps more than you think. Anyway, when my master gives me orders, I follow them, even if all his reasons aren't clear. He wanted me to go with you. There were things he wanted to know."

"What things?"

"It's not important that you know."

Rulalin shook his head. "It was a big risk, coming with us. I can't see any value in it."

"There is one success from that time that I can share with

you. As you all approached the island, my master could sense many things about you all. However, though he is mighty and wise, he does not know all things. So, he sent me along to gather information, but also to see who among you showed promise."

"Showed promise?"

"Yes, even then it was clear to him that some among you could be useful to him."

"Who?"

"You, mainly."

"Me? How can that be? I was as vehemently against your master in those days as any of the other Novaana."

"You were eager to rescue the women, for you loved Wylla, but you should not confuse one passion with another."

"I'm not. Of course I wanted to save Wylla, but I also went to the Forbidden Isle hoping to aid Kirthanin against Malek."

"So you did. Nonetheless, I could see from my earliest days among you, that you held promise. Many of those who have come to Malek's cause were men or women who at first did not want to come. You are not the only one who has come for reasons other than genuine love of my master."

Rulalin shifted uncomfortably. "I said I opposed Malek then, but I'm here to serve him now," he said meekly.

"Don't worry," Synoki continued, the slight, wry smile returning to his face. "My master is aware of your situation. He is no fool. He knows you have come as a last resort, and he will not hold you accountable for blows struck against his purposes earlier in your life, provided you serve him well now. Still, it was clear to me, even then, that you were one who might one day come to the Mountain in just such a situation as this."

"It was?"

"It was."

"How did you know?"

"You showed yourself to me. I saw what lay within you and what could be turned to my master's advantage. I saw it, and I acted accordingly."

"You did?"

"I did. Do you not remember that day on the beach?"

Rulalin's mind sped across the years to another time and place. He saw once more the sandy beach and bright waters and rolling waves of the Southern Ocean.

"I remember."

9

LOOKING BACK

THE SUN HUNG LIKE a glittering jewel suspended above the bright blue water of the Southern Ocean. A soft breeze blew in from the north and made ripples across the surface of the relatively calm water as it rolled gently in. All signs of the storm in the night had passed, and the midmorning warmth had more than succeeded in driving the chill of the soggy trial away. Now, the drops of cold rain that had clung to his body had been replaced by beads of sweat that slid down his smooth, tan skin to join the ebb and flow of the ocean tide.

Rulalin looked down at the water, which was almost waist high now as he continued to wade beside Synoki, some distance from Aljeron, who held a makeshift spear, a knife lashed to the end of a sturdy stick. Though the water was not opaque, it wasn't clear enough to let him see all the way through to the bottom, but the soothing sensation of the sand sliding between his toes brought comfort and happiness that was somewhat surprising given the events of recent days and weeks. It was easy not to dwell on their predicament when the water lapped up gently against his skin and warmed his whole body. If this was what it meant to be stranded and waiting for death, it wasn't such a bad way to go.

He reached down with his hand, dipping it up to the wrist in the cool water. Slowly, he slid down, squatting, until his whole body was submerged in the ocean, save only his head. The water invigorated him. Leaning back, he let his hair float suspended on the water around his face, then he slowly stood again. The water poured off his body in a steady river, and he took his hands and smoothed his hair back as it clung to his neck and shoulders. Rubbing his eyes, he had to stifle a yawn so that he wouldn't startle Aljeron. He stood straight, feeling the sun go to work on the water that coated him. It almost seemed as though he could feel it evaporating as he watched Aljeron maneuver the spear slowly, steadily, waiting for a chance to strike.

Despite internal nagging that he should be paying closer attention to what Aljeron was doing, his mind wandered again, far from the world of fishing. He had vowed to pursue the Vulsutyrim and the women in order to rescue Wylla, and though he would do all he had vowed, he thought he might one day look back at this afternoon with fondness. After all, if they pursued Wylla but never rescued her, his life would never, ever, resemble the dreams he had cherished for so long. What would life be like without even the possibility, even as remote as that possibility might now seem, of seeing her smile with every new morning? Where would he find purpose and joy if she were lost?

Of course, if Wylla chose Joraiem, and it seemed increasingly likely she would, or perhaps already had, then he would still lose her. He might still have occasion to see her smile and hear her laugh, but wouldn't that be worse than losing her altogether? Wouldn't it be harder to know that she lived, but that she didn't live for him as he lived for her?

He squinted at the sun in the clear blue sky, where only the faintest hints of cloud glided slowly across the horizon. Though part of him wanted to be as far from this accursed island as he could be, he nevertheless thought that a place like this is what he would want and where he'd go if all was lost in the end. *If we fail in our mission, or if Wylla be lost to me, I will find a piece of shore like this, where the water beats the shoreline ceaselessly, gently, unchangingly, and I will live there. I will leave Fel Edorath, my family fortune, and my place of privilege in the Assembly, and choose instead a life of solitude and peace. Perhaps I will own a boat and become a fisherman, going out in the darkness before dawn to earn my living like a common man. Yes,* he thought, gazing back down at the gentle waves as they continued to slip in between and around his waist as they rolled ever inward, *I will lay everything aside if she is lost. I will choose life alone if life with her is lost to me.*

A sudden flash of Aljeron's arm disturbed his reverie, and he glanced at the place where the spear had jabbed through the waters. Aljeron jerked the spear back quickly to see if this time he had hit a fish, then splashed the surface of the water with his open hand when he found nothing at all. Mumbling something under his breath, Aljeron stabbed the point of the spear straight into the sandy bottom and let go. It stood quivering from the blow.

"This is a waste of time," Aljeron said, turning to Synoki and Rulalin. "If this is our hope for survival, we are going to starve."

"It takes time and patience to learn to fish this way," Synoki said evenly, dispassionately. He had offered little concrete advice as Aljeron had tried unsuccessfully several times to spear a fish, despite having made it clear he'd survived on the island these past three years through his fishing prowess.

"Hmm," Aljeron grunted in reply, "well, I'll leave the two of you to continue developing your patience with this exercise in futility. I'm heading in."

Aljeron waded past them both, and Rulalin and Synoki watched him head ashore. It was then that Rulalin noticed Joraiem standing there, not far away, watching. He had gone running down the beach earlier that morning, or else Aljeron would have no doubt prevailed upon him to join their fishing venture. As Aljeron reached the shore, he walked up to Joraiem, and the two of them talked before heading up toward the others.

A tinge of envy flashed through Rulalin as he watched them go. He hadn't been especially close to Aljeron before Joraiem had joined them after Peris Mil on the long journey to Sulare. In fact, Rulalin had resented having to defer to Aljeron simply because he was a few months younger. Even so, it had hurt to watch Aljeron warm so quickly to Joraiem, and Rulalin knew he had become an unwelcome third party. Of course, they never said he was unwelcome, but he saw their camaraderie and could well imagine the things they said when he wasn't around.

The pain he felt as they walked up the beach was a faint echo of the pain he had felt at being pushed by Joraiem out of contention for Wylla's affections. What right did he have to ride into Sulare and steal her heart away? He had not wept with her over her father's death in the citadel of Amaan Sul or tried to comfort her in the soft moonlight when her world had become as dark as a starless night. He hadn't waited patiently for the better part of a decade to be together again, this time in a more appropriate place to declare his intentions to love her for a lifetime. Joraiem hadn't suffered as he had suffered, nor waited as he had waited. Joraiem had no right to be first in her heart.

Turning from the shore, he stepped past the still form of

Synoki, who was watching him, and moved toward the spear. "I'll try for a bit," he said to his quiet companion.

"Sure," Synoki said.

He might as well try for a while. There was no point going round and round over everything again. He had struggled with his bitterness night and day since before they had boarded the *Evening Star* to come here, and he had resolved the night of the women's capture that he would put aside his personal struggle with Joraiem for as long as necessary, until they'd found and rescued her. To that end he had sought Joraiem out to make the vow that now bound them, but once they found her, when she was safe, Rulalin would be free of it. When the time was right, he would speak to her one more time, entreating her favor and love, and if she refused then, well, he would look for that peaceful retreat from the cares of this world in some distant corner of Kirthanin. He didn't care who mocked or scoffed; he would put them behind and find a place of rest where he need be reminded of her no longer.

He pulled the slick spear from the sandy bottom and lifted it out of the water. He tapped his fingertip lightly with the end of the knife. It was sharper than he expected and pierced his soft flesh. A small drop of blood formed on his finger. He sucked the drop of blood as he eyed the blade lashed to the stick. His question had been answered. It was plenty sharp to spear a fish, should he find any and be fast enough to jab one.

"Don't worry about the spear. It will do its job if you do yours," Synoki said in the same emotionless tone he had used all morning with Aljeron. "Aljeron didn't fail to get a fish because the blade was too dull."

"Any pointers?" Rulalin said. Aljeron might be too proud to ask Synoki for advice, but Rulalin didn't mind admitting he wasn't an expert at something he had never tried.

"Be patient and keep still. Like a lot of good things in this world, the fish will come to you if you wait long enough."

"The fish will come to me."

"They will come to you."

"And then?"

"The rest, I would think, is obvious."

"Thanks," Rulalin said, barely hiding his lack of sincere gratitude. "That's a big help."

"I don't know how to explain what I only learned through practice. Maybe, when you have been here long enough, and if you are hungry enough, you will learn the patience that only hunger can teach."

Synoki slid closer to him and stood an arm's length behind and to his side. Rulalin fixed his gaze on the water below. Much to his surprise, Synoki, who had barely spoken the whole time they had been out in the water, began a conversation as he stood waiting.

"So, your whole group, you are all young Novaana?"

"Yes," Rulalin answered, glancing over his shoulder at Synoki.

"You have all come to Sulare, and from there you have come here?"

"Yes."

"Where do you come from?"

"I am from Fel Edorath, in Werthanin."

"Fel Edorath? I was there once, many years ago. It is a much larger city than Col Marena. I don't know that I would want to live in such a big place, but in its own way, I thought it was very interesting. I met many fascinating people there. Life so close to the Mountain must be very different."

"It is," Rulalin answered, nodding. "Agia Muldonai casts a long shadow over our lives, from beginning to end. There is a sense, you might say, that life can never be completely carefree, for we fear that if we ever drop our guard, we will fall. So the fathers tell their sons, and the sons tell their own children."

"Do you miss Werthanin?"

"Yes," Rulalin answered, lifting his eyes and gazing out over the ocean. "You do too, I assume."

"Indeed. I have been here long enough. I should like to go home."

"Maybe you still will."

"Maybe. Rulalin," Synoki said, his tone changing a bit, "why come here, where no one ever comes? I ended up here by accident, after a shipwreck. You came here on purpose."

"We did. We followed Valzaan's guidance on that. When a man who is both a prophet and a legend suggests something, it seems hard to say no."

"Ah," Synoki said, letting the word linger alone in the air for a moment. "Valzaan. Yes, I have heard of him. According to the stories, he has been appearing and disappearing for the better part of the Third Age, if not from its very beginning. Despite his past deeds, it doesn't seem like he had such a good idea this time, does it?"

Rulalin shrugged. He wasn't comfortable openly criticizing Valzaan for the decision to come, but it had occurred to him that not much good had come from it. He wondered how many others in the company had thought the same thing.

Synoki continued. "I'd be more wary of Valzaan, if I were you. It's all well and good for him to claim to be a prophet, but how do you really know? What proof is there that he is who he says he is?"

Rulalin looked at Synoki again. This time Synoki met his eyes for a moment before looking back down. "Of course," he went on, "he might well be a prophet, who knows? It just seems suspicious, claiming to be a legend out of the pages of history. If I were you, I'd be careful."

"Well, if we ever get off this island and he asks me to go on another journey, maybe I'll think harder about it."

Thinking that the conversation was over, Rulalin turned

his attention back to the water. A bluish black shape had just flashed past, but it was beyond his reach, so he watched it slip away. A little closer, he thought, and he'd take a shot at one.

"And the women," Synoki continued, apparently not interested in letting the conversation end there. "They are also Novaana from all over Kirthanin?"

"Yes," Rulalin answered softly. He had come out with Synoki to avoid thinking of them, of her, though he hadn't been successful.

"The men, here, seem to be close to one another. Are you all close to them, too?"

"Yes. Some of us have sisters among them. All of us have friends among them. And," he paused, "some of us have dreams of shared lives with some of them."

Another dark shadow darted by, this time closer to Rulalin. He stabbed down quickly, trying to anticipate the fish's speed and direction. The spear slid down into something more or less solid, and a swirl of sand clouded the water. He raised the spear, but there was no fish.

"You were close," Synoki said from behind. "Keep trying."

Rulalin waited as the water cleared around his legs and feet. The silence now between them felt awkward. He hoped Synoki wouldn't return to their previous subject matter, but his hope was vain.

"You care for one of them?"

"Yes."

"I see now."

"You see what?"

Synoki shrugged when Rulalin glanced at him. "All of you care about finding and recovering your friends, that is clear. But, it seems that the matter is even more important to a few of you."

"We may not all have the same reasons for wanting them back, but I'm sure we are all equally determined."

"Oh, I don't doubt it. However, I can see why retrieving

them safely would be of special importance to you, if the woman you love is among them."

Rulalin kept his focus trained on the water below. "I'm sorry if this is a painful subject," Synoki added. "I'm sure it must be hard to be stranded here when she is out there."

"It is."

"At least you can be comforted that it appears they were taken alive. Somewhere, out there, she is probably dreaming of you too."

"Maybe." The word slipped out before Rulalin could stop it.

"Maybe?"

Rulalin tried to focus on watching the water.

"Have you not told her how you feel?"

"I have."

"And she isn't sure?"

Mercifully, another fish darted through his target zone, and Rulalin brought the spear down swiftly, creating another murky cloud on the sea floor. Lifting the spear out of the water revealed the failure of this attempt as well. He resisted the urge to show his frustration, but he could feel the irritation swelling within. This was not the calming exercise he had hoped for. To make matters worse, Synoki didn't seem willing or able to let the conversation go.

"She isn't sure?" he repeated when the water had settled down again.

"It's more complicated than that."

"Oh." Rulalin didn't think he liked the tone he detected, and he was uncomfortable at the thought of where Synoki might be going. "There is another?"

"Yes."

"Someone back home?"

"No."

"Someone here?"

"Yes."

"Oh," Synoki said again. Once more the tone and the discomfort. "It must be a hard thing."

Rulalin shrugged, holding the spear, once again ready to strike. "There are a lot of hard things in the world. We bear what we must."

"True, but some are harder than others. The Novaana assemble in Sulare every seven years for the purpose of building unity, do they not?"

"They do."

"That is what brought you there?"

"Yes."

"Then it must be hard indeed. After all, the difficulty of pursuing a woman's affection, of competing for it with another man, all that is hard enough. I may have been stranded on this island for the last three years, but I have not forgotten such things. How much harder to be going through this in a place where disruption and disunity is most feared and avoided."

Rulalin remained quiet. Surely, Synoki would eventually get the hint that he didn't want to talk about this, about her. "One of the beautiful things about fishing," Synoki said, "especially fishing with a makeshift spear in shallow ocean water, is that it gives you lots of time to think. I have spent many hours out here in the water, more than I care to remember, waiting patiently for my supper, thinking of many things. So while they have been many, the hours have not all been wasted. We may be out here for a while, so why don't you tell me the story? I am an outsider, and it can't hurt the unity of the group if you share your struggle with me."

Rulalin hesitated, but he did not resist for long. Silently, he admitted that he did long to speak of it, to say out loud the things he had been carrying within. It would be a release. He might even be better able to let it go if he could speak of it without reservation.

So he did. He told Synoki of the trip he had taken with his

father to Amaan Sul after the death of Pedrone Someris. He spoke of first seeing Wylla, of how he was struck by her beauty and sadness. He spoke of how his heart had reached out to her, longing to comfort. He explained how he had refrained from declaring himself until the end of his stay, and of the agony he had endured when her response had not been what he'd wanted. He spoke of the long years waiting, hoping, and anticipating seeing her again in Sulare. He spoke of the many prayers he had offered to Allfather that Wylla might return his love for her. And, ultimately, he spoke of Joraiem. He told Synoki of the day by the Barunaan when he had confided in Joraiem about his feelings for Wylla. He spoke of how relieved he had felt to find someone who seemed to understand what it was like to be forlorn in love, recounting briefly Joraiem's own history with Alina. He spoke also of his dismay in realizing that Wylla was holding him at arm's length, and then that she seemed to be looking with favor on Joraiem. Of all the people who had known about his history with Wylla, Joraiem had seemed to understand better than most, and now he was at the center of Rulalin's waking nightmare.

As he finished, a shout from the shore came echoing across the water, and both Rulalin and Synoki turned to look. The twins, Pedraal and Pedraan, were grappling with each other on the beach, and most of the others were standing around watching. Pedraal had lifted Pedraan up off the ground, almost to chest height, and the crowd was watching with amazement at this feat of strength. Standing over on one side was Joraiem with Aljeron. They seemed to be laughing together about something, perhaps the wrestling match. A wave of annoyance and anger rolled through Rulalin, and he was about to turn away when Synoki started to speak.

"Joraiem," he said out loud, though it sounded as if he was speaking half to himself. "The young archer. Look at him." He threw a glance at Rulalin. "How easily he appears to fit in, how calmly he goes about his business. I was certainly fooled by him. How often it works like this. The ones you think you can trust—they are the ones you have to watch out for!"

Rulalin pulled his eyes away from the scene. "I am truly sorry for your suffering, Rulalin," Synoki added. "It is despicable that one could call himself your friend, and then stab you in the back like that. I have had such 'friends' in my life, and I know the pain they can cause. It isn't right. They shouldn't be allowed to get away with what they do. They should be made to feel the pain they cause others. He should be made to feel the pain he has caused you. Such a man, in truth, is little better than an enemy. I don't know how you restrain yourself as well as you do. I certainly couldn't."

Rulalin recoiled at the vehemence of Synoki's language and ideas. Though many similar thoughts had been rattling around in his own head these past few weeks, it sounded strange to hear them expressed aloud by someone else. "I don't know that it is really fair to call Joraiem an enemy. That's stronger than I would put it. I don't think his friendship was disingenuous, and I don't think he set out to take Wylla from me. Even if what he did was thoughtless, maybe even cruel, I don't think it was an act of deliberate malice. Wishing pain and suffering upon him for falling in love with Wylla seems too much. I can't really blame him for finding her attractive also. Besides, for all I know, he didn't even go after her. She may have shown interest in him first, and I don't see how any man could resist that."

"And if she had been your wife? Wouldn't friendship have dictated that he resist any desire he felt for her then?"

"Of course, but she isn't my wife."

"No, but he knew you wanted her to be."

"True, and that hurts, but the two aren't the same. I do feel angry with him, sometimes a lot, but I think you're taking it all too far."

"Hey," Synoki said, stepping up beside him. "You know him a lot better than I do. I don't want to cause any trouble between you. I was just telling you what I thought. Maybe I have it wrong. Maybe he isn't a traitor disguised as a friend. Maybe he hasn't been undermining your chances with her. You know better than I do. I still think it's fair to say he should be held responsible for the pain he's caused you. Even if she's initiated the interest, he could have refused it. Whatever you say, I think a real friend would have done that."

Just as Synoki stopped speaking, two things happened almost simultaneously. First, Rulalin felt Synoki place his hand softly on his back, between the shoulder blades, as though to steady him. Then, a fish came swimming right between his legs. This one was the biggest yet, and he prepared to stab again. This time, though, it seemed as though he was tracking the fish's direction, speed, and trajectory through the water with exact precision. He brought the spear flashing down and felt it strike something other than sand. Now that he had actually speared a fish, he could tell the difference without difficulty. He lifted the spear out of the water carefully, not wanting to drop his catch, and he admired the large, thick fish flopping at the end of it.

The blade at the end of the stick had sliced the fish almost in half. The wriggling tail soon stopped and the fish hung limp, blood dripping down the scales. The blood was dark red, and it ran down the side of the knife and soon started to slide down the stick itself, flowing along the natural grooves and around the knots. He took his left hand and felt the slick, shiny scales of the fish. They felt good. He turned to Synoki and smiled.

Synoki was nodding his head in quiet approval. "Well done."

"Thanks."

"Did it feel good to get one?"

"Yes."

Synoki nodded some more. "When you haven't eaten anything in days, it's a great feeling to get one. If we're here much longer, you'll know exactly what I mean."

Rulalin held the fish, but he looked quizzically at Synoki, whose expression was almost impossible to read, as always. His reply had been straightforward enough, but it had seemed to imply meanings Rulalin could only guess at. He looked back at the fish. He wasn't ashamed to admit it, but it had felt good, really good, to finally get one. He figured it was simply the elation of success, having succeeded at a difficult thing. And it didn't hurt to know that Aljeron had tried and failed. It would be enjoyable to wade in with a fish in hand to show the group that he had done what Aljeron could not.

At the same time, he knew his elation was not completely accounted for by these factors, and he felt a chill inside.

Rulalin looked up across the table at Synoki, who had been sitting there watching him. His mind was reeling as words, images, and the whole afternoon came back to him. It was all so different now. He saw meanings and intentions in words, looks, and actions that he had never seen before. His whole life from that moment until this very second was being reordered by the implications of this new information.

His mind scanned quickly his time with Synoki after that afternoon. From the journey back to the mainland in the garrion carried by Eliandir, and all the way up the Arimaar Mountains, simple statements and looks and nods flashed before him. At least two or three more times, Synoki had come back to Joraiem's betrayal overtly, and every time he had continued to plant seeds and to water the seeds already taking root. Even as they had crouched in the darkness on the edge of Lindan Wood, he had spoken quietly, darkly, of Valzaan's preferential treatment of Joraiem and its unfairness. As Rulalin looked over those days, he saw the progress of Synoki's machinations, and he saw that his insidious suggestions had begun already to reverberate inside him.

"You," Rulalin began, almost unable to speak, now staring hard at the man across the table. "You put that in me."

Synoki, his eyes revealing a hint of a dark smile, answered calmly. "I didn't put anything in you. I simply recognized what was already there, and then I helped you to recognize and embrace it. I helped you, Rulalin. I helped you to understand how you really felt so you could act accordingly."

"Act accordingly? I murdered a man, a friend! I struck him down in cold blood on the beach of the Summerland and held the knife in him as his blood poured out over my hands. I watched him slump to the ground and left him there to die. I am a villain and an outcast because of you. My city, if it isn't already, will soon be in ruins because of the war being waged to avenge that murder. You have ruined me."

"I have saved you," Synoki fairly hissed as he leaned in across the table, his dark eyes glinting now with sparks of rage. "Don't whine to me about your poor hard life. Don't act as though you didn't do to Joraiem exactly what you wanted to do, and don't forget that you are here, in the Mountain, about to swear allegiance to Malek, an act that is likely to preserve your life long after all your old friends have perished, because of a chain of events following directly from 'that murder.' Would you rather have a better reputation among the halfwits and weaklings of the Assembly and certain death when Malek comes forth? Is that really what you want? If it is, it isn't too late for you to die precisely that way."

Rulalin glared across the table at Synoki. The familiarity he had felt when Synoki first entered the room was gone. He was the man they had met walking down the beach on their way to Nal Gildoroth, but Rulalin was under no illusions that he had known Synoki at all. He despised Synoki with all his heart, but he did not dare say any of the things he wanted to. As angry, flustered, and bitter as he might be, he could see the peril his life was in. He kept his mouth shut.

Synoki sat back up, the old impassive expression having returned to his eyes. "Look, Rulalin, I understand that you think I've deceived and manipulated you, but think of it this way: What I did, though it may not seem like it now, was an act of mercy. You couldn't have seen it then, and maybe you still can't see it now, but you will. And, what's more, what you did back then was an act of necessity. You did what you had to do to keep on living. That's what you're doing now. There's nothing wrong with that. Your best interest lies in aligning yourself with Malek. I respect that. He respects that. He doesn't expect you to love following him. He only expects you to follow him fully. You can be a help to Malek, and that's why you are alive today. When we descend from the Mountain upon Fel Edorath, you can bring soldiers from the city over to us. That's all you have to do. Then, with the hosts of Malek at their side, they'll be able to drive Aljeron and his men away from Fel Edorath forever. You're going to liberate the city. That's not so bad, is it?"

Rulalin shook his head. Bringing relief to Fel Edorath was not something he took lightly. He looked down at the table. He knew he should say something conciliatory, but whether because of pride or anger or simple stubbornness, he just couldn't. Synoki had played him like a musical instrument, and he had been duped like a foolish child. He had let an unknown stranger influence his destiny, and he'd reaped abject misery ever since.

Perhaps taking Rulalin's silence as a cue to leave, Synoki rose to go. He walked to the door and opened it. "You would do well to forget about the things in your past that you cannot change," he said, "and focus on the future. You have a great opportunity before you. Don't throw it away because you're pouting about your past."

When Rulalin was sure that he could no longer hear Synoki's uneven footsteps in the hallway, he jumped up from the table. Taking up his chair, he hurled it across the room so that it shattered against the stone wall.

10

FARIMAAL

SORAN FOUND RULALIN sitting in a chair at the small wooden table. A second chair with Rulalin's feet resting upon it sat not far away, while a third lay broken on the floor. "What happened here?" Soran asked.

"Nothing."

"Nothing?"

"The chair broke."

Soran walked toward the table and Rulalin dropped his feet off the only remaining functional chair. "Do you mind if I sit?"

"Go ahead."

Soran settled in at the table. "How'd you sleep?"

"I didn't."

"Not at all?"

"Nope."

"Why not?"

Rulalin traced a crack in the tabletop with one of his fingers. "I had a lot on my mind."

"We're not going to go through all this again, are we?"

"Don't start, Soran," Rulalin snapped, glaring across the table. "You're young, or you'd know better when to keep your mouth shut. I know what we've come to do and what we have to do. Don't worry. You'll get what you're after."

An awkward silence hung between them, until eventually Soran spoke up again, "I'm sorry, Rulalin. I'm just not sure what to say when you're like this."

"The less the better," Rulalin grumbled. He looked up at Soran, who was avoiding his look now. "Look, Soran, I had a visit last night from someone I hadn't seen in a long time. It was a bit disconcerting."

"You know someone here?" Soran looked shocked.

"Apparently."

"What does that mean?"

"It means that someone I knew long ago, or thought I knew, turns out to have been one of Malek's servants this whole time."

"He's a friend?"

"Something like that."

"Well, that's good, right? He's a connection."

Rulalin shrugged. "I don't know what he is. What I know is that it's clearer now than ever that we need to be very careful." Rulalin bent over the table and whispered, "Remember this, Soran, as long as we are here and as long as we are in Malek's service, the only people we can really trust are our people—you and me and those we know personally in Fel Edorath. When we're with anyone else, keep your eyes open and your mouth closed. The more we keep our own counsel the better, understood?"

"Understood," Soran answered. Rulalin sat back, and Soran tried to gauge if it was safe to speak. "Aren't you tired?"

"Not too much. I had a good nap right after we arrived, remember?"

"I do, but I didn't know how long you'd slept before I came by."

"A while, I think. I pretty much went to sleep right away."

Soran nodded, then yawned and stretched. "What do you think today holds for us?"

"Who knows?" Rulalin said, starting again to trace the crack with his finger.

Not long after, a man in simple garb came to the room, bringing a tray with breakfast. The tray had a pitcher, again filled with water, along with bread and butter and two bowls filled with a hot steaming substance like oatmeal. It was strong to the taste but not unpleasant, and both Soran and Rulalin ate hungrily.

After breakfast, Rulalin moved over to the bed and stretched out. Despite his nap the previous afternoon, he was beginning to feel the effects of a full night without sleep. There had been nights on the battlefield when he hadn't slept, but in those situations action and adrenaline kept him going. Here, his mind was utterly fatigued with going over and over his time with Synoki, and he couldn't countenance the thought of it anymore. However, with that stimulus withdrawn and with absolutely nowhere to go and nothing to do, all he felt was weariness.

Soran was sitting at the table with his feet up on the chair. Rulalin looked at him there, twiddling his fingers in boredom, and then turned on his side with his face to the wall. If they were going to spend the day shut in here, he might as well get some sleep.

Just as his eyes were closing, a loud knocking echoed throughout the room. Rulalin sat up on the bed as Soran called out, "Come in."

In walked Tashmiren, his drab riding clothes exchanged for much finer attire. A thick light grey cape hung from his shoulders, clasped under his neck with a bright golden chain.

Under the cape he wore a dark blue tunic with matching pants. A silver hammer was woven atop his right thigh. Other than his clothes, though, nothing had changed.

"Lying abed late, I see," he snorted.

"Not much else to do, is there?"

"Now there is. Put on your boots, you're coming with me."

"And me?" Soran inquired.

"Both of you."

Soran stood and waited as Rulalin got ready. They exited the small chamber behind their guide. It did feel good to be out and walking. He had enjoyed the rest after so many days of travel, but the transition to total inactivity had been a little much.

After they had taken several turns and wound through a quick succession of small hallways, it occurred to Rulalin that he should have been paying closer attention to their course. He chastised himself silently and hoped Soran had been more alert. If for any reason it became necessary to move about on their own, the more they both knew about their immediate surroundings the better.

He tried to focus on the specifics of their route, but with almost no distinctive markings in any of the corridors, it was virtually impossible for him to commit the order of their turns to heart. Frustrated, he gave up and simply followed, watching carefully for anything that might be of use.

Eventually they started moving through wider halls, in most of which they found other men going about their business. All acknowledged Tashmiren with deferential nods and complete silence. No men who had been talking as they approached continued their conversation as long as Tashmiren was within earshot.

After several of these encounters, they passed through a wide opening into another cavernous room, like the ones they had passed through on the way in, except that this one was more brightly lit and full of men. Tashmiren stopped near the entrance, and Soran and Rulalin stopped beside him, looking. Those men close enough to the door gave the same silent nod and, as Tashmiren gave no hint of moving from the place where he was standing, most of them edged away until a fairly wide swath of open space surrounded all three of them.

Rulalin scanned the room, thinking how much the sight reminded him of his army. They had the look of men waiting for something to happen. He looked at them and wondered how they had existed so long inside this Mountain. He had been here only a day, and already he hungered for sunlight and the feel of soft earth under his feet. What about these men? Had they been outside? Did they know what those things were?

"Looking at them reminds me of home," Soran whispered.

Rulalin nodded. "I know."

"I wonder what they're doing, the men."

"Staying vigilant, I hope," Rulalin answered. Then, to Tashmiren he said, "These are the lost children of Nolthanin?"

"They are some of them," Tashmiren answered, looking over the crowd, "as am I." Rulalin looked closely at Tashmiren, whose proud sneer had been momentarily replaced by a look of grim determination. But soon Tashmiren turned from the men to Rulalin, the arrogance back in place. "These are the Nolthanim, the descendents of Andunin's people, faithful to Malek these many years and ready even now to march from here the moment he calls them to service. They await eagerly their return to the northlands, which Malek has promised will be theirs when Kirthanin is his."

Soran looked at Tashmiren with a frown. "Nolthanin is no more. The northlands are empty, a wasteland."

"Yes. When Malek has established his rule over all things, we will return to Nolthanin and live there in peace, alone. Malek promised Farimaal a long time ago. We will answer directly to Malek. The Malekim and Black Wolves will help administer Malek's rule everywhere but in Nolthanin. Not even Cheimontyr and the other children of Vulsutyr will walk the soil of Nolthanin. It will be ours."

"Cheimontyr?"

The smug look on Tashmiren's face spread into a smile. "Cheimontyr," he said again, his mouth forming each syllable delicately and with reverence. "The Bringer of Storms."

Soran looked to Rulalin, but he avoided the younger man's gaze. He didn't understand any more than Soran did. Tashmiren laughed at their looks of bewilderment. "In time you will understand."

Rulalin looked back out over the crowd. "So, all these men have known nothing but the inside of the Mountain?"

"They have all been outside for one reason or another. Many," he added, looking at Soran and Rulalin pointedly, "have seen more of the outside than you would guess."

"Oh, I don't know about that," Rulalin said calmly. "I can imagine some of them have traveled far and wide."

"Indeed they have." Tashmiren grinned as he stared at Rulalin. Rulalin returned the stare. It was only a look, but he felt as if he was wrestling with Tashmiren in a match he was determined not to lose. After a moment, Tashmiren turned away. "Come, let's pass through. There is more I would show you beyond."

They left the large room through the door they had entered, and though they must have at least briefly retraced their steps, they were soon headed in a completely new direction. Rulalin was sure of this because the ground beneath their feet, which had been more or less level, began now to slope downward. Soon the small corridor came to a dead end, where it intersected another, which had a much higher ceiling and was perhaps four times as wide. It cut steeply downward to their left and upward to the right, and in keeping with their general downward motion, Tashmiren turned left.

Soran and Rulalin followed several steps behind him, and soon Rulalin felt Soran's hand gently tugging on the side of his shirt. He turned to look at Soran, who motioned with his head for Rulalin to come closer. "It's a road," Soran whispered. "Maybe the other end of this road leads outside, like that wide road we came in on."

"Maybe this is that same road."

"I will answer any questions you have," Tashmiren called from in front of them.

They stopped talking. Straightening up and walking faster, they drew closer to Tashmiren and stayed close behind the rest of the way, which wasn't far, as just moments later a small side road branched off from the one they were on, and they followed it off to the right. Here, a cacophony of noise rumbled through the tunnel to meet them. It was like the rumble of thunder, or the sound of crashing waters. This assault of sound was accompanied by a powerful and unpleasant smell. The farther in they went, the more intense both the smell and the noise became, until after several moments they found themselves standing high above a deep pit of remarkable dimensions. It was easily five times the size of any of the cavernous rooms they had seen to this point in the Mountain. Tashmiren came to a halt and overlooked the immense chamber.

Rulalin gazed down at the great room far below, and wonder filled him as he saw a dozen or more enormous pens, each filled with flocks and herds of animals. Thousands of pigs, cows, sheep, goats, oxen, and even chickens churned in the teeming sea of animal life below. The noise rose as an undifferentiated mass of squeals and squawks and bleatings, the likes of which Rulalin had never heard before. Both he and Soran covered their ears.

Down in the pit, walking around the great pens, were

Black Wolves, and Rulalin saw that whenever the wolves passed, the animals scrambled and screeched wildly as they tried to claw and trample their way away from them. The Black Wolves seemed not to notice, walking or trotting casually in between and around the pens. A few tables had been placed against one of the walls, and around them sat a handful of men. They must have been either deaf or had cloth strips in their ears, Rulalin thought, for no man could endure that seething tumult otherwise.

They were grateful when Tashmiren turned back from the ledge and led them back to the main road, where he continued their descent. Soran again came next to Rulalin and leaned in. "That one room would feed Fel Edorath for months."

"Yes. That's a good idea." Rulalin called after Tashmiren, who had again moved some distance ahead. "Tashmiren?"

Tashmiren halted and turned to face them. "The people of Fel Edorath are starving."

"I know."

"My ability to persuade their soldiers to follow me, and our master, would greatly improve if I came to them leading wagons of food."

"Will your men not follow you unless you bribe them?" Tashmiren mocked. "What kind of leadership do you call that?"

"Many of my men will follow me, food or no food. However, as I'm sure you know, there are many who would not under normal circumstances follow Malek unless such service promised great reward. These days, a full belly might be the only reward needed. Will you at least consider the idea?"

Tashmiren frowned. "Do you really think Malek had not thought of the attractiveness of food to a starving city? Do not be foolish. When he comes forth, everything will come. The Mountain will empty itself, pouring its inhabitants out upon the world as a storm cloud dumps it waters upon the land. Don't worry about such things. It has all been arranged."

With that Rulalin felt much less burdened than he had for a long time. He had feared what he would bring to Fel Edorath when he returned, but the prospect of bringing food to his people greatly cheered him. Whatever else his coming brought, at least there was hope that when he came the hungry would know fullness again.

After descending a long way, they came to a place where a wide gully intersected the road. A sturdy wooden bridge went over what appeared to be a riverbed, though there was no water in it now. Tashmiren scrambled down the side of the gully beside the bridge, and Soran and Rulalin followed. Together they walked along the bottom of what Rulalin was increasingly convinced either was or had been a channel for water. It passed under the walls that stood on either side of the road they had been following, and Rulalin and Soran walked stooped for a while before the ceiling above them opened up again.

They followed the riverbed until it passed under a great, thick wall, then emerged on the other side into yet another enormous room. Now, though, they did not see a gaping pit below, but a vast space above. They were walking along the bottom of what had once been some kind of lake or reservoir.

"Where are we?" Soran asked, craning his neck upward.

"Up ahead is a small pool of water, and it is all that remains of the waters that once flowed freely from the Crystal Fountain of Avalione. When Malek first came here at the beginning of the Third Age, this lake was full of water, and springs and tributaries ran through many parts of the Mountain. That was long ago, and now we rely on two other sources of water. South of the Mountain, just inside the northernmost reaches of the Forest of Gyrin, there is another large subterranean chamber full of water. The Great Bear who once lived in Gyrin had several wells tapped into it, and it did not take us long to find these and add more. Also, at the northern base of the Mountain is a large basin that stores the runoff of the rains and storms that fall upon Agia Muldonai. From these two places we cart in all our water, though it is an undertaking of almost unfathomable size.

"Even so," Tashmiren said, looking at the large, mostly empty lakebed. "I thought you might want to look upon the place where the famed waters of Avalione once flowed. They are no more, but once they watered the whole world above and beneath just as they watered the Mountain, or so Malek says, for it was he who first showed me this place."

"You came here with Malek?"

"I did. He has shown me many things."

After a few moments, Tashmiren turned and led them back via the dry riverbed to the road. This time, when they had scrambled up out of the gully, they turned not downward but upward. A long time they walked, passing many curious openings and crevices. Ever upward they went, until Rulalin was quite sure they were well above the passageway that had originally brought them into the Mountain.

Eventually they came to a place where the big road intersected another, just as large. Rulalin had figured there must be more than one such avenue, but it had been nice to think for a time that there was just one, and that to find it was to find the way out.

He didn't have long to contemplate his disappointment, for Tashmiren went left at the intersection and immediately into a large room, but by no means as large as the many they had seen to this point. This room was only a little bigger than the Hall of Meetings in Fel Edorath and not nearly so large as the Great Hall in Sulare. It was well lit, and smaller groups of men and Malekim sat in clusters within.

A pair of men near the entrance gave Tashmiren the deferential nod that Rulalin had come to expect, but much to his surprise, they did not stop talking or step away. They continued to converse as they had been when Tashmiren had walked in and seemed not to mind his presence at all.

Again, there wasn't much time to marvel. Tashmiren led them into the heart of the room, and as they walked, Rulalin became increasingly aware of a dais on the far side of the chamber. It stood perhaps three or four hands above the floor, and a simple black chair sat in the middle. In the chair, a tall, gaunt man with dark black hair sat quietly, hunched over to one side as he leaned on his hand. His deep dark eyes stared into the room, and if he took any special note of Tashmiren and his companions, he gave no sign of it.

Tashmiren stopped while they were still some twenty spans from the dais. "Is that him?" Soran whispered to Tashmiren.

"Who do you mean?"

"You know, Malek."

Tashmiren laughed quietly, "Oh, no, it isn't Malek. You will know when you come into Malek's presence, though almost certainly you will not be allowed to look upon him. This isn't Malek."

"Then who?"

"Don't you know?"

"Farimaal," Rulalin said almost involuntarily.

Tashmiren turned and gazed at the dais. "It is."

Rulalin fixed his eyes on the man in the chair. To be sure, he had a disconcerting look. That the man had experienced much was evident, but he could not see the reason for Tashmiren's awe and reverence. From the first time Tashmiren had visited Fel Edorath, he had spoken of Farimaal with almost the same respect and fear granted Malek.

"Will you still not speak of Farimaal, and why you fear him?" Rulalin asked, almost wearily.

Tashmiren looked Rulalin in the eyes and smiled. "All

right, when we return to your room, I will tell you his story, but not here."

Rulalin acknowledged Tashmiren's offer with a nod, and Tashmiren turned to go, but Soran interrupted. "Aren't you going to introduce us?"

Tashmiren turned a bemused look upon Soran. "Unless you are Malek, you don't speak to Farimaal unless he speaks to you, and he rarely speaks."

"Has he ever spoken to you?" Soran asked as they continued on their way out of the room.

"Twice."

"Only twice?"

"Yes."

"How long have you been in Malek's service?"

"My whole life."

"And he's spoken to you only twice?"

"Yes."

"What did he say?"

"Both times he was giving me instructions, and I assure you, I barely slept or ate until I had carried them out."

They followed Tashmiren back out, and soon they were on their way back to their own rooms.

"Problem with your chair?" Tashmiren asked wryly as he pushed the remains of Rulalin's broken chair to the side of the room with his foot.

"Yeah," Rulalin answered simply as Tashmiren settled into one of the two remaining good chairs and helped himself to the pitcher of cool water. Rulalin motioned to Soran to take the other chair, and he sat on his bed with his back against the wall.

He had barely sat down when the weariness of his sleepless night washed over him again. This story had better be good, or he was going to end up sleeping through it. For several moments, Tashmiren showed no interest in anything but his drink. Then he began his story abruptly. "The story, really, begins with the Grendolai," he started.

"The Grendolai?" Soran's voice betrayed his surprise.

Tashmiren shot Soran an irritated frown. "This story is going to take a while, even without your interjections."

Soran's face colored. "I'm sorry. I won't interrupt again."

"Good," Tashmiren said simply. "As I said, the story begins with the Grendolai. The Grendolai were created early in the Second Age with the combined wisdom and power of Malek, last of the Twelve, and Vulsutyr, the Fire Giant and father of the Vulsutyrim. They were fearful to behold, and even their masters wondered at what their hands had created. Though I have never seen one, the stories say they were not as tall as the giants, perhaps three spans high, but ferocious beyond comprehension. Their long arms ended in claws strong enough to shred wood like parchment or to pound stone into dust. Their dark-green skin was more durable than even the hide of the Malekim, not as stiff but denser and harder to penetrate. Their only weakness was their eyes, which abhorred light, making them a natural nocturnal terror. Malek and Vulsutyr created twelve of them, for they were designed to attack the dragon towers of Kirthanin and render them unusable, so the mobility of the Dragons would be limited when Malek returned from the Forbidden Isle.

"History shows they were successful. Ascending the outer walls of the dragon towers in the darkness with claws that pierced the stone, they easily gained access to the dragon tower gyres, and more than one of Sulmandir's children found the Grendolai's powerful claws capable of penetrating their seemingly impenetrable scales. Oh, yes, the Grendolai were shrouded in terror from birth and have lived up to their reputation ever since, all save once.

"But I get ahead of myself. I will enlighten you more

broadly on their history that you may fully appreciate the story I have to tell you. It did not take long for trouble to surface between the giants and the Grendolai. One morning, several Vulsutyrim on the Forbidden Isle were found dead by the hands of the Grendolai, their bodies having been eaten and their bones all but picked clean. Had Vulsutyr himself not finally relented of his fury, Malek would not have been able to prevent the giants, several hundred strong, from making war on the twelve monsters.

"However, Vulsutyr did relent and forged a compromise with Malek. The Grendolai were banished to the high mountain crags of the Forbidden Isle until the invasion of Kirthanin would be ready, and no further incidents took place between the children of Vulsutyr and his own partial creation.

"Unwilling to risk bringing more uncontrollable creatures into the world, Vulsutyr would no longer help Malek, but Malek was not deterred. He set to work on his next two projects, which spawned the Malekim, and then Rucaran the Great, the father of the Black Wolves. These creatures, though useful and fearsome in their own right, were more pliable than the Grendolai, and their numbers swelled until at last Malek and Vulsutyr agreed that it would soon be time.

"Having spent years creating division in Kirthanin, men directed by Malek were able to start the War of Division, and Malek waited for civil war to consume the world. When the conflict was at its height, a vast fleet of men, giants, Black Wolves, Malekim, and of course the twelve Grendolai, crossed the Southern Ocean and brought to pass the worst nightmare of all who stood watch over the southern shores.

"While Malek's main forces progressed into Kirthanin, the Grendolai stole through the darkness across the land to their appointed destinations, and one by one they took control of the dragon towers, just as they had been made to do. Along the way, they brought death and destruction to homes, farms, settlements, villages, and even small towns, as they plundered and feasted on human flesh, their appetites long held in check in their long years of exile. Of all the invaders that came to Kirthanin, none inspired more fear and terror than they.

"The rest, you know. The men of Kirthanin rallied, though almost too late, and with the combined strength of the Great Bear and Dragons, even without the dragon towers, the war was fought to a virtual draw at the foot of Agia Muldonai. There Sulmandir slew Vulsutyr and broke the will of Malek's armies. They retreated here, to the labyrinth of tunnels and caverns beneath the Mountain, where they have remained ever since.

"The Grendolai, however, stayed in the dragon towers. Beneath the gyres were great, dark storehouses where they made their homes. They continued to terrorize the world of men in raids for food, but these raids became infrequent, until it seemed the Grendolai had gone away or perhaps even died. As a matter of fact, the Grendolai were not dead, but merely dormant, holed up in the dark towers they had been sent to conquer.

"And then the day came, perhaps fifteen years after the retreat into the Mountain, when the Grendolai in the dragon tower immediately north of Agia Muldonai refused to answer a message sent by Malek. Three messengers came and went from the Mountain to the tower, and all three returned with the same answer: The Grendolai would not see or speak to them. The fourth embassy, made up of half a dozen men, did not come back at all. A fifth was sent, a pair of Vulsutyrim, and they likewise did not return.

"Malek would not accept this affront to his authority. He sent word to all his remaining host that whoever could subdue the Grendolai would be granted whatever he asked.

"At first it looked as though no one would accept the offer, but then a patrol that had been covertly gathering information from the people of Kirthanin returned to the Mountain. Among them was a captain named Farimaal. Farimaal had been a mid-ranking officer in the army during the Invasion, distinguished by two things: his relative silence and his dedication to leading from the front. Some called him fearless, others foolish, but either way, he accepted Malek's challenge. He vowed not to return until the Grendolai had been subdued.

"A large party of curious onlookers traveled north with Farimaal to the first dragon tower and camped at a safe distance. Farimaal headed the rest of the way on foot. For a week the gathered men waited, but Farimaal did not return. After ten days, they concluded that Farimaal was dead.

"With mirth rather than mourning, they mocked his vain quest and rode back to the Mountain. Malek said little, and most believed he had never really hoped Farimaal would be successful. Life in the Mountain returned to normal, as much as could be considered normal in those early days when the dark halls of stone were being finished to accommodate Malek's purposes. Farimaal's name became the object of ridicule.

"Then, almost three months later, Farimaal returned one morning, dressed in a fantastic armor as black as midnight that fit his every joint with a precision unlike any armor fashioned by human hand. His full body was covered and a grim helmet rested upon his head, so that only his haggard face could be seen. The men at the gate parted as he approached, and he said nothing to anyone he passed into the Mountain.

"Word spread like wildfire as he continued his determined walk into the heart of the Mountain, that Farimaal had returned from the dead. That same word ran ahead of him, and by the time he reached Malek's chamber, the master himself was waiting for his servant's approach.

"Of that meeting, little is known, save that Farimaal did not explain precisely what had taken place within the dragon tower. What did come out was that he had subdued and slain the Grendolai who dwelt in the Tower. Then he had carefully stripped the creature of his hide, which he fashioned into armor. He heated each piece in a stone oven made from some of the stones of the tower itself, until each piece had been blackened and hardened fifty-fold. No blade could scratch its surface, and the keenest arrow couldn't dent it, and yet it was molded perfectly to his body, so that when he wore it he could wield both sword and spear, walk, run, or ride a horse. And in that armor he appeared before Malek to demand his promised reward.

"Before Malek would grant Farimaal's demand, he sent several reluctant men to the dragon tower to investigate Farimaal's story. They returned in time confirming that the tower was empty. Not willing to trust their word alone, Malek sent a second team to ascend to the gyre and bring back some of the stones that surrounded the beacon fires that had been part of the dragon towers' original design. Only then, Malek said, would he know that the Grendolai was gone. Again, the embassy came back with confirmation that Farimaal's story was true.

"At last, Malek believed, and so he granted Farimaal the right to rule at his right hand. With this gift came the long life Farimaal has enjoyed, for the oldest of our men will tell you that he looks not a day older now than he did when they were boys. For the entire duration of the Third Age he has ruled with Malek here in the Mountain, rarely going forth.

"Now you see why no one ever challenges Farimaal, nor do they disobey him. He did what could not be done. He walked into a dragon tower and killed a Grendolai. A Grendolai! With claws that could rip through a dragon's scales and extract the heart from its chest, the Grendolai were surely beyond mortal man, but Farimaal went into that tower and when he came out, the Grendolai was dead. To this day, there isn't a man or beast in this Mountain who wouldn't rather die than incur Farimaal's wrath."

"What about this Cheimontyr you spoke of?" Rulalin asked.

Tashmiren considered this. "I cannot say if Cheimontyr fears Farimaal. But if he doesn't, he is the only one who doesn't, aside from Malek. One might say that if Farimaal is Malek's right hand, Cheimontyr is his left, and it is perhaps foolish to guess which hand is the greater."

"So the dragon towers really do house the Grendolai?" Soran asked, his voice distant as though trying to accept what must have been a very unlikely possibility.

"Yes, save only the dragon tower immediately north of the Mountain, which remains empty to this day. The story goes that after his victory there, Farimaal traveled to the three closest dragon towers to spread the news of his victory and reassert Malek's rule. No Grendolai has defied Malek since then, and though they have not been active in Malek's service, they are amenable to their master's directions."

It was an incredible story, and Rulalin had found it more than interesting enough to hold sleep at bay. It had been hard to imagine what could make the lean figure he had seen so fearful, but if the tale was true, then surely he was a man to be feared.

"Do you understand now?" Tashmiren asked.

"I do," Rulalin answered, and Soran also nodded.

"He will lead the hosts of Malek when we go forth?" Soran added.

"He will go forth with them, though exactly what role he will play has not yet been revealed. The immediate leadership of Malek's armies has been entrusted to Cheimontyr, for this is his hour, but with Cheimontyr before them and Farimaal in their midst, the confidence of Malek's armies is assured. Likewise, it is impossible to imagine who will stand against them. Surely your old friend Aljeron, though he may fancy himself a warrior, has never seen their like. He will fall back, or he will fall never to rise again. So shall it be with all who stand in our way. It cannot be otherwise."

Tashmiren took another long drink. When he had finished, he wiped his mouth and smirked. "Are you still sure you want to meet Malek?"

Rulalin summoned more self-assurance than he felt. "I am to follow him into battle, I would not shrink back from meeting him."

Tashmiren nodded. "And perhaps you shall. That is not for me to decide. Well, I must leave you. I have things to attend to, and when I am ready, I will come again."

"When will we be free to move about on our own?"

"Soon."

Rulalin frowned. Tashmiren rose to go, and he stretched ostentatiously beside the table. "Keep yourselves in readiness, for I cannot say when the master will summon you. Only know that when the time comes, you must be ready."

"We will be ready," Rulalin said, rising from the bed to stretch as well.

"I will give you all the warning you need, for it will likely be me who takes you to him. The rest is up to you."

"We'll be ready," Rulalin repeated.

With that, Tashmiren left the room.

"What do you think?" Soran asked tentatively.

"What do I think about what?"

"About all of it. Farimaal. The Grendolai. The whole thing. Do you think it's true?"

Rulalin shook his head slightly. "I don't know. It sounds fantastic, but why would he lie?"

"So that we fear Farimaal. So that we follow him. Maybe he's just trying to make sure we stay in line."

"Perhaps, though having Malek here would seem to be enough."

Rulalin took the pitcher of water and refilled his cup. "Aside from that," Soran continued, "what do you make of this 'Cheimontyr'?"

"Cheimontyr," Rulalin echoed. "He is even more of a mystery than Farimaal. All we know, I guess, is that he's a giant."

"Yeah, with a name like Cheimontyr, he must be." Soran leaned forward and rested his head on his hands. "What was it that Tashmiren called him?"

"Malek's left hand?"

"No, earlier."

"Ah, 'the bringer of storms,' I believe."

"What do you think that means?"

"I don't know, but if he is going to lead Malek's host out into the world, it could fairly be said that he will bring quite the storm with him."

Tashmiren knelt in the dark room, his face barely above the floor. "You may rise," his master said, and Tashmiren stood.

Malek was seated before him, but as always, he was enshrouded by darkness. A faint trace of light behind Tashmiren cast the slightest of shadows, but it did little more than silhouette Tashmiren's form for his master.

"You have shown Rulalin Tarasir our might?"

"As much as his brief stay has allowed."

"Good. Keep showing him. All lingering doubts must be driven from him before we leave."

"Yes, master."

There was silence in the darkness, but Tashmiren did not try to fill it. When he stood before Malek, he did not speak until spoken to, and he did not leave until dismissed.

"Do you know what happened two days ago in the outer world?"

"Yes, master, it was the feast of Midautumn."

"That's right, one of four days the peoples of Kirthanin

gather to grovel, calling on the name of a God who has forsaken them. It is the last feast they will enjoy in the false security of their current peace. By Midwinter, Werthanin at least will be mine. The New Year will bring the fulfillment of my quest, and at last, Kirthanin will be mine."

"Yes, master."

"But, while my armies prepare to go west, I have a mission for you to arrange in the east."

"Yes?" Tashmiren was curious.

"I want ten men to take twenty Black Wolves and twenty Malekim east to Amaan Sul."

"To Amaan Sul, master?"

"Yes, to Amaan Sul. I want them to bring me the queen and her son."

"The queen and her son, master?" Tashmiren again exclaimed.

"Yes, I want Wylla Someris and her son, the son of Joraiem Andira, brought to me."

"But how can such a small party accomplish this task, and why do we need them?"

"The task will be easier than you think, and I didn't say we needed them. The wolves will be the eyes and ears of the party in the plains between Gyrin and the city, and if a patrol should somehow get wind of them, they will be no match for ten wolves."

"And the city's defenses?"

"Do you know where the royal residence is?"

"Yes, just inside the northern wall."

"It is indeed. Built in the First Age, the potential weakness of such a location was not foremost in the city's design. We will exploit that weakness. When the party reaches the city, the Malekim will breach the gate, and the men will retrieve the queen and prince from the palace, all before anyone knows they are in danger. Then she will be brought to me, even if I am already in Fel Edorath or beyond."

"Yes, master."

"The party you send will ride day and night until they reach the border of Gyrin, where they will need to be careful in daylight, but they must be quick."

"Yes, master, I will instruct them of both their mission and its urgency."

"If the queen is brought to me before I reach Fel Edorath, she will ensure Rulalin's cooperation."

"I see," Tashmiren answered.

"You see what I show you," Malek replied. "The queen's value is minimal. More important is the boy."

"What is important about him?"

"Perhaps nothing, perhaps everything. I will not know until I see him."

"I will arrange it."

"Good. Bring them both to me, then we shall see what we shall see."

11

THE CALM BEFORE

WYLLA LEANED BACK in her chair and looked out the window beside her desk. The sunlight was streaming through and the sky above the city and beyond was a brilliant blue. After so many cold and cloudy days, this relief from the cold and the greyness was most welcome.

She looked around her empty sitting room and through the open door to her bedroom, feeling very much alone. She knew that everyone was leaving her alone because she had work to do, but it was one of the great frustrations of ruling that the details of her work so often isolated her from the very people she was governing. Some of the best advice she had ever been given on the task of ruling a nation had been given to her by her father many years ago. He said that it was necessary from time to time to leave the pressing duties of the day undone and to go out into the city to be reminded of the bigger picture, the reason for the work that lay before them.

She looked down at the papers scattered upon her desk

and sighed. She missed him. She missed her mother too. They had been taken away from her too soon. Missing them brought Benjiah again to mind, for she missed him most of all.

The sound of clattering footsteps in the hallway followed by an eager knock on the door came as a welcome distraction. She rose and went to the door.

"Roslin, Halina, what is it?" She asked with a smile as her two nieces burst in.

"Oh, Aunt Wylla, you have to come down and see because the juggler is finally here. He'd said he would come today and then he didn't come when we were expecting him and we gave up and were very sad but now it looks like he's made it after all. It's so wonderful and Mom sent us up here to let you know that he was here and to see if you wanted to come down, but we know that maybe you can't because you have important things to do but juggling seems like it could be a very useful skill to have and maybe one day you'd find it very handy even though you're a queen and most people don't think of jug-gling right away when they think of queens."

"Well, Roslin," Wylla cut in as her niece paused to breathe. "You are right that I am busy right now, but I will be sure to come down shortly and watch you have your juggling lesson. I'd like to meet this juggler, and of course I'd love to see you and Halina learning. I'm sure you will both be very good at it."

"It looks really hard but I hope you're right because I'd love to be as good as he is. I think it would be great if we went home when all this war is over and I could juggle for Dad like I was a real performer, and maybe Halina and I could even do some of those fancy two-person juggling tricks. Wouldn't that be really great? Anyway, I don't want to keep the juggler wait-ing because he could be really busy and his time must be very important and I want to make the most of the lesson so I need to go." With that last flurry, Roslin took off running back down the hall.

"I hope you enjoy your lesson, Halina," Wylla said to her older niece, who had also turned to head back downstairs, though not as dramatically.

"Thanks," Halina said, smiling. "Maybe we'll see you downstairs later."

Wylla lingered at the doorway after both girls had disappeared. The smile on her face at their excitement faded as she thought of Roslin's words, *when all this war is over.* She and Kyril had agreed that the girls didn't need to know all Valzaan had revealed to them, so they were unaware that the prophet believed Malek was about to come forth. Wylla, too, hoped all this war would be over soon. She hoped the girls would be able to juggle for Evrim to their hearts' content, but she feared that such scenes of domestic tranquility might first become a thing of the past.

She closed the door and returned to the window for a few moments before settling into her chair again. With so much uncertainty hanging over her, over Amaan Sul, over the future of not only her people but the whole world, it was hard to keep her mind focused on the mundane tasks of leadership. Still, she had promised both the twins and the men they had left in charge of Enthanin's defense that she would continue with life as normal. It was important that the news of trouble, if trouble came, be disseminated with wisdom, and now was not the time to be speaking of what might not be for some time.

After a while, she gathered together the many pieces of loose parchment around her, bundled them together, and put them in the large top drawer of her desk. She locked it with a small iron key, one of many on a key-chain that was never out of her control. Slipping the keys into a pocket, she rose, exited the room, and headed down the stairs to seek out the mysterious juggler.

It was now almost Tenth Hour, and she could feel the beginning of rumblings in her stomach. She had skipped lunch as she often did on days when she was trying to be especially productive, an old habit carried over from days when she needed a growling stomach to help keep her from succumbing to the temptation to nap in the afternoon. She didn't struggle with that particular temptation so much anymore, so the empty stomach often proved to be more of a distraction than anything else. It was hard to explain, but sometimes she found comfort in even the unpleasant patterns of her past.

Ignoring the urge to go straight to the kitchen to pilfer an afternoon snack, she followed the squeals of laughter down the corridor to a large open hall. She paused in the doorway, looking in at the scene before her, which was illuminated by the slanted rays of the late afternoon sun falling in through a row of tall windows. Kyril and Karalin were seated in chairs with several of the palace stewards gathered beside or behind them. Halina and Roslin sat cross-legged on the floor, and all were watching a man with thinning white hair and a modest beard maintaining a juggle of some half a dozen colored balls.

Wylla remained where she was, not wanting to disrupt the concentration of the man, who was deftly expanding and contracting the arcs and orbits of the balls. After a few moments, he began to remove one ball at a time from the group by catching each in a different pocket sown into his baggy vest and pants. When he was finished, each of the six was in a different pocket, and he bowed deeply to the assembled crowd, who clapped uproariously.

Wylla caught a clear glimpse of the man's kindly face for the first time, and her impulse to move into the room was immediately checked. The man, perhaps in his mid to late sixties, was barrel-chested with short legs and powerful arms, and his brown eyes glimmered in the flush of his completed routine. As Wylla took all this in, a realization dawned upon her: She knew this man.

For a brief moment, her mind searched for a name to put with the face. She found it and started into the hall with a determined stride. The juggler, facing the entrance, was the first to notice her. When he did, his reaction gave her presence away. Despite the turning heads, Wylla kept her gaze fixed on the juggler, whose face betrayed nervous anxiety.

"Aunt Wylla, you're here, I'm so glad you came down to—"

"Hush, Roslin," Wylla said firmly, raising her hand to her niece while keeping her eyes on the performer. "Not now."

"Welcome to the palace of Amaan Sul, Master Yorek," she began, "Or should I say, welcome back?"

One of the older palace stewards, a woman in her early fifties, gasped when Wylla mentioned the name. She turned to peer at the juggler, who remained where he was, hands at his side, looking at Wylla. Several others also looked back at the juggler, and many exchanged looks of consternation and wonder before turning back to the strange scene.

Wylla, having waited for some sort of reply from the man, continued, "Have I mistaken your name, master juggler?"

"No, my queen."

"Then why do you not answer?"

"Because all the years I have waited to behold my queen again did not prepare me for the encounter. I was at a loss." The man lowered his head humbly, his voice a gentle whisper echoing in the now utterly silent hall. He fumbled with the edge of his vest.

Wylla, for the first time since she had realized who he was, turned from him to a pair of palace guards, who now stood alertly looking with suspicion at Yorek. "I am going to the parlor. Bring Master Yorek to me and make sure that we are not disturbed."

She turned and walked from the room.

She had just enough time upon reaching the parlor to position herself behind her favorite chair before the guards leading Yorek entered the room. She motioned to a chair across from her and he took it. Then, once the guards had left the room, she took her seat, facing him.

"If I am not mistaken, your exile from the city of Amaan Sul was set down in official law, was it not?"

"Yes, Your Majesty."

"And the punishment for violating that law is still death, isn't it?"

"It is."

"Then why have you come here?"

"I was invited."

"To the city?"

"To the palace, by your niece."

Wylla frowned. "I don't remember you as a fool, Yorek. Why play games with me when your life is hanging in the balance?"

"I'm sorry, Your Majesty, I don't mean to offend."

Wylla paused and asked again. "Why are you in Amaan Sul?"

"That is a long story."

"Is there no short answer that would do?"

"I am old, Your Majesty, and the fear of dying was no longer enough to override my desire for other things."

"Like what?"

"Like the hope that I would be able to see you again before I die."

"Me?"

"Yes."

"How long has it been now? Thirty years?"

"Thirty-one."

Wylla nodded. "That's right. It wasn't long after my tenth birthday. I cried for weeks." Memories of a younger Yorek flooded her, his face much the same, save without the wrinkles and with light brown hair that fell in his face, so that her little hands were constantly employed sweeping it away from his kind and laughing eyes. "You have risked death today for me?"

Yorek looked at her, his eyes still kind, but she could see no laughter in them. "You were always precious to me, Wylla, and you still are. I have little left in this world to care about, so in recent years I have not shied away from Amaan Sul."

For several moments they looked at one another, until finally Wylla leaned back in her chair, her arms folded in her lap. "Why did my Father exile you, Yorek? You were his closest friend and adviser. I've never really known why."

Yorek shrugged. "I disagreed with him. Pedrone never liked anyone to disagree with him, and I guess I did it one time too often."

"What did you two disagree over?"

"The people's tax burden for one. Pedrone believed that a people's willingness to pay taxes was an indication of their love for their king, and so he steadily increased it over the time of his reign. I told him that I thought a king's willingness to reduce the burden of taxes upon his people was a sign of his growing love and care for them."

"Father did favor a heavier load than some might recommend, perhaps," Wylla conceded. "But he always poured the money back into the city and the land. He built great public works, remarkable roads, fountains, and buildings with the funds he raised. He turned Amaan Sul into one of the most magnificent cities in all Kirthanin, didn't he? Think of all the beautiful things he built with that money. Do these monuments not outlive and outlast both the King who ordered their construction and the laborers whose taxes paid for them?"

"Yes, and you are right that he spent much of the money he raised on public works, but even so, more than one family went without things they desired and in some cases needed so that his columns and colonnades might be built with the splendor he desired. Though they yield a beauty all might enjoy, it might fairly be said that they were his more than they were his people's."

"It is hard to measure the worth of money spent on a city's structures, or on money invested in a people's pride. Who can say how many have been inspired by the grandeur of their city to aspire to more than otherwise they would have, to achieve more than they had previously thought possible?"

"I cannot, Your Majesty. I don't mean to suggest that such undertakings have no value, only that I encouraged him to lighten the load and undertake fewer of them. Even that, though, was an offense."

Wylla was shaking her head. "Father could be proud, but I can't believe he banished you for this. Surely there was more."

"There was."

"Well, what else?"

"He didn't like that I wanted to remarry."

Wylla gazed at Yorek, remembering things she had not thought of for more than half a lifetime. She had only the faintest recollection of Yorek's wife, a frail but pretty woman who was a close friend of her mother's, even as Yorek was a good friend of her father's. They had one son, also whom she could barely remember. Both had been lost in a fire that burned their home and destroyed several buildings in the city. Yorek had been at the palace, and when he returned home, it was already so swallowed in flames that he could not even get through the front door.

Wylla had been a very little girl, perhaps no more than five. She had never seen Yorek with any woman after that point. That he had been considering remarriage was a revelation to her.

Yorek continued. "Your mother, who might have objected because of her relationship with Eralin, did not. She gave me her blessing, but your father got it in his head that for me to re-marry was to be faithless to the memories of my wife and son. He forbade me to remarry, and I told him that it wasn't his right."

"Did you remarry?"

"Yes."

"Your second wife, is she here as well?"

"No. We were married twenty-two years, but she died too, some nine years ago."

"Did you have more children?"

"No. Allfather never blessed us with children."

Though Yorek's face was still almost completely devoid of emotion, Wylla felt that she could see now the sadness that lined the corners of his eyes where the laughter had once resided. The loss of two wives, a son, and the sentence of exile from a king who had been his closest friend were indeed heavy loads for any man to carry.

"What else?" she asked, more hesitantly this time.

Yorek met her steady gaze with his own, but he kept his mouth shut. She pressed him. "You don't need to be afraid."

Yorek looked into Wylla's eyes, and for the first time since the conversation began, he visibly struggled with his emotions. "I rebuked your father for how he was dealing with you, or not dealing with you might be a better way to put it, and for that he would not forgive me."

"What do you mean?"

"I thought he spent too much of his time with your brothers. You were the firstborn, the one who would rule. I thought he slighted you in favor of them, and I told him it should not be. You were not a boy, but you were his daughter, and he needed to pay attention to you and guide you. You needed a father. You spent too much time with me while he romped and played with them."

Wylla continued to watch Yorek carefully. He did not turn away. "It was a hard thing for me to do, to say this to your father."

"Why?" Wylla asked, her voice sounding distant. "Did you know what it would cost you?"

"No, I had no idea he would take it as hard as he did. It was hard because after all I had lost, spending time with you was one of my chief joys. Though I knew you were not my daughter, it was fun to think that in a way at least, I could be paternal toward you. I thought that I would endure your father's wrath for a few weeks, but ultimately he would see that I was right. I thought I would see less and less of you as he reasserted his rightful role in your life. I didn't know I would be driven from the city and cut off from you completely."

"You stood up for me to my father, and he exiled you," Wylla said quietly.

"I don't know that anything is ever that simple," Yorek replied. "He was not specific in his order to me to go."

"Thirty-one years?"

"Yes, it has been thirty-one years."

"What happened to you?"

Yorek sighed. "Many things. I don't know how to summarize the last thirty-one years any better than you could, I imagine. I did remarry, as I said, and my wife and I traveled to several towns and cities. Eventually, we fell in with a troupe of jugglers and traveling actors. We enjoyed their company because they lightened our hearts and our spirits, and eventually we stayed with them because they became our friends and we saw the value of their work. It was a big change for us, but all in all, it was a happy life, and we asked nothing more of it than that.

"When the troupe would visit Amaan Sul, we would remain outside the city, rejoining them at their next stop. So, for our whole married life together, we never returned to Amaan Sul, even long after your father died. We heard of your marriage in Sulare and your sudden bereavement there, and I wept for you. But I had made my peace with my lot in life and did not consider coming back. Then, when I was bereaved again myself, I felt increasingly that I should come. I did not know if you would remember me, or what you might know of the circumstances of my departure, but I wanted to see you again. So, about three years ago, when some of our troupe came here in Winter Wane, I came with them. I walked the streets of the city, visited familiar places, and walked on more than one occasion by the palace. I didn't have the courage to come in, and in the end, I left without seeing you. This is my fourth trip back to Amaan Sul, and as you already know, I ran into your niece that day in the street, which is why I am here. Perhaps Allfather brought the bird to take my ball that I might meet her." Yorek looked Wylla in the eye. "I am aware that I have violated Enthanin law by coming, and I submit to your judgment. Do with me what seems best to you."

He seemed relieved to have spoken his peace, and he looked neither anxious nor expectant, merely content. She did not doubt from his words and his manner that he was fully prepared to face whatever sentence she might give. Though he had been an adviser to her father and had sported her on his back a thousand times, he was fully resigned to accept her will, as any other subject in her kingdom might be.

"You have ignored the law, and the penalty for ignoring the proclamation of a king without royal permission is death," she said.

He nodded, keeping his eyes on her. "I have."

Suddenly, Wylla smiled at him. "But, I will not execute this sentence. You will be spared, on one condition."

"What condition, Your Majesty?"

"I will let you live, provided that you give up your association with this band of traveling entertainers and settle here, in Amaan Sul. Not only must you do that, but you must also agree to become an adviser to me, as you once were to my father. This is my condition."

Yorek looked perplexed. "You have not seen me in thirty-one years, and even then you were only ten years old. Despite this, you would take me as your adviser?"

"I know you, Yorek. I believe what you have told me. I know you loved my father, and I know you loved me."

"I still do."

"Very well then, what else is necessary? If my father had a flaw, and though I loved him I know he had many, it was his pride. I know that he realized after he exiled you that he had made a mistake, but he never admitted it. Even so, I could see that he mourned your loss and missed your candor. For my part, I can see now some of the reasons for what was. My father did spend more time with me after banishing you. I always thought this was because he was trying to comfort me as I grieved losing you. I see now that he took your admonition to heart, at great cost to you and with much benefit to me."

"I am glad. He was always a loving father when he tried."

"I don't know that I ever thought of him as deficient before you left, but I know that he was more attentive after. For that I thank you."

Yorek nodded. "I also know," Wylla continued, "that you showed my father your love by telling him the truth. What I ask now is that you would do the same for me. Will you be my adviser and speak honestly to me as you did to him?"

Yorek was trembling. "I will, Your Majesty."

"Then it is settled. The penalty for your crime against the throne of Enthanin is service to that same throne, as long as you are able. Do you understand the sentence?"

"I do."

"Then welcome, old friend." Wylla crossed the room to Yorek, hugging him tightly in a long embrace.

Ahead, his uncles were slowing their horses to a walk, though Benjiah could not see why. Benjiah also reined in his mount and eased her to a walk behind them. It was late morning on the twenty-third day of Full Autumn, so he knew they were close to Gyrin. Benjiah looked at the so-called road they had been riding on as his horse welcomed the change of pace and walked contentedly behind Valzaan's. The past few days he had noticed the road deteriorating, but the stretch they had covered today had been positively dreadful. At points, it wasn't clear to Benjiah what distinguished the road from the grassy plains. The distinction must have been clear to Pedraal and Pedraan, however, who rode together in the front without so much as a hint of confusion.

And yet, as they drew ever closer to the forest, the road seemed to reemerge. This phenomenon was somewhat counterintuitive to Benjiah, who had expected the road to be completely abandoned here.

Benjiah moved up alongside the prophet. "Valzaan?"

"Yes?"

"The road, it has been very rough the last several days, but here it is growing clearer and smoother with every span. What is going on?"

"The road in Gyrin is still maintained. No traffic uses it to do trade between Enthanin and Werthanin anymore, but Malek believes, no doubt rightly, that the road may be of service to him one day. However, what he has maintained for himself may prove useful to us too, especially if we should be able to pass through the forest safely and quickly. Beyond that, I have hope that this very road will be once again used for peaceful trade in a world free of Malek."

A movement in the sky attracted Benjiah's eyes, and he turned his face heavenward to see a windhover circling far above them. He smiled as he looked at the majestic bird framed against the blue-grey backdrop of the midmorning sky. He closed his eyes.

Suddenly, the comfortable feeling of sitting astride his horse with the light of day falling on his face was replaced by a strange sensation of moving very quickly. A rush of images flooded his mind and swept through him. Eventually, he realized that he appeared to be looking down over the land from the sky. He swooped over the long wild grass of the green plain below until the continuous image of it was interrupted by the sight of four men on horseback.

His eyes popped open and he stared wide-eyed at his uncles and Valzaan. He had been looking at himself from a vantage point high up in the sky. He moved to speak to Valzaan, but the prophet, whose head was turned in his direction, raised his hand, waving it in an arc between them, and Benjiah felt a rushing in his head and a pulling sensation. He looked from Valzaan to his uncles, and his suspicions were confirmed. He was in *torrim redara* again.

"What's going on?"

"I thought it would be better if we talked here."

"Not that, before. What just happened to me?"

"You saw through the eyes of the windhover. That is one of the ways Allfather helps me compensate for having no eyesight of my own, and it is a gift some other prophets of Allfather have possessed. I'm sorry I hadn't prepared you for this possibility. I am beginning to see now that Allfather intends you to be educated quickly."

"Did my father do this?"

"For him it was a more gradual process, but he did see through a windhover's eyes while we journeyed together."

Benjiah nodded. "Valzaan, while we're here, there is something else."

"Yes?"

"Some time ago, we were resting the horses in the afternoon after a late lunch, near the stream a day or so from Amaan Sul, remember?"

"Yes."

"Well, I closed my eyes while you were talking to the twins, and I think I fell asleep, because I had the strangest dream. I dreamt that I was walking through rolling hills that opened out on a wide plain. The hills and plain were lush, as a deep, thick, soft grass grew under my feet. It was soothing to walk upon. Ahead of me was a city, and I walked toward it across the plain. I was excited to take a closer look.

"As I approached, I noticed that I heard no sounds of life within it, and no one along the road going in or coming out. Soon I found myself outside the gates, and I noticed a man approaching from within the city. He looked like Rulalin, or like Rulalin appeared to me in my vision in Amaan Sul. We looked at each other, and he seemed to both recognize and not recognize me. And then, surprising even myself, I spoke to him. I said, 'Will you not come out?'

"He didn't answer, he only gazed at me. I continued. 'Can you not see that it is better out here than in the city?' And I motioned for him to look at the beautiful grassland and rolling hills.

"He looked past me and at last he spoke. 'How can this be?'

"My words came clearly and surely, but they were from me and yet not from me at the same time. I said, 'Many things now spoiled will be renewed and remade. Come out.'

"He stood watching me but made no move to come out, and I knew then that I was not to enter the city. After a moment, I turned and walked back the way I had come. Shortly after, I awoke. I do not understand what happened."

Valzaan sat still upon his horse, the look on his face thoughtful. "I cannot tell you all that it might mean, but I can tell you that you have been given a powerful gift. Allfather has not granted its like to many. The power to appear in another man's dream is not to be taken lightly."

"I was in Rulalin's dream?"

"Yes."

"Why not say that I saw him in mine?"

"Because that wouldn't be true. Benjiah, before I met your father and his companions on the road to Sulare, I appeared to him in his dreams. Allfather has granted me the same ability, though it is not something I can exercise at will. It happens when He chooses and for His purposes. You were a messenger to Rulalin, and the words you spoke that were yours but not your own were from Allfather."

Benjiah stared at Valzaan. "So what do I do?"

"Keep going forward, and keep looking to Allfather for strength and guidance. I will teach you what I can about all these things, but ultimately you will learn from Allfather all you need to know."

The rushing sensation returned, and the next thing Benjiah knew, his horse was moving slowly forward again.

As soon as they emerged from slow time, Pedraal called out to them and spurred his horse to a gallop. They rushed to catch up, and within moments, Benjiah could see what had attracted his uncle's attention. There were bodies of men and horses lying scattered in the tall grass around the road.

"A patrol," Pedraal said as he dropped from his horse and checked one of the men lying in the grass, his body ripped open. "These wounds were from wolves."

"Not all the wounds were from wolves," Pedraan called from nearby. He pointed to another man lying facedown with an arrow in his back.

"Black Wolves and men," Pedraal said, walking farther from the road, surveying the scene more closely. "And this," he added, "is the footprint of a Malekim."

"Men, Malekim, and Black Wolves have been here?" Benjiah asked.

"Yes, and recently," Pedraal answered. "Some of this blood is still wet."

"I can see them," Valzaan said, his eyes closed. "There are perhaps a dozen men on horseback, along with perhaps twice as many wolves and Malekim. They are headed east, toward Amaan Sul."

"Then we must follow," Benjiah called out. "We must try to overtake them, or at least find a patrol and warn them!"

"We cannot," Valzaan answered as he raised his hand to point in the other direction. "For our road lies that way."

Benjiah looked up, seeing for the first time that Gyrin was now in view. "But Valzaan, my mother and the city, they must be warned!"

"We must leave them in Allfather's hands. We cannot afford the delay. Even as we are beyond their help now, so they are beyond ours."

"But Valzaan," Benjiah started.

"Benjiah," Pedraal said, walking back through the dead bodies to the road. "We have spread the word among the patrols to be alert. The city is strong. Such a small party won't pose much threat to the city's defenses. We must follow Valzaan."

Benjiah turned and stared back over the wide fields. He had thought he was leaving safety to ride into danger. Now danger was riding on Amaan Sul, and he had no way to warn them.

Not far ahead, Koshti slid silently into the fading twilight, the orange in his body eerily illuminated by the rays of sunset, making the contrast with his black stripes all the more pronounced. Aljeron looked up toward the crest of their narrow path, and he could just make out the smoke of a fire coming from inside the ruins of Zul Arnoth.

He pushed his weary horse the rest of the way. Ten days on the road from Shalin Bel, and most of those days they had pressed fairly hard with little rest and no breaks save for meals. He would be glad to dismount tonight, to sit around a fire with friends, and to look forward to a more permanent end, not only to his journey, but to his pursuit of Rulalin.

He looked over his shoulder at the others. Evrim rode with

Caan and behind them came the Great Bear, their dark forms hard even at this short distance to make out clearly in the dissipating light. If he could barely see them, and he knew they were there, how hard must it be for Great Bear to be detected at night by those who weren't looking for them? Their stealth rivaled Koshti's.

The steep ground below him leveled off, and looking ahead Aljeron saw the broken pillars of what once were Zul Arnoth's mighty gates.

Not for the first time, Aljeron wondered what the city might have looked like a thousand years ago. Back then, at the end of the Second Age, Zul Arnoth was a city to rival Shalin Bel and Fel Edorath, a prosperous trade center surrounded by large farms and fertile land. The War of Division brought unprecedented fire and destruction to the city. And, when the War of Division and the war against Malek were finally ended, the Assembly decided Zul Arnoth would not be rebuilt. Its ruin would serve as a reminder to future generations of the danger of division, just as Sularc would serve as a beacon of hope for future unity.

Some disagreed with the decision, but most people of the city had already fled either east to Fel Edorath or west to Shalin Bel. So, while some returned to the area and tried to transform the now trampled ground back into a prosperous farming region, it was hard work and few were able to persist long enough to find a return for their labor. Today, the area was all but deserted.

As Aljeron passed through the broken stone pillars of the old gate, he thought once more about the irony of coming here on his way to finish a war against Fel Edorath. What had made Zul Arnoth a desirable location for armies a thousand years ago remained: It stood on the highest ground for leagues in any direction, and its stone walls, even in ruins, helped to make it even more defensible. Both he and Rulalin had often sought refuge in Zul Arnoth to rest and regroup during the bitter seven-year conflict. Now, he hoped that the next time he passed this way, it would all be over.

The majority of the rubble had long since been carted off for various uses, like strengthening the city's outer wall. Only a few stubborn structures remained within view of the main road. From behind one of those, a dark figure stepped, and called to him, "Aljeron?"

"Saegan?"

"Yes." The figure moved out of the shadow. As Saegan drew nearer, Aljeron could make out his old friend's features more clearly in the light of the waning but bright moon.

"I hoped it was you. We thought you'd be here today."

"Yes, we made good time," Aljeron replied as he dropped from his horse. He clasped Saegan's arm in greeting, and the two men began to walk side by side as Aljeron led his horse the rest of the way.

"You have Great Bear in your party," Saegan said matter-of-factly, as though observing that the air was cool or the night was pretty.

Aljeron smiled. "We do indeed, and that is not the only surprise we have for you."

They emerged into what had once been the town square, and there tall grass and bushes and even a few trees grew. To the east, sheltered by some buildings that were more intact than most of the others, was a large fire with many men grouped around it.

Saegan and Aljeron led the others over to it, and as the men around the fire saw them approach, they stood to greet their immediate superior and their general.

"Sit, enjoy the fire," Aljeron said, acknowledging their tribute with his outstretched hand. "Take your rest while you may. Tomorrow we ride. If Allfather be with us, we will soon be finished with this siege and this war."

A cheer followed, and then the soldiers returned to their seats and their conversations. Aljeron turned to Saegan. "Once, they would have cheered when I said, 'Tomorrow we ride,' not when I said, 'We will soon be finished.'"

Saegan nodded. "But we are wiser now, aren't we?"

"Yes," Aljeron agreed, "we are."

"Well, well, if it isn't another one of my students embroiled in this fine mess."

Evrim and Caan approached. "Caan?" Saegan said with pleasant surprise, "what are you doing here?"

"I've come to help Aljeron finish this job so we can have peace once more. What are you doing here?"

"I am here with a small detachment of Enthanim. We came west at the start of the war and have been here ever since."

At that point, the three Great Bear ambled up and joined the small circle. A hush fell over the soldiers. "Saegan," Caan began, "you remember Sarneth."

"Sarneth!" Saegan said, looking even more surprised. "When I saw Great Bear with Aljeron, it didn't occur to me that you might be one of them. Welcome."

"Thank you," Sarneth said. "I have come with my son and Arintol, whom you will remember from Lindan Wood many years ago."

"Indeed. Your strength and wisdom are most welcome here."

A figure from the far side of the fire rose and approached them slowly. Saegan noticed the approach. "Another of your students is here, Caan. Bryar has also been with us from the beginning."

It was Caan's turn for his eyes to grow wide as Bryar approached. She was dressed in the same riding clothes the others wore and had her hair pulled back tightly into a braid. Her face was hard, even grim. "Welcome," she said simply, nodding to them.

"Well, it's almost a reunion here," Caan said.

"Yes," said Aljeron, his voice both warm and grave. "And it is fitting for we are gathered to find and punish one of our own. It is a shame that this is what brings us together, but so it is. I am thankful to be among friends, even as we look forward to the hard work that remains."

Soon they were gathered around a second, smaller fire, not far from the rest of the Enthanim under Saegan's command. It felt every bit as good to be off his horse as Aljeron had hoped, and it felt even better than he had imagined to be sitting with Saegan, Bryar, Caan, and Sarneth, reliving old memories of the Summerland. Evrim occasionally asked questions, but mostly just soaked it all in along with the other Great Bear. Aljeron could see on Evrim's face the pleasure he himself felt when they talked of the past and of Joraiem's place in it.

Eventually, though, the happy memories gave way to more pressing issues, and the talk turned to the present. Aljeron and Evrim, along with their guests from the southlands, listened as Saegan reported conditions at Fel Edorath.

"The city walls may still be strong, but inside the city is tottering. The people are faint from hunger, and every day citizens slip away by night and flee to our camps. By all accounts, disease and sickness increase as the food supply decreases. Soldiers watch both day and night from the walls, but there have been no attempts to reestablish the food smuggling efforts that we disrupted earlier this month. When we come at them this time, I believe they will surrender quickly."

"Our men are ready?" Aljeron asked.

"Yes, physically and mentally. I will not lie, they are weary. Still, they are eager to have this over, and they know what that will require."

"And Rulalin?"

"He has not been seen since you last left."

Aljeron gazed into the fire. What is Rulalin doing in there?

Why did he continue to lurk behind his walls when he must see that the war was about to end? What was obvious to all of those on the outside must surely also be obvious to him. Aljeron shook his head at the mystery of it all.

He looked up through the night sky at the bright sliver of the failing Full Autumn moon. Whatever Rulalin was thinking, it didn't matter. Neither denial nor hiding would save him. The city was going to fall, and when it did, Rulalin would not escape the justice so long overdue.

"It is time."

Rulalin shuddered, and a chill rippled through his body as he looked from Tashmiren, who stood with only one foot in the room, back to Soran, who sat with him at the table. They both rose, moved to the door, and soon were walking with Tashmiren through the labyrinth of indistinguishable halls and corridors.

It was midmorning, a little after breakfast, just two days after they were given their partial tour of the Mountain. They had spent all day yesterday in their rooms, talking, eating, sleeping, sitting, thinking, and wondering when they would be allowed out again and when they would be brought before Malek. Now it appeared that both things had happened at the same time.

Warm beads of sweat rolled down Rulalin's forehead and dripped on his cheek. He reached up to wipe his forehead, realizing that he must be very nervous. The temperature inside the Mountain was never hot, not even warm, and they had not been walking long. He wasn't surprised, exactly, but he had hoped to maintain his composure a bit better. If he was sweating like this now, what would it be like to stand in the same room with Malek?

Mercifully, their journey passed like a blur, and they stopped in a small, circular room before Rulalin had time to worry much more about it. The room was drab and decidedly ordinary, and essentially empty except for a narrow stairwell ascending through a hole in the ceiling. A handful of men sat in the room, talking softly among themselves. Tashmiren approached them and joined in the quiet conversation.

Rulalin looked at Soran, and he saw in his face the same anxiety that must have been showing in his own. "Ready?" he whispered.

Soran shrugged. "I guess so."

There was no time for more. Tashmiren had returned to them. "All right. We are expected above. Rulalin will come up with me. Soran, you'll stay here."

"What do you mean?"

"I mean you will stay here while Rulalin and I go up."

"Why?" Soran asked, his voice betraying indignation.

A glimmer of rage swept across Tashmiren's face, and he stepped to Soran and looked him in the eye. "You don't question me, ever. I don't care how important you are in Fel Edorath. You're nobody here. Do you understand?"

Rulalin looked at the fury boiling in Soran's face. He reached out his hand and grabbed Soran's arm tightly. "Soran is a good soldier," Rulalin said quietly to Tashmiren while looking steadily at Soran. "He understands the chain of command. Right?"

Soran nodded begrudgingly. "Yes."

"Good," Tashmiren said, not backing away. "I am glad he does. I hope he is able to remember it in the future."

Rulalin held onto Soran's arm until he could see that the danger had passed. It had been a precarious moment. He let go as Soran lowered his head, defeated, and stepped back.

"Is it permitted for me to ask why Malek wants to see only me?" Rulalin asked carefully. "We have always thought we both would have the opportunity to meet Malek, and you have never discouraged that thinking."

Tashmiren shrugged. "I only know what I am told. I was told to bring you both here, but I was also told that only you were to be brought up. I don't know why. It doesn't really matter, though, does it? Yours is the voice of authority, right? Soran will do whatever you decide. His allegiance is to you, and when you swear allegiance to Malek, he will also be sworn, won't he?"

"He will," Rulalin answered, looking at the narrow stairs.

"Well, if we're through with the questions, let's go up. As I told you, it isn't wise to delay when he expects you."

Tashmiren started over to the stairs, and Rulalin followed, nodding slightly to Soran, who stood with his arms crossed, watching them go. The men at the foot of the stairwell parted as Tashmiren and Rulalin started up. Soon they had ascended into the virtual darkness of a much larger room.

Rulalin did not have long to study his surroundings, for Tashmiren immediately directed him to a chair. Two or three torches at the perimeter of the room were the only source of light, as the luminescent stones that typically provided light elsewhere in the Mountain were not to be found here.

Rulalin could see no sign of Malek's creatures, nor any other men. He realized that deep in the heart of the Mountain, there would be no need for a guard. Still, he had anticipated something like a throne surrounded by at least a few of Malek's followers.

The room was large and rectangular, with the opening for the stairs more or less right in the middle. Before being led straight ahead to the chair, Rulalin had managed a quick glance at the other side of the room, and all he could see was a dark, thick curtain with a faint pattern that he couldn't make out.

When they had crossed the distance from the top of the stairs to the chair, Tashmiren sat Rulalin down forcibly so that he faced the dark rock wall. "Sit here and look straight ahead. You will watch this wall for the entire time that the master speaks to you. If you turn around, you will die. It's that simple. Do you understand?"

"Yes."

Tashmiren drew his sword. "Good. It would be a shame for things to go badly now after having come all this way. Besides, you can't see through the curtain anyway. It would be a vain death if you died trying to get a glimpse of him."

"I won't."

With sword in hand, Tashmiren took a seat in another chair right behind Rulalin. What direction he was facing or what he was doing with the sword, Rulalin could only guess. He wasn't about to turn around and look.

For several moments he sat in silence, facing the dark wall. Eventually his eyes adjusted to the darkness, and he could see that the rock was smooth. He reached forward with his hand and slid his fingers across the wall. It felt cool, like polished stone from a riverbed.

As he was contemplating the wall, he heard a slight creaking from the other side of the room. It sounded to him like a door, probably a heavy door, swinging open on an old hinge. The creak was followed by the sound of uneven footsteps, and he thought he could make out a sound like that of something being dragged across the floor. Goosebumps rose on his arm, and he felt the chill as he shuddered again. Then the footsteps stopped, and there was another creaking, the sound of someone settling into a chair.

"Rulalin Tarasir," a voice spoke from across the dark room. The voice was rich, deep, and sonorous. Rulalin found it almost soothing. "You have come to see me at last."

There was a brief silence, and Rulalin, though no question had been asked of him, felt obliged to speak. "Yes, Master. I have come."

Rulalin could hear his voice saying the word, "Master," and though it seemed a strange thing to say, he did not stop himself.

"So, you know me for your Master already. That's a good start. Do you know why it is a good start, Rulalin?"

"No, Master."

"It is a good start because there are only two types of men in Kirthanin. There are those who know me as their Master now, and there are those who will know me as their Master later, and most of those will die learning the lesson. It is good that this is not a lesson you still need to learn, for this is the only difference among men that really matters."

There was another silence, and Rulalin again wondered if he was expected to speak. He wiped sweat from his face again.

"Why have you come to me?" came the question from across the room.

"I need your help."

"Yes, you do, and I do not need yours."

There was another pause, and if Rulalin had felt nervous before, he was terrified now. "It is also good that you know now, Rulalin, that I do not really need your help. My victory is assured, with or without you."

The silence this time was longer, and eventually Rulalin worked up the courage to speak. "Then why did you send Tashmiren to me?"

"I did not say that I do not want the help you offer. I said only that I do not need your help. There is a difference. Kirthanin no longer has the strength to resist me; however, if Fel Edorath comes to me, my victory will not only come easier, it will come sooner. That is why I extended the offer of peace to you, and that is why I want you to extend the same offer to those we are going to face. I know that you are not welcome in the counsels of the Novaana anymore, that you are an exile of the Assembly, but even so, once you were one of their number, and many of the foes I will face are people you once knew. I am authorizing you to bring the same terms of peace that I offered you to them. Do you understand?"

"I do, Master." He hesitated, then added, "I will do what I can."

"Good. Perhaps there are others who will see the wisdom of accepting my offer as you have."

"There may be."

"Now," Malek continued, "there is something that you want from me in exchange for your service, something beyond just being spared from death, is there not?"

"There is."

"And do you really want her that much?"

"I do."

"Is she all you ask?"

"Yes, unless . . ."

"Unless what?"

Rulalin rubbed his sweating forehead on his sleeve. In his head a voice was asking him why he was trying to bargain with Malek, but he continued. "Unless the rumor I have heard is true, that the remnant of Nolthanin will be allowed to settle in the northlands after you have conquered Kirthanin, free to live in a land of only men, a land loyal to you, of course, but a land of men."

"So I have promised Farimaal."

"Then I also ask that I be allowed to take her there when the war is over, to settle among the Nolthanim."

"I will not speak for them or for Farimaal, but if they will have you, then I would not oppose it. Is there anything else?"

"No, Master."

"Then it is time. You are promising me that you will serve me totally, in all that I command and direct from this point forward. You are promising to bring to my aid as many soldiers of Fel Edorath as will follow you. You are also swearing to lead them in my service for the duration of the war, for as long as you live or I demand your service. Furthermore, you will do all that you can as the war progresses to bring others into allegiance with me, that my victory may come as quickly as possible. I, for my part, grant you life. I also grant you Wylla Someris to be your own, whether in Nolthanin or elsewhere. The terms are clear?"

"They are."

"Then swear now the oath. Rulalin Tarasir, do you swear to serve me without question and without fail from this moment, knowing that your life will be duly forfeit if you are false to me in any way?"

Rulalin felt the chill and the shudder a third time, and he rubbed his wet palms up and down along his legs. He swallowed, then spoke, "I swear."

"Good. You are sworn, and you are mine."

BREAKING

1

GYRIN

BENJIAH TUMBLED BACKWARD onto the ground as Suruna flew out of his hand and landed several feet away in the underbrush. He rolled onto his stomach and looked up from where he lay to see the Silent One stepping toward him, sword drawn. His chest ached where he had been struck, but he tried to back up on all fours as fast as he could, unable to think of anything that might save his life. The Malekim drew his long curved blade and gripped it tightly in his powerful hand, glaring down at him with rage and malice. Benjiah had shot two of his companions with cyranic arrows and had been reaching for a third when this Malekim had surprised him from behind a nearby tree, knocking him off his feet with the back of his arm.

Benjiah had more to fear than the back of the Malekim's arm now, and his mind sought desperately for a way out. Fumbling around on the forest floor, he felt a large, solid tree branch and grabbed it instinctively. He doubted he could do any damage with it, but maybe he could defend himself against the Malekim's attack.

But then, just as he prepared to raise the branch in his defense, Pedraal came crashing through the underbrush, shouting. The creature turned to face this new foe, and soon they were exchanging blows with sword and battle-axe. As strong as his uncle Pedraal was, Benjiah could see that he was overmatched. The Malekim lashed out viciously, his sword whistling as it sliced through the air and met Pedraal's axe, which likewise flashed up and down in defense.

Benjiah scrambled for the area where he thought Suruna might have landed. His quiver had slipped down to the crook of his arm as he tumbled backward, fortunately, so he didn't think his arrows had been broken by the fall, but they wouldn't do him any good unless he could find Suruna. Then, as he searched through the undergrowth, he saw the tip of the bow. Grabbing it quickly, he stood, whirled around, and soon had an arrow nocked and ready.

There was no need to fire, though, for as he turned, he saw Pedraal hook the Malekim's sword with one side of his axe-head and yank it from his grasp. He could hear the grunt as his uncle pulled. The creature stepped in toward Pedraal to try to grab him before he could prepare to swing again. Pedraal was ready for him, though, and was already sidestepping away while he brought the battle-axe around in a short, powerful stroke. One of the blades struck the Malekim directly in the waist, and the creature doubled over as blood poured from his midsection, down the thick grey hide of his legs. Pedraal wrenched the axe free and with another swift blow brought the blade down from above, severing the Malekim's head.

Benjiah walked over to where his uncle stood, panting, covered with sweat. "Are you all right, Uncle?"

Pedraal nodded. "And you?" he said after a moment as he straightened up.

"Yes, thanks to you. I don't think I would have been, though, if you'd come along any later."

Pedraal smiled. "I've got to keep you alive. If I don't, your mother will kill me, and I don't stand a chance against her."

Benjiah smiled too, and they walked together back to the Old Mountain Road, which they had been traveling through Gyrin for a week now. Once back on the road, they spotted Pedraan and Valzaan, leading their horses in their direction. When they were all together, Pedraal looked at Pedraan and said, "Well?"

"I caught the one I was after. I smashed him up against a tree with my war hammer and crushed his chest. He's not going anywhere. And you?"

"I caught mine too, but when I got back here, I found one about to hack into Benjiah." Turning to Benjiah, he continued, "Did you miss? What happened?"

"I didn't miss. I hit the other two fine. This was a fifth one. I don't know where he came from. He packed quite a punch."

"Let me see," Pedraal said lifting Benjiah's tunic gingerly. Benjiah pulled it up and over his head, feeling the cool air on his exposed chest. A line of bruising ran across his ribs, and his uncle grimaced as he stared at it. "That's going to hurt for a while. Did you feel anything snap or break in there?"

"Not that I could tell."

Pedraal nodded. "You come from pretty sturdy stock, you do, on both sides of the family."

"So there were five, not four," Valzaan said.

"It looks that way," Pedraal answered.

"If five, why not six?" Pedraan added, scanning the nearby trees.

"No reason," Valzaan answered. "Still, there is nothing we can do about it now. If more have run already, they are long gone now. All we can do is press forward."

"That's the second patrol we've encountered since we

came here, and as far as we know, we've killed every Malekim who's seen us." Pedraal looked back along the road. "The alarm could be raised any day by a hidden foe; no reason to be especially worried about that today. It's out of our control."

"That's right," Valzaan answered, "and whether they know about us being here or not, we must move forward as quickly as we're able. We must be almost directly due south of Agia Muldonai by now. Let's press on, so that the sooner we come through Gyrin, the sooner we may find Aljeron."

"Do you think these two groups of Malekim were headed to Amaan Sul?" Benjiah asked.

"Amaan Sul?" Pedraan asked.

"Yes, like the raiding party whose handiwork we found before entering Gyrin."

"I would think not," Valzaan said. "With so few in both patrols, neither would make an effective raiding party. I doubt they were intended for any destination beyond the wood, and likely they weren't meant to go even that far."

"Either way, they're all dead," Pedraal added. "They won't pose a threat to anyone now."

They mounted in silence, and Benjiah put his tunic back on, covering his aching chest from the chilly air. He put his fingers gently on his wound, but the bruised region was so tender that even the lightest pressure hurt. Riding wasn't going to be any fun, but he was eager to get through Gyrin. He pushed the pain from his mind and spurred his horse onward behind the others.

Despite Pedraal's confidence, Benjiah was worried. He had been worried since they entered Gyrin. He kept thinking of the dead bodies of the Enthanim patrol, some nineteen men and horses. They had been surprised and slaughtered. Perhaps if Pedraal's warning could have reached them sooner, they might have been alert and prepared. Either way, Benjiah had found the troops and their killers often on his mind.

He had tried, every night when they stopped to rest, to see through the eyes of a windhover, in the hopes that he might be able to see Amaan Sul as Valzaan had. He didn't know that this would serve any ultimate good, but he had tried all the same. None of his efforts had been successful. It seemed he was going to have to trust his mother and his home into Allfather's hands as Valzaan had said.

They pushed forward until not long before dark. Of course, there was a kind of perpetual dark in Gyrin under the dense canopy of leaves. Even so, they had all gotten used to reading the varying degrees of half-light the trees did allow, and they did not halt until they had exhausted all the light they could count on for the day.

The remainder of their day had brought them no more difficulties. In fact, they rarely saw or heard anything along the Old Mountain Road inside Gyrin. Except for the two encounters with patrols of the Voiceless, their entire journey in the wood had been eerily quiet. Benjiah, who was no stranger to hunting in the woods, had noticed almost immediately upon entering the forest the near-total absence of any form of life. Some varied species of birds fluttered among the upper reaches of the trees, where the light of day was but a surge of the wings, but down among roots and trunks of the trees, little other than crawling insects and burrowing bugs could be found by Benjiah's watchful eye. He was glad they had entered Gyrin fully provisioned.

Despite the excitement of the day, Benjiah had little appetite for supper, and he did not linger awake for long. They had been riding hard, every day for a week, and Benjiah did not know how much farther they had to go. He didn't even know that getting out of Gyrin would bring a slower pace or rest, for Valzaan was determined to get them to Fel Edorath as soon as possible. And, if the prophet was right, the real work of their journey would only then begin.

The following day passed much the same, silent and slow, riding league after league through the dense wood. At times, Benjiah felt his eyes flutter shut while he rode, and he had to will them open, usually by recalling Valzaan's warning that the apparent emptiness of Gyrin ought not to lull them into complacency or a sense of safety. While few creatures, either good or ill, made their home in Gyrin anymore, almost all the creatures that still passed through the wood were servants of Malek, and most of those could bring death without warning if they lowered their defenses and allowed themselves to be surprised.

And so it was in a moment of temporary alertness, that Benjiah caught sight of something unusual out of the corner of his eye. He slowed his horse to a halt and turned to his right as he peered north off the road into the thick trees. His pause caught the attention of his companions, and soon his uncles and Valzaan had circled back to where he sat silently, and they sat beside him. Benjiah turned to Pedraal and asked, "Do you see anything?"

Pedraal looked intently ahead, then started to nod. "I do," he said, turning to Benjiah, wonder showing in his eyes. "Pedraan?"

"Me too," his brother answered from his other side. "It looks to be a fair piece in, but it is definitely lighter through these trees."

"Lighter, you say?" Valzaan asked, his empty eyes appearing to stare in the direction the others had been gazing.

"Yes," Benjiah answered. "Somewhere north of here, there must be an opening of some kind in the forest. It is not as dark as it is here."

"I wonder . . ." Valzaan said almost to himself before going quiet. The twins looked at Benjiah, and all three turned to wait on the prophet. "We should be far enough along, but I can hardly believe it would still be there. If it is, I should like to go there again. It would bring encouragement to me in these dark days."

"What would?" Pedraal asked as the prophet went quiet again.

"There used to be an open pavilion, not far south of the foot of the Mountain. Men of the Second Age and even the Third, before Corindel, would gather there to call upon Allfather's name and seek direction from His prophets. Of course, since Gyrin fell into Malek's hands, the pavilion has been abandoned. But we are about the right distance into the forest, and the pavilion would be within reach, north of the Old Mountain Road."

"Let's ride in and see," Benjiah said eagerly, for suddenly he felt drawn to investigate the light. "Whatever the explanation, I should very much like to see the sun and sky again, even if we have to go a little bit out of our way."

"I say we keep going," Pedraan answered. "We'll lose the rest of the day if we do this, not to mention part of tomorrow. Besides, who knows what is up ahead? Maybe it is a gathering place for Silent Ones and Black Wolves, even giants. The sooner we get out of Gyrin, the sooner we'll have sun and sky again on a regular basis."

"While normally I would agree with you, Pedraan, I second Benjiah's suggestion," Valzaan replied. "Not every diversion is a delay or distraction, and sometimes rest and refuge in the right place can provide more than you think. I say we go, though quickly and carefully, and if it is the place I think it is, I will be glad of our detour."

Benjiah looked at his uncles, but neither spoke, no doubt not wanting to disagree with Valzaan openly, whatever they might be thinking. So, with their silent assent, Benjiah moved off the road and into the trees.

The way was difficult, for the undergrowth was dense and rough. Thorns pierced his pants and flesh, and he grimaced as he had to remove more than a few along the way. What's more, he had to pause a few times to peel back prickly vines that had lashed themselves to him and his horse. Even so, the light ahead grew steadily brighter, and like a beacon it beckoned him.

At last they arrived at a semi-clearing, where the underbrush was still thick but the trees were not. Looking up, Benjiah saw the sky. It was cloudy, so the sun itself wasn't visible, but it was the sky nonetheless. In addition to the sky, though, and more arresting, was the Mountain, rising above the trees and disappearing into the clouds, closer than he had ever seen it. For several moments, he sat and stared, and the twins stared too, all of them drinking in the air, as though the absence of leaves improved the quality of the oxygen. The sheer magnitude of the Mountain was almost overwhelming. The slope at the bottom was not overly steep, but perhaps halfway up the part he could see, the mountainside rose more steeply. He didn't know if he could have seen the top, even had the day been clear.

While they sat, Valzaan pushed forward, and when Benjiah took his attention from the world above, he saw the prophet on the far side of the clearing, dismounting. Riding toward him, Benjiah realized that Valzaan had found the pavilion. The trees had almost overgrown it, but it was still there, its long, angled roof covering the open meeting place of the Novaana of Kirthanin's past.

Benjiah dismounted and walked into the pavilion behind the prophet. The floor had once been solid, but now weeds sprang up through cracks. Lying among the weeds were shards of wood and other pieces of ancient furniture, long since abandoned but not completely destroyed or decayed. "So this is it," Benjiah said quietly.

"This is it."

Benjiah stooped down and, reaching into the weeds,

pulled out a long, solid piece of wood. It was carefully carved, and grooves wound around it from top to bottom.

"What is it?" Pedraal said as he stepped up beside Benjiah.

"I think it is the leg of a chair."

"Or a table, perhaps."

"Maybe a small table," Benjiah replied. "Whatever it's from, it was well made and has probably lain here almost a thousand years."

"The roof is still mostly intact," Pedraan said, and Benjiah looked up at the sturdy roof overhead. "The things left behind in here have been protected for the most part. Still, it's amazing that anything is left."

"It is indeed," Valzaan added, moving forward through the pavilion as the others followed. "I take it as a sign, for some things do weather the storms of life and come through safely on the other side. Not all that was has passed away, and not all that is will disappear either. Come," Valzaan said, "for now that we are here, there is something else I should like to find if it remains, and the light we have will not last long."

Valzaan moved beyond the pavilion into a patch of undergrowth shaded by the tops of the nearby trees. Several spans from the pavilion, he hesitated, then moved off to his right. Benjiah and the twins followed close behind. A moment later, Valzaan was pulling thick, red-brown vines back to expose a small column of large round stones. The stones had been piled on one another about chest high and half a span across. Benjiah helped rip away the weeds, and soon the small structure was free of the plants that had almost completely concealed it.

"What is it?" Benjiah asked.

"It is a memorial, erected by the Novaana of Kirthanin in the first year of the Second Age. Malek had just been driven from Suthanin across the Southern Ocean to the Forbidden Isle, and the remains of the Assembly gathered here at the foot of the Mountain to seek Allfather's face. Here Erevir, the great prophet of the Second Age, appeared among men for the first time. In the First Age, the Twelve had spoken for Allfather among men and Great Bear, but the Twelve were no more. From that moment until now, Allfather has spoken through prophets, and Erevir was the first."

Benjiah reached out and felt the stones, which were cold and smooth beneath the dirt that had accumulated over the years. "Do the stones represent more than Erevir's appearance?"

"Yes, they were to be a reminder of his message, for he came with a prophecy that was to be spread throughout all the land and remembered thereafter until the restoration of all things."

Valzaan fell silent, so Benjiah prodded him on. "Yes?"

Valzaan closed his eyes and reached out, placing his hand upon the stone. "He rode up from the Old Mountain Road to the place where the men were gathered. They had come from all over Kirthanin to seek each other's counsel and the will of Allfather in the light of the ruin Malek had brought. Those assembled grew quiet as he approached, not only because he was striking in appearance, but because they could sense the presence of Allfather, which was confirmed when Erevir spoke. He announced himself and proclaimed for the first time the commission he had received, saying:

So says Allfather:

There is blood on the Mountain.
It stains the City
And soaks the ground.

The Fountain is defiled.
It no longer flows
And cannot cleanse.

The deep waters will flow again.
And then the stains
Will be washed clean.

But until that day shall come,
The Holy Mountain is
Forbidden to us all.

Valzaan stopped and lifted his hands from the stones, turning to face the others. "When Erevir came, the men of Kirthanin were afraid and overwhelmed. His news was disheartening, for they knew then that the Holy Mountain was closed to them and would remain closed until the blood upon the Mountain could be atoned for. And yet, Erevir's words offered hope, for he spoke of a day when the Mountain would be clean again. They were like us in many ways, for we know that the future before us is grim, but we also know that there is hope. Most importantly, though they didn't know what to do, they knew where to turn. So do we."

Benjiah noticed some stones in the grass near the memorial. Stepping over and stooping down, he confirmed that they were indeed just like those stacked next to them. "Valzaan, there are some stones here on the ground. Do you think they were supposed to be part of the memorial?"

"If they are like the others, yes."

"Then we should put them back, shouldn't we?"

"It would be most appropriate."

Benjiah bent over and picked up one of the stones, which was heavier than he had expected. He hoisted it to the top of the stack and placed it as gently as he could. Pedraal and Pedraan helped, and soon they had added almost two more layers to the top.

As they had been gathered at the memorial, dark clouds moved around the Mountain from its northern side, and soon the sky was dominated by them. A ripple of thunder rolled through the heavens, echoing off the nearby Mountain and rumbling across the treetops. Flashes of lightning appeared, moving both horizontally through the clouds and also falling from the clouds upon the mountainside high above them. The wind picked up and the great trees began to bend and bow, loose leaves flying off and swirling through the Full Autumn air. Suddenly, great drops of rain started to fall, pelting the leaves and making thousands of light slapping sounds all around them.

"Come, let us shelter in the pavilion," Valzaan said as they all turned and made their way the short distance back.

Once underneath the long sloping roof, they saw indeed that it had not weathered the Third Age entirely intact, for the rain exposed several leaks. Nevertheless, they were able to find some reasonably dry patches, and they settled down on the ancient floor. For a long time they sat, watching the storm and listening to the rain. The thunder rolled and peeled, booming sometimes for what seemed like ages, then disappearing, only to return again in greater force. The strikes appeared to be moving down the Mountain, getting nearer. Then a brilliant flash lit up the clearing and a tree south of the pavilion seemed to explode, showering sparks from its crown as the top half tilted and fell, disappearing with a crash into the trees next to it.

"That was close!" Pedraan said, still gazing out at the place where the lightning had struck.

"Too close," Benjiah answered.

But, as close as it was, it was as close as the lightning got, for the storms continued to roll south over the forest, eventually leaving little more than steady rainfall behind. Soon, the attention of the twins was turned to gathering some dry branches that lay under the protection of the edges of the pavilion and building a fire. Dinner was just being served when the sun finally sank behind the distant trees.

Benjiah did not feel much like doing anything more than eating, so he sat quietly, chewing on his supper, while Pedraal and Pedraan talked with Valzaan. They had all fallen into the pattern of riding in silence, for many reasons, and so the evening meal had become for them the only really social time they had. Tonight, though, Benjiah was content to sit and contemplate Erevir and his message. How had it been for him, Benjiah wondered, receiving the call from Allfather to go to the Mountain and speak Allfather's words to the waiting men? Had he felt the burning presence of Allfather flood through him? Had he heard a voice inside his head or in the heavens? With no one there to guide him through the experience, how had he coped with all the questions? Had he slipped into *tor-rim redara* or seen through the eyes of windhovers or anything else? Benjiah had been called to be a prophet, but he was not alone in his call and there had been others before him. Erevir had been the first.

He wondered if Erevir had trained Valzaan, or perhaps Erevir had trained some other prophet who had in turn trained Valzaan. Maybe there was an unbroken line of prophets, going back to Erevir, like the lineage of a royal family. He had thought often in his youth of his royal family, but this was a heritage that was even more remarkable.

Slowly, Benjiah became aware of the conversation around him. They were talking about Aljeron. Specifically, they were discussing what they should do when at last they had found him if Fel Edorath had not yet fallen.

"And what should we do then?" Pedraal was asking. "Aljeron's been trying to lay his hands on Rulalin for seven years."

"Seventeen, really," Pedraan corrected.

"Seventeen," Pedraal acknowledged. "How do we convince him to abandon the siege?"

"Aljeron is not a fool," Valzaan answered. "When he understands what has brought us and what is coming, his first thoughts will be for the safety of Shalin Bel and his people. I don't think it matters much what state we find Aljeron in, because whether he holds the city and whether he has captured Rulalin does not apply to the really pressing questions that Malek's coming raises. A concluded siege may make it easier to turn our focus elsewhere, but a battle not yet fought might mean a greater number of soldiers to stand against Malek's army."

"If the city still stands," Pedraan said, "we could petition Rulalin and the people of Fel Edorath to join us in preparing defenses against the forces that are coming from the Mountain. They will listen to us when they see you are among us, won't they?"

"They might, but I don't know that there will be any use in preparing defenses for Fel Edorath. Aljeron has been starving the city. It will be little prepared to defend itself against the kind of assault that is coming."

"You're saying we should abandon Fel Edorath to Malek?"

"I'm saying that my chief desire is to keep all Kirthanin from being swallowed in darkness. We may have to sacrifice more than Fel Edorath along the way. We may need to entreat Aljeron and all the fighting men of Shalin Bel and Fel Edorath alike to fall back as we search for a plan that offers us hope."

"And where do we fall back to? Even if we retreat all the way to Shalin Bel, is there any hope that we will be better prepared to defend it? Will the soldiers be better rested or better prepared to fight Malek there?"

"I don't know, Pedraal, which is why we need to find Aljeron while there is still time. Malek's coming may take all options from us, for his plans I cannot see. If it is really hope you look for, look not to Fel Edorath or Shalin Bel. Look not to Amaan Sul, either. Your hope is not in any place that you hold dear, for you have not the strength to defend them, nor do we. Your hope is in Allfather, and we will need to look to Him, wherever we flee and wherever we fight, for unless He sends us aid, the best we can do is prolong our demise."

"That isn't very cheery," Pedraan said.

"It depends on how you look at it," Valzaan answered. "You are focusing too much on your lack and not enough on Allfather's power. He has provided for Kirthanin's defense before, and His arm has not grown weaker, nor His eyes less watchful."

The conversation came to a halt, and they sat in the dark, the crackling of the fire filling the void their silence had created. "It has stopped raining," Benjiah said, standing and walking to the edge of the pavilion.

"So it has," Valzaan replied, coming over to stand beside him. "And what has been on your mind, Benjiah? You've been quiet tonight."

Benjiah shrugged. "I don't know, Valzaan. I don't like thinking about what comes next. I have a feeling that it doesn't really matter what we do or even where we go. Malek's actions are going to set the tone for whatever follows. I've been thinking more about the past than the future."

"Yes, what about?"

"Erevir, the Assembly, even Malek's Rebellion. I know the story, of course, at least as much as most people do anymore, but standing here, under the shadow of the Mountain, it makes me wonder what really happened up there. Why did Malek do it? What went wrong in him? And once he decided to rebel, what went wrong with his plans? If he was as strong as everyone says, how could he fail? We've spent so much time these past few weeks wondering how it is all going to end. I'd just like to know more about how it began. Do you know, Valzaan? Or is that knowledge that died with the Twelve?"

Valzaan stood quietly, arms folded, facing out into the night. Pedraal and Pedraan came over and stood beside Benjiah, also staring up at the Mountain. He looked at his uncles' faces, but they were focused out into the starless night.

"I do know what happened on the Mountain," Valzaan said at last, sighing as he turned away from the dark and returned to the fire.

"Will you tell us?" Benjiah asked, also turning back to the fire and sitting as close as the flame allowed. "Or are you forbidden to speak of it?"

Valzaan reached out his hands and warmed them. "I am not forbidden, and I will tell you." He raised his head until his empty eyes rested on Benjiah. "You have been called to play a part in the final chapter of this story. It is appropriate that you know where and how things went wrong, if you are to play a part in making them right. But, I warn you, it will take me some time to tell, and it is already late. If I tell you this tale now, you will still have to rise with the sun in the morning, for I am taking us back to the road at dawn. Do you want to do this now?"

Benjiah didn't hesitate. "Yes, absolutely. I can think of no other time and no other place to hear it. I will be ready as early in the morning as you call, I promise you."

"Pedraal and Pedraan?"

"We're ready."

"All right, then. Listen, and I will tell you things that no one alive but I now know, and what few others in Kirthanin's history have ever known, for I know of them from Erevir himself."

2

BLOOD ON THE MOUNTAIN

HOW EVIL THOUGHTS AND DESIRES first crept into the heart of Malek, who can say? For what is sure beyond doubt is that Malek was created like all the other Titans, majestic and good. Indeed, he was the most majestic of all. Even among the Twelve, he was first in might, first in glory, and first in power. To be sure, each of the Twelve excelled in different skills and together complemented each other perfectly, but in strength and grandeur, Malek had no equal.

"What is also sure, is that at some point, being one of the Twelve failed to satisfy the Master of the Forge. Malek began to crave more. Whether he longed simply to rule all Kirthanin without the aid of his Titan brothers, or whether he thought he could reach into the heavens to pull Allfather from his eternal throne, no one knows. I know only that his mind was bent ever more intently toward wresting control of Kirthanin from the Twelve and setting himself up as lord over all that All-father had made.

"But Malek knew he could not overthrow the Twelve by himself. At least some of the Twelve would have to join and aid him. Carefully, craftily, subtly, he began to plant the smallest of seeds in conversations, looking and listening for any signs that they might take root and grow in the soil of his brothers' hearts. As time passed, he began to despair that any of them would respond to the suggestions he whispered into their souls. Emboldened by desperation, he began to hint more directly at his purpose. This boldness was rewarded in three of his Titan brothers with a readiness to follow his leading. Anakor, Charnosh, and Daegon, awakened to the rebellious hunger of Malek's vision, were ensnared by his words and desires. Soon they had entered into a sinister alliance.

"The other eight Titans were unaware of what was happening, for they did not have eyes to see the temptation that had mastered their brothers. And so they went about their business, both on the Mountain and in the land, oblivious to the storm that was gathering and would soon break upon them.

"Malek also knew that disposing of the other Titans was only one of the challenges before him. He plotted to establish his rule over the other living creatures of Kirthanin. That four Titans could subdue the hosts of men, Great Bear, and dragons, he did not doubt, for even Sulmandir could not have opposed a Titan's will. Malek believed the other dragons would surrender to his desires, seeing the futility of the fight against him. That the Great Bear would never follow him, he knew without question. They would fight to the last and die, and so they would be cleansed from the earth. The hosts of mankind, though, might possibly be subdued with minimal force, if he was careful. Some would willingly join him in exchange for promised glory and power; if he convinced enough men, they could conceivably convert the rest with little resistance.

"This was his aim, for he had no desire to rule a dead and empty world, a wasteland devoid of life. If all went well, dragons and men would live and serve him, even if against their will. He even planned to bring into being new races to do his bidding and worship him. Yes, he had felt it as he worked the forge, the fiery yearning to create, and it was only a matter of time before he figured out how to channel his immense power into the animation of new creatures.

"And then, as Malek contemplated who among the race of mortal man he would first approach, he created in his imagination the weapons that he would offer as a lure. As he sat by the waters of the Crystal Fountain, bubbling forth from the great deep, he saw in his mind's eye the long dark blade of a sword and the sharp, strong tip of a spear, and he laughed. He laughed until the echoes of his laughter rippled throughout the city and down the side of the Mountain. He laughed until the earth shook with the power of his voice. He laughed at the thought of thousands of swords and spears glistening in the noonday sun and at the image of men killing men in his name and bringing destruction, ruin, and fear to all.

"And so it was, in the year 1124 of the First Age, over a thousand years after Allfather first breathed life into him, Malek journeyed from the Mountain to Nolthanin, where Andunin, one of the strongest and most respected of the Novaana of the north lived. He offered Andunin an earthly throne in exchange for his promise to serve Malek and fashion from the men of Nolthanin an army to overthrow the Assembly and subdue mankind. With a mixture of enticement and threat, he ensnared Andunin. The offer was accepted, the deal was made, and the alliance was forged. Andunin gathered the support of the men of Nolthanin while Malek returned to Agia Muldonai, where he retreated to his forge within the Mountain to work in secret on his promised gift to men.

"Seven years passed as Andunin gathered the support of

the Nolthanim, who like Andunin saw both the peril of resisting Malek and the reward of following him. Some said, 'We will rule with Andunin and Malek as lords over the earth,' and others, 'We will perish in rebellion and the birds will eat our flesh and pick our bones.' Whispers spread across the northlands, but follow Andunin they did. None dared defy Malek alone, and all hungered for the promised glory that brought light to their dreams like the sun in the noonday sky.

"At last, in 1131, Andunin met with Malek at the appointed time, and Malek gave him weapons of war, blades designed for no other purpose than to kill. The first Azmavarim were there, and Ruun Harak, the father of spears. These were entrusted to Andunin, as well as the secret to forging more. Malek returned to the Mountain to lay his trap for his brothers as Andunin went home to train his men in the use of those weapons of war. He set the smithies of Nolthanin to work ceaselessly, and night and day the forges glowed hot as plows and harvest tools of every house and barn were fashioned into implements of war. Strong hands, used to wielding sickles and scythes, now learned to jab and thrust and cut with deadly accuracy and force. Soon, thousands of Nolthanim were ready to wield their blades on the battlefield, and Malek determined it was time to move.

"Then, in the height of Full Summer of 1133, two years after Andunin had first received his gift from Malek's hand, Malek visited him one last time. They sat late into the night as Malek gave Andunin his final instructions. In two weeks, Andunin was to amass his soldiers as quickly as possible and move south through a pass in the Zaros Mountains toward Enthanin, where Malek would join them in the march against the Enthanim, having secured Agia Muldonai. Once they had subdued Enthanin, they would proceed from there as needed to bring the remainder of Kirthanin under control. They would celebrate the coming of Autumn with a harvest feast that hailed Malek as lord over the earth and Andunin as his earthly king.

"Malek returned to Avalione. Many of the Titans were away from Avalione, as they often were at that time of year, but Anakor, Charnosh, and Daegon conspired to return from their travels early. They gathered on the Mountain and waited. Gradually, the other Titans began to return one by one to the blessed city. Eralon came first, from his responsibilities in Enthanin, and then came Therin, from the northeastern coast of Suthanin. Then Balimere the Beautiful, the beloved, arrived from the western coast of Werthanin. Malek was ready to act, and he sent the dragons that were then on the Mountain on errands of little consequence to remove them for what was coming. The last of these was no less than Sulmandir, who had brought Balimere back and had been asked by Balimere to remain, since it was the Titan's intent to return shortly to the west. So it was that Malek's command to go to Suthanin for Alazare conflicted with Balimere's command, and for some time after Malek left him, Sulmandir did not know which of his masters to obey. This confusion led to the Golden Dragon's delay, and the delay ultimately led to Malek's undoing, as you will hear.

"Malek called Eralon, Therin, and Balimere to join him and the others in the Council Hall, where the great western window surveyed the land of Werthanin. Malek's plan was simple, yet treacherous. He would offer the three a chance to join him. If they refused as he expected they would—for of all the other Titans, Malek could least envision Balimere accepting his offer—he would kill them. Then, as the others returned, they would face the same choice. Surrender to him, Master of the Forge and now Master of the Mountain, or die.

"When all seven had assembled, Malek declared himself to be first among the Titans, and he put their options before them. Eralon and Therin said nothing, but sat quietly and uneasily as Balimere answered for them all.

" 'Your grandeur and glory are not to be denied,' Balimere

said, 'but the title you claim is not yours to have, for it is not for this that Allfather made you and us. Turn back from this road you have chosen, Malek, for it will but lead you and all of Kirthanin to ruin.'

" 'I will not turn back,' Malek said, 'for I will claim what is rightfully mine. If you will not submit your purposes to mine, you will submit to the power of my hand!' And with that Malek struck Balimere down with his great hammer. Balimere fell to the floor of the Council Hall, dead before he struck the stone. Eralon and Therin tried to resist, but they were no match for the four against them, who wrestled them to the ground in a mighty struggle and killed them with their own hands. Indeed, save for Malek's hammer, there were no weapons wielded in Avalione, for the blades Malek had forged for use by human hands were of no use against a Titan's strength.

"When all three were dead, Malek strode from the Council Hall and dipped his hammer into the waters of the Crystal Fountain. He watched with delight as streaks of blood came off the hammer and spread throughout the clear pool. Again, he threw back his head and laughed until the Mountain quaked and the heavens trembled, for he had struck the first blow, and it seemed to him that his rule was within reach.

"But already his plan had gone awry, for the murder of Balimere had not gone unnoticed. Sulmandir, who had been debating on the northern slope of Agia Muldonai whether to seek out Balimere for guidance about which command to obey, had at last decided to go south. He had leapt from the northern peak and circled around the western slopes when he saw through the Council Hall's great western window something that could not have been. As he flew past at great speed, he saw the glint of metal as Malek struck Balimere in the head. Sulmandir whirled around in a great arc at once, circling at a significant distance to remain undetected, but with each sweep past the window his fear was confirmed: Malek was killing other Titans.

"Sulmandir circled for several moments in a daze, for he had never imagined such a thing was possible. The peace of Avalione, of the Holy Mountain, and of Kirthanin was broken. There was treachery afoot. There was evil at work. There was blood upon the Mountain.

"Turning again south, he flew with greater speed than ever before. He sped all day and into the night until he found Alazare near the southern tip of Suthanin, in what is now called Sulare. When he found Alazare, he wept as he told of Balimere's death, for by then the shock had passed and grief consumed him. Alazare wept with him. He did not allow himself to weep long, though, for Malek no doubt planned the deaths of the other faithful Titans. Sulmandir carried him through the night to the nearest dragon gyre, where Sulmandir entrusted several of his children with the job of finding Haalsun, Rolandes, Stratarus, and Volrain, and bringing them to a meeting place near Agia Muldonai. By the following night, the second night after Malek's betrayal, all five of the remaining and faithful Twelve had gathered and planned their counterattack.

"Sulmandir and the other dragons flew them in their human forms to the southern slope of Agia Muldonai. They arrived in the last hours of the night, in Fourth Watch, for they hoped to enter the gates of Avalione under cover of dark. Alazare, followed by the other four, reassumed their Titan forms and moved north through the half-light of morning into the city.

"As they entered, Alazare halted. A foul odor blew through the streets, and an eerie silence hung over the buildings and the stones that paved the way. He clenched his great fists, feeling anger burn within him for the first time. His blood boiled with rage at Malek for bringing destruction and ruin to their peaceful city. There had been no lack, no deprivation, no absence of any good thing. Malek had never been denied anything of worth or value or necessity. Alazare felt overwhelmingly the need to avenge the deaths of his brothers, who even now lay rotting in the Council Hall where they had fallen.

"But before Alazare could advance, Malek and the others appeared before them on the road. Malek led the others, smiling and holding the hammer that had killed Balimere.

" 'So, you have come together and in the dark of night,' Malek said. 'I thought perhaps I saw a glint of gold out of the window when Balimere fell. Sulmandir will pay for his betrayal, but you, Alazare, will you not join me? There is no need for more to die. You may outnumber us, but we are stronger. I am stronger. You cannot prevail against me, and I will strike you down where you stand if you do not surrender. Decide quickly!'

" 'We may die, Malek,' Alazare answered, 'but we will never join you. You have killed our brothers, and we are here to bring your rebellion to an end. Surrender now and throw yourself on Allfather's mercy, for this is the last chance for mercy you will receive.'

" 'Mercy? You offer me mercy? You fool! You are dead, and you don't even know it.'

"At that, Malek charged Alazare with his hammer raised, but as he swung with all the might he possessed, something remarkable happened. Alazare felt the unseen presence of Allfather move within him in a mighty way, and he caught Malek's arm as it lowered the hammer. Malek's eyes grew wide as Alazare stopped his stroke, successfully holding his hand and hammer still in the air. As they stood, frozen in their struggle, the other Titans fell upon one another. In the dark and confusion, it went ill for those with Alazare. Anakor struck down Stratarus not far from the gate and Charnosh killed

Haalsun while Daegon and Rolandes fell against one another with a mighty crash. The ground rumbled under the weight of the Titans' feet and still Malek and Alazare stood, neither budging, neither swaying, neither advancing.

"And then, the tide of the battle turned, for Volrain, seeing Stratarus fall, leapt upon Anakor and, wrapping his arms around his neck, pulled him to the ground where he squeezed the life out of him. At the same time, Rolandes, who had been struggling with Daegon, felt a surge of strength, and overpowering his foe cast him back several spans until he crashed into the thick and mighty wall of Avalione. Daegon's body cracked the wall and a great chunk off of the top fell outside into the grass that grew around the city, where it sits to this day, the only stone in the blessed city which has fallen from the place where it was set in the very beginning. With Anakor dead and Daegon lying motionless against the wall, and with Malek at an impasse with Alazare nearby, Charnosh turned from that place and fled east and north along the outer wall of the city. Rolandes, still feeling the might and power with which he had cast Daegon, ran after him, and the ground of the Mountain shook under their feet.

"Malek, seeing Volrain rise above the body of Anakor, wrenched his arm free from Alazare, who felt as Malek pulled away, the weariness of both body and mind the struggle had cost him. Malek also turned and ran, charging up through the center of the city toward the place where the Crystal Fountain stood, thrusting the living waters of the Mountain high into the air. Volrain, seeing Alazare's great weariness, gave chase, and Alazare followed as he was able.

"What none of them saw as they ran from that place, was that Daegon was not dead as they had supposed. He rose, and realizing that some had fled along the wall and some up through the center of the city, ran himself along the path that Charnosh and Rolandes had chosen, and again, the tide of the battle shifted. For though Rolandes followed not far behind his adversary, he did not know that Daegon was not far behind him.

"Rolandes caught up to Charnosh in the grove of trees on the western side of the city. There beneath the spreading majesty and deep shade of the great trees, which swayed in the breeze that gusted that morning out of the west across the Mountain, Rolandes slew Charnosh. Feeling still the might and strength that had coursed through his veins as he cast Daegon against the city wall, he struck down his brother. As he stood above Charnosh, looking down at his lifeless form in the grass, he saw the face of a traitor, but also the face of a brother. They had ruled together upon the Mountain for over a thousand years, and now Charnosh was dead by Rolandes's hand. He stood and wept, for though he had done what had to be done, it was an almost unbearable deed.

"He did not have to bear it long, for he never heard the footsteps of Daegon through the thick grass and soft soil behind him. He did not see the great blow come, and if he felt it at all, it was but a moment's pain as he fell atop his brother's corpse. And there he lay, his head upon Charnosh's body, the faithful and the faithless both slain beneath the trees.

"Daegon turned from the grove and ran with all the strength and speed he possessed back into Avalione. Only Alazare and Volrain remained, and if he could reach Malek soon enough, there was still hope the rebellion could succeed. Though they had not expected to lose any of their number, all was not yet lost. With none of the Twelve left to oppose them, Daegon knew that he and Malek could have their way in Kirthanin. Not even the combined might of the dragons could stop two Titans. It would be harder this way, but it would not be impossible. Besides, he thought as he ran, with all the others dead, he would share more power with Malek now than he had ever dreamed of before.

"Meanwhile, Volrain and Alazare had caught up to Malek, who had turned to face them in the open center of Avalione, before the Crystal Fountain. He stood, his hammer held firm in his hand. As they reached the square, they slowed to face their foe, who smiled as they approached.

" 'I will run no further, for I fear no living creature,' Malek said as they approached. 'I am the Master of the Forge, the wielder and the maker. I am the builder and the breaker, the lightning and the thunder. I am the first and the last, stronger than the mountains and more mighty than the oceans. In my hand is the hammer and in the other is the anvil, and whether you be two or two hundred, you will fall before me on your knees and bow, or you will fall before me dead.'

" 'We may fall,' Volrain began.

" 'We will never bow,' Alazare finished.

" 'Then you will die,' Malek said as he charged them with his hammer raised. Even though there were two of them, they were hard pressed to fend off Malek's attack, and soon Volrain and Alazare both found themselves circling around Malek, trying desperately to avoid the blows of his hammer. Around the side of the Fountain he pressed them, until he had driven them the length of the great pool of the Fountain to the northernmost end of the square.

"There they regrouped, and with a sudden surge of energy and coordinated attacks, forced Malek for the time being off guard and pressed him back until he stood with his back against the short wall of the Fountain's pool. But being backed against the pool, Malek lashed out even more ferociously than before, and soon both Volrain and Alazare were giving way before him.

"It was at this point that Daegon emerged from the buildings on the eastern side of the square and brought hope to Malek and despair to the others. They were already weary and losing hope that they could strike Malek down on their own, but with Daegon's coming, they felt hopelessness wash over them. Alazare, who was closest to that side of the city, moved to face Daegon as he ran toward the Fountain.

"With a surge of desperation, Alazare reached Daegon and struck him with all his strength, even as Daegon struck Alazare. The force of the exchange sent Alazare reeling onto the stones of the square, and when he looked up, he saw Daegon also was down. Struggling to pull himself up, he scrambled across the space between them despite the ache in his chest and found Daegon motionless. He was dead.

"Turning to face Malek, Alazare saw the great hammer flashing through the air. It slammed into a stunned Volrain who was slumped upon the low wall of the Fountain's pool where Malek himself had stood just moments before. The hammer struck Volrain's head and drove him tumbling back into the water. Even from where Alazare stood, he could see the blood begin to spread out through the water as Volrain floated by the edge of the pool.

"Malek turned toward him as he walked slowly back toward the Fountain. A gleam of delight mixed with hatred in his eyes. Alazare wondered how he had failed to see it before. He wondered how his eyes could have been blind to all that had gone wrong in Malek. He wondered what had taken place that would give Malek so much pleasure in something so terrible. He wondered what hope he possibly could have now that he was left to face Malek alone. He was weary, not Malek's equal, and he knew it. Malek did too.

" 'I say again, Alazare, you don't have to die. I was willing to share my rule of Kirthanin with Anakor, Charnosh, and Daegon. But now we are the last of the Twelve.'

"Alazare did not speak, and Malek went on. 'I was willing to share with them, so I will share with you. Of course, we will not be equals, but it is better to rule with me as my servant than to be dead, is it not?'

"At that, Alazare found his voice. 'It is not. Nor will you rule. Every living creature will hate you when they learn what you have done. You will have to kill everything you desire to rule, for they will never accept you now, and then what will you do? Will you take delight in ruling an empty world? Will you greet each day with joy, knowing that your greed has ruined the very thing you desired? You may well rule Kirthanin after you have killed me, but you have made a poor trade. You give up a share of the rule of a beautiful and bountiful creation in exchange for a barren and bereft graveyard.'

"The glow of hate burned in Malek's eyes. 'Don't be so sure, Alazare,' he said sharply. 'Not every creature in Kirthanin will choose death over me. I will build a new world with them, and I will fill it with new creations. And when I stretch my hand out to rule it, I will think with great happiness upon this moment, when I threw down my enemy and stood alone upon the Mountain, Master of all.'

" 'That, you will never be.'

"Malek charged. Alazare prepared to receive him. At the last moment, Alazare dove out of Malek's way, rolling across the open square and springing back to his feet with a freshness and alacrity that was not his own. Energy surged in him like a great swell of water in the ocean. Emboldened, he charged Malek, who was still regrouping from his missed hammer stroke. With his head low, he struck Malek in the ribs and knocked him backward onto the smooth stone. Malek's hammer went sliding across the square until it hit and rested against the Fountain wall, and before Malek could shake him off, Alazare was up, on his knees, pounding Malek with all his might.

"The glow of delight had slipped from Malek's eyes, which for the first time filled with fear. He tried to defend himself against Alazare's furious blows and managed to throw Alazare off to the side. He rose to his feet at once and ran to the Fountain. There he paused, gathering his breath, before picking up the hammer at his feet. As he stared at Alazare, and Alazare stared at him, he dipped his hand into the water and splashed some on his face.

"The water that slipped down his face left red streaks of Volrain's blood on his skin. Alazare clenched his fist, the sight of his brother's blood quickening his rage. He started toward Malek.

" 'How did it feel as I beat you? How does it feel to know you have brought such pain on yourself? In over a thousand years, nothing has ever brought you pain like that. You could have continued to live free of pain, free of fear, and free of guilt, but you have thrown it all away. Now pain, fear, and guilt are all that remain to you. Even now, as you stand here guilty of shedding blood on the Mountain, are you not afraid? Do you not know that your plan has already failed? Your companions are dead, and by the power and might of Allfather, I will slay you too.'

" 'I have not failed. I am not afraid, and you will never slay me!'

"This time Malek charged, and his hammer was too swift and furious for Alazare to dodge completely. Though he blocked Malek's arm in midair, he still received a glancing blow to the head. The thud of the hammer hitting his skull shot waves of pain through Alazare's body. Every last nerve howled as his head seemed to explode. His vision blurred and the world went silent. He staggered, seeing little, hearing nothing, and feeling only pain.

"But he didn't fall. As he stood there, Alazare felt a glow, a spreading warmth, and the ringing in his head receded and his vision suddenly cleared. He looked and saw the impossible. Malek was where he had been, standing just a few steps away, but he wasn't moving. He was turning round and round a long slender pole in his hand, examining it like it was something he'd never seen before. Then Alazare recognized what

Malek held; it was the hammer's shaft. The head lay shattered on the ground all around them. Malek's eyes moved from the shaft in his hand to the hammer's head in little bits to Alazare.

"Their eyes met, and Alazare saw all the confidence, all the bravado, all the defiance drain from his foe. Not only fear, but terror showed in Malek's face. Alazare did not understand why, but then he looked down and he saw a radiance emanating from his own skin, as though he had imbibed sunrays and they were now breaking out through the pores of his skin. And then he could not only see it; he could feel it. The light pulsed through his veins, and the ringing in his head faded to a distant echo, and his strength returned. He threw his head back and laughed. He roared with laughter and the sound was like mighty waters tumbling over a cliff.

"Malek turned and fled. Alazare ran after him, and with every step, he felt his body grow lighter and his weary muscles grow stronger. Weaving his way through the city, Malek ran, and weaving through the city, Alazare pursued. Northward they fled, Malek unable to evade Alazare's pursuit. At last they fled beyond Avalione's northern buildings, and still Malek ran, across the rising ground that stretched out toward the twin peaks on the northern side of the Mountain, and up the great stairway at their base.

"Up and up and up they ran. Higher and higher they climbed until they had ascended almost into the clouds themselves. And there, on the uppermost northern ridge of Agia Muldonai, Malek stopped at last, for there was nowhere else to run. He turned to Alazare, terror still with him.

" 'Even without my hammer, I am more than your equal, Alazare. Leave me and this place before it is too late.'

" 'I will leave when I have done what I have come to do.'

"Again they closed on one another. They grappled together, struggling and straining with all their strength on the narrow ridge. Alazare could feel Malek's might, and he wondered how he was not cast backward down the stairs. But the light and strength that had filled him by the Crystal Fountain had not departed, and he felt gradually, ever so gradually, Malek was growing tired.

"And then Malek's foot slipped, and he stumbled backward toward the edge of the ridge that overlooked the sheer drop. Malek looked down at his feet and saw in dismay that he was perilously close to the edge. He looked into Alazare's eyes, his face alive with fear and hate. 'This cannot be!' he shouted. 'I am the strongest!'

" 'No, you're not,' Alazare replied almost softly. 'There is One who is stronger.' And with a sudden shift of his weight, he dropped his shoulder, gained a hold on Malek's exhausted body, and lifting him off the ground, threw him from the Mountain."

" 'Allfather alone is Lord over Kirthanin,' Alazare said as Malek's Titan form plummeted. With a tremendous crash, Malek hit the ground, too far down for Alazare to see with any clarity, but he felt it all the same. The vibrations it caused shook the Mountain from its roots to its uppermost peak, and Alazare struggled to keep his feet as the Mountain quaked. After a moment, though, the shaking was gone, and the only remaining evidence that Malek had been thrown down was a slowly settling cloud of dust.

"Alazare stood for a very long time upon the ridge, gazing down quietly at the place where Malek had fallen. As he stood, he felt the light and warmth that had flooded him slowly slip away. Fatigue and weariness returned to his body, and the great ringing that had filled his head returned until he could hear nothing and think about nothing but the sound between his ears. His vision blurred again, and he sat down on the ridge, letting his feet dangle over the edge.

"And that is the story of Malek's Rebellion. That is how the Mountain was defiled, and why it was closed and forbidden to all. There is blood upon the Mountain still, and it will remain closed until that blood is cleansed away."

Benjiah and the twins stared with rapt attention at the prophet, who sat gazing into the dwindling fire. The flames that had illuminated his face were now so low that his features were covered in shadow. Benjiah looked past him, out beyond the pavilion toward the foot of the Mountain, and he shivered. So much power had once dwelt in this place. So much glory and grandeur had been lost. So much sorrow and suffering begun. So much still unanswered.

"What happened to Malek?" Benjiah asked. "I mean, I've never understood how he survived."

"Indeed," Valzaan answered, "he should be dead."

"So what happened?"

"When Malek struck the ground, his body was broken beyond repair. And yet, powerful and ingenious as he is, Malek saw one chance to live. He knew that his Titan form was dying, but he thought that perhaps, if he could change into his human form one last time, perhaps he could elude death. If his plan worked, he would be trapped in his human form for all time, but he faced a choice between this physical limitation and death. So as his life slipped away from him, he mustered all his strength and changed forms, and to his own surprise, he lived, but at a price: The fall had not only crushed his Titan form but injured his human form as well. He was crippled. And so it is, that while Malek retained most of his Titan powers, he has been crippled ever since, a permanent testimony to his having been cast from the Mountain by Alazare."

"Valzaan," Pedraal said, "years ago, when we were in Sulare, you suggested that Malek might be able to move freely about Kirthanin without being detected."

"I did."

"How could that be? If Malek is stuck in the fragile body of a broken man, how could he travel freely? Wouldn't he be both easily recognized and defenseless?"

"I am afraid he is neither, even though your reasoning may be partially right on both counts. He is not defenseless, for the most part because he has surrounded himself with some of Kirthanin's most powerful creatures since his exile. You are right that he would not strike awe into anyone. He does not have the powerful physique and physical prowess that you possess, Pedraal, or you, Pedraan, but he doesn't need it. Do not be deceived by the fact that he is physically broken, for neither his Titan powers nor his will to rule were broken. He hopes other bodies will fight for him, using in part the powers he has given them.

"As for his identity, you are again partially correct. He cannot change shape at will, but you would be wrong to underestimate his craftiness. All the Titans had the ability to assume multiple shapes when they came among men. They chose to come consistently in the same form because it was easier for men, not because they couldn't have done otherwise. There is no reason to believe that Malek has lost this ability to modify his appearance, even if he cannot reassume his Titanic proportions. For all I know, he has power enough to move about in multiple human forms as different as you and I."

Benjiah pondered Valzaan's words, but his mind went back to the last image in the story, of Malek lying broken and twisted in the crater his impact had created. "Where did he go? How did he join Andunin?"

"When Malek had regained as much of his senses and strength as he was going to, he started moving north and east to intercept Andunin's armies. He found Andunin and informed him of their ruin, for indeed they were ruined. Without Malek's full strength, Andunin's army would be destroyed by the dragons and Great Bear. Their only hope now was in speed. If Andunin and his men could move quickly south and take enough ships from the southern port cities to cross the Southern Ocean, they could take refuge in the great island beyond. Andunin had never heard of such a place, but Malek insisted it was there and that it constituted their only hope.

"Andunin was torn. He wanted to take his men home, to leave Malek alone to face his fate, but Malek convinced him that Sulmandir would know Andunin had been part of the rebellion and so strike him down in his wrath. He also promised Andunin that he still possessed enough power to rescue the rebellion, if he had but time and safety with which to regroup. And he still wielded enough power to kill Andunin and Andunin's son, Tarlin. So Andunin and his army swept south across the land, laying waste to towns and villages and killing any who stood in their way. Some of Andunin's men, including Tarlin, died in the flight, but most lived, and their plan to flee from Kirthanin's shores succeeded. They commandeered over a hundred ships and sailed out of sight and out of all human memory."

"That's how Malek came to the Forbidden Isle."

"Yes, and there he discovered Vulsutyr and his children, and there an alliance was formed between them."

"What about Alazare?" Benjiah asked suddenly. "Why do we never hear anymore about him?"

"Because there is nothing else to tell. Erevir told me when I was very young and first beginning my duties as a prophet of Allfather, that Sulmandir had only talked of Alazare's fate with him once, and that in passing. Alazare sent Sulmandir to gather as many of the dragons as he could. When Sulmandir returned, he found the slain, traitorous Titans exposed upon the southern slope of Agia Muldonai. The seven faithful Titans had been buried, presumably by Alazare, in the grove east of the city. Of Alazare, though, there was no sign, nor has there ever been again. Perhaps Alazare died of his head wound not long after he threw Malek from the Mountain, a victim in the end of Malek's hate and Malek's own hand. Whatever happened, the Titans have passed from the earth, save only Malek, who can no longer wield the full power and force of a Titan. Kirthanin was left under Sulmandir's care throughout the Second Age, until Sulmandir also met his end in circumstances similar to Alazare's, but that is a story for another day."

Wylla adjusted her dress as she prepared to receive Captain Merias. It was late, but this meeting couldn't be put off any longer. She had been putting it off, not because she feared it, but because she didn't have answers to the questions it would raise. She had seen situations where none of the options looked very good, but not since she was a captive of Ulutyr, before she was queen, had she been in a place as devoid of desirable alternatives as this.

Merias strode in confidently, his black tunic and pants a striking contrast to the silver armband that portrayed his rank by its width. Curly haired, bearded, and normally full of mirth, Merias always reminded Wylla of her brothers, but today the captain's face betrayed no hint of laughter. What's more, the thought of the twins brought to Wylla's mind dark images of Gyrin and fears for Benjiah.

The Captain approached the semicircle of chairs and bowed. "Thank you for seeing me, Your Majesty, I know you are busy, especially now that . . ."

Merias stopped midthought, glancing sideways at Yorek, who sat quietly beside Wylla, watching Merias intently. Wylla saw the look and guessed at her captain's hesitation. "Master Yorek is well aware of all we have discussed, Captain Merias, and you need not hold back from speaking your mind. He was an advisor to my father before either of us was born."

"Yes, Your Majesty," Merias said, returning his focus to her. "As I was saying, thanks for making time."

"You're welcome." Wylla smiled. "Enthanin will rely heavily on your skills for the foreseeable future if Valzaan's prophecy comes to pass. Please, sit down and be comfortable."

Captain Merias took a chair on the outside of the semicircle and pulled it around so that he was facing Wylla. "All things considered, the readiness and morale of the army is good, Your Majesty. I am happy with the level of preparation we have already achieved. Who can say how much strength is enough to meet the challenge that is coming? But what strength we have is as ready as it is likely to be."

"Good." Wylla nodded her approval.

"My concern is not military, at least not primarily," Merias continued. "I am more worried about the rumors circulating among the troops about why we have altered our routines and increased our drilling. The men can feel the gravity of the change. They see it in their commanders' faces and hear it in their voices. They know we are anticipating something, but they don't know what.

"I have heard some talk of Malek and the Mountain, but mostly, I hear of the war in the west. Some believe we are going to march to Fel Edorath to help Aljeron Balinor. Some think Rulalin is coming to Enthanin and that we are preparing to defend our borders against him. Still others think Aljeron has defeated Rulalin and is now on his way here to lay siege to Amaan Sul, but who could believe such a bizarre tale, I don't know. Yet two different officers have heard its like in their camps."

Wylla listened carefully, slightly amused by the creative imaginations behind some of the rumors. She could imagine the men circled round the nighttime campfires, discussing the latest theory. "Well," Wylla began, "this is actually better news than I had expected. I'm relieved that the true nature of our peril is not yet known. I had hoped to avoid panic as long as I could."

"That was my initial response as well; however, the more I've thought about it, the more I've begun to worry."

"How so, Captain?"

"Well, while in the short term we may avoid panic, we may have an insurmountable problem if the men are shocked to face a decidedly more fearful foe than anticipated. Preparing to face a presumably weary, even exhausted human army is not the same as preparing to face Malek. If the gap between the perceived and real enemy is sizable, many might be paralyzed when he finally comes."

"But won't telling them now paralyze them also? Isn't this one of those cases where not knowing is a mercy? At least they won't have to face Malek in their daydreams and nightmares between now and then." Wylla shivered, thinking of the dark images that troubled her own waking and sleeping moments.

"There are risks, but if we at least begin to explain the true gravity of the situation, we can begin to prepare them for it, as much as we can prepare for the unknown."

The same questions again. Who to tell what, and when? How to know what to do when, in the end, probably very little could be done? If deliverance for her people was to come, it would almost certainly come from another hand, for no merely human army had ever stood successfully before Malek. Men were all she had under her command, but men were not enough.

"Your Majesty, if I might?" Yorek's voice cut through Wylla's musings.

"Of course, Yorek, that's why you're here."

"I think Captain Merias is absolutely right. If we tell the army of Amaan Sul and Enthanin that Valzaan has prophesied that the coming of Malek is not far away, it will not take long for word to spread throughout the city. The people may panic . . ."

"Then why do it?"

"Because the panic may be unavoidable. Wouldn't it be

better to have panic now? With time, I think the panic will pass, and resolve and fortitude and determination will have a chance to take root."

Master Yorek leaned forward, toward Wylla. "There is another reason why you should tell them," he said, more gently.

"What is that?"

"They have a right to know what is coming. We should tell the people of Amaan Sul that we are taking every step that can be taken to prepare for what is coming. We should model the confidence in the face of danger that we want our citizens to emulate. We will ask them to help fortify the city, but some will choose to go, thinking that the farther away from the Mountain they go, the safer they will be. Whether that thinking is right or wrong, we can discourage it, but it is a choice every father and mother will have to make for themselves. In my opinion, the choice we face now should not be whether we tell the army and the people the truth, but how we tell them."

Wylla turned from Master Yorek to Captain Merias. "And you, Captain Merias, you agree with Master Yorek."

"I do."

"Was there anything else you needed to tell me?"

"No, Your Majesty, that was it."

"You may go, then. I will consider what you have said and summon you when I have made a decision."

"Thank you, Your Majesty." Captain Merias stood and bowed. Turning from them, he walked to the door, and soon his footsteps could be heard disappearing down the hall.

When he had gone, Master Yorek also stood. "Unless you have need of me, Your Majesty, I will also take my leave."

"Go ahead," Wylla said. "Get some sleep. And, Yorek?"

"Yes, Your Majesty?"

"Thank you for your candor."

"You're welcome," Yorek replied, and when she said no more, he left, closing the door behind him.

Wylla rose and stretched. She had been sitting too long, and one of her feet had gone to sleep. She stomped it on the floor to try to restore her circulation, but it was slow in coming. She decided to stretch her legs before going to bed.

She headed out through the courtyard, where the night was clear and cool, and took the stairs up to her favorite walk along the wall. The lights of the city contrasted brightly with the darkness north of the wall. She peered out into the inky black, wondering how much time she had before her people faced their ultimate test.

She paused. Something was moving. She peered more carefully at the open ground northwest of the wall. She was not imagining it. Several forms were approaching, rapidly.

3

INSIDE THE WALLS

"ALARM! ALARM!" Wylla shouted as she ran along the wall. She ducked into the spiral stair and rapidly descended to the courtyard.

Two stewards appeared at the door to the stable and a third appeared at the door to the hallway that led back inside the palace proper.

"Come at once!" she cried, running across the courtyard to the palace. The stewards from the stable ran to meet her and converged where the third waited.

"You," she said, grabbing the tunic of one of the stableboys, "ride into the city to find Captain Merias. He is staying at The Sunny Knoll. Tell him the palace is under attack."

The steward stood for a second, stunned, but Wylla shoved him toward the stable. "Go now!"

She took the arm of the second steward. "Get as many men from the house as you can, grab bows and cyranic arrows from the armory, and return to the wall. Prepare for the worst."

This man moved immediately. He flew into the house, shouting for all to arise and come. The third steward, a middle-aged woman who had been cleaning in the kitchen from the look of her, waited for Wylla's next command. As Wylla began to speak, the first steward streaked by, riding bareback on a light brown stallion. She shouted over the sound of the thundering hooves. "Grab a handful of the older men to start barricading the inner gate. Use anything. Hurry."

Wylla did not wait for her. She sped into the large hall, grabbed a torch from the wall, and ran to the armory. She could begin to hear the palace coming alive. Some thirty men and women lived and served in the palace. She feared they would not be enough.

In the armory, she grabbed one of the smaller bows. She was not the best archer, but at close range, she was good enough. Slinging a quiver of cyranic arrows across her shoulder, she ran back toward the courtyard.

She passed several house stewards, some fully dressed, some in nightgowns, racing toward the armory and the outer courtyard. She called on them to grab torches and to hurry. On her way out, she picked up an unlit torch in her bow hand and ran back outside. As she passed the inner gate, she heard a loud boom come from the outer gate. "Hurry," she repeated as a handful of stewards emerged. The attack was upon them.

Once more upon the wall, she peered carefully over the edge. A dense, dark mass moved below her in front of the outer gate. Large dark forms rammed the gate with a long pole, or maybe a tree. Malekim. She knew by their size. Behind them, on horseback, were men. Wolves weaved in and out of the crowd.

Memories of the bright summer day outside Nal Gildoroth flooded her. She had emerged from the city behind Bryar to suddenly be surrounded by Malekim. A host of images from the weeks that followed flashed through her mind. "Never again," she mumbled. "They'll never touch me again."

Four or five stewards with bows and arrows had come up alongside her. "All right," she said, turning to them. "I'm going to light this torch and throw it down. Aim for the Malekim. We can kill the men and wolves after we've dropped the Voiceless."

She held the unlit torch to the lit one, and when it sprang to light she hurled it into the midst of the dark, teeming crowd below. As fast as the torch fell, Wylla picked out one of the Malekim holding the ram and shot him in the back. He dropped his hold on the pole and spun, trying to reach the arrow. A moment later he was lying still in the grass.

Several other arrows rained down from the wall, and a couple more Malekim dropped. As Wylla fired a second time, a great dark foot came down upon the torch and stomped it out. "Again!" Wylla cried out, grabbing the other torch, which she had set upon the wall, and throwing it down. Again she aimed and fired, but the torch was extinguished more quickly this time, and she didn't see if she had struck her mark.

"Keep firing as fast as you can," she said to the others as she crossed the walkway to look down on the courtyard side. Men and women were moving about, bracing the entry. If the iron-rimmed outer gates were breached, the weaker inner gates would not hold long.

"Use the wagons and carts, in the stables," she called down. "If you aren't moving a cart, go to the armory and bring up all the weapons you can, bows and cyranic arrows especially."

A loud crack echoed up the wall. She ran back across and stared down. The dark flurry of motion was streaming through. The outer gate was broken.

She aimed her bow at a dark form that had stopped short of the outer gate and fired. A grunt of pain confirmed her hit, a man and not a Malekim.

There was pounding now on the inner gate. "Ready your bows!" Wylla called out. She looked down into the courtyard. Two wagons were being rolled in front of the inner gate by half a dozen men.

The wagons were deposited not a moment too soon. Splintering wood shot into the courtyard as a large chunk of the inner gate exploded. A pair of leaping wolves shot through the large hole and landed in the first wagon. One of them was shot immediately. The other managed to get off the wagon but was cut down by a pair of waiting stewards with swords.

More pieces of gate were being broken away, and Wylla called down, "Fire into the gap! Shoot them down!"

With a terrific splintering sound, the Malekim's great ram broke through the gate and the side of one wagon. The wagon moved perhaps half a span, and the great dark forms of the Malekim pushed into the courtyard, pushing the wagons farther out of the way.

"Shoot the Malekim! Drop them with your cyranic arrows!" She fired too, and her arrow struck one of the Malekim in the side of the neck. More arrows flew in, and a number of the Malekim fell heavily.

A flurry of movement on the other side of the courtyard caught Wylla's eye, and she glanced up to see Captain Merias and a dozen other riders on horses fly in from the long lane that led out past the Fountain. Relief flooded her, for now several Black Wolves had slipped under and around the wagons and were running about the courtyard. She even saw one race into the stables.

"Wylla! Your Majesty!" a voice cried out. She looked up to see Yorek running her way. He must have climbed up the other stair at the back of the courtyard.

He drew near and took her by the arm. "Come, we must go and get you to safety."

She wrenched her arm from his. "My place is here." She

drew another arrow and, aiming at a man creeping low beside the shattered wagon, fired the arrow into his crouching body.

"Help has come," Yorek said, gripping her now more firmly. "You must come with me. Now, or I will carry you, queen or no."

Wylla looked at her advisor and saw the fear in his eyes. She looked back down into the courtyard. The fighting was closer now, as both Malekim and wolves were moving past the wagons. There was little she could do with her bow now. She nodded to Yorek and ran behind him along the wall.

They descended the rear stair, and even though they dropped down to the courtyard at considerable distance from the combat, Wylla couldn't be sure that wolves were not lurking in the shadows. She nocked an arrow and held her fingers at the ready.

Yorek and she slipped into the palace and soon were running through the empty building toward the door that led directly out to the Fountain.

A crashing sound from a dark corner echoed down the hall, and they whirled to see a man in a dark tunic running at them with sword drawn. Wylla didn't have time to aim carefully but pulled back her bowstring and let the arrow fly. It struck the man in the shoulder with such force that the point emerged on the other side. The sword he was holding clattered to the stone floor, and he dropped immediately, the cyranic poison already coursing through his body.

Yorek grabbed her hand and again they were running. After a few moments in the front hall, while Yorek scrutinized the Fountain courtyard from the door, he led Wylla outside.

They had started out when two long, lean shapes came padding along the road that led to the rear courtyard where all the fighting was taking place. Close behind the wolves came a pair of men on horseback. They closed in on the animals, and two swords flashed through the night. Both wolves fell dead upon the ground.

Yorek and Wylla had stopped, arrested by the sight. One of the riders rode over to where they stood. Merias.

"I think it's over."

"Over?"

"Unless there are more outside the walls. My men are searching the palace, and others are working with your stewards to repair the damaged gate. I sent your messenger to our encampment outside the city's western gate. A thousand soldiers will be here within the hour."

"Good," Wylla said, relaxing her grip on the bow for the first time since she had picked it up.

"Captain!" a pair of voices called out from behind Merias.

"Yes?" Merias said, twisting in his saddle.

"We have one of the men alive."

The midmorning sky was overcast, and the wind gusted in Aljeron's face as he rode toward his camp just southwest of Fel Edorath. The days had grown successively colder as they had moved east, until now the wind carried a severe bite that made his exposed flesh sting. *The winter is going to be brutal.* He shivered. *All the more reason to wrap this up quickly and head home.*

Close by, Koshti padded along, his movements through the browning grass visible but not audible. Aljeron watched his battle brother glide along and wished not for his stealth or power, but for his thick fur. He knew Koshti must feel the cold, but the only visible sign that the tiger was affected by the temperature was the rhythmic breathing that pulsated from Koshti's mouth in small clouds.

Not far ahead, a pair of men on horseback rode toward them. They wore the purple livery of Shalin Bel and slowed as they drew nearer. When they saw Aljeron and Evrim at the front of the approaching company, they drew up and halted.

"Allfather's blessing upon you, Master Balinor and Master

Minluan. Your return is most welcome," one of them said as they both gave a slight bow while keeping their horses still.

"Allfather's blessing upon you," Aljeron replied. Evrim echoed the words beside him. "We are glad to be back, to finish what we've started."

The eyes of both men glistened as Aljeron spoke. "We will ride before you back to the camp that we might herald your return."

Aljeron acknowledged their words with a nod, and they both wheeled around and spurred their horses back the way they had come. Aljeron and the others kept riding, and shortly the distant shapes of tents covering the hillside rose before them. Round and light grey with a purple stripe around the top, they stretched across the horizon, too numerous to count.

Before long, Aljeron and the others were riding through the midst of the camp, the eyes of all drawn to them. Most waved and nodded to Aljeron and Evrim as they came, then looks of wonder and shock rippled across soldiers' faces as they saw the Great Bear ambling along behind them. Aljeron nodded and waved to many in return, knowing that in a day or two, he would ask these very men to once again offer their lives to finish the work before them.

At last they drew near the command tent, large and rectangular and right in the middle of the camp. Standing outside it were Gilion and Brenim, waiting beside the open doorway. Gilion stood as neat and fastidious as Aljeron had left him, his warm brown cloak drawn together with a sash that hung over his light tan pants. What remained of his receding, iron-grey hair was neatly trimmed and lay smoothly on his shiny head. His dark eyes were serious and focused, and if he thought anything of the Great Bear following Aljeron, it didn't show. Beside him, the wind played with Brenim's short dark brown hair. Though a little shorter than Joraiem, and with darker hair, Aljeron was struck again by the family resemblance. The likeness and difference was most clearly captured in the eyes. In shape and color they were Joraiem's, though harder than Joraiem's had ever looked. At Brenim's waist hung the sword that his father, Monias, had given to him when he had came of age.

"Allfather's blessing upon you both," Aljeron said as he dismounted. "I trust you have kept well in my absence."

"We have, Master Balinor," Gilion answered, his posture erect and perfect as he observed the formalities of greeting his captain. "We have eagerly awaited your return and trust that you will find everything as you desired it."

"I'm sure I will, Gilion," Aljeron replied.

Evrim also dismounted and motioned to the others to do the same. As the Great Bear came forward, Aljeron introduced them. "Gilion and Brenim, this is Sarneth, who accompanied Joraiem and me and the others to the Forbidden Isle. Also with him are his son, Erigan, and his friend Arintol, also of the Lindandraal, who likewise fought with us the night we freed Bryar and Wylla and the others from the Vulsutyrim and Malekim."

"You are most welcome here," Brenim answered, visibly impressed, though Gilion's face remained impassive.

"Your brother's death was a grievous evil, and you and your family have my sympathy," Sarneth replied.

"Thank you."

Aljeron motioned to introduce Caan, but the warrior had already stepped to Gilion. "Gilion Numiah," Caan said, his face breaking into a wide smile, "I knew that if there was trouble up here, you'd be right in the middle of it."

Gilion, a slight grin showing on his face, seemed to relax for the first time. "And what brings you up to these cold and distant climes?"

"I'm here on a mission of peace."

Gilion slapped his old friend on the shoulder. "An agent of peace," he murmured, laughing. "Surely the end is near."

Saegan and Bryar also approached as the horses were led

off in another direction. "Has the midday meal been served?" Aljeron asked.

"Yes," Gilion replied, "but not long ago. There is plenty for you all. Let's retire inside, and I will send for it."

"Very good," Aljeron replied.

Soon the weary travelers were reclining inside the large tent with Gilion and Brenim, enjoying fresh water and warm stew. Even just holding the warm bowl encouraged Aljeron as the heat seeped into his fingers. He looked at the faces of his friends as they ate and talked together. Evrim seemed relieved to be here, talking with Brenim and Gilion about the time they'd been away. Caan was shoveling the stew into his face as he leaned over next to Gilion to hear their conversation. Suddenly he laughed, and smiles broke out on each of their faces. Aljeron hadn't heard the joke, but he smiled too. It was good to be back. The tent felt like home.

"How soon do you think we could move?" Aljeron asked as soon as they were through.

Gilion, who was sitting straight in his chair with his hands resting on his thighs, answered directly, "As soon as you like."

"We thought you might want to rest a few days," Brenim added.

"No," Aljeron answered. "I'm through with waiting. The men are ready. They are invigorated by our return. I could see it. Spread the word tonight; tomorrow we set the plan in motion."

Gilion nodded, approving. "I'll send the messenger right away."

He rose and crossed to the door. He stepped through it for a moment, but only for a moment, and then returned to his seat.

"Now," Aljeron continued, gesturing to Sarneth. "We have some unexpected help, but the plan remains essentially the same. Tomorrow we will all move from camp to the outpost before the western gate. We will make as much noise and create as much commotion as we can. I want men coming and going at regular intervals all day. I want tomorrow to be as chaotic and overwhelming for them as possible.

"When night falls, Saegan and Bryar will take their men around to reinforce the southern gate. If the city is breached, or if there is a concerted attempt to break through and break free, it will come there. With our main force here, little but wilderness to the north, and no gate on the east, the south is the most likely path he would try to take to freedom.

"Brenim, this is our only change of plan: I want you to take an additional company of men with you to reinforce the southern gate as well. I think Rulalin will try to get out when we finally do breach their defenses. I can't see him surrendering. I want you up with the men outside the gate. Make sure, make absolutely sure, whatever happens there, that you do not enter the city. The men will be excited and any number of ruses might be used to draw you in. Stay put. Your job is not to get in. Your job is to make sure no one comes out."

Brenim nodded. "I'll hold the line."

"Caan and the Great Bear will join Gilion at the western gate. The Great Bear especially will be of service there. Their presence will inspire fear when the attack begins.

"When Saegan, Bryar, and Brenim leave to reinforce the southern gate, I will go with Evrim and the men we have set aside to the northern gate. It is the smallest and most lightly guarded, by us and by them. Hopefully, we will be able to push through there and make the breach. We will leave the gate defended and work through the outskirts of the city as quickly as possible to get the western gate opened if it is not already.

"Whether we get in first in the north or not, the most important things remain the same: All breaches must be adequately guarded in the eventuality Rulalin will try to get out. Also, we must press for surrender at the earliest available opportunity. The chaos of battle best affords Rulalin the circumstances he needs to get away. If we are fortunate and Allfather is with us, we will enter the city, and they will surrender rather than face the prospect of total defeat."

"Aljeron," Gilion said, "I asked you before you left if you would allow me to offer favorable terms of surrender immediately upon breaching the gate, and you said you would think on it while you were gone. Have you decided yet?"

"What terms?" Saegan asked.

"Gilion suggests offering food and water to the soldiers, their families, and the citizens of the city, immediately upon surrender. The terms for the army would be simple: They must lay down their weapons, then we will permit them to go free to eat and drink and take provisions to those in need, provided they don't leave the city."

Brenim's eyes narrowed. "You can't be considering this."

"I'm not considering it. I've decided to do it. Our dispute is with Rulalin, not the citizens of Fel Edorath. We will begin to sow the seeds of peace right away, even as the sound of war echoes from other parts of the battlefield. We will offer the people food and water and the supplies they need, and we will stay to help them rebuild whatever is destroyed tomorrow. We must bind the wounds we inflict. If Rulalin is taken, we will eventually return their weapons and withdraw completely."

"You can't trust Rulalin," Saegan said, his voice incredulous.

"I don't. But I believe there are good men in his army, fighting for what they believe to be right because they've been lied to. We are foolish not to think that our behavior after victory is critical to restoring Werthanin unity. We will end this war with mercy as well as finality. I know there are risks to being merciful to the soldiers of Fel Edorath, but there are risks in withholding mercy as well.

"Having said that, no mercy will be shown to any we encounter with sword lifted against the soldiers of Shalin Bel.

Our men must know that their lives are as valuable to us and to me as the lives of those we fight. We will speak of war tomorrow, but we will hope for peace."

They crested the last big hill on the way to Fel Edorath. The city rose before them, its gates shut and sealed tight as they had been when Aljeron had left them at the end of Summer Wane. Before the gates, just out of the city archers' range, a seething multitude of soldiers was gathered. Riders thundered back and forth in front of the foot soldiers, and detachments of men moved forward or to the side, ultimately rejoining the main contingent in another place. Aljeron halted to watch for a moment. He could see his own hand-picked captains and their subordinates waiting in the rear for his arrival. Later, they would move quickly with him under cover of darkness to the northern gate of Fel Edorath. Looking upward, he could see the tiny forms of men atop the city wall. Some stood in groups, gazing over the battlements, while others ran to and fro. He turned to Evrim.

"Do you think the men of Fel Edorath tremble at the thought of the coming night?"

"They should."

"Indeed they should," Aljeron answered, spurring his horse forward.

He rode forward with Gilion and Evrim to the front. Back and forth he rode, up and down the length of the line. He rode with his eyes fixed on his men, calling out words of encouragement and saluting them with the raised fist that they had followed into battle so many times before.

He paused as the sun sank in the west, and he gazed at its disappearing form, thinking of Shalin Bel far beyond the horizon. Wheeling around to face Fel Edorath, he said to the others without looking at them, "It's time."

He spurred his horse again along the line, motioning for

the men to be still and silent. When at last they were, he drew Daaltaran and rode with it raised high, beginning their battle ritual.

"My sword is ready to sing its battle song!" he shouted as he rode.

"And ours shall sing with yours!" came the reply as all drew their weapons.

"My sword is ready to sing its battle song!"

"And ours shall sing with yours!"

"Daaltaran is ready to sing its battle song!"

"Death comes to all!" the men cried, raising their swords high above their heads, almost in unison.

Aljeron brought his horse to a halt and sheathed his sword. The rest disappeared back into their sheaths as well. Absolute quiet fell upon them like the shadow from a cloud sweeping across the noonday sun. "When next we draw our swords, it will be for the last time. We will not sheath them again until Fel Edorath lies in our grasp. So be it?"

"So may it be!"

Turning, Aljeron rode toward the city wall. He had insisted on approaching the city alone, and as he did, he could feel the gaze of thousands upon his back. He wondered how many now stared at him from above as well.

Stopping, he turned his gaze upward. The tops of several heads were visible above the battlements, but no faces. "Men of Fel Edorath, hear me! Too long have we sat encamped outside your walls, surrounding your city. Too many lives have been lost in battle these past seven years. It's time to end this war. If you do not surrender Rulalin Tarasir into my custody that he may be tried before the Assembly for the murder of Joraiem Andira, I will come in and take him."

He paused, allowing the echo of his voice to die away. "These are the terms of your surrender: If you open your gates and lay down your arms, you will be given food and water immediately, as well as medical assistance. We will do all we can as fast as we can to alleviate the suffering your city has endured. We will hold your weapons until we are ready to depart with Rulalin, then they shall be left behind for you to reclaim. Nothing further will be required. The hostilities between us will be over."

Again he paused. He wanted the promise of peace to linger in the air before them like a vision from Allfather. "However," he continued, his voice rising in volume and intensity, "any man found with sword in hand will forfeit his life when we come, and we are coming! With dragon's might and on dragon's wings, we are coming. Our fury will be swift and terrible, and instead of food and water, you will receive only death. The end comes, and the choice left to you is to choose the manner of its coming. I urge you to choose well, and surrender!"

In the ensuing silence he could hear the swish of his horse's tail, and out of the corner of his eye he saw a blur of orange. Koshti was pacing back and forth a short distance behind him. "Your time is running out. My patience will not last forever."

Having said all he had come to say, and having received the reply he expected—nothing—he returned to the front of his waiting army.

"And now?" Brenim asked quietly as Aljeron returned to his senior officers.

"We prepare to go in while we hope they will come out."

Aljeron crouched in the dark beside Evrim under the sparse cover of a grove of leafless trees. The bright stars gave little light on this nearly moonless night. It was just about time for the detachment to retreat from the northern gate. Behind Aljeron, lying among the trees, was the battering ram that had been prepared long before his return and hidden away for this very night.

Peering at the gate, he noticed the torches of his men being extinguished. One by one, the distant orbs of light winked out, and gradually the area became as dark as this distant vantage point. Good, they will be on their way at last.

He looked down at Koshti, lying in the sparse grass. Stroking his soft fur, Aljeron let the tiger's body heat warm his cold hand. "Stay close to me tonight, my brother," Aljeron whispered.

As though in reply, Koshti lowered his head and nuzzled Aljeron's leg.

Evrim tapped Aljeron on the shoulder, and pointed silently out across the field. Aljeron looked but couldn't see anything. He leaned forward and squinted, having learned to heed Evrim's uncanny senses. No wonder he could track almost anything or anyone; he noticed almost as much as Koshti. At last he saw what Evrim had been pointing at: A column of men on foot was approaching, moving silently through the night. A quick glance above them toward the top of the city wall revealed nothing of note.

Aljeron turned to Evrim. "Get the others together and set everything in motion. I want the ram ready to roll out of here as soon as possible. They've probably begun the siege on the western gate by now."

Evrim nodded and glided away through the dark. Aljeron turned back to watch the gate. It was a risk, he knew, trying to penetrate the gate and get into the city with only five hundred men. His hope from the beginning had been that the thousands who would assail the western and southern gates, would discourage Rulalin from trying to slip out either of those ways. He was gambling on the hope that those masses would push Rulalin northward, right into his waiting trap. He had dreamed often of slipping silently up to the northern gate in the dark and smashing it down, only to find Rulalin and his top advisors standing there, befuddled and bewildered.

Then he noticed a change. Lights and torches along the top of the wall were disappearing rapidly. Soon there were only a score, then half a dozen, then none. "Evrim!" Aljeron called, as softly as possible. Soon, Evrim appeared out of the dark.

"Yes?"

"Are we ready?"

"Almost."

"Good, tell them to follow. The lights on the wall have gone out, they may be preparing to escape."

With that, Evrim sprang back into the dark as Aljeron called his detachment of a hundred and fifty men or so to start forward with him. He moved as quickly and stealthily as he could toward the gate, feeling exposed as he left the relative shelter of the wood.

Koshti jogged noiselessly along at Aljeron's side, and from out of the mass of men behind him, Evrim soon emerged. Evrim would not risk missing Rulalin's attempted escape, if that was indeed what was happening.

With that thought rolling through Aljeron's head, a light suddenly appeared, not on the wall but at its base. They had gone less than half the distance to the gate, but Aljeron feared he and his men would be spotted, so he dropped instantly into the grass, and men all around him did likewise. The light remained still, and Aljeron wondered what was going on. Obviously, the gate had been opened, so someone or some group could come out, but what were they doing just standing there?

Then, without warning, the light receded. Aljeron turned to Evrim. "Can you see anything?"

"No. I think someone was standing in the open gate, but they've stepped back inside."

"Can you tell if the gate is still open?"

"No."

They lay there, watching the gate. He reached down to

scratch a place on his side where a coarse stalk of grass had slipped inside his tunic. It was irritating and distracting. He turned back to Evrim.

"We can't just lie here. Did you see anyone actually get out?"

"I didn't."

"We have to move forward, and we'll need to check along the wall in both directions. Some may be out already. I'll—"

Light again appeared at the foot of the wall, this time several lights, hesitantly moving in a cluster. They began to move quickly as the men holding them started to run east.

Aljeron leapt up and signaled his men to follow, and he charged through the dark after the escaping men. Drawing Daaltaran, he pointed in the direction of the gate, and perhaps half the men with him broke off in that direction. As they drew nearer to the figures with the torches, he realized it was a group of perhaps twenty men. He could see a few of them looking over their shoulders, and he knew that at least some of them had realized they were being followed. Several of them dropped their torches and tried to disperse, but Aljeron's men soon had them surrounded. Not one of the fleeing men drew a weapon.

Aljeron picked up one of the discarded torches and approached the trembling men. The light of the torch illuminated his sweating face, and he could see even more fear wash over those who noticed the telltale scars that identified him as surely as his name. Stopping before one of the men, he stepped up close and stared into his eyes. "You know me?"

"Yes." The man's voice was tremulous and hesitant.

"Good, then you know to take me seriously when I ask, is Rulalin Tarasir with you?"

"No."

"Did he go the other direction out of the gate?"

"No, he didn't," the man said, stuttering slightly over the last word.

"Has he been at the northern gate at all tonight?"

"No," came the short reply, the man no longer ambitious enough to attempt more than a monosyllabic answer.

"So, where is Rulalin?"

"We don't know."

Aljeron felt his hand tightening on Daaltaran in frustration. "If Rulalin isn't here, what were you doing?"

"Trying to get away," a second man said when no answer was forthcoming from the first. "We heard rumors that the southern and western gates were under siege. We thought we could slip away without being noticed."

Aljeron snorted, "How could you slip away unnoticed while you were carrying torches?"

"We couldn't see where we were going without them," another man farther back said.

Aljeron turned away and motioned to Evrim to follow him, leaving his men to deal with the captives. As they moved quickly through the darkness to the city gates, he mumbled to Evrim, "If those fools were the best Rulalin could find to man his doors, then Fel Edorath will be ours long before morning."

When Aljeron arrived at the gates, he found that his men had taken custody of more surrendered soldiers, who were debating whether to follow the first group or shut the gate when the Shalin Bel troops surprised them. As it turned out, they were desperately hungry, and when they realized that Aljeron intended to feed them rather than execute them, they brightened considerably.

Meanwhile, the great battering ram had arrived, rolling on an enormous cart. "I guess we won't be needing that after all," Aljeron said.

"Guess not."

"Well, it looks like he hasn't slipped out, at least not here. I suppose we'd better go in after him."

Inside Fel Edorath, Aljeron found the city in disarray. He had worried that if his breach was successful, he might find himself in pitched battles against superior numbers intent on defending every span of the city. In actuality, he encountered hardly any resistance at all. Figures ran through the night, always away from his men, and houses were shut and boarded up tight. He could hear occasionally the din and clamor of shouting coming from the direction of the southern gate, but his business was not there, not now.

Moving through the labyrinth of city streets, he began to grow frustrated. Little disconcerted him like the unexpected, and he had not prepared for this. He had envisioned only heavy fighting or full surrender; what this was or would be, he couldn't tell.

He turned a corner into a wide, well-lit street, discovering a handful of men with swords in hand. When they saw Aljeron's company come tumbling around the corner, they turned and ran, all save one. The man who remained stood facing them, his sword half raised as he backed slowly away down the street.

Aljeron looked closely at the man, realizing that he was little more than a boy, though full grown. He stepped forward, walking steadily toward him, Daaltaran in hand. "Are you aware of the terms I gave for Fel Edorath's surrender, boy?"

"Stop where you are," the boy answered, his voice trembling.

"I said that any man found with sword in hand defending the city would die."

"Then you'll have to kill me," the boy answered, straightening to his full height. "I won't abandon my city to the likes of you."

"Oh no?"

"No, you have no business . . ."

The boy's voice was drowned out by the ring of metal on metal, as Daaltaran's quick stroke knocked his sword to the street, where it slid along the smooth stone. The boy looked up, his frightened eyes growing wider as they caught sight of Koshti. Aljeron held his sword steadily under the boy's chin. "Fortunately for you," Aljeron said tersely, "you are still a boy."

There was no objection from the quiet figure in front of him, who stood with eyes glancing back and forth between the sword and tiger, seeming unsure which he should fear most. "Do you know where Rulalin Tarasir's house or headquarters lie?"

"Yes," the boy said.

"Take me there, and then you may go. I would advise you to be done with this fight and go find food at the western gate. There is more than enough for you and your family. Tell them and your friends that the sooner we have Rulalin in our custody, the sooner we will leave Fel Edorath. Do you understand?"

"Yes."

Aljeron lowered Daaltaran. "All right, take us to the house."

For perhaps a quarter of an hour, all jogged through the streets behind the boy, and at no point did they meet anything resembling resistance. The main contingent of Fel Edorath's army had to be at the southern and western gates, unless they had disbanded completely. At last, the boy stopped before a large, sprawling building of several stories.

"This is it?"

"It is."

"Good, now go." The boy did not linger. Aljeron stepped to the door and pounded. There was no answer, so he motioned to two of his men, who kicked the door down and entered before him with swords drawn. Inside, the front room was completely dark, but a flickering light was headed down a hallway toward them.

"Who goes there?" Aljeron called out.

"The head steward of the house," came the defiant reply. An elderly woman appeared. "I don't need to ask who you are, for you bring destruction wherever you go, don't you?"

"No more than is necessary. Where is your master?"

"Not here, and more than that, you won't get from me."

"This is his headquarters?"

"It was."

"Was?"

She didn't answer, but stared at Aljeron, ignoring the men that now filled the room.

"Check every room, every closet, and every chest," Aljeron said. "Check any space large enough for a small animal, for I wouldn't put it past Rulalin to try to smuggle himself out of the city in his chief steward's pocket."

The men laughed as they lit their torches and moved into the house. Aljeron remained where he was, holding the woman in his gaze. She did not back down or turn away. He admired her strength.

His men soon returned, all reporting the same thing. There was no one else in the house. Aljeron sighed. "All right, we will have to do this the hard way. We will set up our headquarters here. As soon as it is light, have the house fully provisioned from our stores. In the meantime, I want fifty of you to make your way to the south gate, and fifty to the west gate. Report to me on the situations there. If we have not yet gained entrance, do what you can to aid it, but don't do anything foolish if you are heavily outnumbered. When we have taken each of the gates, direct every commander to scour the city. Your purpose is twofold: disarm every man of Fel Edorath, and find Rulalin."

He nodded to his men and the chief steward and then moved into the house.

After looking through the place himself, he finally settled on a comfortable room with a small parlor. He built a fire in the fireplace and warmed himself. He was hungry, but he had seen for himself the bare pantries beside the kitchen and knew there was no food here.

Less than two hours after coming to the house, during the middle of Third Watch, a messenger came from Gilion. Every gate had been secured, almost all of Rulalin's men had surrendered without a fight. The process of disarming the army of Fel Edorath was well underway. The city was being searched, even now, but to this point, there had been no sightings of Rulalin, and there was no news of him. Receiving the news with a grunt, Aljeron sent the man back to Gilion with the admonition that the search go on as long as need be. The man bowed and left, and Aljeron sat back down with Koshti and Evrim before the fire.

"This is worse than battle. Sitting and waiting."

"Yes," Evrim answered, yawning.

"Why don't you get some sleep?" Aljeron said. "I'll wake you if there is any news."

"I think I will, thanks." He stood and stretched.

"There is another room like this next door. I'll send for you there if I have reason."

Evrim slipped out. Aljeron stood and moved to the window that overlooked the city. Gazing out, he wondered where Rulalin was. If he was in the city, why had he not organized a better defense? If he had no intention of fighting, why not just come out and surrender? Again, the disconcerting feeling of facing the unexpected rippled through him. Too many events and pieces to this puzzle made no sense. He returned to the chair before the fire and sat down but did not sleep.

As the sun was rising over the city, a knock came on the door. Aljeron called for the visitor to come in, and he stood to greet Gilion, Caan, and Brenim.

"Well?" Aljeron said.

Gilion began without looking at the others. "We've searched every house, door to door, room to room, closet to closet, and chest to chest. Anything big enough to hold a man has been opened, turned over, and emptied. Rulalin Tarasir is not in the city."

Aljeron picked up a small statue of a child upon a dog, which rested within his reach, and hurled it at the stone wall above the fireplace. It shattered into several pieces that scattered upon the floor. "You've searched the whole city?"

"The whole city."

Aljeron clenched his fists, trying to contain his anger. Evrim appeared in the doorway, his eyes still full of sleep. Turning, he stepped to the window and gazed out over the city. "Search it again."

4

CHEIMONTYR COMES

WYLLA STOOD IN THE COURTYARD, watching the stewards and soldiers, whose number continued to grow as they answered Captain Merias's summons, dragging the bodies of Black Wolves, Malekim, and men outside the gate. The Silent Ones and Black Wolves would be burned, as soon as the piles could be made and fuel prepared, but the men would need to be buried.

"I have a final count," Merias said as he walked up beside her.

"Our losses or theirs?"

"Both. We lost one of my soldiers and three stewards of your household, and there are seven others receiving attention for wounds, only one of them serious."

"I see."

"Your Majesty, we were very fortunate. It could have been much worse."

"Allfather delivered us."

"Yes, by your hand."

"I did what was required. And our enemy?"

"There were nineteen Malekim, twenty-three wolves, and eleven men, including our captive inside."

"So few," Wylla murmured.

"Yes, and yet they managed to breach both gates and gain entrance to the palace grounds. We are fortunate indeed that you saw them approaching."

Wylla nodded, not feeling entirely fortunate. "It still doesn't make sense. Why send so few to assault us? They couldn't have had any aspirations of doing serious harm to the city."

"No, and their presence here would suggest it wasn't the city proper they meant to threaten."

Wylla looked at Captain Merias, who was watching her carefully. "If you are suggesting that I was their target, you may be right, but surely Malek knows that I am an insignificant threat to his plans. Why would he bother?"

"You are our queen. Your death would be a hard psychological blow to start this war."

"I suppose so," Wylla said, sighing.

"Anyway, whatever they were after, one thing is clear: You can't stay in the palace."

"Nonsense," Wylla said. "I'm not going anywhere."

"But, Your Majesty—"

"No. I will model the courage that we will all ask the people of Shalin Bel to show."

"Courage is one thing, foolishness is another."

"Careful," Wylla said sharply.

"I'm sorry, Your Majesty," Captain Merias said quickly.

"I understand your concern. We'll just set a watch on this gate. They won't surprise us again."

"I will move a thousand men here from their training ground by the western gate tomorrow."

"All right," Wylla conceded. She knew this meant an end to her peaceful walks upon the wall, for the open plains would now be crawling with soldiers, but it was the type of loss that war would require.

Wylla watched new arrivals join in the almost finished work of moving the bodies. "Well, it looks like you will get your wish."

"My wish?"

"Yes, I can't really keep our secret from the city any longer, can I? By midday, all of Amaan Sul will know what happened here tonight. We might as well tell them we know worse is coming and get all the panic out there and over with."

"Yes, Your Majesty."

Wylla turned to the palace. "Take me to the captive."

Merias led Wylla inside, and soon she was standing before a large contingent of Enthanim soldiers, all circling one man in black, his hands and ankles bound tightly, on his knees in their midst. Yorek stood nearby.

The soldiers grew quiet as she entered. They drew back, forming something like a semicircle behind the prisoner as Wylla approached. For a moment she just stared at the man, who appeared unconcerned despite the failure of his mission, the death of his companions, and his own capture.

"Do you know who I am?"

The man spat on her dress.

A loud crack echoed in the room, and it took Wylla a moment to realize that the sound had been caused by her hand striking the man's face. She looked at his cheek where a faint, white handprint was fading.

A pair of soldiers grabbed him roughly, and Wylla motioned them to release him. "Let him go," she said. "His mission has failed, and he is a threat to no one."

She waited as they withdrew. "I am Wylla Someris, queen of Enthanin."

"Not for long," the man said.

"We shall see," Wylla said, unfazed. "Why did you come here?"

The question was greeted with silence and a smirk as the man looked away from her.

"He hasn't been altogether helpful on that matter," Yorek said.

"A pity," Wylla answered. "A willingness to be helpful might make things easier for him."

"I don't fear you," the man added, glaring at Wylla. "Do with me what you will."

"I shall." Wylla turned to Captain Merias. "Take him with you and secure him. I'll be in contact with you later. Perhaps he will think better of answering my questions then."

"I'm not going to answer your questions, no matter what you do to me, and it wouldn't matter even if I did. The Bringer of Storms is coming."

"Who?"

"You'll see."

You are sworn, and you are mine. Malek's soft voice echoed in Rulalin's head, and he could feel on his ear the warm breath of whispering lips. He opened his eyes, but Soran was sitting as he had been, leaning back, gazing up at the high ceiling of the large cavern. It had been more than a week since he had sworn allegiance to Malek, but the dark scene still swept over him whenever he closed his eyes.

He pushed back his chair abruptly and stood. "Come," he began, startling his friend. "Let's go again."

"But we just sat down."

Soran looked quizzically at Rulalin. Not wanting the questioning look to lead to any actual questions, Rulalin answered more brusquely than was his intent, "Yes, and now we'll stand again, or are you still a boy that you can't keep up with a man's pace?"

Rulalin could see that his words had stung, but anger quickly pushed Soran's hurt away, and Rulalin knew it would be all right. They had often exchanged hard words before, and Rulalin knew the anger, too, would pass. He drew his sword because he also knew that his more pressing concern was to defend himself against Soran's emotionally charged onslaught.

No sooner had Rulalin drawn when Soran came at him, his own sword moving deftly, pressing the attack with skill and passion. Rulalin, who had practiced with Soran many times, still found it difficult to defend against the more agile movements of his younger companion. He didn't think he would be able to keep Soran from scoring a quick victory, and he had already lost more rounds than he had won. But, just as Rulalin was ready to concede, having already fallen back several spans from the table, Soran made a mistake. He lunged forward to strike Rulalin with the broad side of the sword and score the winning point. His shift in balance was almost imperceptible, but what Rulalin lacked in physical ability, he had always made up for with excellent vision. He saw Soran's miscalculation and the answer, the counterintuitive response to step in toward his opponent. As he did so, he easily deflected Soran's stroke and then countered with a short quick slap to Soran's side, ending the duel.

Soran cursed and turned back toward the table, where he raised his sword as though to strike the nearest chair. Thinking better of it, he cut a large swath through the empty air instead.

"Your mistake—"

"I know my mistake," Soran said. "I don't need to hear it from you."

Rulalin walked around to the other side of the table and sat, ignoring Soran, who had likewise taken his seat again and was staring sullenly in the other direction. Rulalin gazed across the length of the relatively empty cavern. Shortly after swearing allegiance to Malek, Tashmiren had shown them how to come here from their rooms, and they had since spent most of their days here, where the open space helped to ease their growing dislike for their windowless and caged existence. The first day they had been here, men had crowded the large room, but every day since they had seen virtually no one. When asked about it, Tashmiren had explained that most of the Nolthanim had been employed these past several days slaughtering animals and packing the meat in salt for their coming march.

"When we leave," Tashmiren had added, "we will empty every cave and cavern. We will not come back to the Mountain until all Kirthanin has bowed to Malek. When we do return, we will not descend to this place again but ascend to Avalione, where Malek will establish his rule over all things. We will be like the floodwater that swells over the banks of the river and washes over the land, never to return, even when the rains have stopped and the storm is over."

From time to time, two different and equally curious groups of visitors had come and gone through the room while Rulalin and Soran were there. Sometimes, small groups of Vulsutyrim entered through the larger doors on the far side of the cavern, apparently to play a sort of game, a contest of strength that Rulalin did not completely understand. Vulsutyrim paired up, and each pair took turns hurling stones of varying sizes, though all were enormous to Rulalin. How the game was scored eluded him, for he had realized that while distance was important, so was the pattern created by the rocks upon landing, though how he didn't know. Six giants were now engaged in what was at least their third game of the day, for they had been there since he and Soran had arrived a few hours ago. As he watched them, one of the Vulsutyrim launched a smaller rock through the air in a great arc, where it landed with a thud near a couple of the others he and his partner had thrown. It seemed an awesome display, but from the excited calls of the opponents and the body language of the one who had thrown the rock, the result was obviously disappointing.

The giants never acknowledged Rulalin and Soran. They seemed oblivious to the existence of the men. Though he and Soran had watched them for hours at a time, he never observed a single Vulsutyrim looking their way when sitting or standing or even sword fighting.

To the second group of visitors, however, they were not quite so invisible. On the third day after Tashmiren first brought them here, after he and Soran had been dueling for some time, a large group of women entered. The women, perhaps thirty of them, proceeded to walk straight through the cavern from one side to the other, talking among themselves but not shy at all about watching the men, who were reduced to standing and gawking as the sweat dripped down their faces and fell to the stone floor. The pair had recovered only after most disappeared from sight. Neither had suggested going back to their fight, but rather they sat down to have a cold drink. They both admitted to feeling foolish for not thinking before that there must be women, many women, among the remnant of Nolthanin, but the thought had simply not occurred to either of them.

When they next saw Tashmiren, they asked him questions about the women. Tashmiren laughed in his scornful and condescending way at their awkward inquiries. "Of course there are women among the Nolthanim, but they have been busy these past many weeks with preparations of their own for our departure. In addition to the many tents they have sown for our armies, they have fashioned tents for themselves and a grand pavilion, which they will establish just beyond the northernmost reaches of Gyrin at the foot of the Mountain, where they will await the completion of our conquest. For when Malek returns to ascend the Mountain, Farimaal will lead the remnant of the Nolthanim back across the Kiruan River to begin the resettlement of our ancient lands."

Then Tashmiren had smiled a cruel smile. "But why the interest in the women, Rulalin? I thought your heart was given to another, or do you doubt her favorable reception, having killed her husband?"

Rulalin's blood had boiled but Soran, who was sitting close by, restrained him as he moved to stand.

Twice since then, Rulalin saw women pass through the large room, and he ignored them both times, both of which resulted in a foul mood. Soran noticed and said, "Tashmiren is a strutting peacock. Don't let his foolishness bother you."

"I won't, but if he decides to use her as the means for his insults again, I will teach him manners, even if we are both sworn to the same master."

"It might well be the last thing you do."

"At least I will die with a smile on my face."

As Rulalin sat at the table now, watching the Vulsutyrim still playing their game, his mind strayed to Wylla. He knew she would not receive him favorably; he knew she could not. Still, even if she came unwillingly, bound hand and foot, he would protect her from the ravages of the coming war. Perhaps over time she would realize that he was doing this for her as her protector, not her captor.

"Come on," Rulalin said as he stood again. "Let's go back to our rooms."

Seeing that the sullenness had left Soran's face, Rulalin asked Soran to wait for their evening meal with him. He despised sulking in others, perhaps because he despised it in himself, and he would have sent Soran to his own room had he detected even a trace of it in his friend. But one of the things he most valued in his young comrade was the ease with which he let such things go. Soran, for all his vitriol over the war with Aljeron, was good at distinguishing between real offenses and minutiae, a trait Rulalin greatly appreciated.

A knock on the door brought Rulalin to his feet. "The evening meal is here early," he said as he walked to the door.

Before he reached it, however, the door opened and Tashmiren stepped into the room. "Tashmiren?" Rulalin failed to hide his surprise.

"Both of you, come with me. Farimaal has summoned you."

Rulalin glanced at Soran, who was rising hastily from the table. The broad smile was gone from his face, and if the flickering light on the table did not mislead him, he was even a little pale. Rulalin wondered if his own face betrayed the fluttering in his stomach. There was no time to think about it, though, because Tashmiren was already out in the hallway.

The first portion of the journey Rulalin could follow, for he was gradually gaining his bearings in the corridors and hallways near their quarters. They soon passed beyond familiar places, however, and eventually came to an area he had not seen before. High ceilings topped wide halls lined with many doors, and men and women both moved all around them.

They passed through several of these large hallways, and Rulalin did not need to ask to know these were the quarters of the Nolthanim. From their own land, rich and abundant, they had been exiled to the Forbidden Isle, where they lived during the Second Age. From there, they had returned to Kirthanin in hopes of regaining their ancestral home, and they had ended up here, living in caves and tunnels beneath the Holy Mountain. This was where their allegiance to Malek had brought them; did he know for sure that he would not suffer a similar fate? He didn't, but he pushed the question away, for failure in the past did not guarantee failure in the future. He had been taught the corollary to this as a boy in Fel Edorath, namely, that victory against Malek in the past did not guarantee victory in the future, which was why the city had kept vigilant watch on the Mountain. If he had been able to see then the difficulty of defeating Malek's hosts without the aid of dragons and likely without the Great Bear too, could he not now see the probability of Malek's victory? Perhaps the time of Malek's ascendancy had finally come.

Beyond the halls were smaller corridors, now largely empty. Tashmiren led them down one of these to a large door that dominated the wall. Tashmiren pushed the door open without knocking. Inside was a large antechamber with two more doors on either side of the far wall and several chairs around a large table in the middle of the room. Tashmiren motioned for them to sit at the table, and he pulled the door closed behind them, remaining outside in the hallway.

Rulalin surveyed the room silently, not wanting to make eye contact with Soran for fear he might break the silence that Rulalin felt instinctively was better preserved. Aside from the table, there was precious little else to be seen, other than a long narrow table up against the far wall between the two doors. This room was as sparse as either of theirs and felt even more so for being bigger.

The door ahead of them on the right opened up, and both Rulalin and Soran sat up rigid in their chairs. Rulalin felt the tension in his chest, but it quickly dissipated as a young boy stepped into the room with a large tray containing a pitcher and a few glasses. He had seen among the men in the caverns some boys who must have been barely of age, but he had not seen any this young, for the boy could not have been more than twelve. He did not speak or look at either of them but set the tray on the table and disappeared back through the same door. Rulalin raised his arm and wiped his forehead, annoyed with himself. He had almost felt calmer when waiting for Malek.

Then the door on the left swung open and, catlike, Farimaal glided into the room. He seemed to appear quickly, but as Rulalin watched him enter, it struck him that Farimaal moved with an unhurried gait. He was as unimposing up close as he had been when Tashmiren first pointed him out from a distance. Farimaal was not a striking presence, to be sure, but that was not the whole story. He was lean, and the sleeveless tunic he was wearing revealed arms that were taut with muscle. He was unkempt, his disheveled hair a tousled mixture of black and grey, and his face grizzled with the beginnings of a patchy beard. Even so, as Farimaal paused to pour from the pitcher before him, Rulalin looked at his green-grey eyes and found unmistakable authority there. He only caught a glimpse of it, like when the sun peeks out from behind the clouds for just a moment on an overcast day, but it was enough to give him an undeniable sense that the stories about Farimaal were not exaggerations.

Farimaal set a glass before each of them and motioned for them to drink, which Rulalin did only after Farimaal had seated himself opposite them and taken a drink himself. The water in the cup was clear and cold, cold like Rulalin had never tasted. He imagined it had been collected drop by drop off of a large piece of ice and delivered immediately to their table. It chilled him, and he shuddered as he set the cup down.

"You are from Fel Edorath?" Farimaal asked, looking directly at the two men across the table for the first time.

"Yes, we are," Rulalin answered. After their exchange before the meeting with Malek, Rulalin and Soran had agreed that Rulalin would be their spokesman in any similar situation. This was as much for Soran's protection as it was for Rulalin's peace of mind, for Rulalin's value to their new master would not likely protect Soran should he say the wrong thing to the wrong person at the wrong time.

"Your role in what is to come has been explained to you?"

"Yes. I am to persuade as many men of Fel Edorath as I can to follow me as I follow"—Rulalin hesitated for a moment, not quite sure how Malek should be addressed to Farimaal—"the master."

"And after Fel Edorath?"

"I will try to convert as many to our cause as I can throughout Werthanin and indeed all of Kirthanin, though I am likely to be most successful in Fel Edorath."

"In battle?"

"I will do whatever I am entrusted to do as well as I can do it."

Farimaal took a drink from his cup but left his eyes upon Rulalin. When he had set his cup down he continued, looking from Rulalin to Soran and back again. "I am responsible for the movement of all men, Malekim, and Black Wolves both in battle and out. In all things military you are answerable to me, understood?"

"Yes."

"The Vulsutyrim are answerable to Cheimontyr. Follow my commands. Keep clear of them. If for any reason Cheimontyr grows angry with you, even if you are about my business, I will not intervene on your behalf.

"Do as you are told, and you will not face my anger."

Rulalin nodded, and Farimaal rose to go. "We march in two days."

Almost as an afterthought, he paused at the edge of the table and looked down at Rulalin. "I know all there is to know about how things are going in the tasks set before you. I know you have asked to receive a share in the inheritance of the Nolthanim. This request is mine to grant or deny, and your service will determine how I answer it. We are through."

The morning of the second day came, and Rulalin packed his saddle bag and stepped out into the hall only to see Soran emerging at the same time. His young friend looked up at him and smiled. "I won't miss this place very much."

"No, I guess not."

"Tashmiren said we'd get the horses back on the way out, didn't he?"

"Yes. Apparently, the horses are stabled near the upper hall where we left them on the way in."

"Good, I don't especially want to walk back to Fel Edorath."

"No, nor beyond, for I suspect that if we survive long enough, we will traverse most of Kirthanin before we have a real rest."

"Yes, I suppose so." Soran looked at his bag in his hand and at his sword at his side. "I've been so eager to get back to Fel Edorath and give Aljeron what he has coming that I haven't thought much about any more than that. I hope we don't have to fight too many battles outside Werthanin." His smile faded. "It'll be strange to draw my sword beside Malekim against other men, men that haven't done me any harm."

"Yes, it will, but that's the price of our revenge, isn't it?" Rulalin said, looking intently at Soran, who was just beginning to understand why he had not been as ready to rejoice over their allegiance with Malek. "It's also the price of our survival, so don't let it get to you. Our responsibility is first and foremost to the people of Fel Edorath, and this is the path of life for them. We will show the same path to every city we encounter, but if they refuse it, we will fight against them and serve our master well."

"Right," Soran echoed, but Rulalin knew it was an empty reply.

"Come on." Rulalin moved down the corridor toward the hall where they were to assemble and follow the other men of Nolthanin out of the labyrinthine passageways of the Mountain.

They did not have to wait long before the great mass of men and women began to funnel out of the great room through the wide door. The going was slow, for the tunnels had not been built to accommodate such large numbers. At times, the crowd pressed in so tight that Rulalin found it difficult not to push away the strange men who crowded him, if only to breathe. He wasn't used to being herded like a common foot soldier.

After a few hours of this slow pace, they reached the place where some of the men could mount waiting horses, and Rulalin and Soran eventually made their way to their own horses. They did not mount right away, though, for it was apparent that the riders would follow the men on foot. As they waited for the river of men to pass, Tashmiren walked up to them with an extra measure of swagger in his gait.

"Do you see this great host of men? It is but a fraction of our army. The Black Wolves started their descent yesterday, and by now they are no doubt already scouting the path we are to tread. The Malekim are preparing to come behind, as they will be pulling the great wagons of our supplies, stocked with barrels of water and freshly slaughtered and salted meat. As you descend the Mountain, look back over your shoulder and you will see just a hint of the vastness of their number. The silent children of Malek who are ever about his business are like the stars in the sky.

"And," Tashmiren continued, "after they have come out, if you are not too far down by that point, look back again, and you will see the Vulsutyrim, who even now stand assembled beside the gates, welcoming from his resting place their captain, who comes forth to lead them into battle and to victory. Behold Cheimontyr, and know for yourself why he is called the Bringer of Storms."

Eventually, the slow-moving column brought Rulalin and Soran and all the men on horseback back into the outer world. Rulalin breathed the cold but invigorating air deeply. The wind was strong and cold and the clouds thick and grey, but there was light, real light all around them. There was also space, lots of space, for the slope was steep and bare and the road moved in zigzags down the western slope of the Mountain. The Nolthanim moved faster now, for they were able to walk and ride almost ten across. He smiled at Soran, who was himself sitting with a grin on his face gazing down over the host before them. Neither of them spoke. There was no need.

As they exited the Mountain, Rulalin noticed a large level area beside and behind the entrance, a recess in the mountainside. Standing there, holding large axes and great swords, were perhaps a hundred Vulsutyrim, talking among themselves and glancing from time to time at the men streaming out of the Mountain. He had never seen more than perhaps a dozen in one place inside the Mountain, and he wondered how many there were. He wondered if Cheimontyr was standing among them. The road, though, made a sharp turn, and soon the moving tide of men and horses carried him far enough that he could no longer see the Vulsutyrim.

It was perhaps Fifth Hour, their emergence from the Mountain having already taken most of the morning. Rulalin turned his attention to the road. It was indeed steep, so steep that it required his complete focus. The switchbacks were both steeper and narrower than the rest of the road, and the men on horseback had to funnel their lines to two or three at a time as the horses struggled to maintain their footing. Even so, the farther down they went, the longer the straightaway sections became, and the less frequent the switchbacks.

In the middle of one of these more gently sloping segments, Rulalin looked back up the side of Agia Muldonai and almost gasped at the sight. At every level of road above him all the way up to the top, Malekim walked, rank upon rank. Evenly distributed throughout their number were great wagons with high wooden sides and long poles gripped and pulled by some three or four Malekim at a time. How they were negotiating the narrow and treacherous switchbacks, Rulalin couldn't imagine. Still, on they came, a host of Silent Ones far greater than he could ever have envisioned, moving noiselessly out and down the Mountain. He momentarily balked at the thought that he was marching with them, not against them, to battle, but he reminded himself of the very truths he had told Soran.

Downward they went, now walking great distances laterally for every ten or twenty spans they descended. Early afternoon was upon them, and what little warmth the sun had provided diminished as evening approached. Inside Agia Muldonai, Rulalin had not missed this cold weather, but he would willingly pay this small price to sleep beneath the open sky.

"Do you think we'll have to camp on this road and sleep on the side of the Mountain?" Soran asked.

"I hope not, though we might if the cloud cover doesn't break. I wouldn't want to descend this Mountain on my hands and knees alone in the dark, much less risk horses and wagons and who knows what else."

"How big do you think this army is?"

"I don't know. I wouldn't know how to begin to estimate when I can't get a good look at the whole army at once."

"Just looking at the men in front of us, I think there are more men here than in the armies of Fel Edorath and Shalin Bel combined, at least now. Maybe seven years ago we could have put enough soldiers in the field to meet this force at equal strength, but we certainly couldn't now, and that's not even counting the Malekim and the Black Wolves and the Vulsutyrim. Aljeron will have to flee before us, don't you think?"

"I don't know what he'll do. He may retreat from Fel Edorath if he is still there when we come, but how far can he fall back? If he doesn't take the field at all, what will become of Shalin Bel? He is too proud to give up his own city without a fight."

"If he does fight, he won't last long. We'll have to ask Farimaal for a chance to fight in the front, or he may not live long enough for us to see his fall."

"I'm not sure our desire for revenge can influence Farimaal's battle plan. We may have to satisfy ourselves with the knowledge he will surely fall, even if we cannot cause or witness it. As much as I too long to see Aljeron humbled, I will not complain if I am not made to take part in the slaughter of other Werthanim."

The excitement slipped from Soran's face. "Maybe they will surrender after Aljeron falls, and slaughter will be avoided."

"Maybe."

They rode on without further discussion. After a few more switchbacks, they noticed that a rider ahead of them had stopped his horse on the outer edge of the road as the riders passed him by. It was Tashmiren.

"Waiting for us, no doubt," Soran whispered to Rulalin when they realized who it was.

"Yes," Rulalin nodded. "How fortunate for us."

When they reached Tashmiren, he motioned them to join him. With them by his side, Tashmiren extended one arm and pointed back up the side of the Mountain. Rulalin craned his head back and gazed up. The great river of Malekim continued to flow down the Mountain road, but high above, at the still-visible cave mouth, the Vulsutyrim had gathered. Then they opened their mouths, and a great rumbling came from them, and Rulalin could see that they were chanting together.

"What are they saying?"

"Shh."

The mass of giants began to part, and Rulalin was granted a clear glimpse of the open doorway. Then, all at once, swords were drawn and axes raised so that the great blades of the Vulsutyrim dimly gleamed in the overcast afternoon.

At that moment he appeared in the opening, a head taller

than any of the other giants. His hair was dark and thick and long, and even from so far down the Mountain, Rulalin could see his eyes blazing like lightning emerging from a black sky. His complexion was dark, far darker than any of the other Vulsutyrim, and it wasn't skin of one browned by the summer sun, or of the Suthanim, who lived in the sunburnt lands of the far south. It was an unnatural dark, as of pale white skin stretched thin over a blue-black body.

He strode forth into the open air, and the rumble of the Vulsutyrim's voices became a great cry that echoed down the Mountain. He walked out into their midst and stopped, raising his two great arms over his head. His large, cruel hands stretched up to the highest point he could raise them, open with his fingers curled and palms tilted upward. He opened his mouth and his voice boomed like thunder. Over and over he called out the same words, which Rulalin could not understand, and as he did, the clouds grew thicker and darker, and the light around them began to fade, and the shadows grew deeper. Then, with a mighty shout and clap of his hands, the heavens opened up and water fell from the sky as if cascading over a waterfall. It fell thick and heavy in enormous drops, so dense that Rulalin felt he was being pelted by little stones.

Again, a great cry arose from the giants, as though the coming rain was as long awaited as their emergence from the Mountain. The giants closed in around Cheimontyr, and he was lost from Rulalin's view except for the very top of his head.

"Cheimontyr comes forth to finish for Malek what his great father, Vulsutyr, began." Tashmiren spoke reverently, yet loudly enough to be heard above the downpour. "He will bring Kirthanin to its knees, for no one will stand against him."

"How could they?" Rulalin murmured, almost involuntarily, for the image of what he had just seen and the feeling of awe that had washed over him had not departed.

Tashmiren spurred his horse from the edge of the road

back into the river of men, and Soran moved to follow him. Rulalin continued to sit, staring up at the crowd of Vulsutyrim, barely visible through the downpour.

"Rulalin?" Soran called.

"Coming." Rulalin reluctantly nudged his horse out onto the road. It was enough to convince Soran, who moved forward. Rulalin lingered a moment more, staring upward.

Suddenly, he could see the great destruction and desolation that was coming. He saw Cheimontyr striding down the streets of Fel Edorath and Shalin Bel and Amaan Sul. He saw the great walls and buildings in ruin and the men and women and children slain in the streets. He saw the dark clouds that now hung above the Mountain stretched across the whole land, a thick and suffocating roof that blotted out the sun. He saw himself, riding with Tashmiren and Soran behind the unflagging onslaught, helping to destroy all that he had once loved and sworn himself to defend.

All for the uncertain hope of beholding her face again.

He pulled his gaze away from the top of the Mountain and spurred his horse forward. He rode, head bowed low and spirit downcast as the driving rain soaked his clothes and skin.

"What have I done?"

5

THE STORM BREAKS

T H E   W O R K   O N   T H E   O U T E R   G A T E   was almost finished. From the wall, Wylla watched the workmen reinforce the new wooden gate with fitted iron, so that the whole gate would be covered by a single plate.

Beyond, she could see the drilling of soldiers, the new constant outside her walls. She sighed, for as she had feared, the view was no longer the same.

She turned to head inside, and seeing Yorek waiting at the doorway, walked over expectantly. "What is it, Yorek?"

"News has come from Captain Merias."

"Yes?"

"The worst of the panic seems to be over."

Wylla grabbed Yorek's arm. "He thinks so?"

"He does. The chaos at the southern gate has settled down, and while there is still a steady stream of people leaving, there are also merchants and citizens, men and women not in the army, imploring their neighbors to stay and help with the city's defenses. Merias senses a mounting desire to prepare for the coming war. We've turned a corner."

Wylla walked briskly into the large open hallway off the courtyard, seeing a steward of the house inside. "Raynin?" she called to him.

"Yes, my queen," the elderly man answered, coming swiftly over.

"Please get my cloak. I'm going out into the city."

Raynin looked uncertainly from Wylla to Yorek.

"It's all right. The turmoil in the city is dying down."

He nodded and turned, disappearing through the opposite door, and Wylla turned to Yorek. "I should be seen among the people. I should be out there to encourage them."

"I agree. It will do you good to get out, and it will do them good to see you safe and well."

"Has Merias sent any word on our prisoner?"

"Only that he says nothing."

"Let him keep his silence. Valzaan has warned us already."

"He has, Your Majesty, but don't give up yet. Any specific information the prisoner might provide could be most helpful."

"I know," Wylla answered. "I just don't want to be bothered with him, but I'll have to make a decision sooner or later about what to do with him."

"There's no rush."

Raynin returned with Wylla's cloak, as expected, but he was also half running with Kyril beside him, which surprised Wylla.

"Kyril, Raynin, what is it?"

"There is a bit of commotion," Raynin said. "I think you should come with me to the outer wall so I can show you."

"Can't you tell me?"

"I think you should come with me and see for yourself."

Kyril stood nodding beside him.

"All right," Wylla said, and she, Kyril, and Yorek followed

Raynin as he moved off quickly across the room to the court-yard. "I know you are excited, Raynin, but I'm not going to run to the top of the outer wall in this dress."

"Yes, Your Majesty. I'm sorry, Your Majesty," Raynin replied, slowing down a little bit.

"And," Wylla added as she shuffled along, trying to keep up, "I'd like my cloak."

Raynin stopped and held the cloak for Wylla as she slipped it on over her dress. She pulled it to, but he was already on his way again. They quickly passed outside. Wylla noticed immediately that the sky was darker than it had been just moments ago. The wind was also brisker and the cold penetrated her cloak, stinging her exposed face and hands.

They crossed the courtyard silently and ascended the stairs to the top of the outer wall that overlooked the north. Raynin led them to the northwest corner, where several stewards had clustered. Long before Wylla reached them, though, she had seen what they were staring at. The soldiers outside the gate had also seen it, for they stood motionless across the plain, gazing northwest.

"What's happening?" Kyril asked from behind her.

"I don't know. I've never seen anything like it. Yorek?"

"No, Your Majesty, nor have I."

She stopped a few spans away from the others and stared. Great towers of clouds as black as a starless night were expanding and contracting in the distance in odd billowing motions, and lightning was flashing both horizontally and vertically in and around them. On clear days, one could see the Mountain from here, a high distant peak stretching up over Gyrin Wood out of Kirthanin's ancient past and dark present, but these dense clouds totally obscured it. The sky between the city and the great black clouds seemed to change even as Wylla watched it. The thin, wispy light grey clouds floating high in the air filled out with terrible weight before their eyes. A wave of dark grey cloud rolled in on the wind from the Mountain.

As Wylla tried to comprehend how the weather could change so instantly, a great clap of thunder exploded in the distance, and everyone on the wall, including her, jumped as it echoed across the open plain.

"My Queen," said one of the stewards, "what is this?"

Wylla slowly shook her head from side to side. "It is the beginning."

Benjiah dismounted so that he stood beside his uncles and Valzaan. They had reached the western edge of Gyrin after several days of hearing the spattering of rain upon the leaves of the trees, but they had been largely protected from the wet by the thick foliage. Now they gazed out across the open land they had long hungered to see, only to find it dark like Gyrin, but grey and soggy as well.

Valzaan walked to a large stone that rose out of the ground just south of the Old Mountain Road, right on the edge of the wood. Rivulets of water streamed down the side in smooth channels that had been cut by the flow of water over many centuries. Pedraal and Pedraan followed Valzaan to the stone, as did Benjiah.

"A Water Stone," Pedraal said, reaching out his hand and cupping it to catch some of the cascading water.

"Yes," Valzaan said, standing by the rock. "A sign of encouragement in dark times, for Allfather has promised to open the great deep, and the Water Stones will again flow. This storm cannot last forever, but the streams it creates here will return and never run dry again when the time is come."

"Perhaps this storm can't last forever," Benjiah said, "but it has rained the better part of three days. Does no one else find it odd that so much rain would come so continually, when it isn't even the wet season? It is only the fifth day of Autumn Wane."

"It is odd, because the storm is odd," Valzaan said, turning from the Water Stone. "It is unnatural, because it is no ordinary storm."

"What do you mean?" Pedraal asked.

"Some power of Malek's is at work, though what Malek intends to do with this rain, I could not tell you."

"You mean Malek has the power to command the weather?"

"Malek has the power to do many things, and yes, it would appear he has directed some of it to control the weather. But I sense another hand at work in this, and who the second party might be I could not say."

"Well," Pedraan said, shivering, "Malek's storm or not, I'm getting soaked. It's only a couple hours before dark. Should we take shelter here and try to stay dry one more night?"

"We will ride now," Valzaan answered. "We will ride until well after dark. Even if we ride dawn until dusk, it is at least three days to Fel Edorath. The earliest we will arrive is the evening of the eighth, and we must not allow this rain to deter us. If this storm is Malek's handiwork, he may have come forth from the Mountain already. There isn't a moment to lose."

Pedraan did not look pleased with the decision to ride out into the rain, but he mounted without complaint and followed the prophet as he headed away from the wood. Benjiah looked back over his shoulder at Gyrin as they galloped toward the open plain. The trees were only marginally darker than everything else on the whole gloomy horizon, but he felt relieved to have passed safely through, though "safe" might not be exactly the right word to use. He sensed truth in Valzaan's observation that the storm was unnatural. He had felt it that first afternoon when the dusky tree-filtered light had suddenly begun to fade. They had all gazed up at the canopy as the light slipped away and the sound of thousands of heavy raindrops started to slap against the quaking leaves. He had felt more than seen the rushing darkness of the thick clouds that swirled in the sky and spread south over the forest as if blown in by the Mountain itself. He had also heard, or thought he heard, amid the rolling thunder, a deeper, different rumbling. It occurred to him that the rumbling was like words, the earth talking to the sky in a mystical and ancient language, and it frightened him to think of the power they carried. The rumbling had disappeared, but Benjiah's uneasiness continued, and now they were out in the middle of this unnatural rage, with no shelter ahead and no turning back.

Aljeron stood on one side of the long center table in the kitchen, staring across at the grey-haired woman who met his eyes with a level gaze. As useful as she had been in the enormous task of organizing food for the city and finding an effective means to distribute it to the starving residents, she was unrelenting in her dislike of him and was a constant nuisance in pointing out his mistakes whenever she could. She was unimpressed by his physical stature or military accomplishments, and she had stood toe to toe with him on more than one occasion. This chief steward of Rulalin's household would have made a great soldier, and had Rulalin left the defenses of the city in her care, Aljeron might still be looking at the walls from the other side.

"Mistress Brahan, we have done our best to restore regular supply lines to the city and to restore the water supply."

"This rain has restored our water supply," Mistress Brahan sneered, crossing her arms, "and it seems only fitting you should restore our supply lines, since you cut them off in the first place."

"Yes, I did cut them off, but that was war, and now the war is over. I'm trying to restore order here."

"Oh, it's over, just like that, is it? Then why do soldiers

from Shalin Bel still patrol our streets and stand guard over our gates? Why do you still sleep under this roof and eat with your captains at my table? This isn't over, and Shalin Bel will learn that Fel Edorath has a long memory."

Aljeron put his hands on the table and leaned toward Mistress Brahan's face. "This wasn't about Fel Edorath and Shalin Bel. You are talking like a fool."

"I'm a fool? Seven years you've spent making war on my city, and do you have what you came for? Have you got what you were after? Who's the fool, Master Balinor?"

"I said you were talking like a fool, not that you were one, Mistress Brahan," Aljeron said, softening his tone and straightening. "And yes, I have failed to do what I came to do. But my failure to execute justice doesn't mean that my cause was not just. And you may be right, perhaps Fel Edorath will hold all this against me and against Shalin Bel, but neither does that mean my cause was not just. Fel Edorath was a city in rebellion against the Assembly, or have you forgotten?"

"I have not forgotten," Mistress Brahan answered, her certainty and defiance wavering. "But the Assembly didn't have all the facts. The Assembly wasn't going to give Master Tarasir a fair trial."

"That's Rulalin and his father talking. The trial would have been fair, and Rulalin would have been found guilty because he was guilty."

"Of course you say that, you were one of the ones who were out to get him . . ."

"Out to get him? Mistress Brahan, I am a Werthanim like you. Rulalin's crime is also my shame. I was there, in Sulare. I held Joraiem Andira's wife as she wept over her dead husband's body. For two months I traveled with Joraiem Andira's body draped over a horse so I could bring word of their son's death to his parents. Rulalin was one of us. He was . . ." Aljeron hesitated, the words stuck in his throat. "He was my friend."

Mistress Brahan did not answer, but straightened the bodice of her dress and adjusted the bun in her hair. "I will attend to those things you have asked of me. Is there anything else?"

"Perhaps, one day, Mistress Brahan, you will have a chance to meet Wylla Someris and her son, Benjiah, and then maybe you will understand why I have done what I have done."

"Is there anything else, sir?"

"Not for now, though there will be things we need to discuss before we leave."

"Leave?" Mistress Brahan said, looking surprised.

"Yes, whatever we do now, we can't stay forever."

"Of course not," Mistress Brahan answered, her composure regained. "I will be happy to assist in your departure."

"I'm sure you will." Aljeron nodded slightly in respect. He left the kitchen and ascended the stairs with a measure of relief. As much as he wasn't looking forward to dealing with the other issues that lay before him, almost anything had to be better than dealing with her.

Evrim was waiting in Aljeron's sitting room. He looked tired, as tired as Aljeron felt. In the eight days since Fel Edorath had fallen, the work had not ceased. Once the searches had confirmed beyond doubt that Rulalin was not in the city, there had been the disarming of the soldiers, the distribution of food and water, and the organization of a temporary civil authority. Not everyone was as antagonistic toward Aljeron as Mistress Brahan, though many shared her basic attitude. Others, though, seemed relieved the siege was over and eager to put the pieces back together, even if under the supervision of men from Shalin Bel.

Evrim, who had been as disappointed as Aljeron not to find Rulalin, had thrown himself into the work of organizing food and water. Like everyone else, he had been glad to see the rains come and stay, and there wasn't a clean vessel or container in the city that didn't now sit full of cold rainwater. The rain had provided enough water to satisfy the needs of the city while the water supply was restored. That work would be finished today, as it was infinitely harder to stop the flow of a river than to set that same river free.

Aljeron stooped down and stroked Koshti's soft fur while the tiger lay stretched out on the hearth. One eye opened and Aljeron smiled as Koshti looked sleepily at him and then went back to sleep.

"Drink?" Aljeron asked Evrim, pouring himself one from the pitcher on the table.

"No thanks." Aljeron pulled out the chair opposite Evrim and sat down. "They're going to want to make a decision, you know."

"I know," Aljeron answered.

"What are you going to say?"

"I don't know."

"We can't stay much longer. One way or the other, we can't stay."

"I know."

Evrim didn't say anything else, and Aljeron was content to let it go. They'd had the same conversation many times, and as soon as the others arrived, they would have it again. There seemed no need to repeat it now. Discussing it over and over hadn't changed any of the relevant facts, nor had it made clear what they should do. In the end, it was all just talk, and Aljeron didn't know how much more of it he could take.

A light knock on the door elicited a sigh from Aljeron as he stood and went to the door. As he opened it, the others entered. Gilion, Caan, Saegan, and Brenim took seats at the table, and Sarneth sat on the floor by the window, where he could comfortably stretch his legs.

The six men exchanged small talk for a few moments, and a few of them updated the others on things they already knew. All avoided the real issue that had brought them together, and each of them knew it.

"Look," Saegan said at last. "We can't put this off any more. We need to make a decision and get on with it."

"It's true," Gilion added, fastidiously picking a small white thread off his crimson cloak. "This campaign is in danger of falling into inaction."

"This campaign has failed," Brenim said.

"Listen," Aljeron said quickly. He motioned with his hands for each of them to settle down. "We've done what we came here to do. We've taken the city. Rulalin isn't here, true, so now we need to decide whether to go home as planned, or to go looking for him."

"Of course we go looking for him," Brenim interjected. "Otherwise this has all been in vain."

"It was not vain to pursue justice while there was hope of carrying it out," Caan replied, "but it would be vain to lead an army blindly around the country looking for a man who seems to have vanished."

"Regardless of what we decide, we have two realities that we must face," Saegan added. "First, the deadline given for this campaign is still in effect. The Council of Shalin Bel was clear that regardless of success or failure, the army was to return by Midwinter—"

"Did they say the army was to return to Shalin Bel by Midwinter, or that the army was to leave Fel Edorath by Midwinter?" Brenim cut in. "From what Aljeron has said, I think we could fairly assume that the concern of the merchants and the council was that the war with Fel Edorath end by Midwinter so trade could be resumed. No one said Aljeron couldn't continue to pursue justice by tracking a fugitive."

"You may be right," Gilion chimed in, "but your assumption could bring trouble if we keep the army of Shalin Bel in the field without any attempt to communicate with the council. I can't see how it would hurt to seek their permission to pursue Rulalin."

"We will lose weeks waiting for their reply."

"Who said we have to wait? It's still early in Autumn Wane. We have more than two months before the deadline. We can commence our search and tell the messengers where to bring us word."

"We are getting ahead of ourselves," Aljeron cut in. "We have not yet decided to look for Rulalin. Saegan, what is the second thing, beside the deadline?"

"The second thing is this: If we leave, what is to prevent Rulalin from returning? Once we go, we will never again, not in our lifetimes anyway, get permission to lay siege to the city. If we leave and he returns, we will all be reduced to asking nicely that the city hand him over, and that, we all know, seems unlikely."

The men around the table were quiet. They had all considered the possibility that Rulalin's latest evasion might mean he would never be held accountable for his crime, but Saegan's scenario put it before them in images all to easy to envision.

"Look," Aljeron said at last, "we've had scouting patrols combing everything within a two-day ride of here for the last week. We've offered a reward to any man or woman of Fel Edorath who might be able to point us in the right direction. We're doing all we can. We all know it may ultimately prove to be in vain, but we have no choice. When we go, I'm going to give the army of Fel Edorath its arms back, and I'm not going to leave any of my men behind to be the target of their vengeance. We can't all stay, and when we go, we all go."

"There is something else we should probably consider," Evrim said, speaking up for the first time since the others had arrived.

"Yes?" Aljeron asked.

"Well, there is the rumor."

"The rumor?"

"I've heard it from no fewer than two stewards in Rulalin's

own house and from some of our soldiers that over the past several years, Rulalin entertained an ambassador from the Mountain on more than one occasion. Some even say that this ambassador was seen in the city not long before Rulalin disappeared. Don't we need to consider the possibility that Rulalin has fled to the Mountain, to Malek?"

Murmurs broke out around the table, and voices escalated as bickering and dissension began anew. And then Sarneth spoke above the din. "Whether or not Rulalin has fled to the Mountain, it is the Mountain that we must keep uppermost in our thoughts. The darkness that brought the rain came from the Mountain, and as glad as we all were to have it, the storm has yet to let up. Perhaps it is nothing. It does serve, however, as a reminder that more is at stake here than Rulalin. We need to be prudent about restoring Fel Edorath. The city is still the watchman for Werthanin, and if the Watchman sleeps, we are all in great danger."

Again there was silence in the room, and Aljeron saw that the meeting had accomplished all it could today. "Look, we're tired. Go and have an early night. There is nothing else we can do now. Tomorrow we will prepare to leave. The men don't need to know that we are undecided about where to go. Tell them we will leave two days from tomorrow. That will excite them, and the challenge of being ready to go will keep them occupied. I will consider all that has been said, and tomorrow I will let you know what I have decided."

Evrim remained behind after the others had gone. Aljeron saw Evrim watching him from his seat at the table and asked, "Something on your mind?"

"Why the delay?"

"Pardon?"

"You don't need another day to decide what you intend to do; you've already decided."

Aljeron smiled a faint, tired smile as he sat back down at the table. "You know me too well. It is time for this to be over."

"That's not an answer."

"Yes, I've decided."

"We're not going after Rulalin, are we? We're going home."

"Yes."

"Why?"

"Because it's over. I know it. You know it. They all know it, though some of them aren't ready to admit it. Even Brenim knows Rulalin is gone. He doesn't like it—none of us does—but he knows it. He'll probably rant and rave when I tell him we're going back to Shalin Bel, but that's because he thinks that's what a brother is supposed to do. The extra day is for him, and for the others with lingering doubts."

"What about administration of the city?" Evrim asked.

Aljeron waved a hand in front of his face. "Fel Edorath will be fine. It had a civilian council just like Shalin Bel, and several of its members are running the civilian authority already. The leaders will step to the fore; they always do. Our departure will accelerate the process. I'm not worried about the city."

"What about the five thousand soldiers whose weapons are in our care? How do you propose maintaining our security while we return the weapons?"

"I'll hand over the storehouse keys to the officers. They can return the weapons whenever they like."

"It doesn't bother you that you'll be rearming your sworn enemy before you can leave the city?"

"Look, Evrim, they could barely organize a defense of their own city. I'm not really worried that they're going to develop a campaign against us now. We have superior numbers and an intact chain of command. They won't stick their hands in the wasps' nest."

"Probably not," Evrim sighed, "but it just doesn't seem right. All these years and all this work, and now here we are preparing to hand back control of the city as we turn around to march home. It feels like everything has been in vain."

"Maybe it has been, but we can't abandon the pursuit of justice because it isn't always successful. We did what we believed to be right in pursuing Rulalin, and these men did what they believed to be right in seeking to defend him. We've failed and they have been defeated, and it is time for us to begin to repair the damage between our two cities, and that means going home. But we won't give up on finding Rulalin."

Evrim nodded and rose from the table. He walked over and opened the window to look out over the city. Aljeron joined him. "It's strange," Evrim said, stretching his hand out the window to touch the rain, "so much rain at this time of year."

"Yes, it has been quite the storm."

Evrim retracted his hand and wiped it dry on his cloak. "Well, I think I'll take advantage of that early night you were talking about."

"Good idea; we're back on the road soon."

"Yes, but thankfully not for long."

"Speaking of being thankful, I would have thought you'd be happy we were going home."

"Yeah?"

"Yeah. After all those talks about how I needed to end this war so I could find something else to do with my life. Looks like I'll be looking for that something else sooner than we thought."

"Any ideas?"

"Not really. Being a soldier has always felt right to me, so I'm not sure what I'll be when it comes time to lay Daaltaran down. I'd thought, though, that maybe I could begin my military retirement with a little travel. When Kyril and the girls return from Amaan Sul, maybe I could visit you all in Dal Harat and spend some time away from everything."

Evrim smiled. "You'd be most welcome."

"And maybe after that we could travel to Enthanin. It's time I saw Wylla again and introduced myself to Benjiah."

"He'd like that." Evrim slipped out the door, and Aljeron went back to the window and watched the rain fall over the city.

Aljeron sat upright in his bed. An insistent and loud knocking on the door of his outer chamber resounded once more throughout his quarters. He stumbled awkwardly out of bed and fumbled to light his lamp. The darkness led him to estimate it was still well before dawn, though how long he had been asleep he could not tell.

In his outer room, Koshti was pacing warily before the door. Aljeron put his hand on Koshti's back as he reached the door. "Who's knocking at this early hour?"

"It's me, Saegan, with two of my scouts. I think you should hear what they have to say."

Aljeron opened his door and Saegan came in, followed by two dirty, ragged men in their twenties, both with fear etched on their faces. Saegan motioned to them to sit and said to Aljeron, "I'm going to get Evrim. We'll join you in a moment."

Aljeron nodded, rubbing his face. He turned to the table as Saegan slipped out of the room. "You two look like you could use something to drink. Should I send for something?"

"I'm fine," said one, almost before Aljeron could finish his question.

"No thanks, Master Balinor. Saegan gave us something before he brought us over," the other added.

Aljeron nodded and sat down. "Well, what are your names?"

"Tanin," the young man who had answered first said.

"Cyras," the other added.

Aljeron nodded again, but didn't say anything else until

Saegan and a bushy-haired Evrim entered and took seats at the table.

"All right," Saegan said to the two young men. "Tell them what you told me."

"The evening after we took the city," Cyras started, "we were dispatched to search the land east of the city for any signs of Rulalin Tarasir. There were twenty of us in my patrol, and we were to scout out as much of the land between Fel Edorath and the Mountain as we could in a week.

"Well, we didn't see much of anything the first three days, and we had traveled beyond the open grasslands to the more rugged, overgrown land that surrounds the base of the Mountain. Before dawn on the fourth day, when we were to begin the trip back to Fel Edorath, we were attacked."

"Rulalin?" Aljeron said, anger rising in his voice.

"No." Cyras shook his head. "By Black Wolves, lots of them."

Aljeron stared hard at the two men, who stared back. He turned to look at Saegan, who only nodded. "Go on."

"Some of our men were overrun before they could reach and mount their horses, and even those of us who were able to mount were swarmed by the wolves, who emerged in droves from the surrounding undergrowth. Tanin and I and several of the others cut down as many as we could, and our horses trampled several more, but in the end, all but we two were taken down, both rider and horse. Tanin and I took the only chance we had and rode through the mass of wolves until we had broken clear of them all. We didn't know where we were or even what direction we were moving in, but we didn't slow down until we had gone a long way.

"When we did finally stop, we saw we had been heading east and a little north, deeper into the wild lands beneath the Mountain. We moved to the highest ground we could find and carefully surveyed the area. We didn't see any more evidence of Black Wolves, but what we did see was even more shocking. In the distance, southeast of us, a mass of men, some on foot and some on horseback, were moving west along a road. For hours the men passed on out of the east, until at last the men came to be followed by rank on rank of Malekim."

"Malekim!" Aljeron said, standing abruptly. "An army of men and Malekim from the Mountain!"

"And Black Wolves," Saegan added calmly.

"And perhaps more," Cyras said. "We didn't wait to see how many or what might come next. As soon as we realized what we were seeing, we rode hard in a wide arc north and west to avoid the road and also the Black Wolves, and we have ridden without rest since."

"This is terrible."

"It is disastrous," Tanin answered. "The men alone outnumber us. Our doom has come."

"Perhaps not, thanks to the two of you. Come, you have ridden long and hard and need rest for whatever is to come. Evrim will find beds for you in the house. Leave the rest of the worrying to us."

"Thank you," Cyras said as he and Tanin rose to follow Evrim.

"Thank you," Aljeron replied. "Though you did not find what you sought, you have found what we needed."

As they left, Aljeron turned to Saegan. "Send stewards to awaken the others immediately."

"That has already been done."

"Good, we'll begin as soon as they arrive."

That Malek would come forth from the Mountain to try a third time for mastery of all Kirthanin, each of them had known. That the hour of his coming might arrive in their lifetimes, this also they had known. That they would stand in the path of Malek's hosts as they descended upon the world was, however, something they had not anticipated. Their victory over Fel Edorath had been hollow; now it disintegrated completely, turning to ash in their hands. Their prior dilemma now seemed insignificant. The choice before them was all-important.

"We could focus on preparing our defenses here," Gilion said, "or we could retreat to a place that may give us more time to prepare."

"The walls here are strong. Would it not be wiser to take our stand here, rather than run the risk of being overtaken on the open road?" Brenim asked.

"We cannot stay here," Caan said, rising from his seat. "This city is not provisioned for a siege of any length. If Malek's army finds us here, we'll be trapped just like Rulalin's people were."

"Why not retreat to Shalin Bel?" Saegan asked as Caan took his seat again. "It is also a strong city, with ready provisions. We could endure a long siege, if it came to that. Furthermore, we could recruit more men. It sounds like we'll need them."

"I am leery of abandoning Fel Edorath to destruction," Gilion said. "What's more, should we retreat all the way to Shalin Bel, we leave every village and farmer between here and there in great danger."

"We will warn the people about what is coming, and they can flee with us or wherever they will," Aljeron said, "but we will not stay here. This I have already decided, and Caan's counsel confirms it. I don't know that I want to drop back all the way to Shalin Bel, however. It is a strong place, but it is risky to bring battle to the city without knowing the full strength of our enemy. If we have strength enough to win the day in the field, then let us do so somewhere else, lest we bring fire and destruction to Shalin Bel needlessly. I would rather choose a field of battle from which we could organize a retreat, should we be bested."

"If we are bested and have to retreat, where will we go if not to Shalin Bel?" Brenim asked.

Aljeron sighed. "I don't know. But at least if we force a battle between here and there, we will have time to warn the people of the city so that they can flee."

"There is only one place between Fel Edorath and Shalin Bel that could give us any advantage in battle," Gilion said, looking at Aljeron.

"Zul Arnoth," Aljeron said, nodding.

"I thought I had drawn my sword in Zul Arnoth for the last time," Evrim said quietly.

"So did I," Aljeron answered, "but it is the only place."

"It's good ground," Sarneth said from his seat by the window. "The enemy would be visible long before he reached the ruins. The walls on the east would provide good cover for your archers, who are your best chance for success against the Malekim. You also have many possible avenues of withdrawal to the west. It would be wise to go as quickly as possible and to begin preparing for what is coming."

"Are we then agreed?" Aljeron asked, knowing the question to be a formality. They would do what he desired, but he wanted to know now if there were objections. Each man at the table nodded to show his agreement. "All right then. We begin to mobilize now. I want all of my men out of this city as soon as possible. Nobody sleeps in the city tomorrow. We will not be caught in here. Is that understood?"

More nods from the men. "Good, is there anything else?"

"How do you want to inform the citizens of Fel Edorath?"

"I'll take care of that."

Caan leaned over and whispered in Gilion's ear. Gilion nodded as he listened. "You have something to say, Caan?"

Caan looked up. "Aljeron, we should ask the soldiers of Fel Edorath to come with us."

"What?" Brenim said defiantly. "We couldn't trust them."

"We have to ask," Caan persisted. "As Saegan said, we can use reinforcements. We will find none on the road to Zul Arnoth. Here, there are more than five thousand seasoned soldiers. It would be folly not to ask for their help and folly not to accept it if they offered. We must ask, and we must ask now."

6

ALLEGIANCE

THE SUN HAD NOT BEEN up long when Aljeron stepped outside. He made his way a hundred spans or so to the buildings where the commanding officers of Rulalin's army were quartered. He had decided after taking the city that though the lower echelon officers and the regular soldiers would be free to move about, it might not be wise to allow Rulalin's top men to do the same. So the eleven men that he was headed to see had been given good accommodation in separate rooms in three neighboring buildings, each man under constant surveillance by armed guards to discourage secretive communication with one another. They were allowed to recreate in the large parlors of each of the buildings, but those gatherings were also closely attended by Aljeron's men.

However, Rulalin's captains were treated well. They ate better than they had in months, and the constant rain and cold, biting wind made it no hardship for them to stay put. Aljeron had met with them twice already. His reception on both occasions had been polite but strained, and now, as he pulled his cloak tight to protect himself from the rain, he had no idea how they might respond to his request.

Koshti kept up beside him, his fur dripping and matted. Though the rain was not especially heavy, it did not seem to take long to soak them. Aljeron wondered about Malek's intentions for the storm, if indeed he was behind it. Likely it was just meant to be an irritant; Aljeron doubted Malek needed any greater purpose than that when it came to manipulating the weather. Whatever Malek's motives, Aljeron hoped it would be over soon. He did not relish the thought of riding all the way to Zul Arnoth in the wet. But these were worries for tomorrow.

Inside, sitting at a large rounded table, were the eleven men, most of whom he did not know, not even their names. Several of his own men stood around the perimeter of the room. He walked to the open chair closest to the door and Koshti followed him. The officers of Fel Edorath watched the tiger warily, but they did not seem as anxious about his presence as they had a week ago.

Aljeron looked around the table and then glanced at the guards that surrounded them. "Guards, you may wait outside."

The guards left. One of the men a few seats down from Aljeron said, "Something must not be right. You haven't been shy about discussing your plans for us in front of your men before."

"This has nothing to do with my plans for you," Aljeron answered, looking up, "but you are right when you say something is wrong. There is more wrong than you know, and it may well be the death of us all."

Murmurs rippled around the table, and Aljeron let them go. He had intended to unsettle these men from the beginning, hoping this would make the prospect of aligning with their former enemy less of an impossible suggestion.

When the whispers began to settle down, he told them the story his scouts had told him. He told them of the ambush by the Black Wolves and of the army moving toward Fel Edorath. He told them of his own meeting with his officers, and he told them of his decision to withdraw from the city as soon as possible and to march west at first light.

When he finished, no man spoke, and more than a few had looks of stunned disbelief on their faces. As bad as things had looked to Aljeron, he could see that they looked even worse to these men. Their army was smaller and weaker than Aljeron's, their city closer to the imminent peril, and to retreat before the coming enemy was to surrender their homes to destruction. Even so, he had to ask.

"Gentlemen, we have been opponents on the battlefield for the last seven years, and I know there is no love for me in this room. What I have done, I have done in the hope of bringing Rulalin Tarasir to justice. I did not come out of enmity against Fel Edorath, and I do not have any animosity toward any of you. I need your help, and I believe you need mine. My army is not big enough to face this enemy on its own. Your army is not big enough either. Though we have brought food into the city, you are not provisioned for a siege, should you be fortunate enough to keep Malek out. Come with me. Together we will draw up defenses at Zul Arnoth and face Malek on ground we all know well. If we succeed, we will have begun the process of healing the wounds we have caused each other. If we fail, then at least we would have taken our stand together as Werthanim joined by the one thing we all share, hatred of our common enemy. I wish I could give you time to think it over, but there is no time. I need to know now if you will join me."

"If we don't, what will become of us?"

"Access to your weapons so that you may rearm immediately is even now being arranged. You are free to come with us or stay here. As for what will become of you, I cannot say, but I do not have any plans to do anything to you, if that is what you mean."

Again, murmurs started around the table, but one of the men, perhaps thirty, stood at his place. "I don't know why we even need to discuss it. If what we've heard is true, we must join the army of Shalin Bel and take our stand together. Any other course is madness."

"And what of the city? Would you just abandon it to Malek and his hosts? Fel Edorath has anticipated Malek's coming for almost a thousand years. Would you have us not even try to defend it?"

"Not if that defense is hopeless, no I would not."

"Master Balinor," a third man said, "though time is short, is there no way we could be allowed to talk this over together?"

Aljeron rubbed his face with his hands for a moment, then stood up from his seat. "One of my men will let you know when you are free to leave this place and return to your men. We will be on the road to Zul Arnoth by first light, and I hope you will join us. If you wish to come later, I will gladly accept your aid whenever you arrive. Allfather protect you, whatever you decide."

"And Allfather protect you," several of the men echoed as they rose to watch Aljeron and Koshti leave.

Aljeron stood at the entrance to his tent with Evrim watching the activity in the camp. There was perhaps an hour of daylight left, but the men had already packed more than Aljeron had first thought they'd be able to take with them. Their supplies of food and water were already secured in the wagons, and the men were sifting through the various tools and materials they had accumulated during the years of their siege. Though there were some things clearly better left behind, other choices were harder to make. So much depended on unknowns. Aljeron felt a bit like he had when he was just thirty-four and riding out of Shalin Bel at the head of his army for the first time, before he had learned by experience the size and strengths of Rulalin's forces. All the familiarity was gone now, and he knew deep down that more than ignorance separated the battles to come from the ones he had most recently fought. Malek wanted to rule everything, and if he was coming forth now, he believed he had the army to conquer the world, not just one war-worn city.

Bryar, who had taken a mounted scouting party north to look for traces of Rulalin, rode briskly through the camp and up to Aljeron's tent. She surprised Aljeron by remaining in the saddle rather than dismounting, and he noticed for the first time the excitement in her face. "What is it?" he asked.

"Men from Fel Edorath are approaching on horseback. I think you should come."

Aljeron and Evrim exchanged quick glances, and both mounted as soon as their horses could be made ready and followed Bryar back through the camp. When they arrived at the eastern edge, they looked out over the road at the columns of men advancing. "How many, do you think?" Aljeron asked.

"I would say less than half their full strength, two thousand maybe."

"Less than half," Aljeron murmured.

"It is more than none," Evrim replied.

"True."

They rode toward the approaching men. At their head rode three whom Aljeron recognized from his meetings with the commanding officers. In the middle of the three was the young man who had spoken first about the need to join Aljeron. As these three men signaled their company to halt, Aljeron and Evrim greeted them.

"Welcome, are you the first detachment come to meet us, or are you the full strength that Fel Edorath is sending?"

"I have brought two thousand men with me, and we are all," the young officer said, "but Fel Edorath is not sending us. We were threatened on pain of death not to leave and not to take our men, but in the end, the others knew it would be even more foolish to fight amongst ourselves. Still, the road the others have chosen is suicide. Our men have neither the strength nor the morale to face this enemy alone. They were broken before you entered our gates and will not long resist the foe that is coming."

Aljeron looked closely at the officer. "It must have been a hard choice to take your men away from your friends and comrades, not to mention your city."

"The hour has come when all lesser ties are broken and dissolved, and men, all men, are called to stand against Malek and his will. Having chosen to take that stand, my allegiance can no longer be to any particular place. I am a soldier in Allfather's service, and Malek's defeat is my duty. Allfather's will be done."

"Allfather's will be done, indeed." Aljeron dismounted and walked over to the young officer's horse. He looked up at the man and extended his hand. The man reached down and clasped Aljeron's hand tightly. "You have spoken rightly. All lesser alliances and allegiances are now of no consequence. What is your name?"

"I am Corlas Valon."

"Corlas Valon. You are most welcome here. If we fall in battle, we will fall together."

Rulalin shook his cloak in a vain attempt to disperse some of the dampness that clung to him so doggedly. Two days after their departure, he had asked Tashmiren if Cheimontyr's storm was going to follow them all the way to Fel Edorath.

"All the way to Fel Edorath?" Tashmiren had answered with a bemused smile. "Why should it stop there?"

"I don't know," Rulalin had answered. "Why do we need it at all?"

"Ahh, now that is a better question." The bemused smile had opened into a wicked grin. "Cheimontyr is the Bringer of Storms, and you shall see what Malek has called him to summon the storm for, should you live long enough."

That was all Rulalin had been able to pry out of Tashmiren about the steady rain and cloudy skies. Rulalin had no idea of the purpose for the storm, nor of its scope. He didn't know if it was raining all over Kirthanin, or just in areas around the Mountain, or merely hovered overhead, following them league by soggy league. He regretted his complaints about the cramped spaces and lack of sunlight in his little room under the Mountain, where at least it was warm and dry, beautifully dry.

He spurred his horse to catch up to Soran, who rode hunched over like the rest of them, using his back to try to keep his hands relatively dry. They would be within sight of Fel Edorath soon, and then they would find out just what Malek had in mind for their city.

Pulling up alongside Soran, he asked the question that had been bothering him all morning. "Do you know what day it is? I've been trying to count back the days we've been on the march and the days we were in the Mountain, but I'm not sure if I've lost a day somewhere. Is it the ninth day of Autumn Wane, or the tenth?"

"I think it is the tenth," Soran answered, looking down at his hands as he silently counted up to eight on his fingers. "I think we left the Mountain on the first, and this is our tenth day in the saddle. I'm pretty sure that's right."

Rulalin nodded. "I thought I'd lost a day. I'm not sure where though. I guess it doesn't matter."

"No, not unless you're going crazy and you've lost more than a day."

"This rain could easily drive me crazy if it doesn't go away soon, but I don't think I'm crazy yet."

"We're almost there."

"I know."

"Do you wonder what we'll find?"

"Of course."

"If Aljeron is in control of the city, he'll refuse to surrender and ally himself with Malek, especially if the offer comes from you."

"I know."

"He won't let our men surrender either. We might not be able to get anyone to come out and join us. How do you think that will go over?"

"I don't know, but I would think Farimaal and Malek know this. Tashmiren is aware of the siege and the history between Aljeron and me. Surely they know I will only be able to deliver soldiers after Aljeron's control of the city is broken."

"Do you think, even then, that our soldiers will agree to join Malek, just because we ask them?"

"We'll find out soon enough."

Rulalin stood beside his horse and stroked his wet flank as the rain continued to fall. It was almost Ninth Hour and they had been stopped for a while now. The eastern walls of Fel Edorath were visible in the distance, and Rulalin had been searching them for any sign of the story within. He found none.

He looked around again at the vast host now assembled on the plain. Men stretched out north for a long way, many rows deep. Malekim stretched an equal distance to the south. Most of the time he had been standing there, Malekim had been filing in, rolling their great wagons and moving soundlessly through the rain. He wondered how he would feel if he were upon the walls of Fel Edorath, looking at the great multitude of men and Voiceless arrayed against him. Surely the open and bold display of Malek's strength would greatly help his cause.

All around him, heads swiveled as though on cue, and he turned to see what they were looking for. Approaching the rear of their formation came the giants, walking three and four abreast. They were passing now through the open space between the Malekim and men, moving up between the two great hosts until they reached the open ground before them all. They walked with their great weapons, swords and enormous axes, strapped to their backs. When a hundred or so had passed, there came Cheimontyr, walking alone in their midst with perhaps a hundred more behind him. He did not have a sword or axe, but he carried in his hand a great hammer. The hammer was massive, affixed to a pole of perhaps half a span. Both the shaft and the head glistened and gleamed with bright silver streaks as he carried it. Rulalin couldn't tell if his eyes were playing tricks on him or if somehow the hammer was pulsating with some kind of seething energy, but soon both Cheimontyr and the hammer had passed him.

Unlike the other Vulsutyrim, Cheimontyr did not stop but kept going until he had put ten spans or so between himself and any other living creature. He stood motionless as the remaining Vulsutyrim came through their midst and at last stood in a great arc in front of the men and Malekim but behind Cheimontyr. Then he raised the great hammer high over his head, and calling out in a loud voice, words that Rulalin couldn't understand, he brought the hammer down in a furious stroke, striking the ground so that the plain seemed to shudder beneath their feet.

Flashes of lightning began falling from the sky, all converging on the ground where the hammer had struck. The dazzling light was almost too bright for Rulalin's eyes, but he watched in amazement as the ground before Cheimontyr's feet was struck over and over until it began to smolder and smoke rose from the soggy grass into the sky. The lightning strikes gradually stopped, and slowly the smoky haze drifted up and away on the breeze. Through it all Cheimontyr stood still in the constant rain, staring forward at the city.

The scene had been so riveting that Rulalin hadn't noticed Tashmiren's approach, and when he did, it gave him a start. Tashmiren, for his part, smiled condescendingly and said, "It is time for us to learn whether your service is worth anything. Farimaal has called for you. Bring your horse and follow me."

Rulalin called to Soran, who had also been riveted by the events playing out.

Soran turned, saw Rulalin with the reins of his horse moving off behind Tashmiren and instantly comprehended. Soon he was following too, and they moved slowly through the mass of men toward the front. When they passed into the open area, they turned and moved north along the front. Rulalin kept his eyes locked on Tashmiren, for he was uncomfortable with the staring eyes of the men. He had looked into the faces of some of the Nolthanim, and it had been an unpleasant experience. They were like men in a dream, walking in a trance, fixed on the road before them. He had bumped into them and been jostled by them and knew them to be real enough, but their eyes were hollow and faint, like fading embers in the fireplace in the grey hours before dawn.

Eventually they approached a single tent, large but not enormous, with a handful of armed men gathered at the front. Two took the reins of Rulalin's and Soran's horses. The others stepped aside, and Rulalin followed Tashmiren through the flap with Soran close behind.

Inside was a single table, with some light wooden chairs sitting around it. On the far side in a larger chair, wide and simple, sat Farimaal, but not the Farimaal they had met inside the Mountain. This was the Farimaal out of Tashmiren's story, suddenly sprung to life. Armor made from the blackened skin of the Grendolai covered his body. He looked like a monster from a child's nightmare with a human head. The eyes that stared at them from that dark and grizzled face were cold and searing and almost as unearthly as the grotesque skin that covered him. In his right hand Farimaal held a matching helmet, and the fingers of his left hand were drumming it rhythmically. Tashmiren directed them to the seats at the table and then joined them.

Farimaal addressed them, his fingers still drumming on the helmet. "Tashmiren tells me the gate on the eastern wall is not functional."

"Yes, sir," Rulalin answered nervously.

"Yes, sir, what?" Farimaal answered in a steady voice. "Is it functional, or isn't it?"

"It isn't."

Farimaal nodded slightly. "Why do you have a gate that is not a gate on your eastern wall?"

Rulalin rubbed his face with his sleeve, suddenly aware of the water running down it, though the wet sleeve didn't do much good. "When Malek invaded from the Forbidden Isle and took up residence in the Mountain, the elders of Fel Edorath turned the gate into a defensive trap."

Farimaal leaned forward, a look of curiosity on his face. "How so?"

"A gate is always the weakest point of any city's defenses, thus it is the most common point of assault. Knowing this, the city's elders left the gate standing but built a wall of dense stone behind it, a wall that they reinforced with bands of iron and steel. Behind the steel they placed a second layer of stone. It is far and away the strongest single stretch of wall in the entire city. Our elders hoped it might delay invasion long enough for us to inflict heavy casualties from atop the wall while we waited for help to arrive."

A gleam filled Farimaal's cold eyes. "Perhaps you will prove more useful to us than I first thought. Which is the closest functional gate?"

"The northern gate."

"How far?"

"From here, less than an hour."

"You are to take my terms to the city and to return by sundown with their answer. Tell those within that if they surrender by first light and put their soldiers at my disposal, they will live. If they do not, we will tear down the wall and kill every living thing that moves within the city."

"As you wish," Rulalin said. Farimaal waved him away, and he and Soran followed Tashmiren out of the tent.

Outside, their horses were returned and soon they were both mounted. But Tashmiren took hold of Rulalin's horse and would not let it go.

"How does it feel, Rulalin?" he asked as he looked up with a nasty grin.

"How does what feel?"

"How does it feel to know that a trap laid for Malek's hosts almost a thousand years ago by your forefathers will never be used because you, the oh so very proud son of their city, has given away its secret? How does it feel? Are you pleased to know you have frustrated their hopes and dreams?"

Had Rulalin been a younger man, he probably would have drawn his sword and struck Tashmiren down, regardless of the consequences, but he knew Fel Edorath's only hope lay in his ability to convince them to surrender, a task that would be all but impossible if Aljeron was there. He didn't have time to waste on Tashmiren. "I am Fel Edorath's only hope of survival, and if I succeed, I will keep my people alive and my city intact. That alone will please me."

Rulalin and Soran rode hard through the rainy afternoon. They were not far from the gate now, and Rulalin peered up

BREAKING

at the top of the wall to see if there was any activity. It would not do his mission any good if a zealous archer put an arrow through him before he could bring his message to the city. Ironically, his greatest assurance that the soldiers of Shalin Bel would not strike him down if they recognized him was that Aljeron would surely want to take him alive. Even so, he could see no movement above and so gradually allowed his horse to run closer to the wall as they approached the gate.

When at last they stopped, Rulalin wasted no time dismounting but called out, "Watchmen of the gate, we come with a message of utmost urgency! Let us in."

Turning to Soran, he whispered, "This could be a second chance for us."

"Who is it?" a voice from within called.

"Rulalin Tarasir, returned to Fel Edorath in her hour of need."

"Second chance for what?" Soran whispered back.

"Rulalin?" the voice echoed, puzzled.

"To reject Malek," Rulalin said as he heard the great creak of the gate's bolt being pulled back. "We can stay and die defending the city like we were supposed to."

Soran peered at Rulalin. "We would have to pray that we die in her defense, or else the men and women of Fel Edorath would be slaughtered and we'd be taken alive. We'd make a good lesson of the price of betrayal."

Soran stopped speaking as the gate swung open, revealing several soldiers of Fel Edorath with swords and spears raised, peering up at them in surprise. "Master Tarasir, it is you. And Master Nuvaar? Hurry, send word that they are returned."

"We will take word of our coming with us, for we are here on an errand of much haste. Tell me, what news is there of Aljeron Balinor and the army of Shalin Bel? Has the siege been lifted?"

"The army of Shalin Bel left yesterday morning at dawn. The siege is over; they took the city almost ten days ago."

"What do you mean?" Rulalin asked. "They took the city but have already abandoned it, leaving you here as you were?"

The soldier who had been talking hesitated before continuing. "Sir, I don't know any more than this. They took the city, and we were disarmed. They turned the city upside down looking for you. They opened up the waterways to bring water as well as food back into the city. Then, all of a sudden, they started to withdraw two days ago. Yesterday they marched west, along with some of the captains of Fel Edorath and their men."

"What? As prisoners of war?" Rulalin asked.

"No, not that I know of."

"Then what do you mean?"

"The rumor is that scouts from Shalin Bel brought news of an army coming from the east. The rumor also said Aljeron Balinor asked our captains to go with him as they left so they could regroup somewhere else, but our captains refused, or at least most of them did. A few officers led their men out with Captain Valon to join the army of Shalin Bel. That's all I know."

Rulalin pointed at two of the soldiers standing closest to him and said, "You two, summon whatever captains of the city remain and tell them to meet me at my house. Our time is fleeting. Hurry."

The two men started off running through the city as Rulalin turned his horse and started down the familiar streets that would take him home.

"I can't believe Corlas Valon has betrayed his own people," Soran said as they stood at the closed door to Rulalin's house.

"It was the smart thing to do," Rulalin answered. "If word of Malek's approaching army reached them, and if Aljeron was pulling back, then their best hope was to go with him. The others were fools to stay."

The door opened and Mistress Brahan's jaw dropped in surprise. "Master Tarasir? What in the name of the Mountain can this mean?"

"I wish I had time to explain, but I need to talk to the remaining captains of the army when they arrive. In the meantime, I want to dry off. Send towels and fresh clothes to my room."

Mistress Brahan nodded and turned to take care of his request as Rulalin and Soran marched through the house to his quarters. He wondered how it could be that scouts from Shalin Bel had found out Malek's army. Still, he smiled, for though it did not give Shalin Bel any real hope of defeating Malek, Rulalin was pleased to think that favor could still find the Werthanim. He found himself also wishing that news of Malek's coming might have come to him first, weeks ago, so that he could arrange for the defense of the city and the first line of defense for all Werthanin. In another life, perhaps.

Soon they were standing in his room, drying off and changing into the clothes sent by Mistress Brahan. Rulalin sat down in a chair and closed his eyes, appreciating the dryness and comfort. "What are we going to do, Rulalin?"

"We're going to lay the situation before the captains of the city," Rulalin said. "Aljeron is gone, and with him some of our own number. We'll have to find out how many have left, how many remain, and then we will know what our options are."

"Rulalin, there are no options. We need to get back on our horses and take word to Farimaal by sunset that Fel Edorath has agreed to his terms, or we are all going to die. The city cannot be defended."

"This is true, but maybe there is a third way. Maybe we could organize an immediate retreat out the western gate, and if we move quickly enough, perhaps we could catch up to Corlas and Aljeron."

"Maybe, if we leave behind the women and children of the

city, but you know we would be overtaken if we tried to evacuate everyone. Are you willing to sacrifice anyone to Cheimontyr and Farimaal? Besides, even if we do outrun Malek's host, what then? Do you think Aljeron will welcome you like a long-lost brother? Even if he did, what hope is there that the armies of Fel Edorath and Shalin Bel can win this battle? You know they can't."

Rulalin didn't answer. The image of leading a daring retreat down the western road away from the city was slipping from his mind. "Yes, I know." He sighed. "Don't worry about me. I'll put the situation before the others as clearly as it needs to be put."

"The others" turned out to be a group of six men, the only officers of rank that could be found on short notice and were close enough to get to the house immediately. Each looked haggard, exhausted, and completely bewildered to be attending a meeting with Rulalin and Soran. Though questions were many, Rulalin succeeded in silencing them after a few moments.

"I know you have many questions, and there may be time in the days that follow for me to answer them. For now you need to listen. Soran and I have come with an offer, and this offer represents the only chance Fel Edorath has for survival. You have seen the army assembled to the east of the city?"

"Of course," they answered, "and who is that creature who summoned the lightning from the sky like a shepherd calling his sheep?"

"His name is Cheimontyr, and he leads the children of Vulsutyr. He is called by them the Bringer of Storms, and somehow this rain that overshadows us here is his work, but don't ask me how. He and his brethren are only part of your problem. There are enough of them to pull down the city gates and breach the walls many times over. There are also countless men and Malekim waiting to take the city when its defenses are destroyed. Further, there are packs of Black Wolves that were sent out ahead of the army that could be anywhere now. There is no defense for us now. The only way we can save the city and those who live here is to surrender."

"Surrender? To Malek?" the captains looked at each other and at Rulalin in dismay. "Fel Edorath will never surrender to Malek."

"Then you will all die," Soran said, standing to his feet. "What good will all your pride be when the city is but rubble and your wives and children are buried under the stone? I know we've been told for generations that we are the first defense against the Mountain, but we've spent our energy defending ourselves against other Werthanim, haven't we? We no longer have the strength to put up a fight against the power that now comes against us. We will surrender and live, or fight and die. At least if we surrender, there is the hope that Fel Edorath will live on, that we will one day return when the war is over and be allowed to live here in peace."

"Peace, with Malek on the throne, ruling Kirthanin? That is not peace."

"What do we care if Malek rules Kirthanin?" Soran answered. "He was one of the Twelve, and we once submitted to their rule. He will rule again, whether he destroys us or not, so why not join him and be spared his wrath? Allfather has abandoned us."

Murmurs circled the room as the captains talked among themselves for a few moments. "Listen," Rulalin said at last. "I hate the thought of serving Malek as much as you do, but I have already sworn allegiance to him."

Again murmurs spread around the table, but Rulalin raised his hands to silence them. "It was the only way I could save Fel Edorath. If you surrender," he continued, "you will send all our remaining men to aid Malek in his conquest. These men will be at the disposal of Farimaal, the captain of the Nolthanim who follow Malek still, but Farimaal has promised that all soldiers from Fel Edorath will be under my immediate command. If Soran and I return without your surrender, the city will be destroyed at first light, if they even wait that long."

"It seems to me we have no choice," one of the grim-faced captains said. "Our general has sworn himself to Malek and a third of our men have abandoned the city. Allegiance and loyalty are not what they once were."

"Perhaps not," Rulalin answered quietly, "but my allegiance is and will be to whatever keeps you and the other men under my command alive."

The six men at the table did not say a word; they didn't even look at each other. "I will take your silence as agreement. Soran and I must leave right away to take your answer back. You will need to muster our men. How many remain?"

"A little more than three and a half thousand."

"So few," Rulalin said, half to himself. "So be it. I will tell Farimaal this is what remains of our strength, and that Aljeron and his army have fled west. Do we know where they were bound? Shalin Bel, I presume?"

"Unless they change their minds along the way, they are not bound for Shalin Bel but for Zul Arnoth."

"Zul Arnoth?" Rulalin answered, surprised.

"He told us that was where they were headed."

"So be it. We will return with news that the city surrenders, that three and a half thousand men will join Malek's army, and that we know where the army of Shalin Bel is headed."

7

CONVERGENCE

R ULALIN STEPPED RELUCTANTLY from Farimaal's tent. Having spent just over an hour inside his house in Fel Edorath, as well as a short stint in Farimaal's tent before and after, he had a renewed appreciation for life without rain. With an early morning departure looming, he knew his near future held little more save for riding and sleeping in the wet. He could almost have bedded down in the midst of all those Malekim if that meant crawling under one of those wagons they were toting.

"It will be strange to take the field again at Zul Arnoth," Soran said as they walked along in the dark, careful not to step on any of the sitting or sleeping soldiers.

"Yes," Rulalin replied, thinking of the ancient ruin, "I thought I'd fought my last battle there."

"Zul Arnoth hasn't always treated us kindly," Soran said, and Rulalin laughed at the understatement, "but, I suspect this time will be different."

They soon found the place left open for them among the Nolthanim riders, and their horses were there, being taken care of with the others. Tashmiren had dispatched a pair of guards from Farimaal's tent to attend them upon their return. The Nolthanim, in their own quiet way, had made room for Rulalin and Soran from the beginning. Every time they camped, the Nolthanim stopped in the same small groups, and always a patch of ground between the same two clusters of men was left open for Rulalin and Soran. Although Rulalin appreciated the gesture, he was inwardly heartened that from the next day onward, he would be traveling and sleeping among men from his own city. Perhaps the odiousness of his service would not seem so strong when he was surrounded by men he had fought beside for the better part of the last seven years.

There was little left to discuss with Soran, and he was tired. The morning would come all too soon and they would be on the move again. He wanted to be as ready as he could be to greet his captains and assume his command, and so he did not waste time bedding down in the soaking wet grass, his cloak wrapped as tightly around him as he could get it.

He had just started to relax when a hand shook his shoulder firmly. He sat up, startled, to find a grim face smiling down at him out of the darkness.

"Synoki?" he asked, surprised and wary.

Synoki put a finger to his lips and motioned for Rulalin to follow him.

"Now?" Rulalin whispered.

Synoki nodded, the smile replaced by a look of impatience. Rulalin didn't quite know where Synoki was in the chain of command, but it seemed everyone was higher up than he. As much as Rulalin wanted to shut his eyes and lie back down, he didn't want to find out the hard way that Synoki was one of those people not to be offended. So, he did his best to pull his aching, tired body up off the ground, and he followed Synoki as he limped through the camp until they were out in the open plain, several spans from the nearest pair of ears.

"I hear you did well today," Synoki said quietly.

"I did what I said I would do."

"A man of your word," Synoki answered, looking levelly into Rulalin's eyes. Rulalin didn't pick up on any mockery in Synoki's voice, but his answer brought anger to the surface again.

"Why have you come for me?" Rulalin asked bluntly.

"I've come to you because your master has further use of you, and I have been sent to inform you of it."

"Yes?"

"Let me begin at the beginning—or at least, let me give you enough background so that you understand why I'm here." Synoki stopped, clearing his throat as he looked around in the dark. "There is an old prophecy, which is probably little more than empty words, that gives hope to those who despair at the thought of our master's coming. The prophecy speaks of a boy who will do great things against our master, though it is vague on just what these things will be. Those who call themselves prophets speak in riddles and offer hope without really explaining how that hope is supposed to work. Still, though he does not take such things very seriously, Malek thought, or suspected, that perhaps there might be something to the prophecy when he sensed something special about the Novaana who gathered in Sulare seventeen years ago. He even thought that perhaps the young man you so helpfully dispatched for us, Joraiem Andira, might be this boy of prophecy. When word of Joraiem's death came to Malek in the Mountain, the words of the prophecy faded from view.

"Recently, however, Malek has had cause to wonder if Joraiem was not the boy spoken of in the prophecy. He has begun to wonder if someone else in the group might have been the boy. He knows it can't be you, because you are no longer numbered among his enemies, but he wonders if Aljeron might be the one. He wonders, but does not know, for not all things are revealed to him yet. You alone among us, along with myself, would recognize the other men from that group. If and when you see any of them, you are to tell me, or if you are not sure where I am, for I have many responsibilities, you must tell Tashmiren or Farimaal. Do you understand?"

"I think so."

"Are all the Novaana from that trip still alive?"

"No, the younger brother of Bryar, a boy named Elyas, died in the civil war that has been raging in Werthanin. He was never much of a soldier, and he died in one of the first campaigns."

"Ah, so in a sense, you have claimed his life too. You are proving more and more to be invaluable to us."

Rulalin didn't answer, so Synoki continued, "And the others?"

"Joraiem, Kelvan, and Elyas are all dead. The other Suthanim, Darias, I have not seen since I left Sulare. Saegan of Enthanin has served under Aljeron since the beginning of the war, and early on, so did Pedraal and Pedraan, the twin brothers of the queen of Enthanin. I have not seen them in a few years, though, and presumably they remain in Amaan Sul. Aljeron and Saegan, at least, should only be a few days away, and I am here, so half of the remaining men from that group are close at hand."

"Well, when we do catch up to the army of Shalin Bel, let me know if you find Aljeron or Saegan, preferably alive. Malek would like to observe them himself to ensure he has found and eliminated the right person." Synoki paused, gazing intently into Rulalin's eyes. "You spoke of Wylla rather dispassionately just then, calling her the queen of Enthanin. Could it be you have lost some of your zeal for her? As you have named her the one thing you desire in exchange for your service to our master, I hope you have not."

Rulalin looked away from Synoki, gazing out over the dark plain. "I will report anything I see or hear about any of the men who were with me in Sulare. Is there anything else?"

"Not for now," Synoki answered, the dark smile returning as he turned and walked away through the dark.

Rulalin returned to his bed on the ground and again settled in to try to sleep.

"What was that about?" Soran asked quietly.

"Nothing, let's get some sleep."

Rulalin closed his eyes, and soon his mind had drifted away from this cold, wet place to the warm, sunny world of Sulare. He could see the white walls of the Great Hall rising before him, covered with the sinuous yellow vines that grew up out of the rich earth. He knew that inside, the fountain was rising high into the air beneath the opening of the dome, and the water was cool and blue and refreshing, flowing down in terraced pools spread wide around the fountain.

Down the wide avenue from the Great Hall lay the Southern Ocean. Out in the blue waters Merrion flew in the clear blue sky, their white bodies streaking like low-flying clouds, save for the blue feathers that ringed each of their wings. He had stood or sat on that beach for hours at a time, watching the Merrion glide gracefully a hand's breadth above the water, then they would dive under the waves, swimming at times two or three spans underwater before emerging out of the ocean with a fish in their mouths. They were beautiful hunters, graceful in flight and in the kill.

Rulalin opened his eyes in the darkness, catching a raindrop in his eye. He rubbed his lid with his hand. He couldn't think of Sulare or that beach for long without thinking of what he did there, and he had long since grown weary of thinking about that.

Wylla peered over the wall into the courtyard below at the sound of a horse's clopping shoes on the stone. The light from a lamp bounced closer and closer until finally one of her stewards appeared, leading the horse. Even in the dark, Wylla could see the horse was weary, covered with lather and no doubt ready for a feed and some rest.

"Who has come, Raynin?" Wylla called from the wall.

The steward, surprised by the sudden greeting, peered up at the wall as though to make sure he had really heard something. Seeing Wylla, he quickly answered. "A messenger for you, Your Majesty."

"He is waiting inside?"

"He is."

"Someone is attending to him, getting him food and drink?"

"Yes, Your Majesty."

"Good, thank you, Raynin."

"You're welcome, Your Majesty." Wylla watched for a moment as Raynin led the horse to the stable. Looking out over the exterior wall, she looked at the scattered fires in the army's camp, flickering in the dark. She was gradually getting used to the presence of the soldiers.

She descended and went inside, glad to be out of the wind again, for as much as she enjoyed the quiet solitude of the wall, she cared little for the cold bite in the air. At this late hour, there was little activity in the house, so she moved quickly to the kitchen, where she could hear the clink of utensils and the sound of quiet voices.

". . . no, really, this is fine."

"Are you sure? It really wouldn't take long."

"That's all right. I'll just eat this and deliver my message."

"There's no rush on the message," Wylla said as she walked into the room. The messenger, a man not much older than Benjiah, perhaps twenty at the most, stood as soon as he heard

Wylla's voice, and the kitchen steward who had been waiting on him also acknowledged Wylla's presence.

"Your Majesty," the messenger said, bowing slightly, as many of the military officers would when uneasy in her presence. "I was sent to gather information from our patrols near the northeastern shores of the Kellisor Sea, and I have just returned. Captain Merias told me that if I did not find him in when I arrived, I was to bring my news directly to you. I hope I have not disturbed you."

"You have not. Please, you must be tired and famished. Sit and eat while you give me your report."

"I can wait to eat, Your Majesty."

"I'm sure you could, but there is no need." Wylla smiled and motioned with her hands for the messenger to sit down. She took a seat on a stool on the other side of the small table.

"Thank you, Your Majesty," the messenger said, sitting down again and taking a large bite out of the hunk of bread on the plate before him.

"Can I get you anything, Your Majesty?" the kitchen steward asked.

"No, thanks."

"Very well, just ring for me if either of you needs anything," she said as she turned to leave the kitchen.

"We will, don't worry," Wylla answered. When the steward had gone, she continued. "Now, what news from the Kellisor Sea?"

"Well, it is very odd, to be sure," the messenger said, chewing on the bread and swallowing what remained of it. "There is something strange going on with the weather. I spent several days gathering reports, and they are all similar. Somehow, the wind has been consistently blowing northwest across the sea for the last week or so. There are even reports of a strong current also moving in that direction, an undercurrent that pulls any vessel, large or small, unless the men aboard fight hard against it. Some have described it as though the very water of the sea was being sucked away from the southeastern shores. The tide is lower than it has ever been, and does not come in by night or by day. What's more, those who have been in the northwestern part of the sea say that it has been stormy, with lots of rain and strong wind for days. The waves are high and rough the farther northwest you go, and traffic on the sea is slowing to a halt. I have even heard of ships foundering, though the captains and crews were seasoned veterans of the Kellisor and its ways. There is much fear there, for no one can imagine how the weather patterns have altered so much, so suddenly."

As Wylla listened, she grew increasingly uneasy. The news would have been disturbing enough had there not also been abnormalities in the weather in Amaan Sul. Since the beginning of Autumn Wane, the wind had blown constantly out of the east. This was not something she would have noticed had it not been for the rain. Though it had been fairly dry these past several days, the few storms they had seen all behaved in the same odd way: Clouds had appeared off in the east, moving toward the city and bringing with them rain. The rain would come, but never for long, as the clouds soon moved off to the west, toward Gyrin and the Mountain. It was more common for storms this time of year to come north and east from the Kellisor, but nothing seemed to be coming from that direction anymore.

The news from the messenger offered a second piece of the puzzle. It sounded as though there was some kind of weather convergence taking place in the west, drawing the winds and storms from the east and southeast. Wylla shook her head at the thought, for such a thing was impossible and wholly unexplainable.

"Was there more to the message?" she asked.

"No, Your Majesty."

"Thank you for conveying it to me. I will be sure to pass it along to Captain Merias as soon as I can."

"Your Majesty?"

"Yes?"

"Does it make sense to you?"

"No," Wylla said, looking at the young man, and seeing for the first time the anxiety in his eyes. She smiled. "There are many things I can't explain, the weather being just one."

Wylla rose to go and took her leave. Whatever storm was breaking on Werthanin, Benjiah was probably in it.

Benjiah looked up at the blossoming branches. He had seen snow trees in bloom in the summertime and enjoyed their beauty, but the tiny leaves and buds on the branches now afforded little protection from the rain. He felt silly now for being so excited when he realized the small cluster of trees they were making for were snow trees. He would gladly exchange the novelty of them for a plainer, uglier, but better sheltering arbor.

He looked at his uncles, sitting close together with their backs toward Benjiah and Valzaan. They were disappointed, he knew, having failed to produce a fire for the third night in a row. They had been hopeful too, when they spied the trees, but with so little shelter and nothing dry to burn, the failure could hardly be seen as their fault.

"I think it is time you tried again," Valzaan said, pulling Benjiah's attention away from the twins. "I know you are discouraged, but you have made so much progress in controlling your experiences with *torrim redara*, you really should be more patient with yourself in this endeavor. You cannot expect yourself to be able to master all prophetic abilities at the same rate, or even develop the same proficiency in each."

"I know," Benjiah said, scratching his head.

"Relax," Valzaan said, sliding up a little closer. He reached out and took Benjiah's right hand, clasping it between both of his own. "Close your eyes and push everything else away. Think of the soaring flight of the falcon. Imagine a windhover in your mind. Think of them, up there in the darkness and the rain, and concentrate on the rhythmic flapping of their wings. Can you imagine them? Can you sense their majesty and power as they fly into the wind? Their grace and elegance as they glide upon it? Try to see them, feel them, search for them."

Valzaan stopped talking, but he kept a hold of Benjiah's hand. Benjiah again tried to focus, though it was difficult. He had tried this night after night most of the way through Gyrin and since they had emerged. Yes, he had grown in controlling his entrance into and exit from slow time, but he just didn't seem to be able to get this one right. He closed his eyes and thought of birds, over and over, but nothing happened for several minutes.

And then he felt it, faintly at first. The frustration of failure and stupidity went away. It was like a soft echo of a heartbeat inside, but it was not his. It was faster, much faster, and he could hear also the whistling of the wind as it slipped past outstretched wings. He was suddenly very glad that Valzaan had hold of his hand, for he felt as though he were moving very quickly, gliding as though carried by a strong current in a river, but much smoother.

"You are feeling something," Valzaan said more than asked.

"Yes."

"Good."

Benjiah was feeling something indeed, but he still could see nothing. There was only darkness and sound and the smacking of rain, drop after drop. Then there was a shift of light, and the darkness was not quite so dark. He continued to squeeze his eyes shut, but gradually he began to make out a great ocean of darkness below him, with various shadowy forms and shapes floating about in it. He tried to focus, but the sight of things sweeping along underneath him was making him feel sick to his stomach. He fought to hold the nausea down, and soon it passed.

Suddenly the ground below him became much clearer, and he realized he was not as high up as he had first thought, for the windhover through whose eyes he was seeing was only fifteen or twenty spans above the ground. What then were the large shadowy forms? He peered as carefully as he could at them, then gasped as realization dawned on him. "They are Malekim!" he said out loud.

Valzaan's grip tightened on his hand. "Tell me what you see."

"We are flying over hundreds and hundreds, probably thousands of sleeping Malekim. They are stretched out over the ground as far as I can see."

"Do you have any idea where you are?"

"No, it is a dark and rainy open plain."

"Concentrate, Benjiah. I could try to reach out for this windhover too, but it could take me some time to find this particular one. You will need to find some point of reference for me to work with. Ask the windhover to circle higher so you can survey the area."

"How?"

"The same way you have done all that you have done so far."

Benjiah concentrated. *I need to see more, more of this. More of the area around those who are sleeping here. Can you do that? Can you take me higher and show me more?*

Immediately the bird began to bank, and again the sick feeling returned to Benjiah's stomach. Suddenly the ground was tilting and they were moving faster and soon the King Falcon was rising higher and higher until the Malekim were far below. As they flew in ever-widening circles, Benjiah marveled that there seemed to be no end to the host camped below. "There are so many of them, thousands upon thousands. And there," he said suddenly, "a short distance away, what might be men, but we are too high to tell. They are smaller and in rows and rows of clumps, bundled tightly against the rain as we are."

"Can you see any distinguishing geographical features yet? Trees? Water? Mountains? A road? Anything?"

"Nothing yet." Again he concentrated. Wider. Sweep wider. I need to see more. Again the bird responded. Eventually they passed beyond the sleeping forms and all Benjiah could see was open grassland and plain. The falcon continued its arc, and before long, it started back over more sleeping forms. This time he was almost sure they were men and not Malekim. They were smaller and not uniform in color, like many soldiers in different cloaks. The course of the windhover took Benjiah over these men for several minutes, then again it passed out over open grassland and plain. Benjiah was about to say to Valzaan that there was nothing, absolutely nothing, when the bird began to bank and in the distance he saw something large and dark rising up against the nighttime sky. Yes, that, what is it? Go closer. I need to see it.

The windhover leveled out of the banking arc and flew straight and fast toward the large dark form that rose out of the horizon. It was tall and wide and dark. As they drew nearer, Benjiah said excitedly, "It is a wall. Some distance across open ground there is a great wall, like that of a large city such as Amaan Sul." Benjiah broke off as the words escaped his throat. For a moment he panicked. What if it was Amaan Sul? What if Malek's army had gone east and not west, and now his mother and his home were surrounded by the enemy? He looked carefully as they neared the wall and was reassured. It was not Amaan Sul.

"Is there anything else?" Valzaan asked.

"I will try to . . ." Suddenly it was all gone. He tried to concentrate. Where are you? Have you closed your eyes? Are you all right? Can you still sense me? Can you hear me? Nothing. Wherever it had come from, the mysterious link was gone.

Benjiah opened his eyes. He noticed for the first time that Pedraal and Pedraan were sitting beside Valzaan.

"You did it!" Pedraan whispered excitedly, slapping Benjiah on the shoulder.

"Yes, he did," Pedraal answered. "But what does it mean? What has he seen?"

"It must be Malek's army," Pedraan said matter-of-factly.

"Of course it must be, but where are they? What city was it?"

"That is what we must find out," Valzaan jumped in.

"How will we do that?"

"I will do it," the prophet answered. "I will search through the eyes of every windhover I can find until I figure out which city is now surrounded by our enemy, though I doubt that it can be any other place than Fel Edorath. I fear that doom has come already to that city, but I must see what I can see for myself. If it is Fel Edorath, I must scout out the inside of the city as carefully as I can to see if Aljeron is still there."

Benjiah felt the tension building. They had come so far so quickly. They couldn't be too late, not now, not after so much.

"The three of you should sleep," Valzaan said, using that tone he always did when he seemed to feel the need to reassure them that all was not lost. "We may have to leave before the night is over, but it may take me some time to find all we need to know."

Reluctantly Benjiah followed his uncles as they moved back through the trees to the place they had picked out to sleep. They did not speak much to each other, but Pedraan leaned over and whispered to Benjiah before lying down, "What was it like?"

Benjiah shrugged. "I don't know how to explain it. It was, well, like flying."

Benjiah opened his eyes to another cold, grey morning. As he sat up and stretched, yawning, he realized it was much brighter than it should be. They were always awake shortly after sunrise, but if his eyes were not deceiving him, it was mid- or even late morning.

"So, you finally decided to get up," Pedraan said, squatting down to hand Benjiah a piece of bread. Their meals had grown increasingly smaller through Gyrin, and their hopes of eating better once out on the western side had been frustrated by poor hunting, rain, and a need to keep moving as fast as possible. Still, Benjiah took the food gratefully and devoured it.

"I guess it is hard work, flying that is," Pedraan said with a smile. "It must have worn you out. You were dead to the world."

"Why didn't you wake me?" Benjiah asked after he swallowed. "I've held us up and we can't afford to be slowed down."

"Relax," Pedraal answered from behind Pedraan. "We're not going anywhere until Valzaan is ready."

"What do you mean?" Benjiah asked, looking for the prophet.

"See for yourself."

Benjiah followed Pedraal's pointing finger and saw the prophet some distance away under the snow trees, sitting on a rock, right where they had left him the night before. His back was to them, and he sat upright and still. "Has he been there like that since you guys woke up?"

"Yup. Probably been there all night."

"Did either of you go over to see if he was all right?"

"He's all right. If he were dead or something, he'd have keeled over by now. We'll just have to wait until he's ready."

They did wait. The sun rose higher and higher behind the clouds until Benjiah began to feel hungry again. They had given up the midday meal several days ago, both to preserve rations and to maintain speed, but not being in the saddle and having the journey and the land to focus on instead of his hunger left Benjiah little defense against the rumbling in his stomach. Furthermore, despite his long sleep, he was tired again. After so many days riding from sunrise to sunset, this sudden inactivity made him want to sleep some more. He found his eyes closing inadvertently and his head drooping until his chin all but rested on his chest. He jerked up and opened his eyes, trying to stay awake so as to be ready to go when the time came, when he realized Valzaan was standing above him.

"Come," he said, looking down with a calm but serious expression. "We need to go now."

Benjiah rose and followed Valzaan toward Pedraal and Pedraan. As soon as they had seen Valzaan stir, they had immediately untied the horses and were now waiting, reins in their hands. "Ready?" they asked as Valzaan and Benjiah approached.

"Yes, though I am weary of this rain and weary in mind and body. I would gladly sleep if we could afford the delay, but we cannot."

"What have you seen?" Benjiah asked as he climbed into his saddle.

"I have seen many things, and at last a picture of what is happening has formed in my mind. I searched first last night for Fel Edorath, and when I found it, I found Malek's army encamped just east of it. It is a great host of men and Malekim and more. I then tried to search the city, and there I found some activity, though not what I expected for a heavily garrisoned city expecting siege. I did not understand why at first, but as I searched the land west of Fel Edorath, the answer became clear. Aljeron's army was a couple days west, camped beside the road. They have fled the city."

"So they are not trapped," Pedraan said, hope resounding in his voice.

"They are not, but they are still in danger. This morning, as the first rays of light began to appear through the cloud and rain, I saw Malek's host marching around the city. I could not risk making our next move without knowing his. When the army arrived on the western side of the city, the gates opened and men from within marched out to join his army."

"What?" the twins said. The revelation stunned Benjiah.

"Yes, and as the men came forth from the city, the man who greeted them was none other than Rulalin."

"Rulalin was already with the army from the Mountain?"

"Yes."

"Perhaps he had been captured," Pedraal said quietly.

"Perhaps," Valzaan answered. "From what I could see, the men from Fel Edorath were joining him and Malek's host on a great march west, probably in pursuit of Aljeron."

"Rulalin is riding with Malek's army in pursuit of Aljeron," Pedraan murmured. "Then he really has given up his voice."

"Yes," Valzaan said gravely. "His treachery is of staggering proportions. Not only has Malek been strengthened and Werthanin weakened, but Aljeron cannot hope for Fel Edorath to slow the enemy's advance. Malek has bypassed the city and is moving west. Whatever Aljeron has planned, he has less time than he hopes. We must ride with great haste, for he needs our aid now as much as he needs our news."

With that, Valzaan spurred his horse on, and soon they were galloping north and west again.

For three days they rode as hard as they could from dawn until sunset. The ground was often rolling now, in small and big hills, and they passed innumerable rock formations, worn rounded and smooth by hundreds if not thousands of years of wind and rain. They also passed the occasional house and farm, but they tried not to attract much attention and gave any such habitation a wide berth. Though Benjiah understood the need to avoid any potential complications or delays, he found himself at times looking longingly at the barns, dreaming of a roof and dryness. It became his fantasy that one evening, just as they were preparing to stop for the night, they would ride over a ridge only to find a great, abandoned barn rising up before them. Surely then, he thought, even Valzaan would realize it made sense for them to bed down under shelter. But his dreams remained unfulfilled and his prayers unanswered. After several days and nights like this, Benjiah went to bed grumbling that being a prophet would be a lot more useful if he could make a barn appear over the next horizon. Stepping out of the river of time for a few minutes or seeing through the eyes of a bird was all well and good, but right now the only gift he wanted was the gift of shelter.

On the fourth full day after Valzaan's sleepless night, they came to a halt in dramatic fashion. They were following Valzaan, who by this point had turned them almost completely west, when suddenly Valzaan sat up in his saddle and pulled on the reins of his horse with such force that the creature rose on its hind legs and almost threw Valzaan to the ground. Benjiah was surprised at how adeptly the old prophet avoided this potential disaster and, regaining control, turned the animal southward. Benjiah and the twins, having also stopped their horses as quickly as they could manage, followed his lead.

"What are we doing?" Pedraan asked.

"Trying to live long enough to reach Aljeron. Follow me!"

There was no more talk, because Valzaan was moving almost due south as fast as he could ride. For the better part of an hour, they sped south, until gradually Valzaan began to turn them a little, and then a little more, until they were once more riding almost due west. When they had ridden like this for more than three hours, Valzaan slowed his horse to a brisk trot.

"What happened?" Pedraan ventured again.

"Wolves."

"Black Wolves?"

"Yes, a large pack, not far ahead, directly in our path. Had we kept forward, they would have caught our scent before we ever saw them."

"Do you think we have evaded them?"

"I think so. I can see no trace of them. I do not sense them either. If they did catch our scent, they may not have been sufficiently interested in such a small party to deviate from their mission. They are no doubt the eyes and ears of Malek's army, and their concern is for Aljeron's whereabouts, not ours. Even so, it was necessary we take precautions."

"Is it safe to turn north again?"

"I doubt that anything we will do for quite some time will be safe, but it is time. We must move northward, for we need even more than ever to find Aljeron."

The afternoon passed and evening came, and they rode on. It was dusk when Valzaan slowed to a halt again. Just ahead, a river perhaps thirty spans across stretched out as far as the eye could see to the right and to the left.

"I don't know exactly where we are," Pedraal said, staring at the water like the rest of them, "but I have an idea, and I don't remember any rivers in this area of Werthanin."

"This is not a river," Valzaan said.

"What is it?"

"My guess would be that it is a small stream, swollen with the rain. The ground here is rocky, and the cold weather has probably all but frozen it. With all this rain, the stream has flooded its bank."

"But if this is what has become of a small stream, as you suggest," Benjiah said, "what about the great rivers of Kirthanin? What about the Kellisor Sea?"

"I don't know," Valzaan said. "If these rains continue, the flooding could be extensive."

Benjiah ran his fingers through his wet hair as he looked up into the sky. The continuous downpour opened up a well of frustration. "Why is Malek doing this? What purpose can he have for all this rain? I don't understand!"

"Nor do I," Valzaan said. "I am afraid it is but one of many questions about his purposes that we will have to leave unanswered for now. I think we should take our horses gently ahead. I doubt the stream banks are very steep or treacherous, but if you wish to avoid running the risk of floundering, you will be careful."

The following morning, Valzaan told them he had seen Aljeron's army moving north toward Zul Arnoth. Pedraal and Pedraan, who had fought Rulalin in one of Aljeron's early campaigns there, muttered the name of the ruined city under their breath but said nothing further.

"What does that mean?" Benjiah asked.

"It means, I think, that Aljeron means to test the enemy's strength there rather than falling back to Shalin Bel."

"But why? Zul Arnoth is a ruin, and Shalin Bel has strong walls and ample provisions."

"If he is aware of Malek's army, then he has probably sent a messenger ahead to warn the city," Pedraal said. "Perhaps he means to slow Malek down and give the people time to get away."

"Or perhaps he wishes to engage the enemy on ground where he has fought battles before and knows the shape and form of things," Pedraal added. "A loss at Zul Arnoth or a misstep need not be final. There are many paths of retreat from there, and Aljeron has had to pull back from Zul Arnoth before."

"Whatever his reason, Aljeron is moving toward Zul Arnoth. We are close now. Let's waste no more time."

They set out with renewed vigor, for whatever else finding Aljeron would bring, it would bring a rest from the saddle. They rode hard, and about Eighth Hour crossed the western road. Benjiah peered back east. It was cloudy and misty and he could see nothing. Still, it was chilling to know that down that road, beyond what his eyes could see, the hosts of Malek were marching in his direction. Fel Edorath must be empty of all by now, except perhaps for the women and children if they had not already fled before Malek arrived. Beyond the city was the Mountain, also empty after its occupation of almost a thousand years. And beyond the Mountain was Enthanin, Amaan Sul, and home. He was glad to think that Malek's attention was turned this way. Perhaps, if Malek could be defeated here, the shadow of war would never stretch over his homeland.

That night they talked more than usual around the fire, which the twins finally managed to spark, and Benjiah listened to his uncles' stories of their experiences in Zul Arnoth. He had heard them all before, but never while sitting within a day's ride of the ruins. He had tried to imagine the crumbling walls and leveled buildings, the ancient stone fallen in piles all over the high ground, but tomorrow he would not need to imagine. He would see with his own eyes and walk among them with his own feet. And, of course, he would meet Aljeron. He thought of the man in his vision, remembered his intense eyes and the jagged scar across his face. He thought of the man who had been his father's friend and dedicated himself also to being his father's avenger. He wondered what Aljeron would be like in person. Even more, he wondered what Aljeron would think of him. He wanted very much to be accounted worthy of his father's memory. He reached over and took hold of Suruna. He would show Aljeron that he could wield the bow like his father, and that he could be of use to Aljeron's cause in immediate and practical ways. At any rate, all the years of waiting would be over soon. He was both nervous and excited and did not sleep until well after his uncles were snoring loudly beside him.

8

FACE TO FACE

As Benjiah mounted his horse in the morning, he recalculated how many days they had been gone from Amaan Sul to make sure he was correct in thinking it was the sixteenth day of Autumn Wane. He had done the mental calculation often in Gyrin as they rode in the eerie, dark woods. Since their emergence from the forest he had abandoned the habit, but this morning, as they rode on toward Zul Arnoth, the repetition and inward recounting of their journey was a soothing exercise.

The nervousness he felt was mitigated by his growing excitement. The ground was definitely sloping uphill, and he knew they were not far now from the ruin, which rested on the crest of the highest hill between Shalin Bel and Fel Edorath. They had not climbed ground this steep since leaving Amaan Sul, and Benjiah began to understand what his uncles had meant when they talked about armies being exposed on their approach, for there was nothing in any direction to cover their movements.

Just then, Benjiah noticed riders coming downhill, on an angle toward them. "Easy," Pedraan said to Benjiah. "These are probably Aljeron's scouts, out to see who's coming."

Sure enough, as the fifty or so horsemen came closer, Benjiah could see the purple and grey of Shalin Bel on some of them. Valzaan, Benjiah, and the twins stopped their horses and waited as the riders approached and circled them. The riders halted as well, except for a woman, perhaps his mother's age, but with her hair cut short like a man's. She rode up to them, and Benjiah noted her lean muscles and hardened face as she stopped before Valzaan.

"Valzaan, your presence is an honor beyond our worth and aid beyond our hope. You are welcome indeed to Zul Arnoth."

Valzaan nodded in her direction with a slight smile. "Your voice, mistress, is familiar to me, though it has been many years. You are Bryar, are you not?"

"I am."

"You are riding with Aljeron's army?"

"I am. I have served under Aljeron's command since the beginning of the war. In the first year of the campaign I buried my only brother, Elyas, but still I ride with Aljeron and I will ride until all wars cease or until I am laid in my grave."

"May rest from your labors come from the former, rather than the latter," Valzaan answered. "I grieve Elyas with you. He was full of mirth and a good companion."

"He was," Bryar answered, then she turned her attention to the twins. "Pedraal and Pedraan, returned from your leisure in the east? Tired of the life of comfort and pleasure you live in Amaan Sul? We also welcome you to Zul Arnoth. We will need such hardy men as you, and more besides if we are to avoid falling under the hammer."

"We will give you what aid we can, Bryar," Pedraal said, "though we know we alone cannot turn the tide of the coming battle."

Bryar nodded in acknowledgment, then looked from the twins to Benjiah. Benjiah could see the look of mild surprise as she looked him over. "You're Joraiem and Wylla's boy."

"I am," Benjiah said. "I am Benjiah Andira."

Again Bryar nodded, "You are welcome, Benjiah, but it is an ill-fated time you have chosen to journey west. You may well bear witness to the beginning of the end of all things."

"He is more aware of the danger into which he has come than you give him credit for," Valzaan cut in, saving Benjiah from having to respond. "We all are, but still we have come, and farther we need to go as quickly as possible. Can you take us to Aljeron immediately?"

"I will take you to him." Bryar wheeled her horse around and stopped it beside a young rider perhaps half her age, and whispered something in his ear. He nodded and called a command as the other riders turned and rode south and a little west, sidling around the hill. "We are less than an hour from the city," Bryar said when they were gone. "Let's go."

They rode behind Bryar almost directly up the hill, and before long, part of the city's ancient wall came into view. They made for one of the larger openings in the collapsing wall and slowed to enter after Bryar had exchanged a few words with the soldiers inside. Benjiah saw a few glances sent his way as they rode through the camp, but by and large it was Valzaan attracting the attention. Benjiah looked at him, freshly reminded of what a striking figure he presented, his wild white hair sticking out in all directions, his empty white eyes and wrinkled skin, and his dignified carriage.

Soon they halted before a large round tent, which Benjiah knew must be Aljeron's, in part because there were so few others set up, but also because the frenzied activity of the camp radiated outward from this place. Clusters of soldiers sat or stood around the tent, and men came and went from these clusters, weaving in and out around one another rapidly.

"We only just arrived yesterday morning," Bryar said as she dismounted. "Aljeron has been trying to figure out how we are going to do what probably can't be done, so as you can imagine, he's been in meetings since we arrived."

She walked over to the sentries standing before the tent flaps, and Benjiah could easily guess the moment when she first used Valzaan's name, for they both turned in unison to gaze at the prophet, erect and still upon his horse. One disappeared inside the tent and the other came walking toward them. "Master Valzaan and honored guests, let me take your horses. Please, you are welcome here," he said as he bowed.

"Thank you," Valzaan said. He dismounted and turned over the reins of his horse. Benjiah and the twins likewise dismounted and had started toward the tent when Aljeron stepped out, looking weary but excited.

"Valzaan," he said, reaching out to take the prophet's hand. "It really is you. Hail, and well met. I heard my guard say your name, but it didn't seem possible. Not here, not today. Come inside, all of you, come and have a seat."

Benjiah followed Valzaan and the twins, and he noticed Aljeron's eyes pass carefully over him. He could not read their expression though, and he did not know if his name had yet been announced. Inside, the occupants of the tent were on their feet, all save the enormous Great Bear, whose head would have pushed the tent up out of the ground. Two men enlarged their circle with a few extra stools and soon had turned their attention to the newly arrived visitors.

As soon as these two noticed Benjiah, they crossed the floor and threw their arms around him. "Uncle Evrim, Uncle Brenim," Benjiah said in turn as he hugged them.

"What are you doing here, Benjiah?" Brenim asked.

"All that in due time," Valzaan said.

Evrim looked from his nephew to the prophet and back. "You have come from Amaan Sul?"

"Yes."

"How are Kyril and the girls?"

"They were good when I left," Benjiah said, then remembered the envelope from his aunt. "I have something for you from Aunt Kyril. I will give it to you after we're finished here."

Evrim nodded, putting his hands on Benjiah's shoulders and looking down into his eyes. "I will have it then, gladly. It is good to see you, Benjiah."

By this point, Aljeron had closed the flaps of the tent and taken his seat. "Please, everyone, sit, and we will let Master Valzaan introduce himself and the others of his party."

They did sit, and Valzaan did as he had been asked. "I am Valzaan, and I will not belabor these introductions. I have come from Amaan Sul through Gyrin with Pedraal and Pedraan Someris, as well as with Benjiah Andira, heir to the Enthanin throne."

"Through Gyrin?" Benjiah heard a few murmur as one of the older men—a rugged, dark looking man with long braided hair, mostly grey—stood from his seat. "Valzaan, it has been many years, but it is good to see you again."

"Thank you, Caan," Valzaan answered.

"Likewise, Pedraal and Pedraan. I see that you still carry the war hammer and battle-axe."

"Yes, and we can still use them," Pedraan answered, smiling.

"And to you, Benjiah Andira," Caan said, looking at him kindly, "an especially warm greeting. I have long hoped to meet you, and I am pleased to have had the chance."

When all introductions had been made, Aljeron welcomed the twins back into his camp before turning his attention to Benjiah. "The heir to the Enthanin throne is welcome here. Indeed, you would be welcome as Wylla and Joraiem's son whether you were the heir to a throne or not. However," Aljeron said, looking from Benjiah to his uncles and Valzaan, "I must insist that one or all of you take him from this place as soon as possible. I can think of no more dangerous place to be sitting in Kirthanin at this moment than right here. The hosts of Malek have issued forth from the Mountain and are likely moving toward us as we speak. This is no place for any boy, much less a future king and only son."

"And where do you think he should be taken?" Valzaan asked.

"Someplace safe."

"There are no safe places anymore. There are places not immediately under the threat of Malek's power, but those places will eventually come under the hammer too, unless Malek is stopped, and Benjiah may be more important to that end than you think."

"What do you mean?" Aljeron asked, his eyes narrowing.

"This is no time for secrets among friends, so I will tell you plainly what must be kept to yourselves, for Benjiah's true identity may still be unknown to our enemy and must be kept that way as long as we can."

Valzaan proceeded to relate quickly the vision that had led him to Amaan Sul, and the words of the prophecy that he had shared there with Wylla.

With a strength that stoops to conquer
And a hope that dies to live,
With a light that fades to be kindled
And a love that yields to give,

Comes a child who was born to lead,
A prophet who was born to see,
A warrior who was born to surrender,
And through his sacrifice set us free.

The child prophet is Benjiah, and I have brought him with me through much danger and across many leagues to be here in the heart of the storm, because my heart tells me this is where he needs to be."

The men and even the Great Bear stared at Benjiah, and he blushed under their gaze. "You are sure?" Aljeron asked, looking at Benjiah still.

"I am sure," Valzaan answered. "I had thought that the fulfillment of the prophecy might be Joraiem, but it is Joraiem's son. The time of our great trial has come, and it is for this moment that Benjiah has been gifted to serve and to lead. I am here as his guardian and caretaker more than anything else, as are Pedraal and Pedraan. We will of course aid you in the coming battle, but our role must never be misunderstood. We are here to protect Benjiah, with our lives if necessary."

Benjiah looked at Valzaan and then at his uncles, whose gazes had turned sober. He knew that they had felt responsible for him, but he had never heard anyone put the task so starkly before. He shivered to think that Valzaan—the Valzaan of history and legend—was saying that his purpose in life, at least at that moment, was to keep him alive.

"The word of Allfather's prophet is the word of Allfather," Aljeron said. "Benjiah will stay under the care of Valzaan, and everyone in this room will do all within their power to preserve his life, so be it."

"So may it be," the others answered solemnly, and Benjiah looked at his uncles taking stock of him anew. It would have been unnerving to be examined so carefully by those who had known him since birth, had his Uncle Evrim not smiled at him and started shaking his head in good-natured disbelief.

Fortunately for Benjiah, conversation did not dwell on him for long, for soon Valzaan had started reporting to Aljeron about the army coming their way. "How many men do you have here?" Valzaan asked after a moment.

"About twelve thousand," Aljeron answered. "There are ten thousand men of Shalin Bel, and some two thousand from Fel Edorath."

Valzaan nodded. "The men who march under Malek's command alone outnumber you, and included in that number are the remaining men of Fel Edorath."

"That cannot be," Valon said, standing at his seat. "The men of Fel Edorath would never march with Malek. They would not come with me because they would not abandon the city. They were staying to fight!"

"Perhaps, but in the end they did not choose that road. They are marching with Malek, and they are marching under Rulalin's command."

"Rulalin!" Aljeron exclaimed. Aljeron turned to Corlas. "Did you know Rulalin had gone to Malek?" he asked.

"I did not," Corlas said softly, looking ashamed, "and I can hardly now believe it though I know a prophet of Allfather would not lie. I remember when the first embassy from the Mountain came to Fel Edorath to invite Rulalin to seek aid from Malek. It was during the second year of our war with Shalin Bel, and Rulalin dismissed the embassy and the ambassador, a proud swaggerer named Tashmiren. I can't believe that after so many years and lives, he gave in."

"What was or is in the mind and heart of Rulalin Tarasir, none of us can say," Valzaan said. "What we know is that if Malek were bringing men alone, we would be outnumbered. However, Malek has brought more than men, for thousands of Malekim march with him, and many, many packs of Black Wolves are also abroad under his command."

Silence reigned in the tent as Valzaan spoke. Though the news was grim, Benjiah noted in Aljeron's face, as well as in the others, not fear but determination. They did not seem surprised at this news.

"Along with these," Valzaan continued, "comes a foe far

greater than any of them. The children of Vulsutyr are abroad under the command of one who has haunted my dreams. For many years now I have dreamed of him. Several nights ago, I saw him clearly. He leads the children of Vulsutyr and walks in their midst with a great hammer through which, I believe, he is summoning and controlling this perpetual storm we are in."

"So the weather is a machination of the enemy," Aljeron said quietly.

"I believe that it is," Valzaan said.

"And this giant, this storm maker, why does he make it always rain? What purpose is there in the storm?"

"I don't know. Yet his coming casts a shadow over my heart. He will work much evil and do much harm before all is said and done."

"And yet," Aljeron said, "we must do what we can to stop him, and to stop the others with him. We must do all we can to slow down if not stop this advancing force. I have sent messengers west with word of the peril that is coming, but the people in the countryside and in Shalin Bel will need time to flee. We must plan wisely. Have you any hope to offer us, Valzaan?"

"Only this, that we may lose many battles and yet win this war. Our hope for deliverance is in Allfather, and we must look to Him. In the meantime, we must do the best we can. Let us face the coming of our enemy with no illusions as to our chances, but with every confidence that all is not yet known and the tide of many a battle has changed when least expected."

They talked for a long time after, at times going round and round on questions Benjiah began to suspect had no answer. Eventually, Evrim asked permission to take Benjiah to get some food while they continued their planning, and Benjiah was glad to be on his feet and walking with his uncle, even if it meant being back out in the rain.

"Halina and Roslin are well, you say?" Evrim asked as they made their way through the camp.

"Yes." Benjiah hesitated, thinking of the slain soldiers of Amaan Sul they'd left in the grass beside Gyrin. "Uncle Evrim, a raiding party from the Mountain slaughtered a patrol of Enthanim near the eastern border to Gyrin. We think they were heading toward Amaan Sul."

"You saw them?"

"We saw the dead soldiers. The raiding party had already passed."

Evrim nodded. "If Malek's main force is headed this way, then Amaan Sul should be all right. A small raiding party wouldn't pose much danger."

They walked on quietly, coming to the place where Benjiah's horse was being tended, and Benjiah dug the envelope from his aunt out of his pack.

Evrim took it from his hand as if it were made of gold and ran his fingers over it gently before tucking it inside his cloak to protect it from the rain. "Thank you, Benjiah."

"Sure," Benjiah said. "It was the least I could do. Aunt Kyril wanted to come, but Valzaan and Mom convinced her to stay."

"Good, even with the raid, they are likely safer there than here," Evrim said.

"Uncle Evrim, did you know my dad was a prophet?"

"Yes, your mother told me years ago."

Benjiah nodded as they walked. "I'm sorry, Benjiah, but she didn't want you to know until you were older."

"I know. We talked about it. I was just wondering who else knew."

"Not many, just those closest to him and to her." Evrim turned in at a small tent without walls, a large canopy designed to give a fire enough protection to survive the rain. Benjiah waited by the fire while Evrim retrieved two bowls of a thick stew that, despite Benjiah's hunger, were not too appealing. It tasted better than it looked though, and Benjiah ate it gratefully.

"You aren't wearing your father's pendant anymore," Evrim said, looking at Benjiah's neck.

Benjiah reached up and felt the slender golden cord that had replaced it, and looked at his uncle. "Sorry, Uncle Evrim, I know that came from you. I left it with Mom to remember me by."

"No need to apologize; a change every so often is good. I like your new look," he reached over and felt the slender cord that was tied around Benjiah's neck. "If you can't have them here with you, this is the next best thing."

Benjiah nodded, and Evrim took the empty bowl from his hand and returned it. They started walking again, off through the camp.

"Uncle Evrim, what will we do if we lose?"

"We will face that, if and when it comes."

"Do you think we can win this battle?"

"No."

"But it is coming, isn't it?"

"Yes, but we need to do one thing at a time."

Benjiah knew his uncle well enough to know that he wasn't going to get any additional details. "I don't think Aljeron was glad to see me. He thinks I'm a boy who should be home with my head in my mother's lap."

"He's worried for you," Evrim said, looking at Benjiah as his nephew gazed straight ahead. "He feels like he's failed your father, and he doesn't want to see you get hurt or killed."

"He didn't fail my dad."

"I know, but he couldn't do anything to save him, and neither has he been able to bring his murderer to justice."

"Those things weren't his fault."

"I know, and so does he, but it hurts him all the same."

Benjiah stopped and faced his uncle. "I'll show him that I

can do a man's job in battle. I'm as good or better with a bow than most. He'll see."

Evrim looked down at Benjiah and put his hand on his shoulder. "Promise me you won't do anything stupid. Remember what Valzaan said. There are a few people around here who will give their lives to protect you. If you endanger yourself needlessly, you'll endanger them, and we can't afford to have anything happen to any of you. You understand that?"

"I understand."

"Good, let's go back and see if they need us for anything."

Aljeron stood in front of the tent flaps and watched Valzaan and the twins walk away with Benjiah. How much the boy reminded him of his father. It had been a shock to see him at first, but having him in the tent, cradling Suruna in his lap, brought Aljeron the comfort of familiarity. They would need all the bowmen they could get before this was through, and if Benjiah was anywhere near as good as his father, Aljeron would gladly have him in battle.

Turning back inside, he looked at Evrim, sitting by the small lamp, studying him as he went back to his seat. "What's on your mind?" Aljeron asked, sitting down.

"You should just take him aside and talk to him. He's not a ghost, not a memory, and not a hero, at least not yet. He's just a boy."

"I know that."

"Well?"

"Well what?"

"Aljeron, the boy rode all the way from Amaan Sul, through Gyrin, to get here. Sure, he was following Valzaan because the prophet said he must, but I bet meeting you was on his mind as much or more than anything else. You should try to make him feel welcome and not like a burdensome kid."

"I never said he was."

"Your impulse to send him away for his own good could be read more than one way. Maybe he thinks you don't want him here because you think he'll get in the way."

"Why, did he say that to you?"

"Look," Evrim said, leaning forward in his chair. "I'm just saying we could all sense the awkwardness when you greeted him. Maybe he could too. We've been busy today, but maybe you should try to spend a few minutes with him tomorrow, you know, set him at ease."

"All right, I'll see what I can do."

"Good, I know he'll appreciate it."

Aljeron reached over to pick up the pitcher of water, but there was only a tiny bit left. He got up and carried the empty pitcher to the tent flaps and placed the pitcher on the ground outside, picking up another full container just like it off the ground. "At least," he said, returning to his seat and filling his glass, "with all this cold rain around, there's never a lack of fresh water."

"True," Evrim said with a smile, "but I would happily resort to more typical means of getting water if this storm would go away."

Evrim filled his own cup. "How long do you think before the first messenger reaches Shalin Bel?"

"I don't know, several days still, I would guess. All twenty were given destinations along the way, so even the fastest of them, if they barely sleep, must still be leagues away."

"There will be panic."

"Probably. News of Malek's movement will reach Shalin Bel while its army is out in the field. The people will feel exposed and vulnerable, even though we are between Malek and the city. But many will wonder when next they see an army in the distance if it will be us or them."

"I wonder that myself."

"I know. At least the messengers should get through far

enough in advance that most of the people will have time to put many leagues between themselves and the city. There is always the hope that Malek's attention will be so clearly focused on us that the people will be safe. If it is conquest and not extermination that Malek is after, they may live awhile longer yet."

Evrim leaned back in his chair and looked up at the ceiling of the tent. He could see places where water had begun to pool as the tent sagged here and there. "Aljeron, what are we going to do if we lose this battle?"

"We'll drop back and retreat, you know that."

"I do know that; I mean what will we do then? We have no reinforcements. Will we try to wall ourselves up in Shalin Bel and hold out until soldiers from Suthanin or Enthanin come, if they will come? Do we think the walls of Shalin Bel will hold against the Vulsutyrim and this captain of theirs that Valzaan speaks of? We'll drop back, but where to and with what hope?"

"I don't know. We can only do one thing at a time. We'll know more about what we're up against after we've faced it once. Let's hope we'll see enough to see our way ahead."

"Maybe."

"At any rate, we haven't lost the battle yet. Everyone keeps talking about what we'll do when we lose, but we need to give winning a chance too. Right?"

Evrim raised his eyebrows skeptically. "Right."

The flaps of the door rippled, and they turned to see Koshti slip in. "Koshti," Aljeron said, rising to greet his battle brother. "Where have you been all day?"

As if in reply, the tiger sat at Aljeron's feet and lifted his face. "Evrim," Aljeron said quietly, "look at this."

Evrim rose and walked across the tent to Aljeron. Aljeron had his hand under Koshti's jaw and was staring intently at his mouth. The fur around Koshti's mouth was bloody, and small tufts of black hair were stuck to his face.

"Black Wolves," Evrim whispered.

"Yes, and not far away, I would guess," Aljeron answered. He looked at Koshti, "Good hunting today?"

The tiger yawned widely in reply, and when Aljeron let go, he lay on the floor of the tent, stretching himself out. Aljeron stepped away from Koshti and put his hand on Evrim's shoulder. "The wolves are probably scouting out our position to take news back to their master. Koshti couldn't have fought a whole pack by himself, so there might not be many around. Still, send word to our posts that the guard tonight is to be doubled and vigilant."

"I will."

"Good, then get some sleep."

Evrim nodded as he slipped out of the tent. Aljeron stooped beside Koshti, stroking the tiger's wet fur and feeling the heat emanate from his resting body. "You make me nervous when you are gone so long, Koshti. There is no need to go looking for danger. There will be excitement and killing aplenty, coming right here. There should even be enough to wear you out, my friend. So rest now, battle is near."

Most of the next day passed slowly for Benjiah. Valzaan and the twins spent the morning and afternoon in conferences with Aljeron and his captains, but Evrim slipped away to spend part of the afternoon with him. As they wandered about the camp, Benjiah listened to Evrim recount the war with Fel Edorath and their successful conquest of the city. There was sadness mixed with the pride in Evrim's voice.

"It must have been frustrating to take the city and find Rulalin gone," Benjiah said.

"It was, but we know now why we couldn't find him."

"Do you think he went voluntarily to Malek, or do you think perhaps he was captured, you know, maybe kidnapped while on his way somewhere else?"

"I don't know," Evrim answered, looking at Benjiah. "Do you find it hard to believe he could be so treacherous?"

"No, Uncle," Benjiah said. "I just have trouble believing anyone would do willingly what he's done."

"Yeah, me too."

They walked on in silence, and Benjiah looked at the men, sitting in groups on the ground, sharpening their swords and waiting for the summons to battle. "Pedraal says most swords are useless against Malekim. He says that only Azmavarim are of any real use. Do all these soldiers have Azmavarim?"

"No," Evrim said, following Benjiah's eyes and surveying the soldiers around them. "Very few of them actually. First-blades are rare. There are maybe a hundred in the whole army."

"Only a hundred among more than 10,000! What hope is there then? How can a hundred men stand against so many Malekim?"

"Our hope is not in swords alone, for we have a thousand archers who will be much more important in this fight. Cyranic arrows will be our first line of defense. Still, the Azmavarim are important, and Aljeron has hand-selected the hundred men who bear them, and each unit has a handful of these elite fighters with them."

"And if they fall?"

"Then it is up to the men next to them to take up the First-blade and continue the fight."

"If only we had more than one Great Bear here," Benjiah said. "The twins said the Great Bear are ferocious enemies of the Malekim."

"We do have more than one."

"We do?"

"Yes, we have three. Sarneth's son, Erigan, and his friend Arintol are both here."

"Oh," Benjiah said, the brief excitement giving way to disappointment. "Three is better than one, but not much better. Now three thousand, that would be more like it."

"Three thousand Great Bear would indeed be very welcome, but we will have to make do with what we have."

A messenger from Aljeron's tent summoned Evrim back to the meeting, and he bid Benjiah farewell, leaving him to pass the rest of the afternoon and early evening on his own. When it was Twelfth Hour and darkness began to creep over the camp, Benjiah began to wonder what he was supposed to do for supper. Just at that moment, though, none other than Aljeron himself came walking through the camp toward him.

"Hello, Benjiah," Aljeron said, attempting a casual smile.

"Master Balinor," Benjiah said, shifting uneasily and trying to receive his surprise visitor nonchalantly.

"Yes, well," Aljeron stumbled, "you don't really need to call me Master Balinor. Aljeron is fine. No need for formality with me."

"All right," Benjiah said tentatively.

"Anyway," Aljeron continued, "I came to see if you would take supper with me. Would that be all right with you?"

"Sure, but don't you have things you need to do?"

"Eating is one of them. Come and have supper."

Benjiah followed Aljeron to his tent, and when they passed inside, Benjiah saw that the tent wasn't empty. "That must be Koshti," he said as he stopped just inside the flaps.

"Yes," Aljeron said, stepping over and stroking the head of the tiger. "There's no need to fear Koshti. He won't harm you."

"Can I . . . can I touch him?"

"Sure," Aljeron answered, this time smiling for real. "You know, when your dad first met Koshti, he wasn't sure about him at all. He wouldn't touch Koshti for days."

"Yeah?"

"Yeah. As he grew more comfortable with me, though, he grew more comfortable with Koshti. Come feel how soft his fur is."

Benjiah walked over and stooped beside Aljeron, rubbing Koshti's orange and black fur. Koshti looked up at Benjiah for a moment, but soon the tiger's head was resting flat on the tent floor, his eyes closed, enjoying the attention.

"He's beautiful," Benjiah said.

"That he is," Aljeron answered, standing and walking over to a chair at a small table where two plates sat waiting with their dinner on them. Benjiah joined him and soon they were eating and talking, almost as freely as Benjiah might have talked with Evrim. Aljeron told Benjiah story after story about his trip to Sulare and beyond with Joraiem, and Benjiah drank it up like thirsty soil drinks up the first rain after a drought.

"The Summerland sounds beautiful," Benjiah said while Aljeron paused to eat a little. Benjiah had long since finished his own dinner. "Despite what happened to Dad there, it is still one of my Mother's favorite places in Kirthanin. What would you say Sulare is like?"

Aljeron thought for a moment and said, "Sulare is peace. It is like rest, like fullness. If I live through what is coming, I hope to go back before I die."

"Mom says that when Malek is finally defeated, whenever that may be, all of Kirthanin might be like the Summerland. She thinks it is a picture of what Kirthanin was meant to be and might still be again."

"That would be beautiful."

Benjiah could see that the idea of the whole world being like Sulare had taken root in Aljeron. He was staring vacantly at the far wall of the tent. Maybe if he also survived this war, Benjiah would go with Aljeron to see Sulare.

"Aljeron," Benjiah asked after a few moments, "why do you think Rulalin did it?"

"Did what? Kill your father?"

"Yes."

Aljeron shrugged. "I don't know, but I've always assumed

he acted out of bitterness, or envy, or even possibly anger. He loved your mom for a long time, and when she married your father, the rejection pushed him over the edge."

"And why do you think he is helping Malek now?"

"I don't know."

"Did you sense Rulalin lacked loyalty to Allfather back then?"

"No. Rulalin fought as hard as any of us to get the women back from the Malekim. In fact, one of them almost killed him. I never had any reason to suspect he would give up his voice like this."

"Then why?"

"Probably to save Fel Edorath, if not himself. Malek might have threatened to destroy the city if he didn't."

"But you wouldn't join Malek to save Shalin Bel, would you?"

"No, and it may come to that very choice: Let the city be destroyed or join the enemy. But if it does, the city will fall, and I will likely fall with it. I will not surrender Kirthanin to save Shalin Bel or myself."

"Maybe it won't come to that. Maybe we'll win this battle," Benjiah said.

"Maybe we will."

"I'm good with Suruna, Aljeron. I'll make the enemy pay if I get the chance."

"I'm sure you will," Aljeron said, looking at Benjiah closely. "You do remind me of your father."

"Everybody tells me that."

"Sorry, I didn't mean to touch a sore spot."

"No, that's all right. I just wish I could have met him."

"I'd like to see him again myself," Aljeron said.

Benjiah nodded and looked at Aljeron, who was smiling, but with tears in his eyes. "I loved your father, Benjiah, and I'll do what I can to protect you, just like Valzaan and your uncles plan to."

"Thanks," Benjiah said, wondering at how much Aljeron's face had softened just in the last few minutes. "You're kind of like an uncle too. Maybe I should call you Uncle Aljeron."

"I would be honored to be Uncle Aljeron."

"Well, I won't call you Uncle Aljeron in front of too many of the others. I don't want to cause a stir." Benjiah grinned.

"Whatever you like, Benjiah." Aljeron laughed, and they talked until Valzaan came looking for Benjiah.

Before he left Aljeron's tent, he paused at the flaps and looked back. "I know you did all you could to bring Rulalin to justice. I'm grateful for that."

"Thanks," Aljeron said softly.

"I'm also glad to have met you at last, you know, face to face."

"So am I. I'm sorry I never came to Amaan Sul to see you and your mother."

"That's all right; maybe when all this is done."

"That would be good."

Long after, Aljeron sat stroking Koshti, thinking of the bright-eyed, blond-haired boy he had just met—and also of the one he had known so many years ago.

9

ZUL ARNOTH

Wylla looked up at the heavy skies. A great darkness had gathered in the sky in the west and hovered there for days. Now it was creeping eastward like a great black spider moving along its web. Today it not only covered Amaan Sul but the broad horizon as far as Wylla's eyes could see. She closed her eyes and felt the cool drizzle on her face as her horse followed Captain Merias and his men.

"Your Majesty?"

Wylla turned her attention back to the matter at hand. "Yes?"

"We've arrived."

Wylla dismounted and walked up beside Captain Merias. She didn't need to ask where, for the body of the lone captive from the raid lay face down in the wet grass, a host of arrows sticking out of his back.

Wylla stooped to examine him. "He never said anything of any use, did he?"

"No."

"Probably never would have, but still, it is a shame to have lost him."

"Again, Your Majesty," Merias said, "I apologize. The men shouldn't have been so lax . . ."

Wylla waved off the apology. "I was just thinking out loud. I wasn't rebuking you. Mistakes happen. At least no one else was hurt."

"Yes, Your Majesty."

"This leaves us where we were, waiting."

"Yes."

"We've had no further word from the west?"

"No, Your Majesty, save a report from a patrol near Gyrin."

"Yes?" Wylla said, her heart quickening.

"One of our patrols there was found dead. They had been dead for some time, probably killed by the raiding party that attacked the palace."

"My brothers, Benjiah, they were not among them?"

"No, Your Majesty. There was no sign of anyone other than the soldiers."

Wylla walked over to Captain Merias. "They searched the whole area carefully?"

"Yes, Your Majesty. They searched carefully. There was no sign of any other conflict."

Wylla felt the relief, and she patted Merias on the shoulder, grateful for his reassurance.

"We've sent messengers to Tol Emuna?"

"We have."

"Good. I want as complete a muster of Enthanim as we can manage. We must be prepared to defend ourselves or to ride to the aid of our Kirthanim brothers if word of their need comes. The war is begun."

When Benjiah stepped out of his tent on the morning of the eighteenth day of Autumn Wane, he noticed immediately the

BREAKING

change in the weather. The wind had been consistently at their backs on the journey since Gyrin, blowing out of the southeast, but now it was gusting and swirling in all directions and in uneven blasts that threatened to uproot the tents. The rain was also stronger, pouring in sheets that at times came in at a remarkable angle, moving almost horizontally with the wind.

Valzaan stood outside the tent, his face turned upward. Benjiah came up beside him but did not speak. He stood this way for several minutes before Valzaan broke the silence. "He is near. Come, we must bring word to Aljeron. Today is the day."

They started out through the camp, Benjiah's heart beating quickly. "Valzaan, you have seen them coming?"

"Yes, they will be here before dark."

"I have seen him too."

Valzaan did not stop, but he did slow down and turn his face toward Benjiah. "You have seen through a windhover's eyes without my help?"

"No," Benjiah said, sorry to disappoint Valzaan. "I have dreamed of him."

Valzaan nodded. "Tell me of this dream."

"I was standing on a hill, or a small rise, and before me was a great expanse of water. Perhaps it was the shore, or maybe water had risen to cover all things, I do not know. Then, in the dream, I looked to my right, and I saw the giant you have described. He stood with his back to me, facing the water. I heard him cry out, but if he was talking to someone, I could not see him. He shouted, 'You cannot defeat me. You cannot withstand me. You cannot even stand before me. I am the Bringer of Storms.' Then he raised his arms, and lightning flashed between his fingertips, and great peals of thunder began to echo and rumble in the sky. Back and forth the lightning danced and flew. It was a fearful sight. Then, he brought both hands forward in a swift motion and a great ball of sound and light swirled out from between them. The light was so brilliant that I thought it would sear my eyes, and I turned away. When I turned back, the figure was gone and only the water remained."

They had reached Aljeron's tent, and Valzaan stopped and put his hands on Benjiah's shoulders. "It is a vision from Allfather, but of what I cannot tell you, though I have seen its like before. For now, you must not let yourself be troubled. He is coming, this Bringer of Storms, but he has not yet covered the world with water, if that is his purpose. Come, let us do what we have come to do."

Valzaan's visit to Aljeron set the camp instantly in motion. As Benjiah returned with Valzaan to their tent, he watched in wonder as the once-serene camp burst into frenetic activity. Every man packed his horse, as Aljeron had ordered. Everything was to be made ready for a retreat, should such become necessary.

Back at their tent, they found Pedraal and Pedraan sleepily gathering their things. "Oh, there you are," Pedraan said as they came in. "The alarm has been raised. Someone has seen signs of the enemy."

Benjiah laughed. "That someone was Valzaan."

"Oh," Pedraan said, pausing. "You saw through the eyes of one of those birds?"

"Yes," Valzaan said.

"And the enemy, he isn't yet outside the walls of Zul Arnoth?"

"Not yet, but he will be here before dark."

"Well then," Pedraan said, looking fairly pleased, "we should have plenty of time for breakfast."

He pulled a bag containing bread and cheese out of the pack he had been busy getting together. "I secured these from Evrim yesterday in the event that the battle might prevent us from having a proper meal. It really is a nuisance, fighting for your life when you're famished. Eat up, everybody."

They all, even Valzaan, took a large piece of bread and cheese from Pedraan and ate. As Benjiah stood there chewing, a look of satisfaction came over Pedraan's face, and he smiled down at his nephew. "It's nice to have connections, isn't it? I bet not everybody has a bag of bread and cheese to get them through this day."

"No, and you may want to save some of it in case the road to Shalin Bel is more difficult than we expect," his brother added.

"Don't worry so much. I have that taken care of too," Pedraan said, again smiling as he patted his pack.

"Only the two of you could be so fully focused on your stomachs as Malek draws near," Valzaan said dryly. "I hope you aren't too busy eating later to notice that the battle has begun."

"Of course not, Valzaan," Pedraan said, stroking the handle of his war hammer, "I've been waiting to use this on the Malekim again for a long time."

By late morning, the activity in the camp had dissipated. The men had assumed their places, and now the only movement around Benjiah was the swirling rain. He was standing with Valzaan behind the archers, who were behind the front lines. Aljeron had put heavy garrisons in each of the wall's four wide gaps that faced southeast. Several small bands of scouts were outside the walls on horseback, their only job to identify enemy attempts to circumvent their defenses.

The bulk of Aljeron's men waited behind the front lines. Behind this mass of men waited a thousand archers. Most of these were grouped in companies of about a hundred along the back of the line. Because Aljeron didn't know where the concentration of Malekim would be, or if they would be intermingled with men, he was unable to deploy the archers in advance. But several mounds of rock lay against the walls, most of the piles made years earlier in battles between Shalin Bel and Fel Edorath so that archers could ascend at a moment's notice to the top of the wall.

The remaining bowmen, assigned to protect the most likely route of retreat, stood at the back. Aljeron had mapped out several lines of retreat and stationed these archers where they could easily take command of any of these routes. Aljeron and Valzaan had agreed Benjiah could face the coming battle here, for should the battle and retreat prove desperate, Valzaan could take him and flee. Should the battle go well for the forces of Shalin Bel, then he might be able to contribute to the cause with relative safety from this position.

So Benjiah stood next to his horse beside a pile of stones that led to the collapsing roof of a collapsing building. Valzaan and the twins waited with him. Despite his uncles' impatience to kill Malekim, they had not even considered going to the frontlines and abandoning their nephew. "It is entirely too likely that we will have plenty of chances to kill Malekim if we remain with you, so we'll just hang around. It would do us no good to lay waste to a hundred Malekim out there if we returned only to find you dead in the rubble. If any Malekim come this way, you will hear the heartscream of the Voiceless today."

So they waited, and morning became afternoon and afternoon moved toward evening. About Tenth Hour, the clouds in the sky thickened and light faded until it felt almost like night. Horn calls told them that the enemy was coming, and without waiting for anything else, Benjiah scrambled up the rocks to the rooftop and peered toward the city wall. There, men and archers also peered into the distance, where Benjiah could see dark forms moving. Benjiah's heart sank, for though Aljeron's men seemed a great host, what he saw now was indeed a multitude. The lines spread as far as he could see in either direction, and they were advancing up the hill toward the city like waves rolling up the seashore. Pedraal and Pedraan came up too, helping Valzaan to ascend the steep rocks. They also stared silently at the approaching army.

A gap opened in the center of the line, and even from this distance, Benjiah could see that the figures moving forward through the ranks were Vulsutyrim, towering above the Malekim. Then the enemy line stopped moving, perhaps a hundred spans from the wall of Zul Arnoth, and from the cluster of giants strode the one he had seen in his dream, a great hammer held firmly in his hand. Raising his hammer to the sky, he cried out in a loud voice. His words rumbled across the open space toward the city, but Benjiah could not make them out. Suddenly, lightning began to fall from the sky all over that open field, dropping from the heavens and striking the open ground all up and down the outside of the wall. A few even hit the walls, knocking large pieces of stone inside the city and into the midst of Aljeron's soldiers.

Then the lightning stopped, and the army behind the giant rushed forward. As they drew near, Benjiah realized that the army to the right was composed mainly of men, and the army to the left, mainly of Malekim. Benjiah was not the only one who had noticed, for soon their archers had rushed to that side, flooding the mounds of rocks and the walls to fire arrow after cyranic arrow into the approaching Malekim. Arrows flew through the bleak afternoon sky and rain, dropping Malekim all over the field. Benjiah was staggered by the number of arrows unleashed, and yet the Malekim kept coming. Then the Malekim were too close to the wall for him to see what was happening. From the great cry that went up from the men of Shalin Bel and Fel Edorath, he knew that the battle had been joined on the ground as well as in the air. The archers were now firing almost straight down at the ground.

Then, to Benjiah's dismay, great flashes of light lit up the sky, and balls of lightning came hurtling over the heads of the enemy toward Shalin Bel's archers. They smashed into the wall and blew the tops into pieces. Many of the archers were thrown backward ten or more spans, where they fell into the midst of their own soldiers. Gazing out at the battlefield, Benjiah could see the Bringer of Storms with both hands raised. The lightning flashed back and forth between the hammer and his hand before lashing out at the wall, breaching it with every strike.

The battle was changing in too many directions at once for Benjiah to keep track of everything. Below him, the mass of Shalin Bel's men began to lose ground, and the lines that had been well in front of Benjiah's building began to fall back dramatically. Malekim had driven the men back from the wall on their right, and the line on the left was also beginning to sag. Over there, Benjiah caught glimpses of black forms running in and out of small gaps. Wolves had penetrated the walls and were wreaking havoc inside the lines.

The Bringer of Storms redirected his power to the walls where the Nolthanim and Black Wolves seemed to be having more difficulty overcoming Aljeron's armies. There, Benjiah could see more stone being blown backward into the city.

Then it rang out. The sound of the horn calling for retreat. It was calm, orderly, and even reassuring. They had known this would come. The call for retreat was not the call of defeat, but of the next step in the battle. They would fall back while they were still able to protect their lines. They would accept that they had been unable to hold Zul Arnoth, but that they had engaged the enemy and left many of their number dead on the field.

Not far ahead, Benjiah could see Koshti in the center of their own front line, flying back and forth among a cluster of Black Wolves. The tiger seemed outnumbered almost ten to one, but he did not seem to be in trouble, not yet. Even as

Benjiah looked at him, he snatched one of the great black brutes in his jaws and crushed its neck, then flung its limp body away as he turned to roar at a second wolf who had dared to dart too close. The tiger was a flash of orange and black picking off wolves and leaving them lifeless on the ground.

Nearby, Benjiah could see Aljeron on his horse, horn rather than sword in hand at the moment. It was Aljeron who had sounded the retreat, and now surveyed the backward movement of his men. A detachment of Shalin Bel soldiers on horseback surrounded their commander, protecting him from the Nolthanim who were now moving in behind the wolves.

As the men of Shalin Bel dropped back, a figure on horseback at the front of the Nolthanim rode forward into the city. Benjiah stared at his strange appearance. He was covered in rough black armor from head to toe. Even his hands seemed gauntleted with the bizarre black substance. Without looking at his men, he raised his sword and pointed it in the direction of Aljeron.

The horses of the Nolthanim charged forward in and around the wolves and fell upon the retreating men of Shalin Bel, who had braced for this assault. Benjiah, without stopping to think, drew an arrow and shot. One of the men on horseback was knocked off his horse by the force of Benjiah's arrow, and soon a second man had joined him. The lines had crashed together now, and clear shots at the enemy were rare, so Benjiah hesitated.

"We should go down now," Pedraal said. "If we wait much longer, the retreat will pass us by and we will be stranded."

"Not yet," Benjiah said. "I could kill twenty men or Malekim from here before our front line drops back so far." He looked at the line, which was still falling away, though not as quickly now that the archers were pouring cyranic arrows into their midst.

"You could," Pedraan said, "but twenty men and Malekim aren't going to change the fate of this battle."

At that moment, a ferocious thunderclap burst overhead. Benjiah looked over the wall and saw that the giants had come closer, and the one wielding the hammer was raising his hands to the heavens again. "He's coming, Valzaan, what can we do?"

"Only what Allfather empowers us to do," Valzaan said. He raised the staff in his right hand high into the sky and lifted his left hand as well. He seemed to grow pale, even to fade, and when Benjiah looked at his face, he gasped at the sight of flame rolling across the normally white and vacant eyes. "Step behind me, Benjiah, and put your hands on my shoulders. Feel what it is to have the power of Allfather flow through you."

Benjiah handed Suruna to Pedraal and stepped behind Valzaan. He reached out and put his hands on the prophet's shoulders. Instantly he felt a rush of light and energy shoot through his body. It rippled from his fingertips up to his shoulders and into his hair and face as well as down his back and legs until his toes could feel it too. It was a feeling of joy and strength and power and overwhelming peace, all at once. Then Valzaan waved his staff in the air, and the rush of those things slipped away as a wave of intense light and heat shot out from the prophet's staff. It struck the walls of Zul Arnoth and rippled along their length, and what remained of them was blown outward this time. Great blocks of stone flew hundreds of spans, cutting into the hosts of Malek that were still approaching the city. Even the Vulsutyrim staggered backward, and some were severely injured by the flying debris. The giant who had summoned the thunder and lightning picked himself off the ground with fury in his eyes, and surprisingly, with nothing in his hands.

The men and Malekim and even Black Wolves that had been pressing the attack inside the walls hesitated and looked back at the surprising turn of events. The wall was no more, and they saw many of their own number fallen on the field, crushed by its destruction. In that moment of stunned stillness, Aljeron's horn blew again, this time calling for a more hurried and less patient retreat.

"You've knocked the hammer from his hand," Benjiah said to Valzaan.

"Yes, but we must go," Valzaan said wearily, leaning on Benjiah, who had offered his hand to help the prophet down. "We have halted but not stopped the enemy."

Before they descended, Benjiah turned around one more time to survey the battlefield. He saw chaos almost everywhere as the enemy regrouped. The last thing he noted though, was the man dressed in the strange black armor, alone of all the enemy inside the city sitting on his horse, calm and unmoved. His hand was held up as a sign to his men to reassemble and reform their line, and he stared up at the rooftop from which Benjiah was helping Valzaan to descend.

The rest of that day was a blur of rain and riding, as the men of Shalin Bel fled west. They streamed out of the city and fell back down the slope on that side, eventually reaching the road that led to Shalin Bel, which they followed hard through the long dark of that night.

The successful retreat, Benjiah learned later, was the result of two things: First, and most apparently, was Valzaan's remarkable use of Allfather's power to obliterate Zul Arnoth's southeastern wall. As the rear guard reported later, the stunning blow resulted in disarray that lasted several minutes.

The second was the daring work of their scouts, led by Saegan and Bryar. Benjiah was there when Saegan made his report to Aljeron the following morning. As a child he had known Saegan, a friend of his mother and even more so of his uncles, but he had left Amaan Sul for the war when Benjiah was not yet ten years old. Still, Benjiah remembered him as a skilled warrior and tough man who took blows from Pedraal and Pedraan that would have crumpled a man twice his size. Had he not known the character of the man telling the story, he would have doubted its veracity.

Saegan had been outside the city walls with his band of scouts, moving up and down the northern wall of Zul Arnoth to make sure that Malek's army didn't try to flank them. Aljeron had thought it an unlikely maneuver, since the enemy's strength was in power, not speed, but he had sent the scouts just in case. Saegan had been on his way to meet up with Bryar's company and slow down the approach of the Black Wolves when the lightning storm forced him to drop back. The open ground between the city and the enemy's front line had become an impossible stretch of ground to cross, and so Saegan turned his men around and pushed them north along the city wall.

When they entered the city on the far side, they wound their way through the ruins until they came upon the rear lines of Aljeron's men, which by that point had already become the front line of the retreat. They took a defensive stance while the retreating forces passed them, and then formed a rear guard with Bryar's scouts to defend the retreat. Together, the guard formed a number of not more than one hundred fifty, but they were the best riders Aljeron had, and they hid themselves around the passage where their own men had retreated. It wasn't long before several packs of Black Wolves came howling down the road to chase the retreating army, but the scouts surprised them and slaughtered many of the wolves as they ran. The rest of the day and evening, the scouts lingered behind the retreating men, fighting off the resurgent attacks of wolves and Nolthanim cavalry. As the day faded into evening, the encounters became fewer and fewer until it became clear that the enemy had contented itself for the time being to let the fleeing soldiers go. Saegan and Bryar and the eighty-five surviving scouts had diligently held together the rear guard through the night.

For five days now they had been falling back to Shalin Bel. The fear that Malek's hosts would appear out of the darkness was strong, despite the many leagues they traveled each day. By the afternoon of the twenty-third day of Autumn Wane, they had made sufficient enough accounting of their own number to know less than ten thousand remained. Over two thousand had fallen at Zul Arnoth. Benjiah thought that as many or more of the enemy had fallen, but he knew this was of little consequence to such a large army led by a captain of such dread power as that storm-controlling, hammer-wielding giant.

Benjiah had few opportunities to speak with Valzaan alone, but at the first real opportunity, he asked about the remarkable display of power he had seen and felt.

"You wielded more force and more power than the Bringer of Storms. You can defeat him, Valzaan, I know you can."

"The power I wielded was not my own, though the same is likely true of the giant's. The hammer he carries is probably a gift from Malek, somehow imbued with the power to alter and control the weather. My point is that the power you felt and saw was Allfather's gift to me in an hour of need. Allfather does not always give what we think we need when we need it. If I stood before the Bringer of Storms again, I might wield enough power to blow him into oblivion, but I might not. That I cannot know unless Allfather reveals it, and He has not."

"Allfather gave you that power to wield because you are His prophet," Benjiah said, thinking out loud. "Perhaps He could use me to wield His power too. Maybe the two of us together could defeat the enemy!"

"It is possible that you may one day wield that kind of power, or more. That is why I wanted you to feel what it is to have Allfather's power fall upon you."

"I did feel it. It was incredible. It felt as though it was coursing through my veins. I felt strong and powerful and light and peaceful, all at the same time. I felt like I could do anything, see and know and understand anything."

"The liquid analogy isn't a bad one," Valzaan replied. "When Allfather's power falls upon you, it feels as though you have somehow tapped a bottomless well of power and joy. Along with the feeling comes the certain understanding of what you are supposed to do with the power, and it is as though everything suddenly becomes clear. It is almost like moving in *torrim redara,* except the rest of the world has not stopped and you have not stepped out of time. You see what is happening and anticipate what is coming and act with speed and clarity completely foreign to your normal existence. You see and do and never doubt that you have done as you ought. When it is through, normal life feels slow and murky and uncertain. It is hard to return to just being yourself."

"What must I do to be ready?"

"This, Benjiah, we cannot practice. If Allfather chooses to use you this way, you will know."

Benjiah was unable to put the sensation of Allfather's power from his mind. As they rode, league after league, he closed his eyes and saw Valzaan before him on the roof, his body fading and almost pulsating. He could see himself reaching out to touch his shoulders and could feel the surge of power. He felt it even in his dreams, where he envisioned himself uprooting trees and leveling mountains and halting the flow of rivers. He was almost embarrassed to think about the foolishness of those dreams, but the exhilaration kept him hoping when he went to bed that maybe he'd dream again.

On the afternoon of the twenty-third day of Autumn Wane, Valzaan and the twins rode with Benjiah to the front of the column to join Aljeron and his captains. Aljeron had asked them to come so that he could consult Valzaan and Benjiah's uncles. Gilion and Brenim were there, along with Corlas Valon, who had taken to Brenim and could usually be found close by him. Saegan was also there, riding beside Evrim as they talked quietly together. The three Great Bear moved beside the column with Caan.

"Anything new from the scouts?" Aljeron asked Saegan.

"For a half a league or more behind us, there is no sign of enemy movement. They have gone no farther than that, and I would not recommend it."

Aljeron nodded and turned to Valzaan. "Valzaan, have you seen anything about our enemy's movements that could help us?"

"He is coming on behind us, but not very quickly. I have seen the Malekim pulling great carts behind them, and the army moves at a good pace but with no apparent hurry. He drove us from Zul Arnoth in less than an hour, and he knows we are the only significant obstacle between himself and conquest of Werthanin. Malek has waited almost a thousand years to launch this attack; I don't think he is concerned about the day or so between our army and his. He has all the time in the world."

"But he is coming."

"He is coming."

"So the question remains," Aljeron said, looking around at the others. "What next? We have asked this question many times, and the answer has eluded us. By my guess, we can reach the city in three days. I think the time for decision is now, so that we can reconcile ourselves to it before we get there. Does anyone think they see clearly what we must do?"

Benjiah scanned the faces of the men, their eyes forward, heads bowed. "I'm not sure what we should do, Master Balinor," Gilion said at last, "but I think we need to rest our men. Whatever we decide, they will be too exhausted to do it. If the enemy isn't hurrying to catch us, can't we pause for a little longer rest?"

"We can." Aljeron nodded. "We are all weary. Tonight, let's stop at dark, but we will move out before first light. Is that sufficient?"

"Yes." Gilion nodded. "Thank you."

"Anyone else?" Benjiah waited, looking around, but no one spoke. "I see," Aljeron said after a while, "then since all has been said, I have my decision."

The men perked up at this, most of them turning to see Aljeron. Even Benjiah found himself leaning in the saddle, as though being a few hands closer would bring the news to him sooner. "We are headed to Shalin Bel, but we are not going to take up positions there. The city is not to be defended."

Benjiah saw that each of them was stunned by the announcement. Every scenario he had heard anyone discuss since the retreat began involved some sort of engagement near or in the city. He had not heard anyone talk of abandoning it.

"What do you intend?" Brenim asked at last.

"I intend to see how the evacuation is going, and as much as I am able, provide protection for those fleeing the city. The people, not the buildings, are the real city of Shalin Bel. We will protect their retreat and leave the city to our enemy."

The others looked at each other. "I appreciate the desire to protect our people," Gilion said, "but if we do not stand at Shalin Bel, where will we go? Where will we regroup, and where will we face our enemy?"

"We will drop back to Col Marena. We will take all the ships in the harbor that we need, and we will sail south to Suthanin. We will head to Cimaris Rul or wherever Caan says we would be best served by going, and we will join our forces with the Suthanim."

"You mean to abandon Werthanin altogether?" Corlas Valon said. "I came with you so we as Werthanim could band together to fight, not flee on ships to some distant port, leaving our land to be destroyed."

Aljeron turned to Corlas. "This is not about Werthanin anymore, if it ever was. Don't you see that? This isn't about Werthanin or Suthanin or Enthanin. This is about Malek and how he is going to be stopped. We can't do it alone, Corlas. We can't. It's past time we started thinking about the fate of Kirthanin as a whole. Defeating Malek is everything. If we lose Werthanin and Shalin Bel is destroyed, but we defeat Malek, well, then those who survive will have as long as they need to rebuild. Walls can be rebuilt. Buildings can be restored. Roads and statues and pillars and gates, they can all be repaired and replaced. I will not die needlessly to defend them when there is still hope we can save Kirthanin if we join together and stand as one."

"Aljeron is right," Valzaan said. "All that matters now is stopping Malek, and none of us can do that alone. Look at us: We are Werthanim like Aljeron, Gilion, Bryar, and Corlas, but we are also Suthanim like Caan, Brenim, and Evrim, and we are Enthanim like Saegan, Pedraal, Pedraan, and Benjiah. We are already a microcosm of what must be, the union of all servants of Allfather. Besides, if we head south, we may yet be able to convince the Great Bear to join us."

Aljeron looked at Sarneth. "Do you think they might?"

"I think they might. After all I have seen and can tell them, they will have to see that the time has come to put aside past offenses and divisions and join as one. If they do not come, and if Malek conquers the great cities of Kirthanin one by one, it will not be long before the draals are next."

Aljeron nodded. "Then what we need to do is even more clear than I thought. We will seek the aid of the Suthanim and the Great Bear, and perhaps the next time Malek's army engages us in battle, perhaps it will end differently. Are there any objections?"

No one spoke. "Then we are decided. We will go to the city to make sure the evacuation is going forward, if it is not already finished, then we will drop back to Col Marena, defending if need be the people still on the move. When we have done this, we will sail from the shores of Werthanin with the hope that we will one day return to restore what must for a time be lost. So be it?"

"So may it be," the others answered.

"We are decided."

The decision silenced them all, and as they rode on quietly in the rain, Benjiah's thoughts drifted toward the sea. He had come now almost the whole breadth of Werthanin, but they were not finished. They were going farther. He was going to sail south to Suthanin, and maybe, just maybe, he would get his chance to see Sulare. Maybe he was going to see the Summerland.

On the morning of the twenty-sixth, Aljeron was riding with Evrim in front of the column when he saw at last what he had been looking for. "There it is, Evrim. We have returned."

As Evrim looked up at the distant outline of the city, Aljeron mumbled, half under his breath, "I didn't think it would be like this."

"What was that?"

"I thought we'd ride back with news that Rulalin was dead, or else with us in chains. I never even dreamed that we would return fleeing before him."

"We aren't really fleeing from him."

"I know, but he rides even now behind us, knowing as well as we do that we cannot stand before the army he rides with. It galls me to think of him on his horse, gloating at his victory at Zul Arnoth, gloating at his approach to the city, gloating over everything."

Evrim sighed. "He may be gloating, but we don't know yet

the story behind what happened. Certainly, riding in Malek's company would come at a price. He might have been as miserable in victory as we were in defeat."

"Maybe."

"At least," Evrim continued after a moment, "at least we know that Dorant isn't going to be pouring gold into his coffers this winter or spring, profiteering in Fel Edorath."

Aljeron laughed at the sudden shift in subject and tone. "No, I don't suppose he will. In fact, I imagine that the call to evacuate would have been especially troublesome for him. Can you imagine him standing before his great warehouses trying to decide what to take and what to leave behind? He will not be pleased when he learns that we are not defending the city. Of course, with our luck, Malek will come and burn everything in the city but his property, and when we return, he will end up owning everything and all of us."

"If we defeat Malek and live to return, I will not mind if Dorant makes a profit selling supplies for the reconstruction."

"Easy for you to say; you'll be back in Dal Harat."

"I probably will," Evrim acknowledged. They both laughed and looked up at the city again. "Do you think we'll find many people inside?"

"There will be some, no doubt, but probably not many by now."

"It will be strange to see it empty, or nearly empty."

"It will be strange. So many years trying to subdue Fel Edorath, and now it comes to this. Fel Edorath still stands, and Shalin Bel is likely to be destroyed. The future is inscrutable."

10

HOME

R ULALIN GLANCED BESIDE HIM at Soran. He was riding at a good pace, like the rest of them, but he was still slumped with his head hanging low. Rulalin should not have been surprised at how much Soran gave away with his body language; the young invariably betrayed their morale in such ways. He wondered if he was still so easy to read, or if he had learned to cloak his emotions. Transparency was not in itself a bad thing, but they were traveling in dangerous company. The less a man like Tashmiren knew or understood about him, the better.

He had hoped that Soran's funk would pass, but every day since Zul Arnoth had been the same. No doubt the grey skies and steady rains contributed to the pall of silence and dejection that had fallen over them both, especially over Soran. He had hoped, but it hadn't happened. Then again, the battle scars that took longest to heal were not of the body but of the mind.

Their approach to Zul Arnoth had resurrected the best and worst memories of the last seven years. From their early triumphs to their later defeats, Zul Arnoth had played a big part. Rulalin had thought he would never ride to this ground again, unless perhaps in chains. Certainly he had never expected to approach Zul Arnoth once more in arms. Further, he had never expected to ride against a combined force of Werthanim that included men who had served for years under his command. That had been especially hard to reconcile, and their presence at Zul Arnoth is what ultimately affected Soran in such a deep way.

He had arrayed his men on the right of the line as Farimaal directed, along with the Nolthanim. Farimaal rode out in front as they marched up the hill, and Rulalin had seen then in the body language of the Nolthanim the inspiration their general's presence provided. Rulalin had even felt the adrenaline rush of knowing he was following a great warrior into battle, and he had come as close to hungering for battle as he had come in a long time.

As he pushed forward, however, leading the Werthanim under his command into the line of their brothers, the bloodlust Farimaal's presence had inspired began to dissipate. He had of course fought men for years in his war with Shalin Bel, but he had not fought them quite like this. He had raised his sword against men at Zul Arnoth, but never while in Malek's service.

He didn't have long to contemplate the situation, for Cheimontyr's attack on the walls had stunned and surprised him. Suddenly, rock was flying all around him. He had to resist the urge to cover his head or drop to the ground to seek shelter behind his horse. The power displayed was fantastic. He could not believe Aljeron's men would hold out for long, and indeed, the horn sounding the retreat came not long thereafter. He regained his composure and focused on keeping his men together.

As he was preparing to push forward again, a surge of light and heat cast their line into confusion. As he squinted to protect his eyes from the bright and burning light, he had made out, even if only barely, the form of Valzaan standing on a rooftop. He had not been able to see his face clearly, for the light pouring forth from him had made the prophet's features impossible to see, but he had been certain it was Valzaan. The raised staff and wild hair were part of the reason for his certainty, but so too was the wave of light and heat.

It struck him then that Valzaan's attack had been directed against him. Not only him, of course, for there were more fearful enemies than Rulalin Tarasir arrayed against Valzaan that day, but it had surely been directed in part against him and his men. Shame washed over him. Allfather's prophet, whom he had greeted on the road to Sulare as a hero out of the pages of history, was fighting against him. Not only that, but Allfather's prophet was striking blows every bit as impressive as Cheimontyr's.

That thought had led to uncertainty. He had felt uncertain about what he was doing, about whether he could go through with it, but until that moment he had never felt uncertain about this war's outcome. He had never doubted Malek's victory. When he felt the wave of light and heat knock him backward and when he saw what was left of Zul Arnoth's walls, he thought for the first time that perhaps he had underestimated the power aligned against Malek. How much power did Valzaan have at his disposal? How much damage could he alone do? Could he match Cheimontyr? Certainly, as he turned to see Cheimontyr knocked to the ground, his hammer landing many spans away from his gigantic form, it had occurred to him that the Bringer of Storms was not invincible.

Of course, Valzaan's remarkable display had not ultimately turned the tide of the battle. His fears had been somewhat mitigated by that fact, and as Aljeron's army had fallen back in full retreat, he had regained his former confidence. Valzaan was one man, and he was a very old man at that. If stronger than Cheimontyr, why turn and flee? Why not countermand Cheimontyr's storm? Why fall back in defeat? When all was said and done, Cheimontyr and Farimaal had still pushed Aljeron from Zul Arnoth with seeming ease. Could Valzaan's presence have really made that much of a difference when the outcome had been so clearly in Malek's favor?

As Aljeron fled, Rulalin's attention had been transferred to Soran, sitting completely still in his saddle, staring straight ahead with his sword, which was running with blood, held loosely at his side.

"Soran?" he had asked. When Soran did not answer, he had pulled up beside him and called loudly, "Soran!"

He had not forgotten since the dazed and forlorn eyes that turned to him. Soran had looked at him, but Rulalin didn't think those eyes really saw him. He had reached over and taken his young friend by the sword arm and said, "Soran, we must go forward. Aljeron is retreating. We need to follow."

"I killed him," Soran had said, still looking blankly at Rulalin.

"Aljeron?" Rulalin asked, sitting up in surprise.

"No." Soran shook his head slowly.

"Who?"

"I killed him," Soran said again.

"Soran, we have both killed many men in the battles we've fought. That isn't important now. We need to move forward."

It was then that the spell seemed to break and recognition came into Soran's face. "No, you don't understand. It was a soldier of Fel Edorath, and I recognized him. I recognized him, but I didn't realize who it was at first."

"Who was it?"

"That's just it. I can't remember his name. I should know his name, Rulalin. He was only a boy when the war with Shalin Bel started. He used to come out to greet us when we returned from the battlefield. He was always playing at swords in the streets outside your house, and one day, a few years ago, I asked him if he wanted to be a soldier for real. And that was when he joined the army. He was only a boy back then."

"He wasn't a boy today."

"No, and he is no longer a man either. I killed him."

"He might have killed you."

"We'll never know now what he might have done."

"No, we won't," Rulalin acknowledged, then added, his voice softening, "Come on, Soran, there is nothing you can do about it now. We need to press forward."

Reluctantly, Soran had followed Rulalin, but he had needed looking after. By evening he was reasonably sure that Soran had come back from wherever it was he had gone in his mind, but he had fallen into a deep silence and remained there ever since.

"Are you all right over there?"

Soran raised his head a little and looked at Rulalin. "Yeah, I guess so."

"Not too far now to Shalin Bel."

"No, not far now."

Rulalin searched for somewhere to go with the conversation, but he didn't want to bring up what had happened at Zul Arnoth, and any mention of the probable battle to come seemed likely to bring the subject up indirectly. So he searched for a safe question or observation, when Soran surprised him by volunteering the first words he had spoken since the battle.

"I remembered it."

"Remembered what?"

"His name."

"The soldier of Fel Edorath?"

"Yes."

"What was it?"

"It was Danlin. I don't remember his last name, but his first name was Danlin."

"Danlin?"

"That's right."

"Well," Rulalin said, "you may not want to hear this, but it was probably better for Danlin to die by your sword than to fall by the hand of a Malekim."

"You're right," Soran said, looking up at Rulalin. "I don't want to hear it."

Rulalin watched Soran push his horse forward, thought about saying something or trying to keep up, but decided against it and let him go.

Drawing near to the gate of Shalin Bel, it suddenly occurred to Aljeron that it might well be impassable. Looking at the imposing gates, he wondered how he could have drawn so close without realizing that entrance might well be denied him. If the people of Shalin Bel had taken the warning seriously, the gate might be closed, barred, and barricaded, with no one on hand to open it. His mind searched quickly through the options. Knocking down the gate would be hard and potentially foolish, should they need to take up a defensive position inside the city. Getting someone over the wall to let them in seemed wiser, but again, certain difficulties presented themselves. They were not equipped to lift a man so high into the air safely, and while there might be good climbers among them, one wrong step near the top would be a fatal mistake.

He frowned. He couldn't believe that this eventuality, which felt with every passing step like inevitability, was going to find him unprepared. He could not afford to be trapped between an innumerable foe and the strong walls of his own city. No, if the gate was closed to him, he would have to lead the army around the city, even if it meant going all the way on to Col Marena. The thought of not even entering Shalin Bel was disappointing. He hadn't realized until that moment that coming home, even if only to pass through, had been very important to him.

Then, as he came almost within reach of the gate, a head popped out of one of the guard towers above, and a face peered down at him. He was both surprised and relieved to see the man, and he drew up his horse so that he could call up to him. "Gateman, it is Aljeron Balinor and the army of Shalin Bel come home. Open the gate, quickly, for we can brook no delay."

"Yes, sir, Master Balinor!" The man smiled as he called down. "Right away, sir, it is good to see you home again, it is."

The guard's face disappeared from view, and the gates began to swing open almost immediately. "That's a relief," Evrim said beside him. "I thought we might be stuck outside the city if the gates were closed against us."

Aljeron smiled, "Yes, that wouldn't have been good, but never mind; the gates are open and we are home."

"Yes, but what will we find inside, I wonder?"

"We will know soon enough." Aljeron spurred his horse through the gate. Three or four men who all looked like they might have served as city guards ten years ago, when their strength was not yet worn out from many years, stood in the street to greet Aljeron.

"Welcome home, Master Balinor," one of them said as Aljeron stopped his horse near them.

"Thank you," Aljeron said, "though I'm afraid that I will not be able to call this place home soon. Can you tell me of the state of the city? Did our warnings come? Are many still here? By whose command do you still man the eastern gate and why have you all not fled?"

The men looked at each other, perhaps flustered by the string of questions, but the one who had greeted Aljeron in the first place eventually took up the role of spokesman. "Your warnings did come. Messengers arrived several days ago. The state of the city then is that most have fled. I would say that most inhabitants are probably more than a day's journey away by now."

"Good," Aljeron said, turning with a look of relief to Evrim and the other captains who had approached by now. "It is as we had hoped."

"Those who remain, like us," the man continued, "are under the direction of the Merchants' Guild. They have assembled a large caravan in the city square with their most valuable goods and wares and hired many of the men to help them move it all to safety. They are planning on moving out as soon as they are ready, probably tonight or in the morning. That is why we are at the gate, Master Balinor, for they plan on coming out this way."

"What?" Aljeron fairly shouted at the old man. "Did you say that a large caravan of merchants is planning to leave Shalin Bel by this gate? By the eastern gate?"

"Yes," the man said timidly, shrinking back against his friends.

"What foolishness is this? Who could possibly have made such a stupid plan?"

"As I said, Master Balinor, we are under the command of the Merchants' Guild, but I think the plan is Master Dorant's, because it is his estate northeast of the city that the caravan is going to be making for."

Aljeron snarled, "Dorant," and looked over his shoulder at the other captains, whose faces reflected annoyance and disbelief. "Tell me, gateman, is Master Dorant to be found in the city square?"

"Yes, I think so. They are all there, except the men still loading goods out of the warehouses. I think he is overseeing the caravan itself."

"And what of the city council? The elders of the city and

the Novaana of Shalin Bel? Have they given their consent to this madness?"

"I don't rightly know what happened behind closed doors, sir, but I don't think this was part of their plan. Most of the city elders and Novaana have left. They were overseeing the evacuation, they were."

"So the Merchants' Guild has stayed behind and organized this caravan against the express will of the city council?"

"I couldn't say for sure, Master Balinor," the man said, looking to his friends for support, though they looked less than eager to give any.

"Thank you, Gateman," Aljeron said. "You are relieved. This gate is now under my command and control; you may return to the square."

The men looked at one another. "Sir, he told us to stay here until he came," the spokesman added at last.

Aljeron stared down at the man. "Gateman, your devotion to your post is admirable, but I have relieved you. I am headed to the city square myself, so if Master Dorant takes issue with your return, blame it on me. I'd be happy to explain your untimely return."

There were no more objections from the men, and they set off toward the city square. Aljeron turned to Gilion. "Secure the gate with our men once we are all in. Should Dorant cause trouble, we will be ready to hold the gate against him. It should go without saying that you are to allow no one to leave through this gate."

"Yes, sir," Gilion said, spurring his horse off to the side as the column began moving in.

"Looks like Dorant had the same picture of his wares being ruined that we had," Evrim said as they rode toward the square.

"Yes, it looks like it," Aljeron answered. "But I bet you he didn't envision that I would be the one to burn them."

Evrim laughed, but Aljeron continued, "I'm serious, Evrim. If he won't abandon this madness, I'll burn it all. I don't much care if Dorant wants to make a dash for his estate. If he wants to get himself killed, that's his business, but I won't let him lead others into the jaws of the enemy. He's probably promised a fortune to those crazy enough to help. I won't let it happen, Evrim."

"I understand," Evrim said. The city was quiet, and as they rode they noticed the absence of the life characteristic of a big city: the coming and going, the scurrying of men and women and children, the noises of life in and about and often on top of the houses. All seemed gone, until they reached the square.

The city center was every bit as packed with people and carts and wagons as the gatemen had suggested. Men and animals stood and sat all over the field. Every span of the square, except for the Mound, was covered with people or goods waiting to be moved. The activity reminded Aljeron of an army camp, except it lacked the order of a good army.

Aljeron turned to the men behind him. "Saegan, take a company of men north along the outside of the square. Brenim, take another west along the bottom. Evrim, ride with me, and the rest of you come on into the square as you are able. I want Dorant to know that he is talking to the full military might of Shalin Bel. We don't have time to deal quietly with his bullheadedness."

Saegan and Brenim both nodded and began to move men along the outside of the square as Aljeron struck out right into the midst of the commotion. As the men milling about noticed who was riding into their midst, and as they noticed what was going on around the square, they stopped and stared. In this way, a wave of silence slowly swept over the great mass of men and beasts as Aljeron, Koshti, and Evrim moved into the heart of the great square.

It was eerie, coming home like this. As he rode, Aljeron

looked into the faces of the men in the crowd. He saw the respect and admiration that he had often seen when he came home, but today he also saw fear. These men had only just discovered that their security was under immediate and total threat. They had only just come to realize that all they had always taken for granted might not last. He felt compassion swell up within, and along with it, anger. Into this confused and despairing situation Dorant had stepped, but his first thoughts had not been for the survival of the people, but for the protection of his goods. His fury grew as he searched the crowds for some sign of the fool.

Everything in the square had come to a halt and every man stood watching him. He said nothing. He thought of calling for Dorant, but he had learned that silence itself is a powerful weapon. Let them all wonder what he was doing and what he was going to say. Let them all stand and wonder. As the tension and anticipation grew, his dealings with Dorant would play out with all the force required.

Then he saw the open pavilion tent not far from the Mound in the center of the square, where several well-dressed merchants took shelter from the rain. He could not tell yet if Dorant was among them, but he turned his horse instinctively in that direction. As he approached, he saw Dorant, waiting. He could not read exactly the look on his face, but he could see that Dorant was nervous. Good.

Stopping his horse outside the tent, he called in a loud voice that echoed throughout the open square, "I am Aljeron Balinor, captain of the army of Shalin Bel, and I summon the leader or leaders of this assembly to give a reckoning for what is going on here. What means this delay when you have been forewarned about what is coming from the east? Who has dared to controvert the wisdom of the city council, which has already organized the city's evacuation? Who will stand and give an account for what I see here?"

The words rang out above the heads of the gathered men, and he was answered by silence. No one in the nearby contingent of merchants stirred at first, but eventually Dorant shuffled out from under the protection of the tent. But when Dorant opened his mouth to answer, his voice also rang out with confidence, and if he was anxious or nervous, it didn't show.

"The Merchants' Guild has organized this gathering, and the army of Shalin Bel and its captain have no jurisdiction here. We have received the messengers that were sent, and for this timely warning we thank you. Having duly considered the information, we have organized this caravan. Even as the elders of the city have taken responsibility for the preservation of the people of Shalin Bel, so we have taken responsibility for the preservation of the goods and livelihoods of the people. These brave men you see here have volunteered for this dangerous mission, so that if our beloved city is destroyed, all that we have made and accomplished need not perish with it." Dorant paused and scanned the watching crowd before finishing, "I assume that this is a sufficient account of the Assembly and our purpose in it."

"Then the elders of the city and the rest of the city council, they asked you to do this?" Aljeron asked, his voice raised so all could hear. "You are saying here before these witnesses that you were entrusted with this task and given the council's blessing?"

Anger passed over Dorant's face as he answered, "What right do you have to question the legitimacy of what we are doing? I am a member of the city council as you know full well."

"As am I," Aljeron answered, "so answer my question."

"You know that the city council is often divided as to what course should be pursued. At least you should know, seeing how you are often the cause of the division," Dorant sneered. "There were some on the council opposed to this idea, and there were many who supported it. What business is it of yours, anyhow, what I and these men do? The enemy is coming and we have been told to flee, and that is what we are preparing to do."

"What business is it of mine?" Aljeron answered, the rage in his voice escalating. "I'll tell you what business it is of mine." He turned and looked around him. "The time that you have had to organize this caravan was purchased by the blood of my men. Knowing I could not defeat this enemy, I nevertheless diverted him from a direct approach to Shalin Bel and engaged him in the field at the loss of over two thousand lives. Those men did not die so that you could endanger the lives of these men to save your business interests, Master Dorant. Those men died so that you would have plenty of time to put a safe distance between yourselves and this city before Malek's hosts came. This you have not done."

Aljeron pushed himself up so that he was almost standing in his stirrups. "Here me, men of Shalin Bel. There is no time to debate. Our doom has come from the Mountain. A foe beyond our strength approaches from the east, and I have given commands to my men that no one is to be allowed to leave by the eastern gate. It is for your own good. Death lies in that direction, for our enemy has many Black Wolves moving in advance of his main force. You must all flee, now. Go west or south or north, but go. Leave behind these goods and wares, for they are of no lasting value or importance. Take these horses out of their yokes and unhitch them from these wagons and ride them to save your lives. All that rests in this square can be remade, even as the buildings around us can be rebuilt. The glory of Shalin Bel can be restored, but you will not live to see it if you try to go through with this madness. Abandon this folly and abandon this place. My army will watch the eastern gate tonight, but tomorrow we are leaving, for we must ourselves flee to preserve the strength of our army until the time comes to take the field of battle again."

Murmurs swept through the square, and Dorant seemed to know that he was in danger of losing his support. As he opened his mouth, Aljeron dismounted and grabbed him by his thick cloak. "You will say nothing further on this matter, Dorant. There is no one here who can save you from my hand today, so you will do as you are told."

Dorant looked from Aljeron's determined eyes to Koshti, who was sitting alert with eyes keenly focused on him. "Unhand me," Dorant finally said quietly. "The city council will be made aware of the threat you made against me this day."

"I will gladly stand before the council to give a reckoning of my actions and to see you give a reckoning of yours, should we both live to have the chance. I will be sure they are fully aware of your actions since their departure and how you represented them to the men of Shalin Bel in my presence."

Dorant, clearly angry, nevertheless held his tongue and turned away from Aljeron to make his way back to the tent. Aljeron spat on the ground and turned away.

Aljeron walked through the dark and empty corridors of the Council Hall, finding the silence both disquieting and welcome. In the kitchen he gathered some food for the night as well as some wood for the fireplace in his chambers, and he walked with Koshti past the open main hall back through the labyrinth of smaller hallways. His chambers were cold, having been without fire these many weeks, and he set to work right away getting a fire going. It did not take long, for the wood was dry, and he was almost surprised after so many days of trying to kindle fire with soggy wood.

He pulled up his favorite chair and sat before the fire with his cider in his hand, while Koshti stretched out on the hearth. Leaning back in his chair, he thought about how pleasant it was to sit and sip his drink in peace, though the transitory nature of this peaceful moment stole some of his enjoyment. If only Malek had not come then, he could have taken his seat by this fire for as many nights as he pleased without any distraction. He was glad the other captains had insisted he get some rest.

But, even as he thought these things, he knew they were not true. Had Malek not come forth, and had he come home as he had planned, his rest by this fire would not have been so sweet or blissfully peaceful. He would have sat here in bitterness and discontentment, having failed to secure Rulalin. Only now, after weathering so many weeks of this storm and facing the prospect of more to come, could this momentary relief taste so good and feel so welcome.

He sat up and peered into the mesmerizing flames. What was wrong with him that it took such a cataclysmic disaster to awaken him to the normal pleasures of life? He pulled Daaltaran part way from its sheath and gazed at the blade. What was wrong with him that he found so much fulfillment in the wielding of this weapon and so little joy in the things that had marked the peace and security of the First Age?

Running his fingers along Daaltaran's smooth blade, he thought of what lay ahead. If something was wrong inside of him, it would stay wrong for a while yet. If Malek was going to be defeated and Kirthanin set free, a lot of men like Aljeron must take up blades like Daaltaran. It was a strange thing to meditate upon his sword and its use. A great portion of his hope for defeating Malek's evil lay in this instrument, the very tool that had brought so much of Malek's evil to the world. He sheathed his sword and set his cup down, folding his hands in his lap as he gazed at the fire. Perhaps the day would come when he would be able to set the sword down for good, and maybe then he would be content to sit and be warmed by the fire every evening.

Koshti's tail twitched, and Aljeron looked down at the tiger, seemingly fast asleep. He sat back in the chair again and closed his eyes. It was way too early in the day to go to bed for the night, but a short nap wouldn't do him any harm. He settled in, and before long he could hear his own rhythmic breathing and knew he was falling asleep.

A strong rapping at the door startled him, and Aljeron bolted upright. He felt disoriented and, rubbing his eyes, looked at Koshti, who had risen and stood staring at the chamber door. The fire was low, and it slowly dawned on him that he had been asleep for some time. His legs protested as he stood, but he mustered the strength and initiative to cross the floor.

"Evrim?" he started as he opened the door, only to stand surprised as Mindarin and Aelwyn Elathien walked past him into the room.

"No," Mindarin said with a smirk, "but don't worry, I'm sure he will be by before too long. You two can't either one seem to do anything without the other for too long."

"Please excuse Mindarin," Aelwyn said, blushing at Mindarin's flippancy. "By the time we had tracked down Evrim and Gilion to find out where you were, we had already done a good bit of walking, and when they directed us down here, it pushed her over the edge."

"Nonsense, I love a good stroll on a rainy afternoon," Mindarin said, making herself at home in Aljeron's chair. "Now be a darling, Aljeron, and pour me a drink while I dry out and get warm. And pull up a chair for Aelwyn. It's rude to leave a lady standing."

Aljeron, still half dazed, pulled a chair over for Aelwyn without saying a word and poured two more cups of cider. "I'll go to the kitchen for more," he said as he handed them to the women.

"And bring a pitcher of cold water as well, and some bread and cheese if you find any," she said, smiling at him over her cup. "Thank you," she called as he slipped from the room.

The whole way to the kitchen and back, he found himself trying to figure out why Mindarin and Aelwyn might have come to his room. Could it be that they agreed with Dorant's plan and were here to mediate for him? It didn't seem possible, but why else would they still be in the city? If they had come to try to talk him into letting the caravan out through the eastern gate, they would find, old friends or not, that he would not budge.

"Well," he said as he reentered the room, carrying a tray of food and drink. "It looks as though much of the hospitality of this house went with the evacuees."

"That's fine," Aelwyn said with a smile, as he offered her bread and butter with some overripe pieces of fruit. "We didn't come to pester you about food."

"No, we didn't, Aljeron," Mindarin said, her voice and manner calmer. "Though we thank you for this."

"You're both welcome," Aljeron said, pouring a cup of water for himself and pulling up a third chair by the fire. "Now, as nice as it is to see you two, I can't help but wonder why you are still in the city. Were you here when the messengers came?"

"We were, and we thought about going," Mindarin said between bites of bread. "But then we had another idea, and that is why we are here."

"You don't mean this caravan idea of Dorant's, do you?"

"What?" Mindarin said, scrunching up her face. "You don't think we had anything to do with that idiot's foolishness? We agreed completely with our father's rejection of it. Please, give us some credit, Aljeron."

"Your father was against Dorant's plan?"

"Oh yes, everyone on the council was except for some of the merchants, who are basically in Dorant's pocket. They objected in the strongest possible terms, but in the end they did not have any way to compel those who chose to stay behind."

"So why didn't you go with them?"

"We are trying to get to that," Mindarin said, glaring at Aljeron. "If we didn't have to defend our good names against accusations of allegiance with the town moron, we could have told you by now."

"My apologies," Aljeron said. "Please continue."

"All right," Mindarin started. "It's like this. Aelwyn and I have organized about two hundred women to serve as an auxiliary to your army. Now, hold on," she said, raising her hands to stop Aljeron from reacting too quickly, "let us finish."

It took a lot, but Aljeron restrained himself.

"We don't mean as a fighting force," Aelwyn said, "though we are all young and able and would be willing to draw swords if necessary. We knew you wouldn't let us come with you if you thought we were hoping to fight."

"Though you do let that Bryar ride with you like one of the boys," Mindarin said, scowling at him. "You seem to have a double standard there."

"Anyway," Aelwyn said, trying to keep the conversation from being sidetracked, "what we meant was that we wanted to go and help with the necessities of an army on the move. You will need cooking and nursing and all kinds of things just to keep the army in the field, so why not let us come? All the women who have volunteered are of age, none of them have small children, and quite a few have husbands and brothers, even sons, serving with you. It is where we belong, really."

"You should lead the women somewhere safe," Aljeron said quietly to both of them. "The enemy that is coming will destroy my army if he can. I couldn't live with myself if he destroyed you too."

"You aren't listening," Mindarin said. "Where is safe, exactly? We can't stay here. Should we go out into the countryside and hide somewhere, a band of women alone? And what will the enemy do if he finds us there?"

"He is less likely to find you if you aren't with me."

"Can you guarantee that? And if he does destroy your army, will he not cover Werthanin with his rule, and what will we do then? I'd rather die helping you to resist him than live to bear his yoke, and we all feel the same."

Aljeron looked at Mindarin and then at Aelwyn. Though Aelwyn's face was softer than Mindarin's, both wore looks of grim determination. He had known both of these women for many years, long enough to know when their minds were made up. "I suppose that you are going to follow me even if I say no."

"We will," Mindarin said. "You'll have to physically restrain us to keep us from coming with you."

"All right then, I will accept the help you offer," Aljeron began.

"As you should," Mindarin cut in.

"But," Aljeron said quickly, "there is something you especially should know, Mindarin."

"What is that?"

"I don't know what it means or how it happened, but Rulalin is marching with men of Fel Edorath in Malek's service."

The smile disappeared from Mindarin's face and she turned pale. "I don't believe it," she said quietly. "He wouldn't do that. I know him. He wouldn't."

"I'm sorry, Mindarin, but it is true. Valzaan first saw him in one of his visions, but several of our men confirmed his presence among the enemy in Zul Arnoth when we engaged them there."

"He must have been coerced. He wouldn't help Malek unless he had no choice."

"We always have a choice, Mindarin. You yourself said you'd rather die trying to resist him than bear his yoke."

"He is responsible for more than I am. Maybe he did it for someone else, or perhaps for Fel Edorath. Either way," Mindarin said, rising to her feet, "your news doesn't change anything. We are determined to ride with you and oppose Malek, regardless of who rides with him."

"All right then," Aljeron said, rising also. "Go back to Gilion and tell him that you have come to him with my blessing. He will give you the instructions you need. We leave at first light."

Mindarin nodded and moved to the door, but Aelwyn, who had risen with her, remained where she was. "Mindarin, would you wait for me by the entrance to the main hall?" she asked.

Mindarin looked at her tenderly and nodded, then turned to Aljeron. "Aljeron, we appreciate your understanding. We will see you in the morning."

"Very well then," Aljeron said. "And thank you for your help. It will take some getting used to, but we will be glad for your presence on the long road ahead."

Mindarin slipped out of the door, and Aljeron turned to look at Aelwyn, still standing by her seat. "Would you like to sit down again?" he asked, motioning to her chair.

She shook her head, remaining as she was. "When word came from your messengers about what had happened and what you intended to do, I was frightened for you."

"I'm all right."

"I see that," Aelwyn said, blushing again. "I'm so glad." She stepped over to where he was and threw her arms around him. "I'm so glad," she repeated as she hugged him close.

He was taken aback at first, but before he realized what he was doing, he had put his arms around her and was holding her too. If the fire had been warm, it did not compare to the fire of holding Aelwyn close, and he stroked her soft hair as she rested her head upon his chest.

Aelwyn leaned back and looked up at him with tears in her eyes. "You carry too much inside, on your own. Don't fight this war with everything locked up inside, like you fought the last one."

She started to step away and move toward the door when he reached out and caught her hand in his. She stopped and looked back at him, surprised. Her hand felt so small and delicate, and he wondered when he had last touched the hand of a woman. "Aelwyn, thank you."

Aelwyn smiled. "You're welcome, Aljeron."

"I'm glad you're coming with us tomorrow."

"So am I."

"Get some rest."

"I will; you too." Aljeron watched her go, and when the door was finally shut behind her, he sank into his chair. He closed his eyes, and he could still feel her against him. He didn't want to forget that feeling. He sat there for a long time before walking over to the window and peering out into the rainy evening.

He spent the rest of that evening walking with Koshti through the empty halls, and he even went outside and for a short time back up to the rooftop garden where he had run into Aelwyn before the rites of Midautumn. He liked being back up there, thinking of her in the sunlight, but the rain drove him back indoors. He went back in and took another armload of wood to his rooms. By the time he was ready to go to bed, he was eager for a break from all the spinning going on in his head. Why couldn't life throw him one change at a time?

He settled into his bed, and the real mattress with dry sheets and blankets was all he had hoped it would be. He listened to Koshti snoring before the fireplace in the next room and smiled as he drifted off to sleep.

The splash of rain on his face shook him out of the daze he'd been in, and looking up, he saw part of the city wall come smashing inward. Pieces of stone flew around him and over his head, and he saw the Bringer of Storms's face appear in one of the gaps of the wall. He watched as the giant landed blow after blow of his great hammer against the wall and brought it crumbling down.

He remembered then that he been looking for something, but he couldn't remember what. He looked at the people, mostly soldiers, running around him chaotically. The city was in complete confusion. Why had he let them be caught there, trapped inside walls that could not keep their enemy out?

He started running along the base of the wall, and up ahead, he saw some women running in a parallel direction along the top of the wall. He looked carefully at them, and sure enough, Aelwyn was among them. In fact, the rest seemed to be following her as they ran away from the place where the Bringer of Storms was smashing the wall to bits. Aljeron called to them, but as he did, a great explosion echoed through the city as a ball of lightning struck the wall where the women had been running and blew that whole section of the wall into the city.

Aljeron sat up in his bed, disturbed by the image that lingered in his mind. He rubbed his eyes and peered through the darkness. It was pitch black outside the window, and it was likewise dark in the small parlor next to his bedroom, save the little bit of light that came from the dying embers of his evening fire. Then he heard it, a persistent rapping on his chamber door.

Rising from his bed, he walked into the parlor and over to the door. "Yes? Who is it?" he called, thinking that this time he would find out who it was before he opened the door.

"It's Evrim," the voice on the other side said wearily, "We have a problem."

11

INTO THE SEA

ALJERON OPENED THE DOOR and Evrim, followed by Gilion and Valzaan, entered. "Has he come?" Aljeron asked, scanning their faces.

"He? Oh, you mean the giant? No, the eastern gate is secure and Saegan's patrols are outside. They've reported no sign of trouble."

"He is not far away," Valzaan added. "I have seen them. But they are camped for the night. They will not be here until tomorrow evening."

Aljeron felt the relief wash over him. When he had awakened from that dream to Evrim's knocking, he had assumed the worst. "All right, then," he said, "what is it?"

"It's Dorant and the merchants," Gilion said.

"Yes?"

"They've gone."

"They were supposed to go," Aljeron answered, trying to see where they were headed with this.

"Yes," Evrim answered, "they were. But they have ignored your admonition to leave behind their goods. They managed to keep together about half the men they had secured in the first place and have left with about half of their wagons."

"But not by the eastern gate?" Aljeron asked.

"No," Evrim conceded, "not by the eastern gate."

Aljeron, impatient and a little grumpy about being disturbed during his only night in a real bed in weeks, spoke more roughly than he normally would. "Look, you'll need to excuse me. I just woke up. I don't even know what time it is, and I don't have the slightest idea what you're trying to tell me. Dorant and some of the other merchants have left the city by one of the other gates as they were supposed to. What's the problem?"

"The problem," Gilion said, "is where they are headed."

"Where?" Aljeron said, but before one of the other men could answer, he answered his own question, "Col Marena."

Evrim nodded. It was all becoming clear, quickly. "How many men and how many wagons would you guess have gone?" Aljeron asked. "And how do we know they have taken that road?"

The four men took seats by what remained of the fire. "After you left the square," Evrim began, "men started to trickle away, and Gilion and I turned our attention to the men and preparation for the night. When I passed by the square again later I saw a small gathering around the merchant's tent, but I didn't think much of it. I assumed Dorant had made some kind of financial arrangement with the men who had stayed behind and was discussing something like that before hitting the road.

"At any rate, I got caught up overseeing the restocking of our supplies, and I didn't go back by the square. Well, Gilion found me about the end of Second Watch—"

"What time is it now?"

"About the start of Fourth Watch." Aljeron nodded and Evrim continued. "Anyway, Gilion told me that he had been past the square, and at least half of the wagons and all the men were gone. We sent men to every gate other than the eastern one, and fresh tracks were headed out of the western gate. It was then that we realized he might be fleeing for the port at Col Marena to save his wares. If they had left just after dark, they had many hours head start, but we sent a handful of riders anyway. They came upon a man almost a league away from the city with a broken wagon wheel. He was working feverishly to fix it and was evidently pretty unhappy.

"After your confrontation, Dorant did some investigating of his own and found we were headed for Col Marena, which gave him the idea he might save himself and his stuff by going there first. He gathered the remaining merchants and put together their plan. They left after sundown and planned to travel all night to get as much of a jump on the army as they could."

"So he knew we were going to Col Marena?" Aljeron said, feeling the anger boil inside him again.

"We have not made a secret of it."

"And how many men and wagons do you think Dorant has?"

"The man estimated that he has some two hundred wagons, maybe two hundred fifty, and twice as many men."

"You're telling me 500 men and 250 wagons are even now several leagues away along the road to Col Marena?"

"Yes."

"They might as well be a rolling blockade," Aljeron muttered. "If we take that road now, we will inevitably be slowed by them. Those wagons were weighed down beyond all reasonable limits; no wonder one of them has already broken a wheel. It won't be the last wheel they break, either. They can't possibly keep a caravan like that moving fast enough to stay in front of us."

"And we can't let them stay in front of us," Gilion added. "Col Marena is a big port, but I doubt it docks enough ships to accommodate us and Dorant. He'll take what he wants or thinks he needs, and we'll have to deal with what's left."

"But if we go that way," Evrim said, "and pass the caravan by, we may lead Malek's hosts right to them. If we move at his pace to offer them protection, we might all be caught before we reach Col Marena. Either way, the choices don't look good."

"Do we think we have enough of a lead on the enemy to reach Col Marena at the caravan's pace?"

"I wouldn't think so," Valzaan said.

"Why not?" Aljeron asked.

"I think Malek expects you to defend Shalin Bel. That is why his army has been in no particular hurry. When he finds you aren't here, his approach may change. If he pursued you as quickly as he could move, he may overtake all of us if slowed down by the wagons."

"Then we have to bypass the caravan," Aljeron said. "What else can we do? We have to reach Col Marena in time to get the army on those ships. Dorant is a greedy fool. He must realize the danger he has put us and himself in. He may just have to reap what he has sown."

"Dorant is a greedy fool, but will you really give the command to bypass the caravan and ride on by?" Evrim asked. "Could you do it? Could you ride past five hundred men of Shalin Bel, knowing the enemy was following close behind? I'm not even sure that we should. We can't take that road."

"Then what do you suggest, Evrim? Col Marena was my only plan."

"I didn't say we shouldn't go to Col Marena. I only said we can't take that road," Evrim answered.

"What are you saying?"

"I say we leave Shalin Bel by the western gate and, when the road begins to dip south to Col Marena, keep going west across the open country. We can ride right for the ocean, and when we get there, move south along the coast of the Bay of Thalasee to the port. It is a longer route, but if we ride hard and take only what we need, we can still get there before the caravan."

"But could we get there before Malek's army catches us?"

"That," Evrim said, "I do not know. But if taking the road to Col Marena may bring doom to both us and the caravan, then we must get to Col Marena another way."

"But," Gilion said, "how does going around the caravan really save it? Aren't we leading Malek's army to Col Marena anyway? Are we going to leave ships for Dorant? I thought we were going to take all the ships, or at least, I thought we were going to leave no ships behind that Malek could use. So what does the caravan do? They'll roll into Col Marena to find all the ships gone or the enemy already in control."

"I'm talking about giving them a chance," Evrim said, "not holding their hands. They're headed into danger no matter how you look at it."

"Yes, but the solution you offer—"

Aljeron cut Gilion off. "Hold on, Evrim is right. Even if we followed the caravan and then rode with it, we couldn't guarantee its safety. For that matter, we can't guarantee anyone's safety who might be in Col Marena when we arrive, can we? It was always that way. If we come to the city along the coast, like Evrim suggests, the people of the city might still be able to use the road to flee. The caravan would then be forewarned, and they would have the same chance that any refugee from Col Marena would have."

The men were quiet and Aljeron scanned their faces again. "Valzaan?" he asked after a few moments.

"All paths forward are fraught with peril. I don't know that any of our choices will keep anyone safe."

"Maybe not, but we have to try, don't we?" Aljeron asked.

"We do," the prophet answered.

"Then we will try. It is time to start getting everybody up. I'd like the rising sun to find us out of the city."

Though there were no breaks in the cloud cover, Rulalin could tell that the sun had finally dipped below the walls of Shalin Bel. Soran sat next to him, gazing like him at the walls and gate, no doubt with the same questions.

"What are they up to?" Soran asked, confirming Rulalin's suspicions.

"I don't know; maybe nothing."

"What do you mean? They have to be up to something. There's been no movement on the wall, no archers, no anything. There's been no sound from within, no answer to any of Cheimontyr's demands. How are we supposed to offer Farimaal's terms of surrender if they don't acknowledge anything that's going on out here? They're going to leave him no choice but to tear down the gates and probably the walls as well."

"If they are in there, they probably have no intent of accepting Farimaal's terms, so I doubt if they care to hear them."

"What do you mean, 'if they are in there.' Where else would they be?"

Their conversation was cut short by the sight of Cheimontyr motioning to the giants behind him. Picking up great shields made from what appeared to be almost whole trees, they moved cautiously forward. With every step they drew nearer to the city, and still there was no activity on the walls. At last they stood at the gates, and with a sudden, deft movement, they dropped the shields and ripped the massive gates from their hinges.

The wrenching of the iron hinges shattered the early evening quiet. Rulalin winced at the piercing sound and watched as the giants tossed the great gates aside.

"Wow," Soran muttered. "I guess that's that."

"I guess so."

"It really wasn't as satisfying as I thought it would be."

"No, it really wasn't." Soran was still staring straight ahead. As difficult as Soran's experience at Zul Arnoth had been, Rulalin knew that it had served at least this purpose: to take some of the eagerness out of Soran's desire to destroy the enemy. He could see it dawning on Soran, day by day as they approached Shalin Bel, that the antagonism of the past seven years between Fel Edorath and Shalin Bel was but a dot on the timeline of history, whereas the ancient enmity between Werthanin, indeed all Kirthanin, and Malek, was much of the line itself. Soran had not openly expressed regret at their decision to align with Malek, but Rulalin knew that he now understood more of the complexity of Rulalin's own emotions. It was comforting to realize that Soran had a clearer understanding of his own internal struggle, and strangely, it helped him feel more at peace with his decision.

The Vulsutyrim picked up the great wooden shields again and moved into the city. Rulalin and Soran, who had been brought forward through the line to be ready to serve as envoys, followed Farimaal and his guard.

Soon they were inside, and it became quickly apparent that there had been no movement on the walls and no sound within because there was no one anywhere. Street after street was empty, and every building looked deserted.

"They've abandoned it," Soran said with something like disbelief and wonder in his voice.

"It looks that way."

"But how?" Soran turned to him. "I couldn't have abandoned Fel Edorath. If we hadn't gone to the Mountain, gone to Malek, to save Fel Edorath, I would have died defending it. How could they just walk away?"

"Because it was the smart thing to do."

"Like it was smart for Corlas Valon to leave Fel Edorath? What did it get him? The smart thing to do would have been to surrender and align with Malek, like we did. Running may delay their ruin, but they can't escape it."

"Maybe not, but if you were them, and surrender was not an option you'd consider, then fleeing would have been the wisest choice. They saw our power at Zul Arnoth. They had to know these walls could not give them much protection against Cheimontyr. They couldn't save the city, so they decided not to die trying. They are buying themselves time."

"Time to do what?"

"I don't know, perhaps to find a way to fight this war. Perhaps to find a place to fight this war. This is what our captains should have done. When Aljeron offered them a chance to march with him, they should have taken it. Not knowing that we were coming with Malek's army, they thought they were staying behind to die defending Fel Edorath. At least Corlas Valon knew to align himself with Aljeron, because the two of them together were stronger than either alone."

Rulalin stopped his horse in the street, and several of the soldiers following him muttered as they had to go around. "That's it," Rulalin said to Soran. "They've gone for help. We've been thinking too much like Werthanim. They aren't looking for refuge at all. They're abandoning more than the city; they're abandoning Werthanin. They're headed for the sea."

Rulalin saw Tashmiren waiting up ahead, looking back through the advancing soldiers at the two of them. When he saw that Rulalin had seen him, he motioned for them to come up. Rulalin and Soran spurred their horses forward.

"I assume this gives you much pleasure, to ride into Shalin Bel with a mighty host behind you. Surely there must have been times, pinned down as you were, when you dreamt of such a moment."

"I can truly say," Rulalin replied, "that this moment is unlike any dream I've ever had."

"To be sure, for who could dream of such an army unless he had first beheld it?"

"Indeed."

"At any rate, there is unfortunately no time for gloating. Farimaal has sent for you. Come."

They followed Tashmiren to Farimaal. They were on the outskirts of Shalin Bel's city square, and scattered across the open field around the Mound were abandoned wagons and carts, loaded down with goods.

"What do you make of this?" Farimaal asked as Rulalin and Soran came forward.

Rulalin scanned the scene carefully. "This isn't something Aljeron's army would have done. These carts and wagons are not balanced and are too full. They would be impossible to be moved quickly on the run. I don't know why they are here, but he didn't do this."

"That much I had already guessed," Farimaal added, still gazing at the square. He turned to Rulalin after a moment. "Wolves have been sent to examine the gates for signs of their departure. This Aljeron was your opponent for many years. Do you have any theories?"

Rulalin looked at Soran, then back at Farimaal. "I do. I think the wolves will bring back word that the army has passed through the western gate, probably some time ago. They may not have even spent the night here."

"Go on."

"If Aljeron meant to defend Werthanin, he would have taken his stand here. The fact that he has abandoned Shalin Bel tells me he doesn't mean to defend Werthanin at all. He's running for the sea. He can't defeat us alone. He will try to find help."

Farimaal looked around him at the empty square. "How far to the most likely port?"

"The closest port large enough to accommodate an army

and possibly refugees from the city would be Col Marena. It's about a three day's hard ride from here."

"Three days."

"Yes."

Farimaal continued to stare at the empty square. "If the Black Wolves confirm your theory, we will ride immediately."

"Can we make up such a gap?"

Farimaal turned to Rulalin with a grin that chilled Rulalin to the core. "There are few things that can't be done if you have the strength and the will to do them."

Aljeron gazed out over the water. He had not been to the Bay of Thalasee, indeed, to the sea at all, in at least ten years. The water, despite the grey clouds and unrelenting rain, looked wonderful, and the salty smell was invigorating. After three days of hard riding, it was an even more beautiful sight than he had remembered.

"The thirtieth of Autumn Wane," he said to Evrim, who stood beside him.

"Yes, the last day of Autumn."

"Yes. Only a day away from winter, and only a day away from Col Marena."

"Less on both counts. If we followed the coastline now, we could be there by nightfall. And, as it is now almost Third Hour, we have just more than half a day to winter."

"True, to be sure, but irrelevant now." Aljeron turned to Valzaan and the others behind him, who were watching him carefully. "You are sure?"

"The enemy will catch us within the hour. I have seen them coming, and it is so."

Aljeron shook his head. "How could they make up almost a day's gap?"

"They have left the Malekim behind. They have brought only the wolves and men on horseback, and of course the Vulsutyrim, who can run for days at great speed. They have not rested by day or by night, save to feed and water their horses, and they have tracked our every move through the well-trained eyes and noses of their wolves. It was inevitable, once they decided to catch us before we reached Col Marena, that this moment would come."

"Then why did you not say so?" Aljeron said, frustrated. "Why did you even let us try?"

"Because it had to be tried. Besides, I have only said that it was inevitable they would catch us. What will happen when they do is not inevitable, for those events have yet to take place and I have not been granted the ability to see them."

Aljeron laughed ruefully. "If we turn south, they will catch us before Col Marena and will attack our rear guard with impunity. If we stand and fight, we have little hope of ultimate success, and the whole journey west, all the way from Fel Edorath, will have been for naught."

"We have tried running," Brenim said impatiently. "Let us now stand and fight. We can at least do the rest of Kirthanin this favor and take as many of the enemy with us as we can. If they have no Malekim, we can do much damage before we are overrun."

"Perhaps," Caan said, "but without the Malekim, the enemy may well unleash the Vulsutyrim to do more of the front-line fighting than we saw at Zul Arnoth. If they are unleashed, it will go more ill for us than you think."

"There is no time for debate," Aljeron said to prevent the others from taking sides in the argument, for he could see the familiar divides within his own council preparing to surface again. "I am committed to getting as many men to Col Marena as I can, but we cannot simply flee. I will take two thousand men and draw up defenses here, while the rest of you will move south with the others. We will hold them as long as we can, then we will do our best to outrun them when holding

BREAKING

the field becomes impossible. This is not a suggestion, nor is it a recommendation. This is my command."

"I am staying with you," Evrim said. "You will not remain behind alone."

As several of the others began to make the same protest, Aljeron raised his hands and silenced them. "We cannot all stay, and we cannot all go. Caan, you and Gilion will lead the retreat to Col Marena. Caan knows the south, and Gilion knows our men. Brenim, I want you to go also. You are likewise a Suthanim and may be of use to them. No arguments. Corlas, I want you and your men to go too. If you make it through, I want the Suthanim to know that both Fel Edorath and Shalin Bel have sent some of their sons to join them against Malek. Evrim will stay with me. Saegan and Bryar and the scouts will also stay. We will need their help if any of us are to make Col Marena when we eventually fall back. It will be hard work, even harder than at Zul Arnoth, Saegan, but I will need you."

"I will also stay," Valzaan said when Aljeron had finished. "Or else I fear, you will not hold out long without me."

"Then I am staying too," Benjiah said.

"I am against it," Aljeron said, shaking his head.

"As am I," Valzaan agreed, and Aljeron could see the surprise on Benjiah's face. "If all goes well with us, I will catch up to you in Col Marena or later, on the sea. But if all does not go well, I want you with Pedraal and Pedraan, safely out to sea and far away from here."

"But—"

"There is no time for debate," Aljeron repeated. "Perhaps Valzaan, you could talk further with Benjiah while we organize our defenses."

Valzaan nodded, and put his hand on the boy's shoulder. Aljeron scanned them all quickly. "I hope to see you all soon in Col Marena, but don't wait for me in the city. Take every ship out to sea, only leave enough ships for our men behind, but with full crews ready to sail should we never come and the enemy come instead. Some of us may not meet again under this sun, but when the story of the world has been told in full, perhaps then we will meet again when Allfather restores all things. The Fountain will flow again, so be it?"

"So may it be."

As Benjiah turned to face Valzaan, he felt the pull of *torrim redara*. The transition to slow time was by now familiar, and he did not feel any of the nausea that had once accompanied the change.

"Benjiah, there isn't much time for you to put a safe distance between yourself and this place, so we will talk here," Valzaan said. "And furthermore, there are some things that I must say that are not for all ears."

"Valzaan, I should stay," Benjiah said meekly, not really holding out much hope that his protest would move the prophet. "I can help you."

Valzaan stood quietly, his empty white eyes appearing to gaze at Benjiah's face. "You can help, meaning Allfather has told you that you will be of service here? Or you can help, meaning you think possibly that you could do some good if allowed to remain behind?"

Benjiah lowered his eyes. "Perhaps Allfather has called me all the way from Enthanin for just this moment."

Valzaan stepped closer to Benjiah. "I know it is hard. I have told you that Allfather has called you to play a role in this war. I have dragged you through Gyrin and all the way across Werthanin to this place, and now I am sending you away from danger to be kept safe. But, Benjiah, you need to learn the difference between Allfather's specific and clearly revealed commands and the desires of your heart. Exercise your prudence and wisdom. If Allfather had shown me that this was the day and the place for which you had been raised up to serve, I would tell Aljeron in no uncertain terms that you could not be sent away. However, Allfather has shown me no such thing, and I don't believe he has shown you either. This day is shrouded in mist and mystery. In fact, I have had nothing but uneasy thoughts about it. I am troubled in spirit and in heart, and my wisdom tells me that the farther you are from this, the better. The prophecies that Allfather gives me always come to pass; they are infallible. I am not. My insights are not always accurate and my decisions sometimes are mistakes, but I have to use my knowledge the best I can and trust Allfather despite my limitations. In short, all this is to say that my heart tells me you must go, and go quickly."

"But what about you?"

"I must stay. Aljeron will be overmatched, and if he is to succeed in delaying the enemy so you may reach Col Marena, he will need my help."

Benjiah sighed. "What good does it do anyone if I survive and you do not?"

"It could do a lot of good, a world of good in fact. If things go badly here and something happens to me, then all those who oppose Malek will need the guidance of a prophet of Allfather."

"But what could I do without you?"

"You could do all that Allfather empowers you to do. Your calling is not from me, it is from Him, and He does not need me to help you. He has been pleased to grant us this time together, but there was no guarantee that you would have me with you every step of the way. But do not lose heart; I have not fallen yet. I may well come riding with Aljeron and the others into Col Marena not long after you. You must not despair. Hope remains." •

Benjiah nodded. "Should something happen to you, Valzaan, I will do my best to serve Allfather and the enemies of Malek."

"I know you will." Valzaan smiled. "I would like you, when we return to real time, to take my staff with you."

"But Valzaan, you need it," Benjiah said, stepping back, surprised.

"I will be fine without it. Remember, the power I sometimes wield comes from Allfather, not the staff. It is useful more as a symbol of my authority than as a weapon of war. If I do fall, it may serve you well the same way. If I do not, then I will receive it back from your hand and your care when I catch up to you, all right?"

"All right."

As the words were coming out of Benjiah's mouth, he felt the pull of real time, and soon the world around them had returned to life. He heard the sounds of men and horses and messengers bustling around Aljeron. Valzaan extended the hand that held the staff, and Benjiah took it with trepidation from his hand. It was solid but light, and the smooth wood fit easily into his hand, much like Suruna. He looked at the windhover carved at the top, and as he gazed at the bird's features, he suddenly saw the thundering ride of thousands of men, with a sea of Black Wolves running before them. As quickly as the image came, it was gone.

"They are coming," Benjiah gasped, looking up at Valzaan.

"I know. It will not be long. You must go."

Benjiah nodded and saw Pedraal and Pedraan waiting for him. "I will keep this until you come," Benjiah said, lifting the staff.

"Thank you," Valzaan answered. "Allfather's blessing be upon you." As Benjiah turned to pass with his uncles to their horses, he heard Valzaan add, "Always."

"Here they come!" Aljeron cried out as he steadied his horse to face the mass of Black Wolves thundering across the sparse grassland. He had arrayed his men as strategically as the land allowed, using the sandy beach on his left and some elevated but rocky ground to anchor his right. It was little more than a bump and certainly not a hill, but it was the best the topography had to offer. His line formed on a slight diagonal, facing mostly north but also east. He knew that it would not be hard for the enemy to go around his line, but he had done his best.

Then the wolves were upon them, and as the first one leapt through the air at his horse, Daaltaran cut through both the air and the wolf. But on they came and kept coming, until the ground in front of them and all around them was filled with black fur and snarling teeth. The Werthanim were not able to keep their horses steady, for terror of the wolves had come upon them, and Aljeron saw a couple of his men nearby thrown off and pulled mercilessly down into the sea of angry jaws that ripped them apart.

Behind the wolves came the men, and Aljeron spurred his horse forward to meet them. His men did the same, and the two lines of horsemen met with a mighty clash. Swords flashed in the misty midday, and soon sweat mingled with rain poured down Aljeron's face as he fought with all his skill to keep his horse and his place in the line.

Overhead, lightning began to run back and forth horizontally in the clouds. He could see in his peripheral vision a remarkable display of laterally moving strikes. They seemed to ripple through the clouds in every possible direction. Then, as Aljeron feared, they began to fall from the sky onto the plains. The Bringer of Storms marched forward with several Vulsutyrim, and the enemy's line opened up to allow them through.

And then they were really in it, for the giants brandished their swords and axes and blades as big as men, cutting down men and cutting down horses. Volley after volley of arrows flew over their heads at the giants, but each giant pulled from his back a great wooden shield almost a span long and nearly as wide. They were enormous, Aljeron realized, though against the Vulsutyrim they did not seem so big. Many of the arrows struck the wood, though some slipped past and found their mark, and the giants were at least slowed by the raining arrows.

Aljeron knew that the arrows could not long forestall them. Even had they been poisoned, cyranic arrows did not have the same effect on giants that they did on Malekim. In fact, they did not have the same effect on anyone that they had on Malekim, not really. Cyranis would kill a man, to be sure, but not so swiftly or brutally as it killed the Voiceless. A Great Bear would be made quite sick by a cyranic arrow, but it probably wouldn't kill one, unless he was hit by many. Vulsutyrim were even harder to drop with cyranis. The quantity of poison required was too large to make it a useful approach. It was a better strategy to hit the Vulsutyrim in vulnerable places, like the eyes and throat, where single arrows could do a great deal of harm. So Aljeron had ordered the archers to send their cyranic arrows with the others. They would be needed when they engaged the Malekim again. For now, accuracy was their only hope. Unfortunately, the shields did a good job of protecting the giants where they were weakest, and not one of them fell.

At last the Vulsutyrim penetrated Aljeron's line. The men in the middle dropped back to one side or the other. Aljeron found himself on the beach side of his divided force, and he wheeled his horse instinctively as his side of the line formed an arc with the sand and sea at their backs. Step by step they gave ground, and Aljeron could feel loose sand now below his horse's feet. A handful of giants pressed them all backward toward the water.

Then, one stepped directly at him, and Aljeron dove from his horse just ahead of a great stroke of the giant's axe, which cut clean through the poor animal. Aljeron felt himself hit the sand, and he rolled to his feet with Daaltaran ready. A wolf running across the sand leapt at him, and with a short, deft stroke he cut the brute in half. The Vulsutyrim that had killed his horse moved closer, and another great swing of the axe sent Aljeron leaping backward into shallow water. His body dropped below the surface, and the stroke missed him by less than a hand. Salt water flooded his throat and nostrils, and he popped up coughing. He looked up at the giant towering over him and realized he was about out of options, when suddenly Koshti leapt from behind the giant, so high that his claws dug into his back.

The Vulsutyrim was knocked off balance by the tiger and tipped forward, tumbling facedown into the water with Koshti still on him. Aljeron jumped sideways to avoid being crushed, and then, just as quickly, brought Daaltaran down on the giant's neck with all the force he had. The blade of the Azmavarim did its job and severed the giant's head, which embedded itself in the sand just under the water so that his long dark hair floated and swirled at the surface. The rest of the body lay mostly in the water, with the tide falling away just enough to reveal every so often the giant's feet.

Aljeron had started back up the beach with Koshti at his side when Valzaan appeared and reached down, helping Aljeron up onto his horse's back. "You must sound the retreat, Aljeron. You can do nothing further here. Pull the men back, down the beach, and I will do what I can."

Aljeron grabbed the horn that hung around his neck and poured out the water inside it. He lifted it to his lips and blew, loud and long. The note rang out over the battlefield. Valzaan had somehow dodged the heaviest pockets of fighting and they were now down the beach, below the engagement, looking back north at the two segments of his former line, fighting furiously. Eventually he saw what he was looking for, for the men, some on horseback and some on foot, began to move in their direction, holding together as best they could.

"There is no time, so you must listen," Valzaan said as they waited. "Far to the northeast in the wastes of Nolthanin, there is a mountain that is known to some as Harak Andunin, or 'Andunin's Spear.' You will know it when you see it. It is a long and difficult journey, but you must go, for it may harbor Kirthanin's best chance to defeat the Bringer of Storms."

"Valzaan, what are you talking about?"

"Listen! When Sulmandir flew north from the Holy Mountain after killing Vulsutyr, it was believed by most that he flew away to die. I know that he did not die, at least not right away, for I saw him once thereafter, in his lair in Harak Andunin. More than nine hundred years have past since I left him there, and I have kept his secret all those years. But now Allfather has bid me reveal it to you. I know not if the Father of Dragons still lives, but we must pray he does. Only he can rouse what remains of his children to come forth from their dens and lairs in all their might and splendor. Sarneth may be able to raise the aid of the Great Bear, but I fear that without the dragons, we may still be lost. You must go. Promise me you will go."

"Valzaan—"

"Promise!"

"I promise!"

As soon as Aljeron said the words, Valzaan leapt down from the horse and started walking up the beach toward the roiling mass of men. Valzaan lifted up his hands and raised them to the sky, and suddenly a great cloud of swirling sand rose behind the enemy and came down the beach behind them like a great fog. It swept up around the heads of the giants, and soon the Vulsutyrim were struggling desperately to keep the flying sand out of their eyes. What's more, beneath the paws of the Black Wolves, the beach was beginning to give way. Aljeron could see wolves being sucked into the churning sand all around him. They scrambled furiously, their eyes wide with fear as they were sucked down into the very ground.

The enemy men on horseback had lost control of their horses, which were rearing and leaping like wild beasts all over the battlefield. All of this came upon Malek's armies at once, and Aljeron again blew his horn of retreat. His own men, eyes wide with wonder, ran down the beach on foot and on horseback. The sand under their feet did not give way. The sand above their heads did not blow into their eyes, and the horses they rode upon did not throw their masters. They passed Valzaan, who was left standing in the gap between Aljeron and his men, and the enemy. And as they reached Aljeron, he called out to them all. "Double mount! We all ride, and we all ride now. Head south. Go!"

Wasting no time, the men on foot climbed up on horses, and quickly the horses took off down the beach, but Aljeron lingered. Valzaan still stood there, his hands raised, showing no signs of joining them.

"Valzaan, we must go!" Aljeron called.

The prophet stood his ground. The minutes passed and before long Aljeron could not see the men that he had sent away. All that time, Valzaan sustained the terror and confusion of the enemy. "Come on!" Aljeron called again.

"Go now," the answer came. "You have promised!"

Aljeron hesitated, but Valzaan's wishes were entirely clear. He started to ride away, back down the beach. He rode for a hundred spans or so, then stopped and turned around. He was alarmed to see the cloud of sand had dissipated, and the Bringer of Storms, still rubbing his eyes with his free hand, had stepped in front of the rest with his hammer in his hand. Rearing back, the giant hurled the hammer across the beach at the prophet, who leapt sideways toward the water to avoid it. The hammer flew past him and landed in the sand.

Valzaan drew himself up at the edge of the water to face the Bringer of Storms. The great giant walked down the beach until he stood directly inland from Valzaan.

"I am Allfather's prophet," Valzaan called, "and I have a message for you. For your service to Malek, your life will be required. And yet, if you turn now from him, your brothers may be spared."

For a moment, there was silence on the beach, but it did not last long. The Bringer of Storms threw his head back and laughed. His long dark hair fell around his shoulders and his body shuddered with the laughter. Then he raised his arms above his head, and instantly lightning danced between his fingertips. "You cannot defeat me!" he shouted. "You cannot withstand me! You cannot even stand before me! I am the Bringer of Storms!"

Then Aljeron gasped, for with a single forward movement of his arms, an enormous ball of lightning shot out from the giant's hands and struck Valzaan, hurling him back over the water more than fifty spans into the sea.

EPILOGUE

FLAMES ROSE FROM Col Marena. The port had been largely empty when they had arrived earlier in the evening, the ships having sailed and the citizens having fled. Still, here and there they found those hiding in the dark corners, hoping not to be found.

Cinjan stood over one of them, a large muscular shopkeeper. "You should have gotten on one of the ships or rode south with the rest," Cinjan muttered as he freed the long slender knife he had buried up to the hilt in the man's chest. He wiped the blade across the man's tunic to clean off the blood, and then returned the weapon to its sheath.

Cinjan walked over to the window of the shop, which was located nicely on the wharf, overlooking the harbor. The fires in the city reflected on the water, the flickering light dancing jovially. He could still make out the many sails holding off shore, not far away. What did they think, he wondered, of the flames?

He stepped out the door, back into the steadily falling rain. Had he not known his master was there, waiting in the shadows, it would have been hard to see him resting with his back against the front of the shop. "The building is secure."

"Good," came the simple reply.

"What do we do now?"

"Now?" The man replied. "Now we wait. While our soldiers search for a seaworthy ship, we wait. If we don't find a way to go out to them, I will have the soldiers withdraw, and we will hope some of them come back to us."

"Isn't it risky, either way? Won't they suspect you if you row out to them or if they row in and find you here?"

"I don't see why they should. Some among them will remember that I claimed this was my home. I will tell them I am a sad victim of this war. I will sell them my sorrow and my woe, just like I did last time. They will take me in and shelter me. They will offer me refuge and relief. Both of us, for this time you will come with me. And you and I, we will get close to Aljeron this time. We will get close and stay close, and I will find out if he is the child of prophecy."

"If he is?"

"We will kill him."

"If he isn't?"

"We'll kill him anyway."

Synoki laughed, and he and Cinjan moved away through the night.

When darkening skies and storms arise,
    Blow, wind, blow!
When lightning flashes and thunder crashes,
    Rage, storm, rage!
When the heavens storm and whirlwinds swarm,
    Swell, waves, swell!
When clouds surround and rains pour down,
    Fade, light, fade!
When all looks lost and we're tempest tossed,
    Then sail, ship, sail!
Fly the storm and escape the gale,
    Find safe harbor and never fail
To find a haven where no winds assail.

—"The Song of Storms," a familiar lyric of sailors, sung
to a traditional melody.

The End
of the Second Book of
The Binding of the Blade

GLOSSARY

Aelwyn Elathien (ALE-win el-ATH-ee-un): Novaana of Werthanin, Mindarin's younger sister.

Agia Muldonai (ah-GEE-uh MUL-doe-nye): The Holy Mountain. Agia Muldonai was the ancient home of the Titans, who lived in Avalione, the city nestled high upon the mountain between its twin peaks. Agia Muldonai has been under Malek's control since the end of the Second Age, when he invaded Kirthanin from his home in exile on the Forbidden Isle.

Alazare (AL-uh-zair): The Titan who cast Malek from Agia Muldonai at the end of the First Age when Malek's Rebellion failed. Severely injured in his battle with Malek, Alazare passed from the stage of Kirthanin history and was never seen again.

Aljeron Balinor (AL-jer-on BALL-ih-nore): Novaana of Werthanin (Shalin Bel), travels with his battle brother Koshti.

Allfather: Creator of Kirthanin, who gave control of Kirthanin's day-to-day affairs to the Council of Twelve. To accomplish this task, He gave great power to each of these

Titans. Since the time of Malek's Rebellion, Allfather has continued to speak to His creation through prophets who remind Kirthanin of Allfather's sovereign rule.

Anakor (AN-uh-core): Titan, ally to Malek, killed by Volrain in the Rebellion.

Andunin (an-DOO-nin): The Nolthanim man chosen by Malek at the Rebellion to be king over mankind.

Arimaar Mountains (AIR-ih-mar): Suthanin's longest range, which runs between Lindan Wood and the eastern coast of Suthanin.

Assembly: The official gathering of all Kirthanin Novaana who are appointed to represent their family and region.

Autumn Rise: See seasons.

Autumn Wane: See seasons.

Avalione (av-uh-lee-OWN): Blessed city and home of the Crystal Fountain. It rests between the peaks of Agia Muldonai and was once the home of the Titans. Like the rest of Agia Muldonai, the city was declared off limits by Allfather at the beginning of the Second Age.

Azaruul butterflies (AZ-uh-rule): Green luminescent butterflies.

Azmavarim (az-MAV-uh-rim): Also known as Firstblades, these swords were forged during the First Age by Andunin and his followers.

Balimere (BALL-ih-mere): Also called Balimere the Beautiful. The most beloved of all the Titans to the lesser creatures of Kirthanin. It is said that when Allfather restores Kirthanin, Balimere will be the first of the faithful Titans to be resurrected.

Barunaan River (buh-RUE-nun): Major north-south river between Kellisor Sea and the Southern Ocean.

Bay of Thalasee (THAL-uh-see): Bay off Werthanin's west coast.

Benjiah Andira (ben-JY-uh an-DEER-uh): Joraiem and Wylla's son.

Master Berin (BARE-in): Master of Sulare.

Black Wolves: Creatures created by Malek during his exile on the Forbidden Isle.

Mistress Brahan (BRA HAN): Rulalin's housekeeper and chief steward.

Brenim Andira (BREN-im an-DEER-uh): Novaana of Suthanin (Dal Harat), Joraiem's younger brother.

Bringer of Storms, the: See Cheimontyr.

Bryar (BRY-er): Novaana of Werthanin, Elyas's older sister, who fights for Fel Edorath under Aljeron's command.

Caan (KAHN): Combat instructor for the Novaana in Sulare.

Calendar: There are ninety-one days in every season, making the year 364 days. The midseason feast days are not numbered and instead are known only by their name (Midsummer, Midautumn, etc.) They fall between the fifteenth and sixteenth day of each season. These days are "outside of time" in part as a tribute to the timelessness of Allfather; they also look forward to the time when all things will be made new.

Calissa (kuh-LISS-uh): Novaana of Suthanin (Kel Imlaris), Darias's sister.

Captain Merias (mer-EYE-us): High-ranking officer in the army of Amaan Sul.

Charnosh (CHAR nosh): Titan, ally to Malek, killed by Rolandes during the Rebellion.

Cheimontyr (SHY-MON-teer): The Bringer of Storms, most fearful of the Vulsutyrim who can control the weather.

Cimaris Rul (sim-AHR-iss RULE): Town at the mouth of the Barunaan River where it pours into the Southern Ocean.

Col Marena (KOLE muh-REEN-uh): Port near Shalin Bel.

Corindel (KORE-in-del): Enthanim royal who attempted to drive Malek from Agia Muldonai and betrayed the Great Bear at the beginning of the Third Age.

Corlas Valon (KORE-las vah-LAHN): Fel Edorath captain whose troops join Aljeron's to face Malek.

Council of Twelve: The twelve Titans to whom Allfather entrusted the care of Kirthanin. The Council dwelt in Avalione on Agia Muldonai, but frequently they would transform themselves into human form and travel throughout the land. The greatest of these was Malek, whose Rebellion ultimately brought about the destruction of the Twelve.

Crystal Fountain: Believed to be the fountainhead of all Kirthanin waters, this fountain once flowed in the center of Avalione.

cyranis (sir-AN-iss): A poison of remarkable potency that can kill most living things if it gets into the bloodstream. Consequently, the cyranic arrow—the head of which is coated in cyranis—is one of few weapons that the people of Kirthanin trust against the Malekim.

Elder Curran (cur-AN): chief elder, Shalin Bel council.

Daaltaran (doll-TARE-an): Aljeron's sword, a Firstblade whose name means "death comes to all."

Daegon (DAY-gone): Titan, ally to Malek, killed by Alazare during the Rebellion.

Dal Harat (DOLL HARE-at): Village in western Suthanin, Joraiem Andira's home.

Darias (DAHR-ee-us): Novaana of Suthanin (Kel Imlaris), Calissa's brother.

Derrion Wel (DARE-ee-un WELL): Town in southeastern Suthanin.

draal (DRAWL): A tight-knit community of Great Bear.

dragon tower: These ancient structures were built in the First Age as homes away from home for dragons who naturally live in the high places of Kirthanin's mountains and prefer to sleep high above the ground.

dragons: One of the three great races of Kirthanin. All dragons are descended from the golden dragon, Sulmandir, the first creation of Allfather after the Titans. All dragons appear at first glance to be golden, but none except Sulmandir is entirely golden. Three dragon lines exist, marked by their distinct coloring: red, blue, and green.

Eliandir (el-ee-AN-deer): A red dragon.

Elnin Wood (EL-nin): Suthanin forest south of Vol Tumian.

Elnindraal (EL-nin-drawl): The draal of Great Bear living in Suthanin's Elnin Wood.

Elyas (eh-LIE-us): Novaana of Werthanin, Bryar's younger brother, who died fighting for Amaan Sul in one of the first campaigns against Fel Edorath.

Enthanin (EN-than-in): Kirthanin's eastern country. Residents are Enthanim.

Eralon (AIR-uh-lahn): Faithful Titan killed by Malek and his allies during the Rebellion.

Erevir (AIR-uh-veer): Major prophet of Allfather in the Second Age.

Erigan (AIR-ih-gan): Great Bear, Sarneth's son.

Evrim Minluan (EV-rim MIN-loo-in): Joraiem's best friend and close friend to Aljeron.

Fall Rise: See Seasons.

Farimaal (FARE-ih-mal): Leading general of Malek's, who brought the Grendolai into submission.

Fel Edorath (FELL ED-ore-ath): Easternmost city in Werthanin; the first line of defense against attacks from Agia Muldonai.

Fire Giant: See Vulsutyr.

First Age: The age of peace and harmony that preceded Malek's rebellion. Not only did peace govern the affairs of men in the First Age, but the three great races of men, dragons, and Great Bear coexisted then in harmony.

Firstblade: See Azmavarim.

Forbidden Isle: After Malek's failed Rebellion at the end of the First Age, he was driven from Kirthanin and took refuge on the Forbidden Isle, home of Vulsutyr, the Fire Giant.

Forest of Gyrin (GEAR-in): Forest south of Agia Muldonai.

Full Autumn: See seasons.

Full Spring: See seasons.

Full Summer: See seasons.

Full Winter: See seasons.

Garek Elathien (GAIR-ick el-ATH-ee-un): Novaana of Werthanin, Aelwyn and Mindarin's father.

garrion (GARE-ee-un): Mode of transport common in the First Age used by the Titans and some Novaana. Garrions came in many shapes and sizes, but they all functioned similarly: A dragon would pick up the garrion with his talons as he flew.

giants: See Vulsutyrim.

Gilion Numiah (GIL-ee-un new-MY-uh): Captain of Shalin Bel's army.

Great Bear: One of the three great races of Kirthanin. These magnificent creatures commonly stand two spans high and are ferocious fighters when need calls. Nevertheless, they are known for their great wisdom and gentleness.

Grendolai (GREN-doe-lie): Rumored to have been the joint creation of Malek and Vulsutyr, these terrifying creatures were reportedly used to attack the Dragon Towers when Malek invaded Kirthanin from the Forbidden Isle. They have not been seen since, and some believe their existence is wholly legendary.

gyre: A manmade dragon den built on top of a dragon tower.

Gyrindraal (GEAR-in-drawl): Clan of Great Bear inhabiting the Forest of Gyrin south of Agia Muldonai.

Haalsun (HAL-sun): Faithful Titan killed by Charnosh during the Rebellion.

Halina Minluan (huh-LEE-nuh MIN-loo-in): Evrim and Kyril's older daughter.

Harak Andunin (HARE-ack an-DOO-nin): Mountain in Nolthanin whose name means "Andunin's Spear."

Hour: See time.

Invasion, the: Malek's second attempt to conquer Kirthanin.

Joraiem Andira (jore-EYE-em an-DEER-uh): Novaana of Suthanin (Dal Harat) and a prophet, murdered by Rulalin.

Karalin (CARE-uh-lin): Novaana from Enthanin (near Amaan Sul), crippled left ankle.

Kellisor Sea (KELL-ih-sore): The great internal sea of Kirthanin that lies directly south of Agia Muldonai.

Kelvan (KEL-vin): Novaana from Werthanin who died on the Forbidden Isle while battling Malekim and Black Wolves.

King Falcon: See windhover.

Kiraseth (KEER-uh-seth): Father of the Great Bear.

Kirthanin (KEER-than-in): The world in which the story takes place. Kirthanin comprises four countries on a single continent. Each country is defined by its geographic relationship to Agia Muldonai.

Kiruan River (KEER-oo-an): Marks the boundary of Werthanin and Nolthanin.

Koshti (KOSH-tee): Aljeron's tiger, battle brother.

Kurveen (kur-VEEN): Caan's sword, a Firstblade whose name means "quick kill."

Kyril Minluan (KEER-il MIN-loo-in): Novaana of Suthanin (Dal Harat), Joraiem's younger sister and Evrim's wife, mother of Halina and Roslin.

Lindan Wood (LIN-duhn): Forest in eastern Suthanin, just west of the Arimaar Mountains.

Lindandraal (LIN-duhn-drawl): Clan of Great Bear that resides west of the Arimaar Mountains in Lindan Wood.

Malek (MAH-leck): The greatest of Titans whose betrayal brought death to his Titan brothers and ruin to Kirthanin. Since the end of the Second Age and his second failed attempt to conquer all Kirthanin, he has ruled over Agia Muldonai and the surrounding area.

Malekim (MALL-uh-keem): Also known as Malek's Children, the Silent Ones, and the Voiceless. These creatures were first seen when Malek invaded Kirthanin at the end of the Second Age from the Forbidden Isle. A typical Malekim stands from a span and a third to a span and a half high and has a smooth thick grey hide. "Malekim" is both a singular and a plural term.

Marella Someris (muh-REL-uh so-MAIR-iss): Wylla's deceased mother, former Novaana and Queen of Enthanin.

Merrion (MAIR-ee-un): White sea birds with blue stripes on their wings that can swim short distances underwater in pursuit of fish.

Mindarin Orlene (MIN-duh-rin ore-LEAN): Novaana of Werthanin, Aelwyn's older sister.

Monias Andira (moe-NYE-us an-DEER-uh): Novaana of Suthanin (Dal Harat), Joraiem's father.

Mound: Central feature in the midseason rituals that focus on Agia Muldonai's need for cleansing.

Nal Gildoroth (NAL GIL-dore-oth): Solitary city on the Forbidden Isle.

Nol Rumar (KNOLL RUE-mar): Small village in the north central plains of Werthanin.

Nolthanin (KNOLL-than-in): Kirthanin's northern country, largely in ruin during the Third Age.

Novaana (no-VAHN-uh): The nobility of human society in Kirthanin who at first governed human affairs under the direction of the Titans but have since adapted to autonomous control. Every seven years the Novaana between the ages of eighteen and twenty-five as of the first day of Spring Rise were to assemble from the first day of Spring Wane until the first day of Fall Wane. Sulare is commonly referred to as the Summerland. "Novaana" is both a singular and a plural term.

Nyan (NYE-un): Novaana of Suthanin (Cimaris Rul).

Pedraal Someris (PAY-drawl so-MAIR-iss): Novaana of Enthanin (Amaan Sul), Wylla's younger brother, Pedraan's older twin.

Pedraan Someris (PAY-drahn so-MAIR-iss): Novaana of Enthanin (Amaan Sul), Wylla's younger brother, Pedraal's younger twin.

Pedrone Someris (PAY-drone so-MAIR-iss): Last king of Enthanin, deceased.

Peredin Terasir (PARE-uh-din TARE-us-ear): Rulalin's deceased father.

Peris Mil (PARE-iss MILL): Town south of Kellisor Sea on the Barunaan River.

Ralon Orlene (RAY-lon OR-lean): Mindarin's late husband.

Rebellion, the: Malek's first attempt to conquer and rule Kirthanin by overthrowing the Twelve from Avalione.

Rolandes (roll-AN-deez): Faithful Titan killed by Daegon during the Rebellion.

Roslin Minluan (ROZ-lin MIN-loo-in): Evrim and Kyril's younger daughter.

Rucaran the Great (RUE-car-en): Father of the Black Wolves.

Rulalin Tarasir (rue-LAH-lin TARE-us-ear): Novaana of Werthanin (Fel Edorath), who murdered Joraiem in jealousy over Wylla.

Ruun Harak (RUNE HARE-ack): A spear given to Andunin by Malek.

Saegan (SIGH-gan): Novaana of Enthanin (Tol Emuna) who fights alongside Aljeron.

Sarneth (SAHR-neth): A lord among Great Bear, one of the few to still hold commerce with men.

seasons: As a largely agrarian world, Kirthanin follows a calendar that revolves around the four seasons. Each season is subdivided into three distinct periods, each of which contains thirty days. For example, the first thirty days of Summer are known as Summer Rise, the middle thirty days as Full Summer, and the last thirty as Summer Wane.

Second Age: The period that followed Malek's rebellion and preceded his return to Kirthanin. The Second Age was largely a time of peace until a massive civil war devastated

Kirthanin's defenses and opened the door for Malek's second attempt at total conquest.

Shalin Bel (SHALL-in BELL): Large city of Werthanin.

Silent One: See Malekim.

slow time: See *torrim redara*.

Soran Nuvaar (SORE-an NEW-var): Friend and officer of Rulalin.

span: The most common form of measurement in Kirthanin. Its origin is forgotten but it could refer to the length of a man. A span is approximately 10 hands or what we would call 6 feet.

Spring Rise: See seasons.

Spring Wane: See seasons.

Stratarus (STRAT-ar-us): Faithful Titan killed by Anakor during the Rebellion.

Sulare (sue-LAHR-ee): Also known as the Summerland. At the beginning of the Third Age the Assembly decreed that Sulare, a retreat at the southern tip of Kirthanin, would be the place where every seven years all Novaana between the ages of eighteen and twenty-five were to assemble from the first day of Spring Wane until the first day of Fall Wane.

Sulmandir (sul-man-DEER): Also known as Father of the Dragons and the Golden Dragon. He is the most magnificent of all Allfather's creations besides the Titans. After many of his children died during Malek's invasion of Kirthanin at the end of the Second Age, Sulmandir disappeared.

Summer Rise: See seasons.

Summer Wane: See seasons.

Summerland: See Sulare.

Suruna (suh-RUE-nuh): Joraiem Andira's bow, previously his father's, whose name means "sure one."

Suthanin (SUE-than-in): The largest of Kirthanin's four countries, occupying the southern third of the continent. Ruled by a loose council of Navaana. Residents are Suthanim.

Synoki (sin-OH-kee): A castaway on the Forbidden Isle.

Tarin (TARE-in): Novaana of Enthanin, Valia's cousin.

Tashmiren (tash-MERE-in): Servant of Malek, originally from Nolthanin.

Tergan Dorant (TER-gin dor-ANT): Wealthy Shalin Bel merchant and council member.

Therin (THERE-in): Faithful Titan killed by Malek and his allies during the Rebellion.

Third Age: The present age, which began with the fall and occupation of Agia Muldonai by Malek.

time: Time in Kirthanin is reckoned differently during the day and the night. Daytime is divided into twelve Hours. First Hour begins at what we would call 7 AM and Twelfth Hour ends at what we would call 7 PM. Nighttime is divided into four watches, each three hours long. So First Watch runs from 7 PM to 10 PM and so on through the night until First Hour.

Titans: Those first created by Allfather who were given the authority to rule Kirthanin on Allfather's behalf. Their great power was used to do many remarkable things before Malek's rebellion ruined them.

torrim redara (TORE-um ruh-DAR-uh): Prophetic state of being temporarily outside of time.

Ulmindos (ul-MIN-doss): High captain of the ships of Sulare.

Ulutyr (OO-loo-teer): Vulsutyrim captor of the women on the Forbidden Isle.

Valia (vuh-LEE-uh): Novaana of Enthanin, Tarin's cousin.

Valzaan (val-ZAHN): The blind prophet of Allfather.

Voiceless: See Malekim.

Volrain (vahl-RAIN): Faithful Titan killed by Malek during the Rebellion.

Vol Tumian (VAHL TOO-my-an): Village along the Barunaan River between Peris Mil and Cimaris Rul.

Vulsutyr (VUL-sue-teer): Also known as Father of the Giants and the Fire Giant. Vulsutyr ruled the Forbidden Isle and gave shelter to Malek when he fled Kirthanin. At first little more than a distant host, Malek eventually seduced Vulsutyr to help him plan and prepare for his invasion of Kirthanin. This giant was killed by Sulmandir at the end of the Second Age.

Vulsutyrim (vul-sue-TER-eem): Name for all descendants of Vulsutyr; both a singular and a plural term.

War of Division: Civil war that weakened Kirthanin's defenses against Malek at the end of the Second Age.

Water Stones: Stone formations created by the upward thrust of water released from the great deep at the creation of the world.

Werthanin (WARE-than-in): Kirthanin's western country. Residents are Werthanim.

windhover: Small brown falcons that are seen as "holy" birds in some areas of Kirthanin because of some stories that associate them with Agia Muldonai.

Winter Rise: See seasons.

Winter Wane: See seasons.

Wylla Someris (WILL-uh so-MAIR-iss): Queen of Enthanin and widow of Joraiem.

Yorek (YORE-ek): Royal advisor.

Zaros Mountains (ZAHR-ohss): Mountain range bordering Nolthanin on the south.

Zul Arnoth (ZOOL ARE-noth): Ruined city between Shalin Bel and Fel Edorath; sight of many battles during Werthanin's civil war.

ABOUT THE AUTHOR

L. B. Graham was born in Baltimore, Maryland, in 1971. He loved school so much that he never left, transitioning seamlessly between life as a student and life as a teacher. He and his wife Jo now live in St. Louis. They would like one day to have a house by the sea, which he wants to call "The Grey Havens." His wife is Australian, which he thinks is appropriate since his grandfather was Australian and his father was born in Melbourne. The fact that he has these Australian connections and that his father grew up in Ethiopia all make him think he is more international than he really is. He went to Wheaton College outside of Chicago, where Billy Graham went, but they aren't related. He likes sports of all varieties, especially basketball and lacrosse. His biggest sports achievement was scoring 7 goals in a lacrosse game when he was a junior in college (a 10–6 win against Illinois State). He and his wife have two beautiful children, Tom and Ella, who love books, which pleases him immensely.